8⁰⁰

The Light
of the Morning

a story of beginning

The Light
of the Morning

a story of beginning

Elaine Stienon

ENSIGN PUBLISHING HOUSE , GLENDALE , CALIFORNIA

Library of Congress Cataloging in Publication Data

Stienon, Elaine
   The Light of the Morning
   1. Title

JS 661S53 813'.5'4 88-81302

ISBN 0-929328-00-0

Printed in the United States of America

—*And...they (the ancient ones) did leave a blessing upon this land in their prayers, that whosoever should believe in this gospel, in this land, might have eternal life.*

...And now, behold, according to their faith in their prayers, will I bring this part of my gospel to the knowledge of my people. Behold, I do not bring it to destroy that which they have received, but to build it up.

And for this cause have I said, If this generation harden not their hearts, I will establish my church among them.

     —The Lord to Joseph Smith
     Harmony, Pennsylvania, 1828

—*For as the light of the morning cometh out of the east, and shineth even unto the west, and covereth the whole earth, so shall also the coming of the Son of Man be.*

     —Matthew 24:27
     Inspired Version

1

Hands. Gentle hands on her. Touching her forehead, smoothing back her hair. Straightening the covers. Even now, bedridden as she was...the gentle hands, the caring...

"Emma?" Her voice, no longer strong, quavered a little.

"It's all right. I'm right here." Emma, her daughter-in-law, was leaning over her. The large, dark eyes met her own. "Are you feeling better? You look better today."

"Yes. Better." Lucy drew a deep breath. "It's so late. I should have been awake...oh, hours ago. But I'm so tired."

"There's no hurry. It's all right to rest...rest a bit longer." Emma straightened up. "I have to get back to the kitchen now. I'll send David in with some breakfast. Then I'll come back and help you get into your chair."

Again they exchanged glances, the two who had been through so much together. What hadn't they endured, Lucy wondered? Loss, persecution, countless moves from one place to another...

The road wound from western New York to Kirtland, Ohio, and then to Missouri and back to Illinois...Nauvoo, the beautiful city, the brief years of prosperity...and at last, the final, unbelievable sorrow. Her sons. Two splendid sons (one of them Emma's husband). The brothers Hyrum and Joseph, slain at the same hour...murdered by a mob at Carthage jail...

Time heals, so they said. But it was always there, the memory of what had happened...like an extra shadow in the room.

Lucy's lips moved, a whisper.

"'Who shall separate us from the love of Christ? shall tribulation, or distress, or persecution...or famine, or nakedness, or peril, or sword?...Nay...'"

"What?" Emma asked. "What did you say?"

"Nothing, dear. I was just thinking. Quoting scripture again, like they always say I do."

"Joseph said he would be stopping by later this morning. But that won't be for a while. You rest now."

Lucy lay musing on the quality of Emma's voice...the power it had to bring comfort and reassurance.

...the times Emma had opened her house to take strangers in, the times she had even given up her own bed to the sick and had nursed them. Emma, the same girl Joseph had brought home so long ago...spirited, vivacious, a mind of her own...not always easy to get along with. A beautiful girl, with hair as black as a crow's wing, and dark, luminous eyes...

Lucy had thought she was a bit spoiled, in those early days. An exotic creature in a house full of common folk. Who would have thought she'd have the stamina to endure all she had? Joseph had chosen well.

Joseph. She thought of what Emma had just said...something about Joseph stopping by. The young Joseph...Emma's son, now a man grown.

Turning in her bed, Lucy thought of the other Josephs...the first Joseph her husband, father of her nine children...the tall, powerful man, toughened by a life in the woods and fields. And then Joseph her most extraordinary child...the slain prophet. But who would have thought he was different from all the rest?

A picture rose in her mind...Joseph as he was growing up.

...a sturdy boy, big for his age...quick blue eyes and hair the color of light sand. But beyond the physical

6

*strength, the quickness, there was something more —
the open quality of his spirit, the peculiar innocence...as
if he could not believe there was such a thing as deceit
or cruelty in the world...*

And again the shadow moved in the room.

Emma's comment...no painting could catch his
expression... always changing in reflection of his
thoughts and feelings. Like light and color, his emotions
crossed his face, for all to read.

Even the memory of Emma's voice...a soothing effect.
Lucy felt secure, safe at last, as if she were resting after
a hazardous journey. And because she was relaxed, her
mind went spiraling back down the ins and outs of that
journey, to the place where it had begun...far from
Nauvoo (empty almost deserted now) and her daughter-
in-law's house, where she lay hospitalized...

*...Gilsum, New Hampshire. The place of her growing
up.*

And the years dropped away; she was young again,
a girl in her parents' house.

Like spring, her youth was...green and sweet with the
scent of forestland, like the New Hampshire hills. But
spring was full of rain.

"Hush, Lucy," her mother said. "Don't make too much
noise. You know Lovina is resting. No; you can't see her
now."

Her older sisters Lovisa and Lovina...both dying of
consumption when they were young women.

"Lovina..."

Lovina she loved especially; Lovina was her friend, her
playmate, her companion. They were almost inseparable.

But the separation came, and Lovina was gone. Lucy was left desolate. The colors and hues of spring were muted, tinged with gray; she thought the rain would go on forever.

Then, out of the grayness, voices:

"It's been two months since Lovina died. And Lucy is not herself."

"She's still grieving, poor child. It's too much for her... it's like a deep melancholy."

"I think she needs a change of scene." Her brother Stephen's voice. "Let me take her to Vermont for a while, to live with me."

She went with Stephen to Tunbridge, in Vermont.

In the midst of her melancholy, she had prayed and read the Bible, hoping her spirits would lift. She thought of joining a church, but each clergyman claimed that his own church was right and all others were wrong.

"Do you know what, Stephen? All of these churches... by their contention, all they do is witness against each other. How can any of them be the true church of Christ?"

"I don't know, Lucy. I was never much for religion, myself. Everyone has to find his own way, seems to me."

"But don't you believe in prayer?"

"Indeed I do. You're looking better, and taking an interest in things again. If I prayed for anything, it was for your health."

Dear Stephen. As she looked back, she thought how fortunate it was that her brother had cared for her enough to take her to Vermont. For it was there she met Joseph Smith, whom she married.

But in the sixth year of her marriage, with two sons already born to her, she fell ill... the same consumption which had taken the lives of her older sisters. The doctors even told her she was about to die. All she could think

8

to do was pray...she pleaded with the Lord all that night and promised him her service.

Then, with the first light, she heard a voice:

Seek, and ye shall find, knock, and it shall be opened unto you. Let your heart be comforted; ye believe in God; believe also in me.

In the morning she felt better.

As she got stronger, she thought more and more of religion. Again she began going from church to church, seeking someone to instruct her.

"I'm just not satisfied with any of their answers."

"That doesn't surprise me," her husband replied. "You probably know as much as they do."

"I guess I will just have to keep the Bible as my guide. But someday I shall find someone who will baptize me — you'll see! I shall be baptized according to the New Testament, without being required to join any of these congregations."

"I don't think it'll happen too soon," her husband said.

Joseph was of a skeptical turn of mind. To keep peace with his father Asael, he stopped going to meetings with her. She began to pray that the true gospel would be presented to her husband, and that he would accept it.

Then, she had a strange dream...someday, the thing she had prayed for would come to pass. Incredible as it was, she believed it...she tried to have patience.

Who would have thought it would come through one of their own children? *Joseph, her third son*...and suddenly he was alive again, there in her mind...the tall, blue-eyed youngster.

He looked much like his older brothers, Hyrum and Alvin. She thought of the many times she had been asked about Joseph's early childhood...if there had been anything unusual about it. But she could remember nothing out of the ordinary. He was a quiet boy, she would tell people... "remarkably well-disposed."

Then, when he was seven years old, the dread typhoid fever swept through their family. Hyrum came home from school with it, and each of the children fell ill. The doctor even gave up on Sophronia, their oldest daughter. The girl was saved, Lucy knew, because of the prayers she and her husband had offered at the bedside.

The boy Joseph was ill with the fever only about two weeks, but then complications set in. First there was the pain in his shoulder. It was treated as a sprain, even though the boy insisted he had not injured his shoulder. Then they found it was a large abscess. It started to heal when it was lanced. Then the pain and swelling began in his leg.

With closed eyes Lucy could see the two brothers Hyrum and Joseph together on the low bed, for Hyrum would not leave his brother. Joseph lay for two weeks in agony; much of the time Hyrum braced the afflicted leg in his hands to help ease the suffering. The surgeon which the Smiths called in (whose name was also Smith, but no relation) operated twice on the leg. It relieved the pain only until the wound began to heal.

Then the surgeon returned with an associate and eleven others. The decision had been made to amputate. Lucy remembered the doctor's words:

"My poor boy, we have come again."

But Joseph utterly refused. Finally Lucy insisted that they try to cut out the part of the bone that was diseased, and give the leg one more chance to heal.

Joseph refused to be tied down, and he would not take brandy for the operation. He insisted that his mother leave the house, and go where she could not hear his screams. She put folded sheets under his leg and then went out a little way into the woods.

10

A shadow stirred in the Nauvoo room where she lay, a breeze moving the curtains. From outside came the scent of pine needles and damp earth, as if it had just rained. It was like this, the day she had gone off into the woods, leaving her child inside with his father and the doctors. A slight wind was shaking the branches, making the shadows move on the forest floor. There was the smell of the damp woods. And then she was back there on that day, kneeling in the dirt under a large pine, trying to fight back the helpless, sick feeling inside her.

She put her hands over her ears. *I must be strong for him, she thought. He believes God will help him.* But the first scream struck her in spite of the distance, the cupped hands. It was like a knife wound to her heart.

She scrambled up and ran back to the house. Bits of dirt and pine needles clung to her skirt. She didn't stop to brush them off. She burst into the room, her heart pounding. The boy shouted,

"Oh, Mother! Go back! Go back! I don't want you to come in!"

He was shouting something else, something about "toughing it out." She turned and rushed out of the room. She felt faint and sick, and the pounding in her chest wouldn't stop. She started to go out of the house again. Then the weakness hit her. She stopped and leaned against the wall for support.

The screams began again, rushing over her. After a moment they seemed to come at her from a distance, as if she were in a dream. She bit her knuckles, the tears hot on her cheeks. There was one final scream and then silence.

11

She hurried back into the room. Through the haze of her own faintness she saw her child in his father's arms, lying deathly pale. His leg was open, and his bed was soaked with blood.

"It's all right, Missus," the surgeon said. "The worst is over."

His recovery was slow, but his leg was saved. Lucy remembered how thin he was, and how she could easily carry him. He walked with crutches for three years, and had a slight limp the rest of his life.

She had tried not to worry about him...they were, after all, in the hands of God. But she remembered the trip from Vermont to Palmyra, New York, and the unscrupulous man whom her husband had hired to bring herself and the children to their new home. Caleb Howard, his name was...and all too soon he had spent her husband's money drinking and gambling at the inns. Lucy was grateful when they met the Gates family, traveling in the same direction. They decided to travel together; Lucy and her sons were in different wagons and got separated.

Later she heard that Howard had made Joseph get off the Smith wagon to make room for the Gates' daughters, whose company Howard enjoyed. Joseph was forced to walk for miles with his lame leg. When his older brothers protested, Howard knocked them down with the butt of his whip.

A cruel man... Lucy remembered how he had thrown their goods into the street in Utica, New York, and prepared to drive away with their horses and wagon. Her oldest son came to her with the news.

"Mother, Mr. Howard has thrown the goods out of the wagon, and he's going to start off with the team."

12

She remembered the anger, how it rose up in her...she had had enough. There were voices outside her bedroom window in Nauvoo...a shout, a horse neighing. Like the sounds outside the inn, on that day long ago. Then she was back there on that morning; she tried to keep her voice steady.

"Alvin, you go right out and tell Mr. Howard to come in here. I wish to speak with him."

The boy went back outside. Lucy made her way into the barroom. The place was full of travelers, both men and women. There was the murmur of voices, a burst of laughter...boots stamping on the rough wood floor. Outside, a horse neighed. Then Caleb Howard himself was coming toward her, his eyebrows raised quizzically (insolently, she thought). One of her sons was on either side of him. The other children, she knew, were not far away.

"What is it now?" he asked.

Lucy spoke in a loud voice, trying to sound firm.

"Mr. Howard, why have you thrown our goods out of the wagon?"

People stopped talking and began to listen. He shrugged.

"Well, ma'am, I thought you knew. All the money Mr. Smith gave me has been spent. I can't go any further without money."

"But why are you taking the team? My son said you intend to take the team and the wagon. Now you *know* that belongs to my husband."

He shuffled his feet. "Like I said, Ma'am. I already spent more than your husband gave me."

"Yes. On drinking and gambling."

Mr. Howard's mouth twitched at the corners. Lucy glanced over at the nearest group of people. She didn't know she could speak so loudly.

"Gentlemen! Ladies! Please listen to me! As sure as there is a God in heaven, that - that team of horses and those goods belong to my husband! This man says he's taking them from me...at least the team! Here I am with eight children, and no means of going on with my journey!"

Her words seemed to ring out, filling the whole room. She looked at Mr. Howard.

"Sir, don't you even touch that team! You shan't drive it one step further! You can go your own way; I don't need you any more. I shall take charge of the team myself!"

Mr. Howard was looking around, uneasy. A group of men started to move toward him.

"Now, wait a minute-" he said. But his words were lost in the sudden murmuring of the crowd.

"Come on, children," Lucy said. She started to walk out. One of her boys said,

"Mother, that was magnificent."

Another said, "I didn't know she could yell that loud."

Strong hands helped load the goods back on the wagon, the hands of men who had heard her story. Then she did indeed take charge, driving the team to Palmyra and arriving with two cents in cash.

Looking back, she wondered that she'd had the strength to go through it...a mother with eight children, one of them (Don Carlos) just born the past spring, and her own elderly mother who traveled with them as far as Royalton. Toward the end of their journey, they were bartering everything they had, even their clothes, so they would have enough to keep going.

Palmyra...the frontier village of wooden huts, log cabins...population about six hundred...the Erie Canal was going to be built; it was 1816 and everyone's hopes were high. The Smith family, having lost everything

14

in business and farming ventures, would make a new start. Lucy remembered the family council, held after they were reunited. They decided to do everything they could, with everyone helping, even the younger children — working and saving to buy a good piece of land.

'Cake and Beer Shop,' the sign at their door proclaimed. Gingerbread, root beer, pies and boiled eggs, little cakes, other goodies...they were all offered for sale at the shop. Cakes were sold from a pushcart. Lucy remembered one of the boys or their father manning the pushcart wherever crowds gathered in the village, and later, at the revival meetings.

Lucy painted designs on oil cloth, and sold enough table covers to furnish a house. Her husband Joseph was skilled as a cooper. In addition, he and his older sons, Alvin and Hyrum, took any jobs they could find...well-digging, gardening, harvesting. They helped feed the family by fishing and trapping. The boy Joseph, only eleven, hired out to work on local farms.

In two years they had done it. Her husband contracted with a land agent for one hundred acres in Manchester. They were able to settle themselves on their own land, in a comfortable log house. Then they worked harder than ever.

Clearing sixty acres of heavy timber...gathering sap from fifteen hundred sugar trees...making one thousand pounds yearly of sugar, molasses, and maple syrup (one year they won the county prize for production of maple syrup)...selling cord wood and vegetables...making and selling baskets, brooms and barrels...peddling cakes from the pushcart...

How could anyone say they were lazy? It was only afterwards, when the neighbors heard of her son Joseph's visions, that word got about they were lazy and shiftless. Until then, the local people accepted them as "decent

15

folk" and even allowed Lucy to "doctor" their sick, which she did as a kind, neighborly gesture.

"Uneducated," they said Joseph was. Very true, for with the depression after the War of 1812, there was no money to give anyone a formal education. And while Joseph spent much time meditating, he didn't read the Bible as much as the others did.

Still, they had a good religious upbringing. Prayers and hymns morning and night, and urgings for each child to seek his soul's salvation, or to "get religion." Lucy, looking back, had told someone she had raised them all "in the fear and love of God, and never was there a more obedient family."

William did balk a little, she recalled. When the boys saw their father reaching for his spectacles, they knew, as William said, they were "in for it."

Religion...getting religion...it was the subject of intense excitement in those days. Revivals, fiery exhortations in the groves...circuit riders...preachers saying,

"If you embrace wrong doctrines and unite with a corrupt church, you may expect coldness and darkness all your lives."

What was in young Joseph's mind as he stood on the outskirts of the crowd with the pushcart full of cakes? Lucy and three of the children, Hyrum, Sophronia, and Samuel, joined the Presbyterian Church. Yet Joseph did nothing.

Lucy remembered the feeling of dissension in the family...the conflict. Her husband refused to join any church. Her son Joseph was partial to the Methodists.

Then, in response to scripture, the boy had gone out into the woods to pray.

She was doing some household task — she couldn't even remember what it was — when Joseph had come in and

16

leaned up against the fireplace. His face was pale, and she thought at first he was tired or ill. Then he said,

"Mother, I know one thing. I'm not going to join the Methodist Church."

"Oh? All right."

"I'm not joining the Presbyterian Church either. But I won't keep you from going."

"That's good."

Later, much later, he told of the vision he'd had, out in the woods...it was early morning with the light filtering down through the trees, and he was walking out to the thickest part of the maple grove to pray. He looked around, making sure he was alone, and then he knelt down to begin his prayer. Suddenly a strange power seized him, and thick darkness surrounded him; he could no longer speak.

"I was terrified. Then I saw this pillar of light, right over my head. It was brighter than the sun...it came down slowly until it was on me."

Then he was delivered of the power which had bound him.

"When I looked, the Lord was standing before me, in the light... it was so bright I can't even describe it to you. He said I must not join any of the churches. For he said...and these were his words:

"'They draw near to me with their lips, but their hearts are far from me. They teach for doctrine the commandments of men, having a form of godliness, but they deny the power thereof.'"

In Joseph's first descriptions of the vision, he quoted the Lord Jesus as saying he was coming soon, clothed in the glory of his Father. Later on, Joseph told other details of the vision... how there were two personages in the light, and how one had called him by name and pointed to the other, saying,

17

"This is my Beloved Son; hear him!"

He also told them how the light was so bright he marveled that the trees were not burned by it.

Light... the return of the Lord Jesus, as promised in the scriptures. God was speaking again, as He had spoken to the ancient prophets, to the New Testament Christians. For Lucy, this was the most wonderful thing about the vision. *Light, and a voice in the woods, bringing order and harmony to their family, to their world.*

Many years later, when Joseph was at work on an inspired revision of the Bible, she remembered a favorite passage. It was from the twenty-fourth chapter of Matthew.

"For as the light of the morning cometh out of the east, and shineth even unto the west, and covereth the whole earth; so shall also the coming of the Son of Man be."

The King James version read, "...as the lightning cometh..." but Joseph, under the inspiration of the spirit, had corrected it to read, "the light of the morning." *How beautiful, how calm... as gentle as the first coming of the Lord, to the stable at Bethlehem.* Lucy, looking back, liked to think that Joseph's first vision was the beginning of that light... the dawn that would lead to the Lord's returning.

Although Joseph didn't tell his family right away, he felt he should discuss it with somebody. He tried to tell one of the Methodist clergymen about the vision a few days afterward. His report was treated, as he said later, "lightly... with great contempt."

Lucy smiled. She remembered the clergyman; she could imagine what had happened. And while she felt sympathy for Joseph, she could understand the reaction of that particular clergyman... startled... unable to deal with anything so completely outside his own experience.

She turned in her bed to face the window...the light of early morning. She could smell the scent of damp earth, of crushed pine needles. Then she was back in Palmyra on that day when Joseph was young and anxious to share his vision. *So long ago*. She closed her eyes, thinking of how it might have happened.

2

That afternoon the Reverend Buckworth was tired. There had been two buryings that morning on the other side of town, a child and an old man. Now he sat hunched over the table, thinking of his people and what he should say to them in the meeting that night.

He didn't have much time. Ford's daughter Polly was coming back soon, and she would want to talk. He liked listening to her; she was lively and more intelligent than most of the young people. But he wanted to get his work done first.

He closed his eyes and tried to concentrate. But other thoughts drifted in. He thought of his people, how few there were, and how he had to be prepared to give comfort or share their joys at a moment's notice. It was hard, boarding about with different families and having to be careful not to offend any of them. He wondered when the people would get around to building a church, so they wouldn't have to meet in the grove or the schoolhouse. It would be easier for him then, or for whoever was in charge. For a young man, it would be different. But forty was no longer young on the frontier.

He looked out the open window. He could see the field bright with sunlight, the tall grasses waving. Pines rose in the distance, on the edge of the forestland. He looked down at the table, which was bare except for last week's *Palmyra Register* and the Bible. The Psalms were open before him. He leafed through them, looking for one he could use that night. Then he heard the noise, the footsteps on the porch outside.

"She's back early," he thought. He ran his hand over his tie and collar. There was a knock.

"Come in," he said. He turned as the door opened.

It wasn't Polly after all, but a boy from one of the farms. The reverend gave a faint, surprised smile.

"Oh, hello, there, Joseph. We haven't seen much of you lately."

The boy stood blinking, unused to the dimness. He was a tall, stocky boy with blue eyes and light blonde hair. The man liked him; he pushed the Bible away and waited. The boy came closer.

"It's a busy time for us, reverend. We're just finishing up the planting. We did get to some of the meetings, though." He paused. "Say, I thought you could tell me where to find Reverend Lane."

"Why, land, boy, he left two days ago. He doesn't stay around one place too long. He's got a lot of territory to cover."

"Oh," the boy said. The man looked at him, wondering why he wanted the circuit rider.

"Anything I can do?"

"I don't know." The boy brushed his hand against a large pine chest. On top of it, a half-grown white cat rose and stretched. Joseph said,

"That looks like one of our kittens."

"Belongs to Mrs. Ford. Don't know where she got it. It's a nuisance. Eats, sleeps. Does everything but catch mice."

"Sounds like one of ours, all right." The boy stroked the top of the cat's head. It arched its back, purring. The man smiled, but he didn't really care for cats. Suddenly the boy gave him an intent look.

"Reverend Buckworth, if something very important happened to you, you'd want to tell it, wouldn't you?"

The man stopped smiling. "Well, yes. I reckon so."

21

The boy frowned, as if uncertain. Buckworth pointed to the long wooden bench by the table. He said,

"You can sit there, if you want."

The boy pulled out the bench and sat down. As the reverend leaned forward, he noticed that the boy's shoes and faded overalls were dusty from the road. The boy's eyes darted around the room, and the man tried to think of something to put him at ease.

"Well, now, what's on your mind?"

There was a thump as the cat jumped to the floor. The boy's hands gripped the edge of the bench. "It's about this strange thing that happened."

"Strange thing?"

"Yes. I-" He hesitated. The reverend nodded, to encourage him. The boy said,

"Mr. Buckworth. Do you believe in revelation?"

The man frowned, puzzled. "Divine revelation? Well, yes. I mean, certainly. I mean, what sort of revelation?"

Just then the cat jumped up on the boy's knees. The boy stroked its head and said,

"Well, have you ever had the feeling that, if you went out alone into the woods, and made your mind very clear and still, God would speak to you?"

"No. I can't say I have."

"It's the same sort of feeling you have when you're walking through the woods, and suddenly everything seems full of the spirit of God. The trees, the grass — you feel God in everything."

The reverend was uncomfortable; he wondered how to change the subject. "Yes...I think I've felt that. Anyway, let's get to the point. You said something about a strange thing that happened."

"I'm coming to it. You remember Mr. Lane's sermon, the last one he preached? It was about the different sects, and which one we should join."

22

"I remember it, all right. One of the best we had. Better than any of those other groups could offer."

"I thought so too. But the best part was when he said we should go out and ask God about it. I felt a good feeling when he said that, sort of a warm feeling in my chest. It was like an answer to something that had confused me."

"And what was that?"

"Well, how was someone like me to know which of the churches was right? All three of them said they had the truth."

The reverend nodded, sneaking a look at his watch. Twenty to four. "Uh, yes. You have to decide which is closest to your idea of truth."

"But if there was one church that was right above all others, you'd want to join it, wouldn't you?"

"Uh - that's an interesting question. You want to be careful about embracing wrong doctrines. But if churches are similar, one idea is to go with the group that needs you the most. I mean, if we had a few more converts, for instance, we could get a church built here."

The boy frowned. "No. I think Reverend Lane's idea was better. Right after I heard him, I went home and looked up the passage in my father's Bible. Let's see, it goes like this:

> If any of you lack wisdom, let him ask of God
> That giveth unto all men liberally and upbraideth not
> And it shall be given him."

Buckworth nodded quickly. "From the first chapter of James."

"That's right. I couldn't get it out of my mind. I read it over and over, thinking about it. Finally I decided to do it."

Buckworth leaned back, nodding. "Did it help?"

23

The boy smiled briefly. "Yes, but wait. I'd better start at the beginning. Do you know where our maple trees are? There's a whole grove of them; I showed you the first time you came out. There's a place there, where there's lots of undergrowth — a secret place where I sometimes go. I went out there three days ago. It was early morning. You remember that morning, when it was so clear and still? I could even see each leaf against the sky; it was that still. I remember lots of things — the way the grass felt, nice and cool, and the smell of the woods. But the thing I remember most is when I started to pray. I looked around, to make sure I was alone. Then I knelt down. I started to pray out loud, and I remember how strange my voice sounded. That was when it happened."

The reverend folded his arms across his chest. "When what happened?"

The boy kept his voice low. He seemed to be trying not to hurry.

"Well, suddenly I felt this power, like a great force all around me. I was terrified; I couldn't even speak. It grew dark, as if I was in some sort of cloud. This power was so great — I can't explain it, but I've never felt anything like it. I was ready to give up. I thought I was about to die."

Buckworth tried not to look startled. His mind was working, searching for something to say to the boy. The boy said,

"Just then I saw something...a pillar of light, way up over my head."

The man broke in. "A - a pillar?"

"Yes. It was tremendously bright, brighter than the sun, even. As soon as I saw it the fear went away. I kept watching the light, and it came down, closer and closer. Finally it was right there in front of me, and all

24

around me. It was like fire, but when I looked at the trees, they weren't burned. They weren't even singed."

As the boy spoke, he no longer looked at the man. He seemed to be looking at the open window. Buckworth turned, wondering, but all he could see were the fields and the distant pines. The man felt perspiration break out on his forehead. The boy spoke faster.

"This is the part that's hard to tell. I looked, and when I got used to the light, I saw — well, it was like a man, only larger. And there was a brightness, a tremendous brightness. It seemed to come from him. He was just above me in the air, and the whiteness, the light all around...I can't describe it. It dazzled my eyes."

The reverend sat in a stunned silence. He knew he should stop the boy, but he didn't know how. He shook his head, trying to drive away the weak, dazed feeling.

"Well...and then what happened?"

"As soon as I could speak, I asked which of the churches I should join. That was what I wanted to know. And the voice said-"

Buckworth shifted in his chair, uneasy. "Now, just a minute, son. I'm sure you meant well. All this talk about light, that's all very well. But a figure in the light, that spoke to you — why, that's too much."

"I know it sounds strange. That's why I had to tell you." The boy was sitting on the edge of the bench. "Don't you see? The trouble is, nobody has much faith any more. That's what the Lord said. 'They draw near to me with their lips, but their hearts are far from me.'"

"Don't tell me that was the answer you got."

"He said I shouldn't join any of the churches, for their creeds were — he used the words 'an abomination.' I think it means that people have forgotten about the power of God. With all these different churches, they're too

25

confused to come close to him. He said it plainly: 'Go not after them.'"

Buckworth nodded and let his breath out slowly. He would have to say it now, and he didn't want to. The boy was saying,

"After a while I came to myself, and I was lying on my back. It was the same beautiful clear morning again, and that's when I saw the leaves against the sky. I lay there awhile. Then I got up and went home."

The reverend tried to make his voice sound patient and kind. "Well, I suppose you're lucky. Not everyone has such a good imagination."

The boy looked at him, startled. "What do you mean?"

The reverend waved his hand. "What do you think I mean? You came in here and told me this thing, and I agree. It's a fine story. Now let's be serious."

The boy's face was pale. "But I told you. It's the truth."

Buckworth gave a nervous little laugh. "Oh, all right, then. I might as well tell you. I've had dreams, hallucinations, too. Not quite as dramatic as all that. It depends on what I've eaten the night before."

Still the boy didn't smile. He gave Buckworth a long look. Then he seemed to understand, and looked down. The cat gazed up at him, purring. When the boy spoke, his voice sounded forced.

"You don't believe me, do you?"

Buckworth laughed again, but he felt sorry for the boy. "Of course not. Did you think I would?"

"I was hoping you would."

The reverend glanced toward the door. "Sister Polly should be back in a few minutes. Now, let's get a few things straight. In the first place, there are no longer such things as visions or revelations. All that stopped with the apostles. You know that, don't you?"

The boy started to nod. "But after what happened-"

"Forget what happened. It sounds like a- a delusion, a bad dream. I mean, even if it really happened, it would be the work of the devil. All this talk about everyone being wrong; it's preposterous."

The boy's eyes rested on Buckworth, and for a moment the man was struck by the peculiar force of them. The boy's voice was tinged with anger.

"You said you believed in revelation. When I first came in, you said you did."

The reverend smiled nervously. "But I meant revelation long ago. Land's sakes, boy. I mean, it's all been said, back at the time of Christ. There's no need for anything else."

The boy put the cat on the floor. "Then why are things so confused?"

"*Things* aren't confused, only people. You, for instance."

The boy got up and moved around to the other side of the bench. It was warm in the room, and there was a faint musty smell in the air. Buckworth pointed a finger at the boy.

"Tell me, supposing the Almighty were to reveal himself. Just supposing, you understand. Why would he appear to *you*, of all people? Why not to Reverend Lane, for instance? Or one of the others, like Reverend Townsend?"

The boy drew a deep breath. "I don't know. I honestly don't know." He brightened. "Maybe if they asked Him, He would."

Buckworth felt his face growing warm. Things had gone far enough. He stood up. The boy was watching him carefully, waiting. Buckworth smiled as he put a hand on the boy's shoulder.

"You haven't told anyone else about this, I hope."

"Why not?"

"Well, it'd be a good idea if you didn't say too much about it. I mean, I don't want you to make a mistake."

"Mistake, sir?" The boy moved away from him a little.

"You know how folks are around here. If word of this gets around, why, it's not going to be easy for you."

A puzzled look crossed the boy's face, as if he hadn't considered such a thing. The man took advantage of the pause.

"Come on, now. Admit it. Isn't it time you changed your story? I won't tell anyone else."

It was quiet in the room. Buckworth could hear the cat purring as it rubbed against the bench leg. The boy was gazing out the window again, and his eyes had a brooding, distant look. For a moment the reverend wondered if anything had really happened in the woods. Leaves against the sky, a strange, dazzling light...but of course it was impossible. It couldn't happen — not in these woods, in this out-of-the-way place. The man leaned forward for the boy's answer.

"I can't," the boy said simply.

Buckworth felt a sudden, irrational anger. He took his hand away and moved to the window.

"I can't help you then."

The boy waited, as if wondering what to do next. Suddenly Buckworth felt laughter rising inside him. He tried to control it, but it came from him in sharp bursts.

"Voices from heaven. That's pretty good. Wait till Reverend Lane hears about this. And the Fords."

The boy was looking at him, open-mouthed. Buckworth tried to avoid his eyes.

Just then there was a noise at the door. They turned as Polly came in. She was tall, a handsome dark-haired girl, not yet eighteen. Her pretty mouth curved in a smile.

"Hello, Reverend. Oh, hello, Joseph. I haven't seen you for awhile. How's your mother?"

The boy swallowed, as if speaking were an effort. "Fine. She's fine, thank you." He didn't look at her. "I'm just leaving."

"Oh. I hope I'm not interrupting anything," she said, looking at Buckworth.

"Not at all," the man said quickly. "Say, you want to hear something funny?"

"Goodbye, Mr. Buckworth," the boy said.

Buckworth chuckled. "Don't you want to tell Miss Polly what you told me?"

But the boy didn't stay. Polly drew back with a puzzled smile as the boy brushed past her. He went quickly across the porch, down the steps.

"What is it?" the girl asked.

The reverend knocked the cat away from the door with his foot. "The boy. You know what he just told me? He says he isn't going to join any church because he had a revelation from God telling him not to."

"Oh?" She laughed pleasantly. "That's a strange notion."

For a moment the sunlight seemed too bright, and the reverend started to close the door. He could see the boy starting across the field toward his home.

"What did you tell him?" the girl asked.

"I don't know." The reverend paused, his hand on the door. "I mean, he just sat there, sober as you please, and talked about seeing visions, hearing voices."

She gave a little shrug. "He's a rather nice boy, too."

Suddenly he didn't want to talk about it any more. She moved closer to him.

"You figure if someone else talked to him, he'd change his mind?"

"I don't know." He didn't meet her eyes.

"Well, don't let it bother you any. He's just a boy. Maybe he'll get over it."

29

"Who said I was bothered?" he said, but his tone was annoyed. Polly looked at him, puzzled. He tried to think of something pleasant to say, to make things right again. But he was tired, and there was a vague uneasy feeling in his stomach.

"Would you like me to brew up some tea?" she asked.

He smiled weakly and nodded. She went toward the kitchen, but he stayed where he was, looking out.

Sounds of late afternoon drifted in — cattle lowing over the hills, a horse neighing. Somewhere a voice called to children, and a dog barked. The reverend could hear the wind stirring in the tops of the trees. He felt the breeze on his face, and for a moment he caught the scent of the woods, of pine and fresh damp earth.

He drew back, feeling the weariness rush over him.

"Like as not I'm getting old," he said. "That's what the trouble is."

Then he closed the door.

* * * *

She was a small-boned, pretty woman, looking younger than her twenty-eight years. She sat in her maple rocker with a shawl around her shoulders. The parlor, sun-lit, still had the chill of early morning about it.

"Please sit down," she said to the man. He was older, in his forties, wearing a dark suit of broadcloth. "You say you're a missionary? You put me in mind of a missionary I knew, back when-"

"No, ma'am," Jesse Stokes replied. "I'm not a missionary. I'm actually a writer — that is, I write articles. I'm doing research for a newspaper."

"A newspaper! How interesting. That puts me in mind of-"

"Mrs. Cox, I wanted to get some information about the Smith family." He took a seat on the wooden bench by the rocker. "The Smith family, from Palmyra."

"Oh, yes. The Smith family. In truth, they lived closer to Manchester. The village was...well, let's see, there was the Harrises and the Jacaways, and the-"

"About the Smith family. I understand they were your neighbors."

"That's right. My father owned a farm right near theirs, in New York. My parents were friends of the Smith family. And let me tell you, it was one of the best in that locality. They were honest, you know...religious and industrious. But poor. In fact, they were so poor that-"

"Excuse me, Mrs. Cox. Would you say they were - uh - lacking in intelligence?"

"Well, no. In fact, the father of the family was, I'd say, above the average in intelligence. I heard my parents say he looked like he'd descended from royalty. A tall, well-favored man. His wife was called 'Mother Smith' by just about everybody. Children loved to go to her house. It was a big house, and she would listen to us, and give us good rye bread to eat, the best I've ever had-"

"All right. What about Joseph Smith? The son of these people. Do you remember anything about him?"

"Joseph? Oh, yes. My father loved young Joseph Smith. He often hired Joseph to work with his own boys."

"Do you recall when that was?"

She pressed her thin lips together. "Oh, it must've been when I was about six years old. Yes. I was six when he first came to our home. In fact, I remember going into the field one afternoon to play in the corn rows while my brothers worked. I played all afternoon. When evening came, I was too tired to walk home. I cried because my brothers wouldn't carry me. Well, then Joseph lifted me to his shoulder. He threw his arm across my feet, to steady

31

me. I put my arm about his neck, and he carried me to our home. He was so kind, and just lifted me up... you can't believe how tired I was, just a little girl, and he-"

"I see. All right. Let's get on to something else. Mrs. Cox, do you remember anything about his having visions?"

"Oh, let's see. Oh, yes. I remember...yes, Joseph's first vision. There was a lot of excitement about it...some of the people were all stirred up. My father said it was only the sweet dream of a pure-minded boy. Isn't that a nice thing to say? I thought it was. Anyway, one of our church leaders came to my father and said he shouldn't allow such a close friendship between our family and the 'Smith boy' — that's what he called him. My father — I remember him saying that Joseph was the best help he'd ever found. He told the churchman he always fixed the time of hoeing his large field to when Joseph Smith could come and help. That was because of the influence Joseph had over the wild boys of the neighborhood. You see, when these boys — I should say 'young men' — worked by themselves, they'd spend a lot of time arguing and quarreling. Like as not they'd end up in a ring fight. But when Joseph worked with them, they'd work steady, without fighting. That way, my father got the full worth of the wages he paid."

"So," Stokes said. "So Joseph was able to influence the others to keep working. That's interesting."

"I remember the churchman saying, oh, in a very solemn tone...he said the very influence the boy carried was a danger. He said not only the young men, but all who came in contact with Joseph, were likely to follow him."

"I see. And did your father listen to the clergyman?"

32

"No. He certainly did not. Well, then Joseph had a second vision and began to write a book. Now, this book drew many of the best people away from the churches. Intelligent people, that you wouldn't think could be misled. Then my parents realized that the churchman had told them the truth. Why, my aunt Allie, she said-"

"Excuse me, Mrs. Cox. What did your parents do then?"

"What did they do? Well, of course they cut off their friendship for all the Smiths. Would you believe *all* of that Smith family followed Joseph? Even the father, intelligent man that he was — why, even *he* could not discern the evil they were promoting."

There was a faint musty smell from the parlor, which had been unused over the winter. Stokes shifted his position on the bench.

"So your whole family turned against him?"

"Yes. My parents lent all the aid they could to help stop Joseph Smith, but it was too late. He had run his course too long. He could not be put down."

She shook her head, and her eyebrows drew together in a frown. She sighed and said,

"I don't understand. He was so kind, you see. There never was a truer, purer..." She smiled then, and a softer look came over her face. Her eyes still looked troubled. "Noble. Yes, he was noble. There never was a nobler boy than Joseph Smith, before he was led away by superstition."

3

Imagine that it is mid-morning on a day in September, 1823. It is Monday, and the date is September 22. The place — a hill in western New York state, near the village of Manchester. Later, people will call it "Mormon Hill" and the "Hill Cumorah," and they will put up a monument and trim the lovely foliage and even have a pageant there every year, with loudspeakers and colored lights and busloads of singers and actors.

But the boy climbing the hill that morning knew nothing of such things. For him it was just another hill, and there were no monuments or signs or trimmed bushes all in a row. In the year 1823 it was a wilderness, and for those people who think wild places are beautiful, it was very beautiful indeed.

There were white pine and maple and oak, the leaves of the hardwoods just beginning to turn yellow and orange. The sumac was already flaming red by the forest path. The boy pushed through the underbrush, the tangled growth of young popples and ferns. There was the crunch of last year's leaves underfoot, the crackle of twigs breaking.

The only other sounds were bird voices…a jay calling somewhere, a crow, the chattering of chickadees. The boy knew all these sounds; they were as familiar to him as waking and breathing. Raised in the wilderness, he had no formal education as we know it, but he had a sense of the woods and wild places. For him, going into the forest was like putting on an old, familiar coat, with every button and pocket known.

As he climbed, part of his mind was tuned to his surroundings — the bird calls, the thicket of brush ahead. But most of his concentration was on the strange thing that had happened.

He had seen another vision. In fact, he had been awake all night; he had experienced the same vision four times. By now, it was indelibly printed on his memory.

Somewhere near the top of the hill (so he was told), there was a stone, and under that stone was a book written on gold plates, an account of other people who once lived on this continent. Buried with the plates, there was also an ancient breastplate with two stones set in silver bows, something used by seers in former times.

Marvelous as that was, and eager as he was to see those things, there was something else which puzzled and troubled him. According to the angelic visitor, who had come to him four times, God had a work for him to do. Because of that work, his name would be had for good and evil among all nations, kindreds, and tongues. The visitor had also warned that he would be tempted, because of the poverty of his family, to get the plates for money.

Joseph, almost eighteen, was six feet tall, powerfully built, well developed from his work outdoors. Right now he was feeling tired, light-headed from his lack of sleep...it was as if the vision of the night before was still with him. When he had gone to the fields that morning with his father and brothers, he had felt too exhausted to work. His brother Alvin had admonished him to keep working. His father had looked at him and told him to go home.

Then, as he had tried to climb the fence by the edge of the field, he felt dizzy; he fell to the ground. The next thing he saw was the angel standing above him in the light. The same vision of the night before was repeated (the fourth time), and Joseph was asked why he had not told his father.

"Well...I was afraid he wouldn't believe me."

"He will believe every word you say to him."

Joseph had returned to the field and told his father. His father had listened, then nodded.

"Be assured...the message is from God. You'd better go and do as you are commanded."

He had gone immediately to the hill which had been shown him in the vision...the largest hill in the neighborhood, just east of the mail road from Palmyra to Canandaigua.

Why did he think his father wouldn't believe him?

From the time he had his first vision, at the age of fourteen, he had known nothing but ridicule from the people who should have sympathized and tried to help him. The religious leaders, the young people in the churches...all had turned away from him.

He thought of the weekly trip into town to pick up his father's *Palmyra Register*, and how he had tried not to hear their voices.

"There's Joe Smith. God speaks to him; did you know that?"

"Hey, boy. What's God saying these days?"

He knew that because of his vision, the whole family had suffered ridicule and persecution of various kinds.

But this latest vision...so new and strange. He wasn't sure what to make of it himself. That, and his feeling of unworthiness about receiving such a thing, had made him hesitate to tell anyone in his family.

It had not been easy for them, as Joseph knew only too well. Along with the general ridicule and scorn of the "Christian" townspeople, there was the poverty, the constant drudgery, the struggle to survive. Many mouths to feed, bills to pay, chores to do...hard work required

36

of every able-bodied family member, from dawn to the last light. He wished he could do more to ease their burden.

But all he could do was hire himself out...and he had been hired to work at many things. Farm hand, day laborer, wood chopper, money digger...for that was the current fad — the belief that there was ancient treasure buried in the hills. Most of the time these treasure hunts came to nothing, but Joseph collected his wages and took them home to his family.

Now he was on the strangest treasure hunt of all. He tried to hurry — he had seen the place in the vision; he thought he knew where it was. Would he know the actual spot when he reached it?

The summit of the hill was still ahead. He thought briefly of the events which had led to this last vision.

Rejected by the "decent folk" of the town, he had fallen into friendships and habits that he felt were not in keeping with the call of his earlier vision.

Vices and follies. A light and vain mind...a foolish and trifling conversation. For Joseph was fond of people; he loved jokes and stories, and even wrestling. He liked debating and arguing too. And it was impossible to grow up on the frontier and not learn self defense. Whenever he was forced to fight anyone, or lay hands on them in anger, he felt sorrow and a sense of shame. Hadn't his parents told him that fighting and quarreling were "sins that are beastly?"

So Joseph had decided once more to engage in earnest prayer, asking for a manifestation of his standing before God.

Retiring to his bed for the night, he had begun his prayer. While he was praying, he had become aware of a light in the room.

Light increasing...filling his world...he remembered how it was brighter than the noonday sun. Brighter than the pools of light on the forest floor. Then he was back there, in his room, with the light all around him, gazing with astonishment at the place where the light was brightest.

It was just beside his bed. His heart gave a leap. There was a figure in the light's center, a being of light. The being was standing in the air, for his feet did not touch the floor. He had on a loose robe, which was whiter than anything Joseph had ever seen. An exquisite whiteness. The robe was open around his chest; his head and neck were bare. His hands were also bare, and his arms to a point just above his wrists. The robe extended almost to his ankles and feet, which were naked.

Not only did the robe glow with an unearthly whiteness, but the whole aspect of the being seemed to radiate a glory beyond anything Joseph could imagine. The being was looking at him; the expression was not unkind, but steady and piercing. Joseph's initial fear began to leave him. Then the personage was addressing him, calling him by name.

He said that he was a messenger sent from the presence of God; his name was Moroni. Then Joseph was told about the work God had for him to do — that his name would be had for good and evil among all people.

A shadow came between Joseph and the light. He felt a rush of air on his face. He looked up; it was the morning again, and he was on the hill. A sudden breeze was stirring in the tips of the trees. A branch was shaking in the wind; the shadow moved over him.

He thought of the many other things the being of light had said in the vision. After telling of the book written on gold plates, with the "fullness of the everlasting gospel" contained in it as delivered to the ancient

38

inhabitants, the messenger had started to quote passages of scripture.

"'For behold, the day cometh that shall burn as an oven...' 'I will reveal unto you the priesthood by the hand of Elijah the prophet before the coming of the great and dreadful day of the Lord...' '...the hearts of the children shall turn to their fathers; if it were not so the whole earth would be utterly wasted at his coming...'"

What kind of day would "burn as an oven?" How could the whole earth be utterly wasted? Joseph had no idea. He only knew that he was very tired; the events of the night had exhausted him, even though every detail was clear in his mind. He must somehow find the place where the book was buried, for apparently it was his work to bring it to light.

He was nearing the top of the hill. He was very close to the spot where he believed the book was hidden. A shifting of light and shadow, trees rustling in the wind...and he was there, in the place shown in the vision.

On the west side of the hill...not far from the top. There was the stone, just as in the vision...thick, rounding in the middle on the upper side. Only the middle was visible above the earth...the edges covered with soil.

He knelt, digging at the edge of the stone, scraping away the dirt. In the underbrush he found a stout stick, which he used as a lever. Finally he pried up the stone, and there indeed, in a kind of stone box, were the articles described by the messenger.

Sunlight glinting on the ancient metal...the plates, "of curious workmanship," held together by shining rings. The breastplate was alive with light; a thousand tiny sparkles danced on the surface. There was a brightness all around. As he reached to take the plates, he looked up to see Moroni standing beside him in the light.

* * * *

"What, Joseph? You didn't get them?"

"What do you mean, you weren't allowed to take them?"

"Why not?" William asked. "Why didn't you just grab 'em?"

"Be quiet, William," his father said.

William Smith was only twelve the day his older brother came back from the hill.

Memory is a funny thing. Seen through the haze of years, events take on colors and hues that never existed at the actual time, or they become jumbled and juxtaposed with other events. Looking back from a vantage point of old age, William couldn't really remember whether Joseph asked the family to gather together before he went to find the plates, or later on that evening, after he returned.

But at any rate, they gathered, sitting in a little circle in the main room. His mother later said it was the evening after the visit to the hill, when the family members were together.

Joseph made an attempt to tell them what had happened. But it was late, and he was tired. His face was pale, and he seemed to speak with an effort. It was Alvin who said,

"I have an idea. Why don't we go to bed now, and get up early in the morning? We can finish our day's work an hour before sunset. Then we can have an early supper, and a fine long evening. You'll have plenty of time to tell us about this vision."

"Let him tell it now. He can do it now."

"Be quiet, William. Can't you see how tired he is?"

William wasn't tired. He was impatient to hear the rest of it, and to know why Joseph hadn't brought the plates home with him. But he had to wait with the rest of the family until the next evening.

At last sunset came, and the family gathered again. Then Joseph charged them not to tell anyone outside the family what he was about to say.

"For I have been warned...the world is so wicked that when people hear about these things, they'll try to take our lives. And when we do obtain the plates, most people will think we are lying."

Then he went on to tell about the plates, and how he had found them in the very place where the angel had directed him to look.

Why wasn't he allowed to take them? William wanted to know.

"I was told the time wasn't right...I wasn't ready. I am to go to the hill next year at this same time. So we must wait until then."

"A whole *year?*"

William didn't think he could wait that long. But he didn't have a choice. And the secret, the most wonderful secret of gold plates buried in the hill, was carefully kept by the whole family. It was something they shared and carried together — the knowledge of the ancient book in the earth that would soon be in their hands, and their responsibility to help keep it safe.

As the time approached for Joseph to visit the hill again, William found it hard to keep his mind on his chores. The whole family waited with excitement. Everyone expected Joseph to come home with the plates.

But he returned empty-handed, looking troubled and shaken. As he came in the door, his father asked if he had obtained them.

"No, Father. I couldn't get them."

"Didn't you see them?"

"Yes. I saw them, but I couldn't take them."

41

His father said, "Well, I would have taken them, if I were in your place."

"So would I," William said.

"You don't know what you're saying," Joseph replied. "I couldn't get them, for the angel of the Lord wouldn't let me."

Then he told them what had happened.

He had lifted the stone and uncovered the plates. He had reached for them to take them up. As he was lifting them out of the stone box, he wondered if there might not be treasure buried with them. The instant's greed made him lay the plates down, so he could cover the box and conceal what was left in it from any passing stranger. He covered it carefully, but when he turned around, the plates had vanished.

Alarmed, he knelt down and asked the Lord why the record had been taken from him. Then the angel appeared, and told him he had not done as he had been commanded. For he had been told not to lay the plates down or put them out of his hands even for a moment until he had taken them home to a safe place. Instead, he had laid them down in hopes of securing some fancied or imaginary treasure that remained.

Finally Joseph was allowed to raise the stone again, and there the plates were as he had first seen them. He reached to take them. Suddenly he was hurled back upon the ground with great violence. When he managed to get up, the angel was gone. Joseph went home weeping with grief and disappointment.

When the family heard it, everyone wept. They began to worry that he might never obtain the plates. They doubled their diligence in prayer and supplication, all praying that Joseph might be obedient and faithful enough to receive the ancient record.

Then the series of instructions began, with Joseph meeting the messenger each year at the place where the plates were buried. In turn, Joseph told his family the things he was learning. The ancient inhabitants...their dress, mode of traveling, the animals upon which they rode...their cities, their buildings, their mode of warfare...their religious worship — all these Joseph described at the evening meetings.

But the most serious part — the thing that William never forgot — was that the book about to come forth had the "fullness of the gospel" as given to the ancient people of the land.

What did that mean? They talked about it in their evening meetings. Their father had read where John Wesley the reformer had said,

"'The times which we have reason to believe are at hand (if they have not already begun) are what many pious men have termed, the time of 'the latter-day glory;' — meaning, the time wherein God would gloriously display his power and love, in the fulfillment of his gracious promise that 'the knowledge of the Lord shall cover the earth, as the waters cover the sea.'"

The family was unified as never before, and prayed anxiously about the great thing that was about to happen.

William, looking back through the mist of years, could never think of that time without remembering his brother Alvin. For Alvin became ill suddenly with abdominal cramps, and all efforts to save him were in vain. William remembered how his brother requested his father to go immediately for a doctor. Their family doctor was not available, and their father came back with another doctor, Dr. Greenwood. He prescribed a heavy dose of calomel, which Alvin at first refused to take. At last he was persuaded to take it.

The family believed that the dose of calomel lodged in his stomach, and all the ministrations of his family doctor three days later, and four other skilled physicians, could not undo the damage.

William remembered the family gathering at Alvin's bedside...they listened to his last words as the candle flickered beside the bed.

"Hyrum...I have done all I could to make our parents comfortable. I want you to go on and finish the house, and take care of them in their old age...don't let them work hard..."

To all the children, including William, he said, "Be good...do all you can for Father and Mother — never forsake them...Be kind to them, and remember what they've done for us."

But to Joseph, he said, "...be a good boy, and do everything that lies in your power to obtain the record. Be faithful in receiving instruction, and in keeping every commandment that is given you..."

He asked to see his young sister Lucy for the last time, and his mother went to get her out of bed. The two had a special fondness for each other. When she was brought in she cried and clung to him.

Soon afterward, he breathed his last. The child Lucy continued to cry for "her Amby." The others were numb, in shock; it had happened so fast.

Alvin was one of those people who are universally liked; the whole neighborhood mourned him. But his family was especially stricken.

After that, it was hard for them to talk about the record, for they remembered how zealous and anxious Alvin had been in regard to it — more so than any of the rest of the family.

In time their sorrow grew less. There was always the work to be done, the chores, the bills to be paid. They worked on finishing the new house, and even refused an offer for it from the principal workman.

William thought less and less about the golden plates. He figured Joseph probably never would be good enough to get them anyway. In their circumstances, who wouldn't have thought of seeing if there were treasure buried with them? But the plates, he knew now, were not to be used for the purpose of "getting gain." Even the thought was wrong.

About this time their mother became interested in a movement to unite the local churches. Most of the family went to the meetings with her, and even their father went a few times. But Joseph refused to have anything to do with it.

"Why, I can take my Bible, and go into those woods...I can learn more in two hours than you can in two years, even if you went to meeting all the time."

One day he said,

"You look at Deacon Jessup, and you hear him talk very piously. I bet you think he's a very good man. Now, just suppose that one of his poor neighbors should owe him the value of a cow, and that this man had little children. Let's say the neighbor should get sick and die. He leaves his wife with one cow, and no other means of supporting her family. Do you know what? Deacon Jessup, religious as he is, wouldn't hesitate to take that cow from that poor woman, in order to secure the debt. He would do that, even though he has more than enough of everything."

"Oh, Joseph, no," his mother said. "How can you say that?"

To William's amazement, within two years Joseph's statement was literally fulfilled.

Just before the house was completed, a Mr. Josiah Stoal came from Chenango County, New York. His name was really 'Stowell,' but most everybody spelled or pronounced it 'Stoal.' He had stories of a lost silver mine.

Mr. Stoal claimed to have an ancient document which showed the location of the mine, supposedly opened and abandoned by the Spaniards, in the Susquehanna Valley. Stoal had already done some work on the site.

He had come looking for Joseph, the family learned, because of Joseph's reputation as a clairvoyant and a finder of lost objects.

William could hardly contain his excitement. A lost silver mine! Treasure left by the Spaniards! This was better than gold plates which you couldn't get unless you were especially good. He couldn't understand why Joseph was reluctant to go help locate the mine.

But Joseph did hang back, and even tried to talk Mr. Stoal out of the project. William wished he could go in Joseph's place. But Mr. Stoal was insistent; he particularly wanted Joseph to help him.

"I'm prepared to offer you fourteen dollars a month!"

The family did need the money. Finally it was agreed. Joseph would go and work for Mr. Stoal, along with his father and a few of the neighbors. It was arranged that Joseph and his father would board with Mr. Isaac Hale, in Harmony, Pennsylvania, near the site of the mine.

William, not yet old enough for such a venture, had to watch while his father and older brother set out. It was hard to be only fourteen, and to have to wait at home while his brother Joseph got to do such exciting things. It wasn't fair.

But again he didn't have a choice. Maybe it wouldn't be that much fun anyway. William hoped it might not be.

Then he sighed and turned back to his chores.

4

That's right. Josiah Stowell's my name. Oh, some folks write it 'Stoal' or 'Stowel.' But I never did care much how they spelled it. As long as they came close.

Let's see, now. You wanted to know about Joe Smith? Oh, yes. I knew him well; matter of fact, he worked for me. His family called him Joseph, though — like his father. They was good workers, he and his father. I guess the brothers were, too. But they didn't work for me.

What's the question? Did I think he was a prophet of God? Well, not when I first knew him. Oh, later, sure — when he translated the book from them gold plates and organized that church. They called it the Church of Christ back then. But when I first saw him, he was just a young lad — about twenty, I'd say. Handsome chap. Tall — he was six foot at least, and he could wrestle just as good as his old man. He had sandy-colored hair — auburn, I think they call it, and blue eyes.

Tell you what, though. There *was* something different about him — I can't quite put my finger on it. It wasn't his looks — but both my daughters told me he was uncommon handsome. And they was experts in such matters (they told me so themselves). Maybe it was his eyes — he looked at you direct, not shifty-eyed like some folks. When you was with him for a little while, you got the feeling you was in the company of a straight-forward, honest feller.

What did I mean by that? Oh, let's see...well, I would say he sure wasn't one to put on airs. Not him. There

47

was something about him that made me want to believe anything he said.

I first went lookin' for him because I'd heard he had spiritual gifts — "keys" by which he could discern lost objects. And I had a lost object I wanted to find — a silver mine. I knew it was there (left by the Spaniards, it was). I even had the map with the location marked. I had done some diggin' myself, there at the site. But it was a large area, and I needed some extra help.

Now, about them "keys." There are lots of people in these hills who put great stock in "seer stones" or bits of glass, same as there are folks who witch water. Some have the gift, and some haven't. So Joseph's ability in this line warn't so unusual. "Glass-lookers," they called them. And you can bet he wasn't the only one who was doing it. Why, folks up and down these parts swear there's buried treasure left in those hills — silver and gold left by the Spaniards. Spaniards, Vikings, Indians...God knows who else was here. Even Israelites, according to Joseph. You see, people were in a frenzy at the mention of buried treasure. I ought to know — I was one of them. Why, I'll wager on certain days you could go out and find someone diggin' at every mound in the Susquehanna Valley.

My stars, there's nothing wrong with glass-looking, or trying to find buried treasure. But later, when Joseph was trying to start his church, people would laugh at him and say, "The money-digger's up to his old tricks."

I felt bad then, when I heard those things. You know, Joseph got himself in a bit of trouble down here, when he was working for me. He rubbed someone the wrong way, is all I can figure out, and he was brought to trial as an impostor. Nothing came of it, of course. There was all this talk of his claiming to know where certain treasures were, but men trying to find them couldn't get

48

them. The thing I remember most is, Joseph's father got up and said,

"Joseph and I are mortified that the wonderful power, which God has so miraculously given, should be used only in search of filthy lucre."

So, you see, even his family thought he had special powers.

Well, I never did find that filthy lucre. Joseph convinced me I should stop looking for it. But he stayed on and worked for me, after the other diggers had gone home. He did a lot of work on the farm...odd jobs...he could do anything. He was a good, dependable worker, and all this talk of his being lazy and shiftless is just a load of— well, there just ain't any truth to it.

But now comes the interesting part. I have to tell you about Emma, and the Hale family

Now, this Hale family was an interesting bunch. A good family. I liked them, Isaac and Elizabeth, even though they was devout Methodists and I was Presbyterian. You had to say they were generous. Their home was always open to the traveling ministers, the circuit riders. In fact, they had opened their doors so often to the Methodist ministers that folks started calling it the preacher's home.

Now, Isaac was good to others, too, not just preachers. He was a skilled hunter, him and his boys...expert woodsmen. Why, he'd take his boys and go up the Starucca — that's a creek branching off the Susquehanna, goes way up into the wild country. And he'd shoot elk. He'd salt that meat and pack it home...and half the time he'd leave it at the door of some needy family. That's the kind of man he was.

Folks said he warn't afraid of anything, he and his boys. The story was that they'd heard Ethan Allen swear, and after that they wasn't afraid of any bears, no siree!

49

Isaac and his wife had nine children. I told you a little about the boys. Now, they had a daughter named Emma. She was one of the youngest — I think she was the seventh, but I might be mistaken. Emma was tall and dark-haired, real purty. Big dark eyes. And she loved to sing — she sang most all the time, around the house. Somewhere along the line she'd had music lessons. She had book-learning too; she was a school teacher. And she could ride a horse about as good as any of her brothers.

You can imagine how proud Isaac was of this daughter. Why, any man would be. Folks thought she was proud too, but I figure maybe she was just quiet. Reserved...that's the word. She could act real dignified-like, probably because of all the school-teaching. And as far as young men were concerned, she was most particular.

Now, I had arranged for the Smiths and some of the other diggers to board at the Hale's home, over in Harmony. Little did I know what was going to happen. I reckon no one ever does, unless they're a prophet.

Well, as far as I can figure, Joseph took one look at this handsome school-teaching daughter of Isaac's, and he was gone for sure. Set his heart on her, if you know what I mean. If I'd known, I would have told him to give it up. After all, she had all this culture, this book-learning. Her family was well-to-do... not the richest folks around, but they sure weren't dirt poor. And he had nothing. No learning, no schooling. No money except what he earned as a day laborer.

Well, he might have been poor, but he was determined, too. When he stayed on to work for me, he went over to see her whenever he could. And he even attended school. I think he was trying to get some learning, on account of Isaac saying he was poorly educated.

50

You see, Isaac was bitterly opposed to the whole idea of Joseph's keeping company with his daughter. I've thought about it some, and I think part of the trouble was that Isaac was just too respectable. I would have been proud to have Joseph Smith as a son-in-law. But Isaac couldn't see beyond the money digging and the glass-looking...things that Joseph only did for a short time. Isaac didn't like any of those boarders...he said one of them ended up owing him $12.68. But it wasn't one of the Smiths.

Isaac said Joseph was careless and insolent to his father. If he was, I sure didn't see it. But I guess it was the lack of education and the money digging he objected to most. That's what he said, anyway, when Joseph asked for Emma's hand. He said Joseph was not well enough known to the Hales, and they disapproved of his business.

Joseph had told his own parents about his intentions to marry Emma, and they had approved. His friends did all they could to help. Joseph Knight — the old man — lent him a horse and cutter so he could go visit Emma in style. Martin Harris went and bought him a new suit of clothes, so he'd look good before Emma and her father.

Joseph said it was his religion that Isaac Hale really objected to. All these rumors about his seeing visions, and gold plates buried in that hill. But whatever the reason, things didn't look too good for those two. Her father finally forbade her to see him anymore, and even locked her up... kept a close watch on her so she couldn't sneak out and see him.

Joseph tried to pretend it didn't make much difference, but you could see him sort of moping around. He was over working for Joseph Knight at the time, trying to save enough money to get married. So you see, he hadn't given up. But we all figured it was going to be a cold day in hell before Isaac ever agreed to that marriage.

51

Now, as I was saying, things looked pretty bleak. But I'll be darned if the lady didn't have a mind of her own. Would you believe she was just as stubborn as Isaac? Well, shucks, she was over twenty-one — old enough to decide for herself. She knew what she wanted. And she didn't want the 'respectable' young feller her father had picked out for her.

Well, she was over visiting my daughters about this time, and Joseph just happened to be there. He started in begging her to marry him, and I must say, I urged it too. They must have planned the whole thing then. They waited until old Isaac was off at church, then he just went over and got her. She left everything she had; the only things she took with her was the clothes she was wearing.

Mr. Hine and his wife — they was neighbors of the Hales. Well, they looked out of their winder that morning — mid-January of 1827, as I recall — and they saw Joseph riding past on an old horse with Emma up behind him. They were married later that day at Squire Tarbill's house in South Bainbridge.

We was all relieved to get it over with. The only person that wasn't happy was Isaac. He was furious. It was some time before he accepted the fact that she'd run off with Joseph. In his opinion, she woulda been better off dead. That's how grieved he was. Meanwhile, Joseph and Emma went over to live with the older Smiths, near Manchester.

Whenever I saw them together after that, I remember thinking what a good match it was. They were a good-looking pair, to begin with. They seemed happy and lively, and as far as I could tell, they was always nice to each other. They went through some pretty hard times too, like we all do.

Later, when Joseph was a church leader, I heard tell his enemies were saying he stole his wife. Well, land of Goshen! What choice did the man have? He did everything a body could have done...tried everything to get around that old man. And I guess she was trying everything too, at her end. The only thing left for them to do was run off together.

What's that you say? Oh, yes; I've heard them rumors. You mean, about Joseph having other women...actually marrying other wives besides her? Well, all I can say is...not if *she* had anything to say about it.

It don't seem likely, somehow. See, he had to go through so much trouble to get her, like I just told you. I know he really cared about her. He cared too much to do something that would grieve her, or make her uneasy. You see, he was one of the kindest men I ever knew; I never saw him do anything that wasn't kind. Why, he even treated dogs and horses better than some folks treat other people.

Why, shucks...that plural marriage business. That's the kind of talk you hear about every religious community these days...every new group. So I'd discount it, if I was you.

No, I just can't believe them stories. It wouldn't be like him.

5

It was after midnight when they started. Emma had glanced at the clock as she hurried through the front room in her bonnet and riding dress.

Only Joseph's mother was still up. The rest of the household, including the guests (Mr. Knight and Mr. Stowell), had long since gone to bed.

Joseph had Mr. Knight's horse and wagon just outside. He held the lantern as Emma climbed up into the seat.

He swung up beside her and took the reins.

"Ready?" he said smiling.

"Yes," she whispered. She marveled that he could remain calm when the time he had been waiting for was so close. Her own heart was beating fast, and she felt a strange agitation in the pit of her stomach.

For this was the anniversary of Joseph's visit to the hill. For three years he had climbed the hill, according to commandment, and met the angel at the designated spot. Now, this fourth time, he fully expected to be given the sacred record and the Urim and Thummim.

"If I don't get them now, I don't think I ever shall," he had told her earlier.

They were moving now, going slowly down to the main road. The wagon was creaking, and the horse's hooves crunched in the dirt. The lantern threw a feeble light on the road. It cast strange shadows on the fence posts. She could see the tufts of grass in the light, and the deep ruts other wagon wheels had made.

Out beyond the circle of light, it was pitch dark. The moon had set two hours after sunset. Emma thought of sitting alone with the horse and wagon while Joseph took the lantern and went on up the hill. An uneasiness gripped her. She hoped he wouldn't be gone long.

Then she was annoyed with herself. Of all things, to be afraid of a little dark. Hadn't she only a few months before braved the wrath of her father and left her mother, brothers and sisters, not knowing if she would ever see them again? With just the clothes on her back, she had left.

All too vividly the memory came back...the hurt and pain of leaving her home, her family...the greater hurt if she had not been able to marry Joseph. She had chosen to go with Joseph, for better or for worse. She remembered sitting up behind him on the old horse as they rode away to be married.

It must have taken some kind of courage, she reflected, although she hadn't thought much about it at the time. To go with her husband to a strange place, to live with a family she had never seen. If she could do that, sitting in the dark alone was nothing.

Nevertheless, she moved closer to Joseph, as if to draw strength from him. They made the turn onto the main road. He put his arm around her.

"Are you warm enough?"

"Yes. I'm fine, thank you."

"It can get chilly this time of year."

They spoke softly and then lapsed into silence. The darkness was their friend; she knew that. With what they were going to do, it was best to keep it secret as long as possible.

She remembered Joseph's mother's face, just before they left the house. They had told no one where they were going, not even Mother Smith. Just before they left, Joseph had gone to his mother and asked if she had a chest with a lock and key. She seemed to know

55

immediately what it was for, and the distress showed in her voice; she didn't have a chest which locked. Emma heard Joseph say,

"Never mind. I can do very well for the present without it. Be calm. All is right."

Then, as Emma had walked through the room, she was conscious of Mother Smith's eyes on her. Emma had turned, and in an instant read the distress, the anxiety...the years of waiting. Emma had tried to smile, but the older woman was too preoccupied to notice.

She was most likely at home praying this very moment. Mother Smith was one of the kindest persons Emma had ever met, and probably the most devout. The old lady prayed about everything, or else had an appropriate passage of scripture for it. Emma smiled. At the same time, she was strangely touched...reassured at the thought of Mother Smith praying for their safety, and the success of their mission.

She realized too, for the first time, how the whole family was concerned about the plates. It wasn't just Joseph, as she had assumed when he first told her.

During their courtship, she had heard it...the story of the gold plates in the hill, and the angel's visit. She remembered how strange it had seemed to her at first. It was his honesty and sincerity that had convinced her...if it was true (and she believed it was), then this man had a most extraordinary mission. Now she, too, was part of that mission.

One of the remarkable things about him, she had decided, was not his good looks nor his persuasive sincerity (both of which he had in abundance). It was his willingness to do what he considered to be God's will. She knew many so-called "men of God" who could only do things their own way. Here was one — unlettered, unschooled — who was anxious to do things God's way, and not his own.

Emma, with all her schooling, could not even think of a word for such a quality — perhaps there wasn't one. But the quality itself was real, and perhaps it was more important than either of them had guessed. She had a feeling it might be so.

The shadow of the hill was ahead of them, its outline dark against the sky. Everything seemed hushed; there was no wind. Joseph guided the horse just off the road into a small flat area behind a stand of trees.

"You'll be safe here," he said. He handed her the reins. Then he got down and reached for something in the back of the wagon.

"There's an old blanket back here, if you get cold. I'll be back as soon as I can."

With the sound of the horse's hooves stopped, a deep silence seemed to hover around them. It was a stillness greater than any Emma had ever known. She wanted to speak, to say something. But Joseph took the lantern, and she heard his footsteps in the dried leaves going further and further away. She followed the glimmer of light with her eyes as far as she could. Then she was left alone. There was only the silence, and the light of the stars.

An owl hooted, and some small animal made a rustling in the underbrush. Her eyes were becoming used to the dark; she could see the jagged edges of trees against the sky. Joseph's words came to her, his last words to his mother.

"Be calm. All is right."

She tried to pretend it was just an ordinary night in the deep woods. She looked up at the stars, the Big Dipper inverted at a strange angle (how late was it now?) She remembered how her father and older brothers had pointed out the constellations, naming them for her.

She felt a sudden wave of homesickness for her family. Not that she regretted leaving them; she could not have stayed there. But sometimes she did miss them, and wished she could see them again, just for a little while.

Her brother Alva...she thought of how he loved to tease; he was never serious. He and the other brothers had gone out of their way to tease Joseph, and 'vexed' him at every opportunity. Once, on a fishing trip, the teasing had gone too far. Joseph had thrown off his coat and offered to fight them all.

The Smith family was very different from her own. They never made light of one another, or teased each other without regard for feelings. They were supportive of each other, and even the opinions of the smallest child were treated with consideration. And they seemed to stay in good spirits, in spite of all the trouble concerning the house.

For their frame house, which they loved so much, had been taken from them by a stratagem.

According to Mother Smith, the carpenter Stoddard had offered them fifteen hundred dollars for the house, but they had refused to sell. Then, he and his accomplices had told the land agent in Canandaigua that the two Josephs had run away, and that Hyrum was defacing the property, cutting down the sugar trees. Stoddard, with this story, had persuaded the land agent to give him the deed to the property, upon immediate payment.

Stoddard had then offered the deed to the Smiths for a thousand dollars. The family had tried desperately to raise the money, but failed. The best they could do was to persuade a Quaker gentleman by the name of Lemuel Durfee to buy the property. He did so, taking ownership in December of 1825. He had treated the Smiths kindly, and had leased the house to them so that they could stay there for another three years.

Emma knew the loss of the home was a blow, especially to the elder Smiths. Joseph's mother had said several times that every corner of the house reminded her of Alvin. They had hoped to live the rest of their lives there. But all their hopes had come to nothing.

In spite of the disappointment, they still managed to treat each other (and her) with kindness and concern. Work went on as usual, with a certain attitude of forgiveness and acceptance. She wondered if her own family, with their greater material wealth, would have handled things as well. She somehow doubted it.

Where was Joseph? She hadn't thought it would take so long. She was getting cold, sitting there in the dark.

She hoped he wouldn't be disappointed this time. He had been to the hill several times before, she knew, and had returned empty-handed. Suppose something had gone wrong, and even now he was being reprimanded for some oversight on his part?

She remembered an incident not long after they were married. Joseph's father had sent him to Manchester on business, and he had not returned by six o'clock in the evening. Hours later, he came in and threw himself into a chair, exhausted.

"Joseph," his father said. "Why are you so late? You should've been home three hours ago."

Joseph was silent; he was breathing fast.

"Joseph? Why don't you answer me? What's happened to you?"

His mother said,

"Now, Father. Let him rest a moment. You can see he's home safe. He's very tired, so don't bother him now."

Finally Joseph smiled, and said in a calm voice,

"I've just taken the severest chastisement that I ever had in my life."

His father was angry, thinking that it was from some of the neighbors. "I'd like to know what business anybody has to find fault with you!"

"Stop, Father! Stop!" Joseph said. "It was the angel of the Lord. As I passed by the Hill Cumorah, where the plates are, the angel met me. He said I had not been engaged enough in the work of the Lord…the time had come for the record to be brought forth. I was told I must be up and doing, and set myself about the things which God had commanded me to do."

He took a deep breath, then went on. "But, Father. There's nothing to worry about…I know what I'm supposed to do. Everything will be all right."

The horse shifted his weight from one side to the other, lifting a hoof and stamping it down again. The crunch seemed to echo in the stillness. Emma strained to listen. But there was no sound from the hill.

The rustle of branches. A slight breeze was stirring in the tips of the trees. Emma shivered. She secured the reins, then climbed into the back of the wagon. She found the blanket and settled down with her back against the wooden side. She pulled the blanket up around her. At least now she would not be cold, and she would be ready to move into the front seat at a moment's notice.

She was sleepy. There was a warmth stealing all through her. She must be careful not to go to sleep. Joseph might need her. She wondered how heavy the plates would be, and indeed, if he could manage to carry them and the other articles by himself. Maybe he would need two trips.

She thought of her family, and what they would say if they knew what she was doing now. Not that she cared; she would do it anyway. But she thought of her father raising his eyebrows and staring.

"You're doing *what*? In the middle of the night, you're waiting while that glass-looker does *what*?"

She sighed. Maybe someday her husband and father would get along. The first steps had already been taken.

A few months after her marriage, she had written to her father. She had left behind everything she owned when she eloped. In the letter she asked if she could have her belongings...the rest of her clothes, a few pieces of furniture, and several cows. Her father had agreed. In August, she and Joseph had gone to her parents' house to collect her property.

To her joy, there had been a reconciliation. According to her father, Joseph had agreed not to do any more "glass-looking." He was to bring Emma back to Pennsylvania to live, and to accept her father's offer of help at getting started as a farmer. Joseph was reconciled with Alva too. Alva had said he would come later and help Joseph and Emma move back to Harmony.

Emma had hopes that they all could be happy together and live in peace. But she had doubts too. Somehow she had the feeling her father never would understand about the angel, or the gold book that would have to be translated.

She would not worry about that right now. She would leave it in God's hands. She tried to keep her eyes from closing. But the hard boards of the wagon felt comfortable and far away. For a moment the stars and tree branches seemed to blur and blend together.

Starlight. A steady gleam. Light, coming down from the side of the hill. She raised her head, wondering.

61

Then she saw the glow of the lantern growing brighter and brighter. The trees outside the circle of light were no longer in total darkness. She could just make out their shapes, shadowy outlines in a dim half-light.

She climbed back onto the wagon seat. She could hear Joseph's footsteps in the dried leaves now, not as fast as when he started up. He seemed to be carrying something heavy.

In a moment he was beside the wagon. He had something wrapped up in a piece of cloth.

"You've got them?" She thought she had whispered it.

"Hush. Yes. Let's be off."

He put the bundle in the wagon, just behind the seat. Then he hoisted himself up onto the seat and took the reins. He clicked to the horse and guided it out onto the road. The familiar clopping of horse's hooves echoed in the air.

Emma leaned back against the seat. She was just beginning to realize how anxious she had been. But now it was all right; he had the plates in his possession at last.

There was a noise behind them, a twig snapping. He started, and looked around. She looked back too. But there was nothing.

"Deer, most likely," he said. But he kept casting glances over his shoulder as they rode.

It wasn't until they were almost home that he said,

"The angel...he stood by and said...he said, 'Now you have got the record into your own hands, and you are but a man...therefore be watchful, faithful to your trust, or you will be overpowered by wicked men...'"

Another glance over his shoulder. "'...they will lay every plan and scheme that is possible to get it away from you. If you do not take heed continually, they will succeed.'"

She could see the outlines of the fence, the tall grass even now touched by a faint light. The road to the farm was just ahead.

"'While it was in my hands, I could keep it, and no man had power to take it away...but now I give it up to you...'"

He reined in suddenly, and the horse stopped. Emma looked at Joseph, but he was glancing around behind him again.

"I thought I heard something..."

But there was only the sound of leaves stirring gently in the wind.

As Joseph turned, his face looked resolute in the light of dawn. Already he seemed older, less carefree. He urged the horse forward, and they made the turn onto the little road.

"'Beware, and look well to your ways...and you shall have power to retain it, until the time for it to be translated.' Those were his last words to me."

Emma nodded. She was beginning to understand about his anxiousness, his uneasy glances.

"You'll have them safe at the house in just a few moments," she said. "Then I can see what they look like."

He looked at her, and a stricken expression darted over his face. She wondered what was wrong.

He waited, then said,

"Emma, my dear...you must understand. I would give anything if you could see them too. But I am forbidden to show them to anyone."

"What? I can't even see them? But why not?"

"I - I don't know. But I've been commanded...no one is to see them. Not you, not my father — not anyone. Maybe it will be different later on. But for now...I just can't."

63

He spoke deliberately, as if he were very tired. She was silent. He took her hand.

"Please try to understand."

She made an effort not to let the disappointment show. "Of course, Joseph. I - I understand. It's all right. I don't have to see them."

Her voice had a forced cheerfulness that she hadn't intended. She patted his arm.

He smiled then, but he still looked troubled. She said, "There must be a good reason for it."

"There is. We must exercise faith as never before, and try to do everything as I was instructed."

She nodded, feeling suddenly the lack of sleep. She hoped they would be able to get some rest before anything else happened.

They rode the rest of the way in silence.

6

The public house in Palmyra was buzzing with the news.

"That's right," one grizzled old citizen declared. "I heerd it with my own ears. He's found a book up on that hill — a book written on gold plates!"

"Oh, come on, Josh," someone said. "There ain't any sech thing, and you know it."

"I heard it from Martin Harris hisself. And you know all them stories — everybody knows there's treasures up there, just waitin' to be dug up."

"The trick is knowin' where."

"He's right," someone else said. "Why, back in 1810, it was, why, De Witt Clinton hisself, *he* told about finding copper kettles and other old things, in a buryin' ground. Near Canandaigua, he said."

"So young Joe has found himself a gold treasure," the innkeeper said.

"Why not? He's been lookin' long enough, I hear tell."

"I wonder what it says — I mean, the writin' on them plates?" old Josh said.

"It beats me," the innkeeper said. "If they're really made of gold, I don't think he'll be able to keep 'em long enough to find out."

* * * *

The family knew little of the excitement sweeping the neighborhood. They were overjoyed that Joseph had the plates at last. His father asked,

"What, Joseph? Can't we see them?"

"No. I disobeyed the first time. But now I intend to be faithful. I was forbidden to show them to anyone until they are translated."

They were allowed to handle them through the cloth covering. When William handled them, he felt thin sheets of metal that could be riffled like the pages of a book. He said they were heavier than wood or stone, and seemed to be a mixture of copper and gold. He estimated they weighed about sixty pounds.

Emma went over to them where they lay on the table. She touched them through the cloth, tracing their outline and shape. They were pliable, like thick paper. She moved the edges with her thumb; they rattled with a metallic sound.

Joseph did allow his mother to see the interpreters, the two stones set in silver bows. Soon after his return from the hill, he said to his mother.

"Don't be worried, Mother. All is right. See here? I've got a key."

"A key?"

"A key to the translation. An aid."

He showed her the strange object.

It appeared to be two smooth three-cornered diamonds set in glass. The glasses were set in silver bows, which were connected to each other in the same way as old-fashioned spectacles.

"I don't understand, Joseph. How is that a key?"

"Well, you see, the plates are written in a language that is now lost. No living person has any knowledge of it. The only way it can be read and translated is through these interpreters. The angel said it was used by seers in former times. That's why I call it a key."

Joseph Knight, Sr., whose horse and carriage had been borrowed for the expedition, said to Josiah Stoal,

"Seems to me he thinks more of them fancy glasses than he does the plates. Why, he described all them things to me, those gold plates and the spectacles, and he says, 'It's ten times better than I expected.' He tried out those spectacles and he says to me afterward, he says,

"'I can see *anything*. They are marvelous!'"

"If that don't beat all," Stoal said. "You know what I just heard? Old Martin Harris, he's gone up there diggin' on the hill hisself, to see what he can find."

"Once word gets out, they'll tear that place apart."

In the next few days, people started coming to the Smith place, asking to see the plates. Joseph told them it was impossible; he was not permitted to show them.

"It's gettin' worse," Joseph Knight said to Stoal. "People are insisting; they're offering money and property, jest to see those things. Joseph, he keeps right on saying he can't do it. And some of them folks, they're gettin' pretty mad. Some are actin' downright ornery."

"I hope they don't take *this* place apart."

* * * *

"A chest," Joseph said to his mother. "We have to get a chest made."

She told him to go to the cabinet-maker who had made some furniture for their oldest daughter, and tell him they would pay him for making a chest.

"Just as we did for the other work...one half in cash and one half in produce."

Joseph said, "Very well, I'll tell him. But I don't know where the money's coming from. There's not a cent in the house."

The very next day a Mr. Warner came to him, and said that a widow over in Macedon needed some labor

67

done on a well. As the earnings would pay for the building of a chest, Joseph went over right away and started work.

With Joseph gone, the rest of the family was left to deal with the neighbors. One of the neighbors in particular began questioning Joseph's father. Soon an alarming piece of news came to light.

Ten or twelve men, the father learned, were clubbing together with one Willard Chase, a Methodist class-leader, at their head. They had even sent away for a "conjuror," who was supposed to tell them where the plates were hidden.

The Smiths thought the part about the conjuror was ridiculous, but they were afraid the mob might accidentally discover where the plates were hidden. Joseph's father decided to verify the stories the next day, and set off to visit among the neighbors. At the very first house he came to, he found the conjuror, with Willard Chase and the rest of the group.

On the pretext of an errand, he listened to their plans with rising alarm. When he returned home, he asked Emma if she knew where the plates were. She wasn't sure. He told her what he had just learned.

"I don't know what to do," Emma said. "It seems to me, if Joseph is to get the record, he *will* get it, and no one will prevent him."

"Yes. He will, if he is watchful and obedient. But, you see, for only a small thing, Esau lost his birthright and his blessing. The same thing might happen to Joseph."

Emma waited, then said, "If I had a horse, I'd go and warn him."

The Smith team was gone that day. But there happened to be a stray horse on the place, and William was sent to fetch it. In a short time William brought up the horse. He had put a large hickory withe around its neck (to mark it a stray, according to law).

Soon Emma found herself riding for Macedon, on the back of a stray horse decorated with a hickory withe.

She rode in haste, concerned not only for the safety of the record, but for her husband — for the worst thing she could think of was that something should happen to Joseph. He was waiting for her a little ways from the place where he was working. Later he said he'd had an intuition something was wrong.

She told him the news about the mob, and he decided to return with her. At first the lady who had hired him wouldn't agree to his leaving. Finally she consented and sent for a horse for him.

Still wearing the coarse linen frock he used for working, he mounted the horse. Together he and Emma hurried home, riding through the village of Palmyra on the way.

At home Joseph found his father pacing the ground, greatly agitated. Joseph said,

"Father, there's no danger. All is perfectly safe. There's no cause for alarm."

Nevertheless he sent his youngest brother, Carlos, over to Hyrum's house with the request that Hyrum come over immediately. When Hyrum got there, Joseph told him to get a chest with a good lock and key, and to have it there by the time he got back.

Then Joseph started for the plates.

He had secreted them about three miles from his home, in an old birch log. The log itself was much decayed, except for the bark. Joseph had cut the bark carefully with his pocket knife. He had made a hole big enough to hide the plates. Then he had replaced the bark and had thrown some branches across it.

When he reached the hiding place, he took the plates from the log and wrapped them in his linen frock. He put them under his arm and started home.

He went along the road for a while. Then, uneasy, he left the road and headed into the woods. He tried to move as quickly as possible without making any noise. He thought he heard a twig snap somewhere ahead of him. He froze, listening. There was no other sound.

He pushed aside the overhanging branches. Just ahead was a pile of trees uprooted by the wind. He began to climb it, picking his way over the logs.

He jumped over a log. A man sprang up on the other side.

Before Joseph could even cry out, the man raised his gun and swung it down with great force. Joseph tried to dodge. The blow caught him on the shoulder.

Joseph whirled around. Using his free hand, he slammed his fist into the man's face. The man staggered back and fell down among the logs.

Joseph ran. He held the plates close to his chest, dodging trees, leaping over logs. Leaves and twigs crackled under his feet.

He thought he saw something move behind a tree. He tried to turn in another direction. It was too late.

The second assailant was upon him before he could even draw a good breath. Joseph managed to dodge the blow from the gun. He tripped the man and sent him sprawling in the leaves.

Running again. Which way? His shoulder ached, and the load of plates was heavier than he had ever imagined. He was almost home. But he was frightened; who else was waiting for him? And how close behind were the others? The farmhouse and its clearing were just ahead through the trees. He *had* to reach it. Panting, he tried to run faster.

The third man met him at the edge of the woods. Tired now, Joseph swung and missed, then swung again. The man grappled with him. As Joseph struggled to protect the plates, he felt his thumb being bent back. Finally he managed to knock the man down.

With the last of his strength he pushed on, keeping to the woods. There was the house at last, the familiar fence of split rails.

He could go no further. He threw himself down beside the fence, panting, trying to catch his breath. His shoulder ached; he felt bruised all over. Then he noticed the pain in his thumb. He had dislocated it in the last encounter.

He got up and went over to the house. Surely *now*, in his home, he would be safe.

His mother met him at the door. For a few moments he could not speak; the fright and fatigue were too much for him.

After resting, he asked her to send his brother Carlos for his father, Mr. Knight and Mr. Stoal.

"Tell them to go immediately...see if they can find the ones who were chasing me."

Then he wanted Carlos to run to his brother Hyrum's house.

"Tell him to bring the chest. Hurry."

It happened that Hyrum's wife had just given birth to a daughter (Lovina) two days before, and was still confined to her bed. Hyrum was having some tea with two of his wife's sisters, who were visiting. Carlos came in, and just as Hyrum was raising the cup to his mouth, Carlos touched him on the shoulder.

Immediately Hyrum jumped up, dropping his cup. He caught up the chest, turned it upside down and dumped the contents on the floor. He rushed out of the house with the chest on his shoulder. Carlos raced after him.

"Jerusha, your husband has gone crazy!" said one of the sisters.

Hyrum's wife laughed. "Oh, not in the least. He just thought of something which he forgot to do. It's just like him to fly off on a tangent when he thinks of anything like that."

When Hyrum arrived at his parents' home with the chest, Joseph locked up the record.

By this time a number of people had gathered in the kitchen. There was the family, Mr. Knight and Mr. Stoal, and some of the more sympathetic neighbors. Joseph went in and told them what had happened. He showed them his thumb.

"I must stop talking, Father, and get you to put my thumb in place — it's very painful."

His father, with Mr. Knight and Mr. Stoal, searched all through the woods. They could find no sign of the persons who had made the attempt on Joseph's life.

After this incident, Joseph stayed close to home, working with his father and brothers on the farm. His mother believed that through the use of the interpreters, he was given knowledge as to whether or not the plates were in danger.

One afternoon he came in and requested her to come downstairs immediately. She left what she was doing and got downstairs. That was when he handed her the breastplate.

It was wrapped in a thin muslin handkerchief, so thin that she could see the glistening metal. It had a concave pattern on one side and convex on the other, and was big enough to extend from the neck downward to the mid-section of a large-sized man. It had four straps of the same material attached to it. Two of the straps ran back to go over the shoulders, and the other two were designed to be fastened to the hips. Lucy measured the straps; they were two finger-widths wide. They had holes in the ends of them, so they could be fastened.

"Joseph," she said, incredulous. "It must be worth at least five hundred dollars!"

He took it and put it in the chest with the other objects. Then he went out again.

Not long afterward, he ran into the house, breathless.

"Mother! Has there been a group of men about?"

"Why, no," Lucy said. "No one's been here since you left."

"A mob will be here tonight, if they don't come before that time. They intend to search for the record — we have to get it to a safer place."

What should he do? He began pacing up and down, looking around the room. There were hoofbeats outside, the sound of a horse slowing to a walk. He sprang to the window.

"It's only Mr. Beaman," his mother said, opening the door. "I know it's safe to let *him* in."

It was indeed Mr. Alva Beaman, an old friend of the family. He had come in from the village of Livonia.

"What's the matter?" he said, once he was inside.

Joseph told him his fears for the safety of the record and breastplate, and also his belief that a mob would be there that night.

"We must be prepared to drive them away," Joseph said. "But first we must get the plates to a secure place."

"Hm," Mr. Beaman said. He spoke deliberately, taking his time. "What about — why not put them under the floor? Pull up them boards over here-"

"The hearth!" Joseph said. "That's it! We'll take this portion up. There's an old wooden box out in the shed. I'll get it."

In haste they pulled up the bricks. Joseph put the articles into the box, which he nailed shut. They buried the box and relaid the bricks on top of it. By this time Joseph's father and brothers had come in to help.

73

The hearth was scarcely relaid when there was a shout from outside. Lucy drew back against the wall. The men moved toward the window. There were the sounds of someone running, a shot from the edge of the woods.

"There's your mob, all right," Mr. Beaman said.

"They're all armed," William said.

"How many do you reckon there are?"

"There's no more time!" Joseph said.

He threw the door open. Then he began to shout and halloo as if he had a whole legion at hand.

He gave the word of command at the top of his lungs. At the same time all the male portion of the family, from the father down to little Carlos, dashed out of the house.

They rushed out upon the mob, whooping and shouting. One of them yelled,

"Rush on! Rush on, boys! We'll get 'em!"

The mob fled before them into the woods. Once in the woods, the mob began to disperse.

For the moment the record was safe. Lucy remembered the story of her father Solomon Mack and how he had saved his life by a similar stratagem. Alone in the woods, he had come up against four Indians armed with tomahawks, scalping knives and guns. But he had fooled them into thinking he outnumbered them.

She had told her family the story many times. Now the trick had worked once again.

"It's not over yet," Joseph said as the family gathered back inside. "They'll be back. But not for a while." He glanced around. "We've got to get the plates out of the house."

Toward the end of the afternoon he dug up the hearth again. He opened the box and took up the objects, wrapping them in clothes. He carried them to the cooper's shop, just across the road.

He hid them in the loft, in a large quantity of flax. Then he tore up the floor of the shop and dug a place just big enough for the wooden box. He nailed up the empty box and put it in the depression, then replaced the floor.

The mob was there as soon as it was dark. The family could hear them milling all around the house and in the woods. There was the cracking of twigs, the smashing sound of rifle butts against wood. They swarmed everywhere, ransacking, searching, but made no attempt to enter the house. They moved along the fence, tripping over things in the darkness. Then Joseph heard them out in the cooper's shop.

After a while they left. In the morning, Joseph hurried out to the cooper's shop. The floor had been torn up, and the wooden box shivered in pieces.

Later, the Smiths learned that Willard Chase's sister Sallie had found a piece of green glass, and by looking in it, claimed to "see" where "Joe Smith kept his gold bible hid." She had directed them to the cooper's shop, and the box under the floor. The plates themselves remained safe overhead, in their bed of flax.

Joseph knew that the next task was to translate the record, with the help of the interpreters. But how was he to accomplish it, with all the greedy and curious neighbors?

The answer was simple. He had to get away, to a place where his discovery was not yet known. They would go back to the home of Emma's family, in Harmony, Pennsylvania.

Alva Hale, Emma's brother, came out to help them with the move. Joseph was concerned about money for the journey, and how they would manage. He went ahead with plans for the move. But their poverty weighed on his mind...they had very little, and the persecution was so heavy that he couldn't see how things would ever be otherwise.

He and Alva were settling some business in town the day Martin Harris came up to them.

"How do you do, Mr. Smith?"

They shook hands. Then Mr. Harris took a bag of coins out of his pocket. He put it into Joseph's hand.

"Here, Mr. Smith, is fifty dollars. I'm giving it to you to do the Lord's work. No, I give it to the Lord for his own work."

After the initial surprise, Joseph said, "No. We'll give you a note. Mr. Hale, I presume, will sign it with me."

"Yes," Alva said. "I'll sign it."

"No, no," Mr. Harris said. "I want to give the money to the Lord. I must insist."

To the others gathered in the public house, he said,

"I call you to witness; I give this freely. I ask no compensation. This money is for the purpose of helping Mr. Smith do the Lord's work."

Joseph managed to thank him. Fifty dollars! It was enough to help them with the move.

Not long after, they started for Pennsylvania. It was mid-winter, and Emma was in her first pregnancy. They made the wagon trip of one hundred and twenty-eight miles, with the box of plates hidden in the bottom of a bean barrel.

7

Martin Harris truly wanted to serve the Lord. A seeker after truth, he had sought it in various denominations. First there were the Quakers (his wife Dolly was one). Then he had investigated the Universalists, Restorationists, Baptists, and Presbyterians.

For all his religious wanderings, he had a great knowledge of the Bible and was able to quote verses and whole chapters from it. But still he was not satisfied.

He was in middle age when he first heard of Joseph's visions. He had a sturdy appearance, with sideburns and chin whiskers. Hardworking all his life, he had married his first cousin, Lucy Harris, who was known as Aunt Dolly to their circle of friends. Together they managed their 240 acre farm. Their endeavors included growing wheat and manufacturing worsted and flannel cloth.

In addition, Martin had served his community as a commissioner of common school and an overseer of highways. He had a reputation as an honorable man and a good neighbor.

He had first heard of the gold plates from Joseph's father. His imagination was immediately fired.

"Plates of burnished gold, Dolly! With hieroglyphics engraved on them!"

"What's that you say?"

"Hieroglyphics. You know...strange figures engraved on the plates."

"You don't have to shout, Martin. I can hear you."

"Mr. Smith says it's the record of an ancient people with the knowledge of the truth. Imagine that, Dolly.

Secrets of past ages, hidden in the earth! What do you think of that?"

"I think the hot spell's gone to your head."

Martin said, "Oh, no, Dolly. Mr. Smith's a reputable man. A good neighbor. He wouldn't make up something like that."

"I'd have to *see* those plates before *I* believed it. You say one of the boys found them in that hill?"

"Yes. Joseph...one of the older ones. He— why, he used to work in my fields for fifty cents a day. He was around ten years old then. Who'd ever think he'd find something like that?"

"Well, like I said. I'd want to see them first."

Now it was rumored that Joseph actually had the plates in his possession.

Martin's first reaction was to go digging on the hill himself, in the hopes of finding more treasure. When his efforts came to nothing, he wanted to know more about what Joseph had found, and if, indeed, he could help.

Martin wanted to serve the Lord, especially in this matter. But things kept getting in the way. To begin with, his wife Dolly remained suspicious of the whole thing. It was her deafness, of course. Whenever anything was said that she didn't hear distinctly, she became annoyed. She had demanded to see the plates. But Joseph had refused. That had angered her, and now she was determined to see them.

Martin couldn't figure out about Dolly. One moment she was over at the Smiths', saying she'd seen the plates in a vision and they were indeed of God. Then the next day she'd turn around and say it was all a scheme to get their money from them. He wished he had something definite to show her, to convince her once and for all.

"It's just that you must have *faith*, Dolly. Joseph was forbidden to show them to anyone."

"Ridiculous! I have faith in what I can see!"

"Well, when he gets some of those characters copied for me, then you'll have some proof that-"

"What? What's that about copying the - the what?"

"Characters. The letters in the strange language. He's going to make a copy of some of them. Then I'm going to take the copy to someone who knows about ancient languages — maybe some expert in New York City-"

"Good, good. That's a good idea. And he'll be able to tell if they're real or not."

"He'll be able to tell maybe what language it is, and if-"

"I bet the whole thing's just a hoax, it is. I want to go with you, Martin. I want to hear that expert tell me himself those letters are genuine."

"But, Dolly, I can't- I'm not prepared to- That is, I think it's better if I go alone."

"Well, how ridiculous. I insist — I'm coming with you."

"Really, Dolly. I - I can be more help to Joseph right now if I go over there alone."

"So you're in cahoots, are you? Trying to deceive me, and take my money!"

"No. Oh, no. That's not true. It's just that - well, it's a four-day journey to Harmony, in the first place-"

"That's fine. You don't have to shout. I'll be ready. And I intend to see those plates, as long as I'm about it."

Martin thought it best to leave without her knowledge. Together he and Hyrum Smith made the trip to Joseph's house in Harmony.

They found Joseph and Emma living in a small frame house about four hundred and fifty feet east of the Hales' home. It had a beautiful maple floor, and three rooms — a kitchen-living room, a bedroom, and an upstairs room. Part of the upstairs was partitioned off into a room with a window to the east. Here Joseph sat to do his work of translating.

It was February of 1828 when Martin and Hyrum got there. Martin immediately wanted to know about the plates and how the translation was progressing. To his dismay, things were not going very fast.

"I did some work on the translation in December," Joseph said as they sat around the small table. "I began it then, as soon as we were settled from the move. The main trouble is, I can't write very well."

"You can't write?" Martin asked.

"I'm a poor writer. It takes so long, you see, and-"

"It takes him a long time even to write an ordinary letter," Emma said.

"So for that reason, I needed a scribe."

"A scribe," Martin said. "Oh. You mean, someone to write for you."

"Yes, while I dictated the words. Now, Emma did some of it for me."

"Reuben helped too," Emma said. "My younger brother."

"But it's slow work. It requires a degree of patience, and we need to keep at it."

Martin thought of them sitting there hour after hour, Emma writing while Joseph spoke the words. Such a thing indeed would take time. But Emma had her housework to do; she said herself there was not enough time for her to write for him. And Joseph had to work in order to support both of them, as they had no money except what he could bring in.

"Do you need money now?" Martin asked.

"We still have a little bit left," Joseph said. "Our friend, Mr. Knight — you remember Joseph Knight, from

Colesville? He saw that we had a few provisions, and some extra money."

"He even brought Joseph's father and brother Samuel to see us," Emma said. "And he gave you money for paper, remember?"

"Yes — that was later. He handed me some money and said to go buy paper for my work."

Emma said, "I don't know what we'd do without friends."

"I'm glad not everybody looks at things the way your father does," Joseph said. "We'd really be in trouble then."

They told Martin what had happened when the box was first taken out of the bean barrel. Emma's father had looked at it, then wanted to know what it was.

"I told him he could lift it, but that he couldn't look inside. He said... what was it he said?"

"Oh, he was angry," Emma said. "He said, 'You'd better get it out of my house, then, or I'll open it for sure! I never heard the like...something *I'm* not supposed to see!'"

While Martin was there, he tried his hand at writing for Joseph. He wrote just enough to become fascinated by the content of the book: he wanted to do more. But first it was agreed that he should take the page of characters, together with a translation, and find a reputable linguist.

Martin had a friend in Palmyra, the Reverend John A. Clark. He went to this friend with the transcript. From Reverend Clark, and others, he learned about the leading authorities on ancient languages and where he could find them.

He went to see Assemblyman Luther Bradish in Albany. Bradish had traveled in Egypt and knew something of antiquities. From there he was directed to Charles Anthon of Columbia College, and Samuel L.

Mitchill, professor, classicist, physician and United States Congressman.

He called on Professor Anthon in his Manhattan study. Professor Anthon was a bachelor living alone on the Columbia College campus.

Martin, awed by the rows and rows of books, introduced himself. He described the gold plates found in the hill, talking fast because he was nervous. He produced the transcript from his pocket.

"And some of the characters have been translated," he said. He handed the transcript, together with the translation, to the professor.

Professor Anthon was middle-aged, his hair gray at the temples. He had a wide mouth and a strong, determined set to his chin and jaw. When he spoke, his voice was cordial.

"Do sit down, Mr. Harris."

Martin preferred to stand. Professor Anthon took the pieces of paper and sat down at his desk. He put on a pair of spectacles. Then he bent over the transcript, studying it in silence. He read the translation, then turned back to the characters.

From where he stood, Martin could see the characters Joseph had copied with such care.

Martin waited, trying not to fidget. Professor Anthon's eyes behind the thick glasses were intent; they made his whole face seem alive with interest and curiosity. Martin had never met a professor before, but he had a sudden flash of insight...this man loved his work — his books and his ancient languages — as much as he, Martin, loved the open fields and fresh-turned earth.

Finally the professor looked up.

"Well, I must say, from what I've seen, that the translation appears to be correct. More so, in fact, than any I've seen from the Egyptian."

82

"Egyptian?"

"Yes. Now, these — I presume these down here have not yet been translated. They certainly look Egyptian, yes, and Chaldaic. I see some that look Assyriac and Arabic. It's fascinating."

"Are these - uh - those things you just said...I mean, are they the true characters?"

"Yes. From what I can see, it would appear that they are."

"Well, you see, I wish you would put that in writing."

"Writing?"

"Yes. You see, I need to show the people back in Palmyra — they want to know if what we've found is real."

"Real. I take it you mean the plates with the inscriptions?"

"Yes. I may have to help with the printing of the book, and I'd like some sort of, well, proof that it's not a hoax. I mean, I may have to sell some of my property to help get it printed."

"I see. You need some sort of certificate. Well, let's see what we can do."

While the professor was writing, Martin could hardly contain his excitement. A certificate! He would have something in writing, to show Dolly and the rest of the townspeople. As for himself — well, he had known all along the characters were genuine.

"This should be of some help," Professor Anthon said. "It certifies to the people of Palmyra that these appear to be true characters. It also states that the translation of the characters I have seen appears to be correct. I don't know what more I can do for you."

"Thank you very much," Martin said. He took the various papers — transcript, translation and certificate. He folded them separately and put them in his pocket.

"You're welcome. I'm glad to have been of service. Now, I'm busy here, so I'll let you find your own way out."

They shook hands. Martin went out of the study and down the hall to the front door.

"Mr. Harris?"

He had his hand on the door knob. Professor Anthon called again.

"Mr. Harris? Could you come back here, please?"

Martin turned and went back into the study.

"I was just curious. About these gold plates in the hill... how did the young man find out they were there?"

"Well, sir, an angel of God revealed it to him. That's how he knew where to find them."

"An - an angel of God?"

"That's right."

Professor Anthon got up from his desk. His mouth tightened at the corners.

"Let me see that certificate again."

Martin fished the certificate out of his pocket and unfolded it. He handed it to the professor.

Professor Anthon took it and began tearing it up. Martin watched in astonishment; he took a step forward.

"I'm sorry to have to do this," the professor said. "But there's no such thing now as the ministering of angels. You see, I can't have my name be used-"

He stopped, then looked at Martin.

"If you will bring those plates to me, I'll translate them myself.

"But - but I can't. I'm forbidden to bring them. And part of the plates are sealed."

"Well, I certainly can't read a sealed book. Good day, sir."

* * * *

"He said that?" Joseph said. "'I cannot read a sealed book?'"

They were in the kitchen of Joseph's house. Joseph had just pulled out a chair for Martin, and now he stood holding Martin's greatcoat.

"The certificate was in my hands...I - I swear it. And he tore it up."

"'...a sealed book.'" Joseph hung Martin's coat on the coat-rack beside the door. Then he sat down beside Martin at the table.

"If only I hadn't given it to him. But I didn't know...I had no idea-"

"Martin, it's all right. I'm not surprised. Look." He reached for the Bible. "Isaiah...here we are. Isaiah 29:10. Read this."

Martin read,

> For the Lord hath poured out upon you the spirit of deep sleep, and hath closed your eyes; the prophets and your rulers, the seers hath he covered.
> And the vision of all is become unto you as the words of a book that is sealed, which men deliver to one that is learned, saying, Read this, I pray thee; and he saith, I cannot, for it is sealed.

He looked at Joseph, open-mouthed. Joseph said, "What about Dr. Mitchill? Did he say the same thing?"

Martin looked down at the table. "He said exactly what Anthon had said, respecting both the characters and the translation. I didn't get a certificate from him either."

Joseph gripped him by the shoulder. "There's no call to be discouraged. This - this is more than I expected from either of these gentlemen. Martin, don't you see? We don't need their certificates. We *know* the thing is true. And soon others will know it too. You'll see. Here. Here, read the rest of this passage."

Joseph pointed to the text. Wondering, Martin read,

> And the book is delivered to him that is not learned, saying, Read this, I pray thee; and he saith, I am not learned.
>
> Wherefore the Lord said, Forasmuch as this people draw near me with their mouth, and with their lips do honour me, but have removed their heart far from me, and their fear toward me is taught by the precept of men:
>
> Therefore, behold, I will proceed to do a marvellous work among this people, even a marvellous work and a wonder; for the wisdom of their wise men shall perish, and the understanding of their prudent men shall be hid.

Martin stopped reading. His eyes flicked back over the passage.

"That's uncanny," he said.

"What?"

"It's strange. I mean...after what Professor Anthon said. I can't-"

"No," Joseph said. "It's not so strange." He leaned back in his chair. "I wish I could go ahead with the translation a little faster."

"But that's the *book*. That's the book it speaks of. It's—it's right there, in Isaiah."

Joseph sighed, and a shadow crossed his face; he looked tired. "I *know*."

"How is the work going?"

"It's going very slowly. Emma doesn't have the time to write for me, and she's not feeling too well these days. My father-in-law thinks I'm crazy. No one in his family understands what I'm trying to do...except Emma, of course. And somehow I have to provide for my family."

"Well, then, let me help you. I can do some more writing."

Joseph smiled; in the firelight he looked less tired. "Splendid. We'll start in the morning."

* * * *

There was the clink of glasses, the sound of wine being poured. There was the murmur of well-bred voices, the rustle of taffeta. Above the muted sounds, he heard the laughter.

The girl was laughing, a high tinkle of sound. She was a pretty young thing, about seventeen. She had blonde hair, and the rosy freshness that certain young girls have. Her companion was young too; he looked to be in his early twenties. They were coming toward him, guided by his hostess.

He stood waiting, a glass of the red wine in his hand. He still had work to do for his lecture the next day. He had intended to make excuses to his hostess and retire early. But looking at the girl, he was glad he had stayed a little longer.

"Oh, Professor Anthon," his hostess said. "I want you to meet my daughter, Catharine. Katie, this is the distinguished Professor Anthon, who revised the famous *Classical Dictionary*. It's gone through six printings already."

"My dear Mrs. Tibbs," Professor Anthon said. "You flatter me." To the girl he said, "A pleasure to meet you."

Mrs. Tibbs introduced the young man.

"...a friend of Catharine's. A student at the college...he'll probably be in one of your classes next year. Professor Anthon...Mr. Peter Carter."

They shook hands. Professor Anthon was looking at the girl. He said, "You mentioned *A Classical Dictionary*. As a matter of fact, I'm thinking of enlarging and expurgating the work."

"Expurgating the *Dictionary*?" his hostess said.

"Yes. It is my belief that Lempriere's work is frequently marked by a grossness of allusion, which makes it quite unfit for the young."

"Oh, really?" the girl said, blinking.

The young man was saying, "Sir, in the book you made reference to Champollion's *Pieces du Systeme Hieroglyphique...*"

Erudite noises. The young student trying to impress him. Professor Anthon smiled at the girl.

Then he stopped smiling. The girl was saying,

"...the Mormons actually claiming that you declared Joseph Smith's 'characters' to be-"

"I know," he said quickly. "Ancient shorthand Egyptian." He took a sip of wine.

Mrs. Tibbs smiled. "Those Mormon hieroglyphs are a sore subject right now."

The professor managed to smile. "Well, the newspapers are having their fun, of course. What really happened..."

His listeners waited, intent. The girl Catharine leaned toward him, her eyes eager. He tried to keep his mind on what he was saying.

"What really happened is that this Harris, this plain and apparently simple-hearted farmer, came to me...it was back in the spring of 1828. He had a letter from somebody...Mitchill, I believe. He said something about being asked to contribute toward publication of the translation of these gold plates. And also — I believe he intended to sell his farm. He wanted to seek the opinion, as he said, of 'the learned.'"

They laughed together, and the professor sipped the wine.

"What did the writing look like?" the young man asked.

"Well, let's see...it was a singular scroll. It consisted of all kinds of singular characters, disposed in columns.

It had evidently been prepared by some person who had before him at the time a book containing various alphabets...Greek and Hebrew letters, crosses and flourishes, Roman letters inverted or placed sideways. The whole ended in a rude delineation of a circle — evidently copied after the Mexican calendar, given by Humboldt."

"That's interesting," the young man said. "They actually went to the trouble of mixing alphabets."

"You must have a wonderful memory," the girl said. "All these years, and you describe it so clearly."

The Professor gave a little cough; he took another quick drink. It *had* been some time ago, to be sure.

"I have had frequent conversations with my friends on the subject — ever since the Mormon excitement began. I can assure you, that paper contained anything else but 'Egyptian hieroglyphics!'"

They laughed again. Mrs. Tibbs said,

"Let me fill your glass, Professor.

"The Mormons are making vile use of my name," Professor Anthon said, handing the glass to his hostess. "I've had to write in answer to some of the inquiries...trying to describe what really took place."

The girl said, "They mentioned a certificate-"

"Oh, yes. The certificate. What I wrote for Mr. Harris was to demonstrate that the characters were a hodge-podge in imitation of various alphabets. I really don't- Thank you," he said to Mrs. Tibbs, who had refilled his glass.

"Incidentally, I saw the man again, just a few years ago. Martin Harris, the countryman. He showed up at my door and tried to give me a printed copy of that golden Bible."

They laughed. "Did you ever hear the like?" Mrs. Tibbs said.

89

"Whatever did you tell him?" Catharine asked.

"I told him I was too busy to bother with such things."

Mrs. Tibbs waited, then said,

"Oh, Professor, you simply *must* try some of my little cakes. They're from a French recipe."

"I'd be delighted."

"And, Katie, don't monopolize him all evening. I'm sure he'd like to talk to some of his colleagues."

"That's quite all right," he said.

Someone on the other side of the refreshment table spoke to Mrs. Tibbs, and she moved over to answer. The two young people had already started to move away.

He reached for one of the cakes. The wine was doing things to his vision; the candles wavered unsteadily.

The Mormonite inscription. Strange how the thing kept surfacing. Years since the incident...he couldn't really remember those characters. He recalled not being able to decide what language they belonged to.

He had done the proper thing, as far as his professional reputation was concerned; he had covered himself well. If an 'angel of God' had anything to do with it, it was best that he dissociate himself from it as quickly as possible. Which he had tried to do.

The odd thing was that he'd rather liked Martin Harris. The man was an amazing mixture of hardiness and credulity. The upstate farmer, full of superstition and old wives' tales. All of those country folk were a bit touched anyway...the light, perhaps. The colors and shadows...the changing hues of the lakes region. Anybody could see angels if he looked long enough.

He finished the cake and wiped his fingers carefully with a linen napkin. It was time to leave.

He started toward the front hallway, where he had left his hat and greatcoat.

8

No man could have dictated the writing of the manuscript unless he was inspired...when returning after meals, or after interruptions, he would at once begin where he had left off, without either seeing the manuscript or having any portion of it read to him. This was a usual thing for him to do. It would have been improbable that a learned man could do this; and for one so ignorant and unlearned as he was, it was simply impossible.

—Emma Smith

Martin Harris began to act as scribe for Joseph in April of 1828. First he tried to settle his affairs back in Palmyra.

Dolly was in one of her states. She was furious that he had gone off without her. She had made up a bed for him in another room, which she refused to enter.

He made an effort to restore some semblance of peace. But Dolly would only storm and say,

"I know how to protect my property."

For she was still worried that the wealth they had worked so hard to collect would be wasted on something foolish.

Martin knew her concerns; he wished he could reassure her. But it was becoming more and more difficult to reason with her.

One thing about Dolly was that she hated to take second place; she liked to take charge and run things herself. But when she'd first offered help to Joseph, he had said,

91

"When it comes to assistance, I would rather deal with men themselves, and not their wives."

Martin felt Joseph had an instinct about such things. With Dolly's disposition, how could she be trusted? But perhaps with time, she would come around.

When he set out for Pennsylvania, Dolly insisted on coming with him. This time he didn't try to stop her.

That was his first mistake. He brought her along, even though he had heard rumors of how she had called on Lucy Smith and told her, "I have property, and I know how to take care of it." Lucy had protested that her family had never asked the Harrises for money, but Dolly had seemed not to hear.

Martin reasoned that it wouldn't do any harm to let her go over to Pennsylvania and stay for a few weeks. Then he could bring her back, return to Harmony and resume the writing.

But to his dismay, she had no sooner reached Joseph and Emma's house, when she began raising a fuss. She told Joseph that she had come to see the plates and would not leave until she had done so. She then started to ransack the house, searching everywhere. Joseph removed both the breastplate and the record from the house, finding another hiding place for them. Finally Dolly began searching out-of-doors, in spite of the snow and cold weather.

All this Emma and Joseph bore with patience. One afternoon, after searching out in the woods, Dolly came rushing into the house. She warmed her hands by the fire, stamping her feet impatiently. Emma, looking up from her work, wondered what was wrong now.

"Tell me," Dolly said. "Are there any snakes around here?"

"Snakes?"

"Yes, snakes. In this country, in the winter, do you have snakes?"

"Well, no. Not when it's this cold."

"I've been walking around in the woods to have a look at your place, and as I turned around to come home, a - a tremendous big black snake stuck up his head before me, he did, and started hissing at me!"

Shortly after the snake episode, Dolly packed up and went to stay with a near neighbor of the Smiths. She told the neighbor that just as she thought she had found the place where the plates were buried, she encountered a horrible black snake. It gave her a terrible fright, and she ran with all possible speed to the house.

While Dolly remained in the neighborhood, she did all she could to injure Joseph in the estimation of his neighbors.

"He's a grand impostor, he is. And he has seduced, yes, seduced my poor husband into believing that he is some great one, a prophet, of all things — just to get hold of my husband's property."

After two weeks in Pennsylvania, Dolly went back to Palmyra with Martin. She pleaded with him not to have any further part in the publication of the record.

"I'm sorry, Dolly. I know how you feel. It's all right; I'll be very careful. But I *must* go back."

To other entreaties he turned a deaf ear. When they reached home, Martin left again for Pennsylvania.

Martin wanted to believe in the truth of what they were doing. On certain days the story of the gold plates, so miraculously found, seemed plausible to him, even wonderful. On other days he had his doubts, especially because of his wife. *If only he could convince Dolly,*

93

beyond a shadow of a doubt...then he, himself, would never question it again...

Martin was willing to believe many things. Like most back country people, he lived in a world of magic, of superstitions and old wives' tales. It was a time when witching water and folk medicine were prevalent, when supernatural creatures and spirits roamed the hills, at least in the minds of the people. Creatures guarding certain treasures, benevolent and evil spirits — all were possible, and believed to exist. So Dolly's "black snake" did not surprise him very much. It was not intended that she should find the plates.

She *had* to be convinced that the work was truly of God. He began to plead with Joseph, as they worked, to let him show the manuscript to Dolly. Joseph inquired of the Lord.

"I'm sorry, Martin. I can't do it. The Lord has forbidden it."

Again Martin asked. He kept at Joseph, asking and pleading. Again the request was met with refusal.

Doubts. Was Joseph an impostor? Once, to test Joseph, Martin substituted another stone for the small dark "seer stone" which Joseph was now using. To Martin's joy, Joseph declared that all was dark and he could not translate. This incident served to convince Martin that Joseph's gift was from God, and not something of his own doing.

At last one hundred and sixteen pages of foolscap were completed. Martin pestered Joseph constantly for the privilege of showing the manuscript to his wife and a few friends.

"I *know* they will believe. I *know* it. If only they could just see it."

Joseph went to the Lord a third time. This time Joseph received a revelation giving Martin permission to show

94

the manuscript to his wife and four others — her sister Abigail Harris Cobb, Martin's brother Preserved, and his parents.

"Those, and no more," Joseph told Martin. "You mustn't show it to anyone else. I can't tell you how important that is. You must swear in solemn covenant with the Lord — no one else must see them."

Martin bound himself in solemn covenant to do as he was commanded. Then he set off for Palmyra with the only copy of what had been translated, one hundred and sixteen pages of foolscap. It was June 14 of the year 1828.

* * * *

The very next day, Emma had her baby, after a long and difficult labor. The child, a boy, lived only three hours. Sorrowing, they buried him in the little cemetery east of the house.

For two weeks Emma lay in bed, so ill that they feared for her life. Joseph was too concerned about her to think of anything else. As she began to recover, his thoughts turned once more to the manuscript. He wondered why there had been no news from Martin.

He didn't speak of it to Emma, not wanting to upset her. But she sensed something amiss. Finally she urged him to go to Palmyra.

"I shall not be at ease until I know something about what Mr. Harris is doing."

Seeing that her health was improving, Joseph prepared for the journey. He left Emma in the care of her mother and set off.

* * * *

Joseph was almost at the end of his strength.

For two weeks, waiting at the bedside of Emma, he had not had one hour of undisturbed rest. When the worry about her had subsided, another fear took its place...where was Martin with the only copy of the manuscript?

Now, as he sat in the stage bound for Palmyra, the anxiety filled his mind. *What had Martin done with it*? If it were lost, the only way it could be recovered was through the power of God — and it was hardly to be hoped that such a thing would be granted again. He had taken a most terrible risk...perhaps, by asking three times, he had fallen into transgression, and the manuscript was now lost forever.

Exhausted, Joseph was in such a state of worry that he could not sleep. Eating was out of the question. He felt that he had somehow done wrong; *he* was responsible for the loss of the manuscript, if it was indeed lost. How great his condemnation was, he could not imagine.

When the stage stopped for refreshment, he made no move to get off. He sat staring straight ahead, lost in the horror of what he had done. When the ride began again, he was hardly conscious of it.

A voice, speaking to him. It was a kind voice; he turned, wondering.

There was one other passenger on the stage, an older man. The stranger was asking him the cause of his affliction...even offering to assist him if his services would be acceptable.

Joseph was touched. He realized how he must have appeared...pale, haggard from lack of sleep.

"Sir, I thank you for your kindness. I've been watching some time with a sick wife and child. The child has died, and my wife is still very low."

96

The other trouble he did not mention. But it pervaded his thoughts; it swirled in his exhausted brain and made a hard knot of anxiety in the pit of his stomach. Toward the end of the journey, he felt the shadows of night closing around him. He stared out into the darkness.

It was almost ten o'clock. He had twenty miles to go on foot before he reached his parents' home. As he was about to leave the stage, he remarked to the stranger that he still had a twenty-mile walk ahead of him.

The stranger said,

"I've watched you since you first entered the stage. I know you've neither slept nor eaten since that time. You shouldn't go on foot alone this night."

"I must," Joseph said. "I have to reach my parents' house."

"All right. If you must go, I'm going with you. Now, tell me...what is the trouble that makes you so dispirited?"

Again Joseph mentioned his wife, and the child which had died — their first and only child. He said nothing about the missing manuscript, for in truth, what was there to say?

The stranger said,

"You have my sympathy. But I fear you're not strong enough to go much further. You'll be in danger of falling asleep in the forest, and Lord knows *what* might happen to you then."

Joseph thanked him, and they started off together.

As they made their way through the forest, he felt sleep overtaking him. He stumbled, and would have fallen. But there was the stranger's touch on his arm, the voice beside him in the darkness. Toward the end of the journey, he was falling asleep every few minutes as he walked along.

They reached the farmhouse just before dawn. The stranger said to Joseph's parents,

"I've brought your son through the forest, because he insisted on coming. But he's not well, as you can see. He needs rest, as well as refreshment. He ought to have some pepper tea to warm his stomach."

When the stranger had directed them in the care of Joseph, he said,

"After you've attended to him, I'll thank you for a little breakfast for myself. Then I must be on my way again."

As soon as Joseph had taken a little nourishment, he asked them to send immediately for Mr. Harris. Lucy sent someone over to fetch Martin Harris. She gave the stranger his breakfast. Then she began preparing breakfast for the rest of the family.

She set a place for Mr. Harris, as they expected him to be there at any moment. He usually came hurrying over whenever they sent for him. But eight o'clock came, with no Mr. Harris. They waited till nine, then ten and eleven, but he was still not there. By this time, even the youngest members of the family sensed something was wrong. Not knowing what the trouble was (as Joseph had not expressed his fears to them), they waited, uneasy.

* * * *

Martin Harris had truly intended to honor the solemn promise he had made. When he had shown the manuscript to Dolly and the others, she had let him lock it up in her bureau. There it was safe, until another friend pressed him to see it. Then the promise was forgotten.

When he went to open the bureau, the key was missing. Dolly was out that day; she had probably taken the key with her. In his eagerness to show his friend the manuscript, Martin picked the lock, damaging the

98

bureau. The manuscript was safe; he showed it to his friend.

Dolly was furious about her damaged bureau. Martin, having showed the manuscript to one person not specified in the covenant, began showing it to anyone who happened to come along.

Then came the message from the Smith household. He had not shown the manuscript to anyone for a while. He went to the bureau that morning, opened it — the manuscript was gone.

Alarmed, he searched the bureau. There was no sign of the manuscript. He ransacked the house, ripping open beds and pillows. All morning he searched, and searched again.

As the sun rose higher in the sky, he realized the awful truth. He had broken his solemn word, and the worst had happened. He would have to go over to the Smiths' empty-handed, and tell not only Joseph but the whole family.

* * * *

About half-past twelve they saw him walking with slow and measured tread toward the house, his eyes fixed on the ground. When he reached the gate, he stopped. Instead of coming through the gate, he climbed on the fence. He sat there with his hat drawn over his eyes.

At last he came in the house. Soon afterward, the whole family sat down to the table, and Martin took the place that had been set for him.

The family began eating. Martin took up his knife and fork, then put them down again.

Hyrum said,

"Martin, why aren't you eating? Are you sick?"

Martin put his head in his hands and cried out,

"Oh, I have lost my soul! I have lost my soul!"

Joseph sprang up from the table.

"Martin, have you lost that manuscript? Have you broken your oath, and brought down condemnation upon my head, as well as your own?"

"Yes. It's gone," Martin said in a muffled voice. "And I don't know where."

"Oh, my God!" Joseph cried, clenching his hands. "All is lost! All is lost! What shall I do? I have sinned — it is *I* who tempted the wrath of God! I should've been satisfied with the first answer I received from the Lord. He told me it wasn't safe to let the writing go out of my hands." He was weeping now, clenching his hands together, walking up and down the length of the room. He gave a deep, anguished groan.

The family members looked at each other, wondering. They had heard rumors that Martin Harris had taken some of the manuscript. In a flash they realized what had happened.

Joseph turned from his pacing.

"Martin, you must go back and search again."

Martin looked up, his face tear-stained.

"No. It's all in vain. I've ripped open beds and pillows, and I *know* it's not there."

Joseph began walking and groaning again.

"How can I return to my wife with such a tale as this? I dare not do it. It would kill her at once. And how shall I appear before the Lord? What's the angel going to say to me now?"

By this time the whole family was in tears. Lucy managed to say,

"Oh, Joseph, don't mourn so. It was a mistake. Surely the Lord will forgive you. I mean, when he sees how humble and repentant you are-"

Joseph looked at her, but the attempt to comfort him was in vain. For everyone else was weeping now; sobs and sounds of grief filled the room.

Joseph was more distressed than the rest, as he understood more fully the consequences of his disobedience. He kept pacing back and forth, weeping and grieving, until about sunset. Finally Lucy persuaded him to calm down and take a little nourishment.

The next morning Joseph set out for his home in Harmony. His parents hugged him tearfully. As they watched him walk out toward the main road, Lucy said to her husband,

"It doesn't seem possible. All we had hoped for…gone in a moment. I - I often thought, when I was doing some tedious thing… I'd think about the plates, and the work he was doing. And then I'd feel better."

"I know," Joseph's father said. "He should've been more careful."

"And now that's all gone. That feeling I had. It's like… it's lost forever."

"I know. And I'm sorry…we have to make the best of things. And so does he."

"I hope he'll be all right."

"I think he will."

He put his gnarled, sunburnt hand on her shoulder. They stood looking at the road until Joseph was out of sight.

9

Behold, thou art Joseph,
And thou wast chosen to do the work of the
Lord
  But because of transgression
    If thou art not aware thou wilt fall.

But remember
  God is merciful.

  Therefore,
Repent of that which thou has done
    And he will only cause thee to be afflicted for
a season,
    And thou art still chosen
      And art again called to the work.

  Except thou doest this,
Thou shalt be delivered up and become as other
men
      And have no more gift...

                              —Book of Commandments

Joseph's father, being of a skeptical nature, thought
it strange that the words could have such an effect on
him. Here he was, skeptic, agnostic, refusing steadfastly
to attend any church. A direct contrast to his wife, mystic,
visionary...at times he thought she would believe
*any*thing.

Now, through a series of events, he was becoming
convinced that his son *was* an instrument in the hands

of God, that he did indeed have a gift that made him different from other men.

Was it his great love for Joseph that made him feel such a thing? Was it a father's fondness for a beloved son? Or was it his imagination, his hopes that one of his own could possibly be gifted in such an unusual way?

As he worked, making the necessary repairs to his fences and outbuildings, chores of spring, he mused on the events of the fall.

For two months he and Lucy had heard nothing from Joseph. They had become increasingly anxious. Finally they had gone to visit him.

Memories touched his mind...how, when they were about three quarters of a mile from the house, Joseph had come to meet them. They learned later he had discerned they were on their way; as he left the house, he had said to his wife,

"Father and Mother are coming."

It was a joyous reunion. He showed them a red morocco trunk on Emma's bureau. In it, he told them, were the Urim and Thummim, and the plates.

Then he told them what had happened after he had left them and returned to Harmony.

Lucy was full of questions. Joseph,Sr., remembered how he'd tried to keep her quiet so Joseph could talk. He remembered the anxious expectation on his own part as Joseph related his experiences.

Feeling completely at a loss, expecting no blessing at all, Joseph had gone to pray once more.

"All I could think of was my grief at having been so stupid, and what it meant. I asked the Lord for his mercy and forgiveness...I don't know what I expected, or even deserved. I just prayed, intending to do what I could to atone for what had happened. As I was praying, an angel stood before me."

The outcome was that Joseph was reprimanded and told to prepare for a time of waiting, after which he would be able to resume the translation. At the time of his parents' visit, Joseph had again received the interpreters, which had been taken from him by the heavenly messenger.

He was told not to retranslate the missing manuscript pages, as the people that had taken them were planning to alter the words and use them later to discredit the book. He was to work on another portion of the record, which gave a fuller account of the same events.

In the words of the Lord, Martin Harris was referred to as a 'wicked man.' Joseph's father remembered how puzzled Lucy had been.

"But the writings are no longer even in his hands."

"I only know what I was told, Mother. I was told that he sought to destroy me. He sought to take away the things I had been entrusted with, and sought to destroy my gift — the gift of translating. Maybe he didn't know that's what he was doing."

"It's Dolly. She's a bad influence," his mother said.

"As for Martin, you shouldn't have trusted him," his father said. "I hope you don't have to depend on him again."

"I'll be careful, Father. It might be that Martin will repent — he could be a big help to us. After all, he's helped me before. But I'll not give him any of the manuscript again. What I need now is a full-time scribe. The angel said the Lord would send one to me. I hope it happens soon."

Joseph's parents stayed for three months. During that time, they got to know Emma's mother and father, and the rest of their family.

"Well, Mother," Joseph's father said, just before they were to leave. "Do you feel better about things now?"

"Oh, yes," Lucy said. "The time has passed so fast. I feel that a tremendous burden has been lifted. It's a good thing, too — I no longer had the strength to carry it."

"I remember how grieved we were when he left us last spring."

"Our tears have surely turned to joy. But I wonder where he's going to find a scribe?"

The skeptic was amazed at his own answer. "Well, now, if God has blessed him so abundantly with these other things, forgiveness and so on, then I suppose somehow he'll find a scribe too."

* * * *

He was a young man, just a year younger than Joseph, and his name was Oliver Cowdery. Lean with hollow cheeks, he had a gentleness about him, a certain tenderness of expression.

He had been hired to teach the district school in Palmyra. As was the custom, he prepared to board with different families in the neighborhood. He began to hear rumors about the gold plates and the book that was being translated.

When he reached the Smith household, he felt at home immediately. He even called them "Mother" and "Father." They in turn treated him as one of the family, with one exception. They were reluctant to talk about any such things as angels or gold plates.

Oliver began to question Joseph's father on the subject, but for some time didn't get any information from him. At last he gained Father Smith's confidence, and learned the whole story.

Plates buried in the hill...inscribed with characters from a lost language... Oliver could not stop thinking

105

about it. He couldn't get over the uncanny feeling that he himself was somehow connected with it...that his future was already bound up with the plates of gold in the strange language. Didn't Joseph's father say Joseph needed a scribe? It struck him with great force; he, Oliver, would eventually be that scribe!

"It seems working in my very bones," he said to Father Smith. "I can't get it out of my mind, not even for a moment. Do you know what I'd like to do?"

"What is it?"

"Well, you just mentioned yesterday about Samuel going down to Pennsylvania — going to stay with Joseph for the spring."

"Oh, yes. He's been planning that for some time."

"Well, I'd like to go with him. We can leave just after school closes. You see — I've been praying about it. I really think I'm supposed to have something to do with that ancient record. Maybe I'm the scribe he's looking for." Here Oliver looked earnestly at Father Smith. "What do you think of that?"

Joseph's father didn't seem as eager as Oliver was. "Well, all I can say, Oliver, is that you must make your own decision. I suggest that you seek a testimony for yourself, as to whether it's the right thing to do."

"Yes. That's a good idea. Yes, I will."

After that, Oliver was completely preoccupied with the subject of the record.

"Land's sakes," Lucy said to her husband. "It's hard to get him to talk about anything else."

Lucy tried to point out to Oliver that the way would not be easy...that he might be liable to misfortune if he should turn his back upon the world, and set out in the service of God.

"Now, Oliver," she said. "You see this house?"

"Yes. It's a handsome house."

106

"Jest look at it. See how comfortable it is? Every child has taken pains to make us as comfortable as possible."

"I can see that," Oliver said. "They've done a good job."

"There's only one thing wrong."

"What's that?"

"We can't stay here. We're about to lose our home."

"*What*?"

She told him how it was now time for them to move out, according to the terms of the lease.

"I don't think we would've lost our home, if the neighborhood hadn't been so stirred up about Joseph's visions. So it's for the sake of Christ and his work that we have to leave. Do you understand, Oliver?"

"I - I see," he said.

"I hope you understand also why we can't keep you with us much longer. We'll be moving — you'll have to board with someone else."

He was alarmed. "No, Mother! Let me stay with you. I don't care about a big house — I can live in any log hut where you and Father live. But I don't want to leave you. Don't even mention it!"

"All right, then, Oliver. We just wanted you to know how things stood. You can stay if you want to."

"I want to," he said.

* * * *

In April, Oliver and Joseph's younger brother Samuel set out together for Pennsylvania. They pressed on in spite of bad weather — it had been raining, freezing and thawing, which had made the roads almost impassable. But Oliver was determined to get through.

When they reached Joseph's home in Harmony, Oliver learned that Joseph indeed was in great need of a scribe.

The work of translating was almost at a standstill. Three days before their arrival, Joseph in desperation had asked the Lord to send him a scribe, as the angel had promised.

Oliver was overjoyed; his skills were needed, just as he had somehow known they would be. He was tired from the journey, but he wanted to know more about the plates and how Joseph had found them. They stayed up talking until late in the evening. Joseph told Oliver the things that had happened to him, filling in the details his father had left out.

The following day they talked some more, and Oliver helped Joseph with some things of a temporal nature. The next morning they began the work of translation together.

If there was an inspired period in Oliver's life, a time to be remembered with wonder and gladness from the vantage point of middle age, it was the time of translation. Day after day he sat writing while Joseph dictated. Oliver was convinced that the words he wrote down were dictated by the inspiration of heaven. The ancient record, the plates of gold, contained a story as fascinating as any he had ever heard. To be actually engaged in such a work filled him with a joy and gratitude beyond anything he had imagined.

He continued to write, uninterrupted, as Joseph translated the words that were to form the history (or record) called the Book of Mormon. He believed both in the seer and the mechanism of translation, accepting eagerly whatever Joseph announced as revelation from God. For Oliver believed that Joseph would die before he would lie.

Provisions were scarce that spring. Joseph and Oliver walked to Colesville in an attempt to find Joseph Knight, Sr. He wasn't at home. For several days they searched for work. Not finding any, they returned home.

There they found Mr. Knight with his wagon full of supplies. Gratefully they helped unload a barrel of mackerel, ten bushels of grain, six bushels of potatoes, a pound of tea, and some lined paper.

"What do you do with a whole barrel of mackerel?" Oliver asked Joseph.

"Oh, Emma will think of something. And it's better than starving."

When everything had been unloaded, Mr. Knight said,

"It's a good thing I happened by. You was just about out of everything, warn't you? With two extra mouths to feed, too."

"We sure were glad to see you," Joseph said.

"Well, now you can git to work and git that translation done."

While Joseph and Oliver worked together in the upper room, Emma kept the house going and provided meals from the bounty Mr. Knight had left. Samuel helped with the outside chores, doing the work on the farm that, according to Emma's father, Joseph should have been doing.

"Will you look at what he's doing now?" Isaac said to his wife. "Bad enough I'm not even allowed to *see* those plates — how do I know he's even *got* any? Now he's spending day after day with that skinny young fellow — that school teacher. They sit up there in that room, and they say they're 'translating,' but you know they're just wasting time. He should be out taking care of his fields...but, no. He sends his brother out to do that. And how does he feed his family? He has to depend on the charity of others. If it wasn't for that Mr. Knight — that miller from Colesville — why, they wouldn't have *any*thing. My own daughter, on charity."

109

* * * *

The work of translating the ancient record went on, in spite of poverty, complaints from Emma's family, and growing opposition from the neighbors. And Oliver, told to "be diligent; stand by my servant Joseph, faithfully, in whatsoever difficult circumstances he be for the word's sake," was completely dedicated to the truth of what they were doing. When he wasn't helping with the translation, he found time to write letters. He wrote to his friend David Whitmer, who lived with his parents, brothers and sisters on the family farm in Seneca County, New York.

In one letter to David Whitmer, Oliver wrote that he was convinced Joseph had the record of an ancient people, and a revealed knowledge of their truth.

In the earliest days of their association, Joseph had received the word of the Lord for Oliver.

"Behold, I am Jesus Christ, the son of God. I am the same that came unto my own and my own received me not. I am the light which shineth in darkness, and the darkness comprehendeth it not.

"... Verily, I say unto you, if you desire a further witness, cast your mind upon the night that you cried unto me in your heart, that you might know concerning the truth of these things; did I not speak peace to your mind concerning the matter? What greater witness can you have than from God? And now, behold, you have received a witness, for if I have told you things which no man knoweth, have you not received a witness?"

And Oliver remembered the night at the Smith farmhouse in Palmyra, when he had first heard of the plates, and had prayed to know the truth. Joseph's father had urged him to "seek a testimony for himself," and he had done so. As he later confessed to Joseph, the

110

Lord had manifested the truth to him. But he had told no one at the time, and neither Joseph nor anyone else could have known what had happened, unless the Lord had revealed it to him.

Oliver was also told, "And behold, I grant unto you a gift, if you desire of me, to translate even as my servant Joseph."

But when Oliver tried to translate as Joseph did, nothing happened.

In answer to his bewilderment, came the following:

"Behold, you have not understood; you have supposed that I would give it unto you, when you took no thought, save it was to ask me; but, behold, I say unto you, that you must study it out in your mind; then you must ask me if it be right, and if it is right, I will cause that your bosom shall burn within you; therefore, you shall feel that it is right; but if it be not right, you shall have no such feelings, but you shall have a stupor of thought, that shall cause you to forget the thing which is wrong; therefore, you can not write that which is sacred save it be given you from me.

"Now if you had known this, you could have translated; nevertheless, it is not expedient that you should translate now."

It sounded so simple, Oliver thought. He should have realized it. The process of translating was more than just looking into the interpreters, or the "seer stone." Joseph was no longer using the ancient interpreters, as he said they made his eyes sore. Instead, he translated with the aid of a single light-colored stone he had found. The material device was apparently not as important as the heart and mind of the translator.

Oliver found himself wondering if the complete knowledge of the ancient language had been given to Joseph, or only the specific word or phrase that he needed at the time.

Other people were to wonder too. As Oliver looked back on this time, years later, he remembered the many questions that were put to Joseph on that subject. But Joseph would not satisfy anyone's curiosity. He would only say that it was translated through the mercy of God, by the power of God.

Perhaps Joseph himself did not know more than this, or could not have put it into words. Oliver knew that they were both caught up in amazing events, happenings which they could only witness and recollect with wonder.

On May 15 of the year 1829, one of these extraordinary events occurred.

According to their understanding, the power of priesthood had been lost through human carelessness in the early centuries of the Christian church. They had just reached that portion of the record where baptism for the remission of sins was mentioned.

"But who is there to baptize us?" Oliver asked. "Such authority no longer exists on the earth."

"Let's go out in the woods," Joseph said, "and make it a subject of prayer."

Oliver remembered how they had walked together out into the woods, and how the sunlight lay in bright patches on the forest path. They found a secluded place. There they knelt and prayed, each one in turn, calling upon the Lord.

Oliver remembered how the intensity of the light seemed to increase as he was praying. There was the touch of Joseph's hand on his arm. He opened his eyes to see the dazzling cloud, and the figure, all in white, descending in the cloud. At first he felt afraid; he glanced at Joseph. Joseph was looking straight ahead, unmoving, his face pale.

Then they heard the voice.

"I am thy fellow-servant."

It was not a harsh voice; it was gentle, but it seemed to pierce Oliver to the core of his being. His fear left him; he felt a deep sense of reassurance.

The heavenly being laid his hands upon their heads.

"Upon you, my fellow servants, in the name of Messiah, I confer the priesthood of Aaron, which holds the keys of the ministering of angels, and of the gospel of repentance, and of baptism by immersion, for the remission of sins..."

This Aaronic priesthood, the messenger told them, did not have the power of laying on of hands for the gift of the Holy Ghost; that power would be conferred upon them later. The messenger said his name was John, the same that is called John the Baptist in the New Testament. He said that he acted under the direction of Peter, James, and John, who held the keys of the Melchisedec, or higher, priesthood.

The messenger commanded them to go and be baptized, directing that first Joseph should baptize Oliver, and then Oliver would baptize Joseph. After that, they were to ordain each other to the Aaronic priesthood, first Joseph laying hands on Oliver's head and ordaining him, and then Oliver doing the same for Joseph.

Joseph listened intently to the instructions, as if he were making careful mental notes; he had experienced manifestations of this kind before. But Oliver was completely caught up in the sound of the messenger's voice, in the light and the dazzling appearance of the heavenly being. He could not get over his amazement that an angel of God was actually standing before him

113

and speaking...conferring upon them the very spiritual authority they had sought to find.

As the messenger's hands were resting on his head, he thought of the world outside...the millions of people groping for spiritual meaning, as blind men grope for a wall. Masses of men and women, distracted and uncertain, while in that secluded bit of woods, all doubt had fled...they knew, he and Joseph; for their eyes and ears were not deceived. Here was the truth, coming to them from the lips of a pure personage, and all the religious deceptions and superstitions of his day seemed to wither and fade away beside it.

He was aware then of the overwhelming love of God for them, and for all people, even the people he had just seen in his mind. It seemed to glow with the radiant light, encircling them, enkindling a similar flame in his own heart. Oliver felt warmed, as if bathed in all his being by a spiritual fire. At the same time, he felt a peace beyond anything he had yet experienced.

They set about baptizing each other, as they had been commanded. As they were coming up out of the water, another gift was given — the gift of prophecy. Oliver couldn't remember much of the details, but as he emerged from the water, he felt such peace and joy that he began to speak. He prophesied concerning things that would soon happen to them.

Joseph, after his own baptism, prophesied concerning the rise of the church, and other things connected with the church. Rejoicing, they ordained each other.

As they went home, Joseph said,

"I think now we'll be able to read the Bible with more understanding."

"The Nephite record might be easier to understand, too."

"There're mysterious passages in the Bible — things I never could figure out. I'll show them to you."

114

Oliver said, "When you think of all the people out there...people just waiting to hear the things we have witnessed-"

"Oliver. Wait. It might be better if we didn't tell a lot of people — I mean, if we just kept it to ourselves for a while-"

"What do you mean, 'keep it to ourselves?' All the things that just happened-"

"Well, we can tell Emma, of course. And possibly my brother, Samuel."

"How can we just forget it?"

"Of course we're not going to forget it. But right now we have to deal with the spirit of persecution-"

"But we know there's going to be persecution. You prophesied it yourself, right back there."

Joseph said patiently, "The most important thing we have to do right now is translate the record. Then somehow we have to get it printed. Don't you see? If we stir up more trouble now, we might even delay the publication-"

"It's true we've been threatened," Oliver said. "We've come close to being mobbed...to think it was instigated by those who profess religion."

"You know why they didn't mob us? It was because of my wife's father."

"Old Isaac?"

"The same. He's become very friendly to me, and he hates mobs. He said that if I wanted to translate, I should be allowed to do it without interruption."

"Another miracle."

"Call it what you will. But as long as he's giving us protection, we'd better not upset him."

"All right. You're right. We'll keep quiet about it."

"We can reason out of the scriptures, of course. We can talk with our acquaintances and friends...that's our duty."

"Yes. I feel that it is."

"We might even find a candidate for baptism," Joseph said.

They pushed through the underbrush and found the road that led up to the house. As they walked along the side of the road, they saw Samuel going in the back door with his arms full of firewood.

"There's one now," Joseph said.

"He looks as likely as any."

They spent the next few days talking to Samuel and reasoning with him out of the Bible. Finally Samuel retired to the woods to seek his own confirmation of the things they had told him.

Oliver baptized Samuel, and he started the journey back to his father's house, eager to tell his family what had happened.

The growing persecution was a cause for concern. Joseph told Oliver he had received directions to go to Fayette, to the Whitmer household, and continue the work there. Oliver sent off another letter to David Whitmer, telling him to come down to Pennsylvania and take them both to his father's house, as they had received a commandment to that effect.

* * * *

David wasn't sure what to do. He had read Oliver's letters with curiosity and excitement, especially the news about the ancient record. Now they needed help — immediate help.

But he was pressed with his work on the farm. He had twenty acres left to plow.

116

He decided he would finish his plowing and then leave for Pennsylvania.

He got up that morning and prepared to go to work. He walked out to the field.

To his amazement, some of the work was already done. Between five to seven acres of his ground had been plowed during the night.

Who had done it? His father and brothers were all busy with other things. The work was done just as he would have done it himself, and the plow left standing in the furrow.

Wondering, he finished the plowing. With so much of the work done, he was able to start his journey sooner.

As he pulled into Harmony, he saw Joseph and Oliver walking to meet him. He was still some distance from the house

To his astonishment, Oliver was able to tell him when he had started from home, where he had stopped the first night, and how he had read the sign at the tavern. Oliver knew where he had stayed the next night, and that he would be there that day before dinner.

"That's why we came out to meet you."

"But - but how did you know all these things?"

"Joseph told me."

"But - but how-"

"Didn't he get it right?"

"Exactly. It's all just as it happened. But-"

"Just wait," Oliver said. "You haven't heard anything yet."

David shook his head, incredulous.

The next day Joseph packed up the plates, and they started the trip back to David's father's house.

10

David pulled the horses to a stop.

"There it is," he said. "Our home."

Two deep ruts, made by wagon wheels, led up to the farmhouse. The house itself was made of wood, one and a half stories.

David clicked to the horses and they pulled ahead. The wagon creaked. Joseph could hear the tall grasses swishing against the bottom of the wagon.

"We're right between the lakes here," David explained.

Joseph had a glimpse of lake water shimmering through the trees, of rolling hills and fields. The fields were sweet with the scent of crushed grass. Beyond them rose the pines and hardwoods, the stretch of forestland.

He was struck by the solitude, the quietness of the place. Here, for a time, they were safe. Here, at last, there was no mob gathering, no grumbling disapproval from the neighbors.

"This is truly a place of peace," Joseph said.

"That's because you haven't met the family yet," David said.

Even as he spoke, the front door opened. Two young men and a girl came out and stood, waving. The men hurried toward them, but the girl stayed by the door.

Oliver was looking at the girl, his lips curved in a half-smile.

"My brothers and sisters," David said. He drew the horses to a stop. "Oliver, why don't you introduce him to Peter and the others? I have to see to the horses."

"What?" Oliver was still looking at the girl.

"Oh, never mind. Joseph, this is Peter and Christian, and Jacob's out in back somewhere. That's Elizabeth Ann, and here comes our father-"

In a very short time, Joseph and Oliver found themselves part of a whole household of young people, all curious, eager to hear more about the ancient record. Even the neighbors were receptive.

They resumed their work of translation the next day. To work with the support of friends, in an atmosphere no longer hostile, was like stepping from night into day. This time, there were many others to help.

* * * *

David Whitmer remembered how in the mornings there would be the service of scripture, singing, and prayer. The whole family would join in. Then, at the end, there would be a special prayer, just before the session of translating.

He watched, marveling, as Oliver and Joseph sat together at the table. Oliver would write as Joseph dictated. With eyes darkened, Joseph slowly enunciated the words that were to form the Book of Mormon.

When Oliver needed a rest, there was usually someone else to assist. Both John and Christian Whitmer acted as scribes; Emma (who had joined them as soon as she could) and Martin Harris did also. But most of the work was done by Oliver.

As the work went on, David was intrigued by Oliver's devotion to it. His friend seemed caught up, absolutely on fire with it, as if he had undergone some deep experience in connection with it. David sensed Oliver's feelings for the translator too; it was hard to mistake them.

"You really think the world of him, don't you?" David asked.

"I know that what he's doing is of God," Oliver replied.

"I've seen how you defer to him. Do you really think he's right all the time?"

Oliver looked uncomfortable. "He hasn't been wrong yet. Yes, I suppose, it's possible he could make a mistake, just like any of us. But in the matter of the translation, he seems to be especially blessed."

"I'll agree with that. The whole thing is amazing. Especially when you think of how many people there are under one roof — more than we've ever had. And yet there's very little quarreling...everyone seems unified."

"It's not so strange," Oliver said. "With what we're doing, if it was truly of God, I would expect a high degree of communal harmony."

David, through his fondness for Oliver, began to believe more and more in the validity of the work. The translating progressed, but not always smoothly. Joseph told David that sometimes his mind was too much on earthly things, and he would be unable to translate until he went out to pray.

One morning Emma did something that angered Joseph, and they "had words." He found that he could not translate a single syllable as long as he was irritated with his wife. Finally he walked outside into the orchard and prayed. Then he went and asked Emma to forgive him. After that, he was able to proceed with the translation.

When Joseph and Oliver weren't busy with the translation, they found time to meet with the neighbors. Many homes were opened to them, and people gathered to hear of the strange new things that were happening.

In the month of June, David was baptized in Seneca Lake, along with Hyrum Smith and Peter Whitmer, Jr.

Oliver said to Joseph,

"Would you have thought so many would become believers, all at once?"

"Four more have asked for baptism this week. And six others want to meet with us, to learn more about it."

In the course of translation, they found that three special witnesses were to actually see the plates with the ancient engravings upon them, and were to testify that they had seen them. Almost immediately, David, Oliver, and Martin Harris (who was visiting at the time) began to ask Joseph if they might have this privilege. Finally Joseph put the matter before the Lord, and received the following:

"Behold, I say unto you, that you must rely upon my word, which if you do, with full purpose of heart, you shall have a view of the plates...and it is by your faith that you shall obtain a view of them, even by that faith which was had by the prophets of old."

They were instructed to bear witness of what they were to see. "...and if you do these last commandments of mine, which I have given you, the gates of hell shall not prevail against you; for my grace is sufficient for you; and you shall be lifted up at the last day. And I, Jesus Christ, your Lord and your God, have spoken it unto you, that I might bring about my righteous purposes unto the children of men."

One morning, at the end of the Whitmer family service of singing and prayer, Joseph stood up.

"Martin, you must humble yourself before your God this day, and obtain a forgiveness of your sins. If you do, it is the will of God that you should look upon the plates, with Oliver and David."

* * * *

David remembered how the four of them left the house
and went out into the woods. They sat on a log to talk
for a while, and Joseph instructed them about praying
each in turn. Then they knelt down and began to pray
aloud, first Joseph and then the others.

They waited, listening. There was only the rustle of
the wind high in the tree tops. They began the prayers
again.

Finally Martin got up. His voice was subdued.

"It's my fault. It's because of me that you receive no
answer. I haven't enough faith...it's - it's no use..."

He raised his hands in a helpless little gesture. Then
he turned and walked away from them, his head down.
He disappeared into the woods; David could hear his
footsteps growing fainter.

The three others renewed their prayers, each man
praying in turn. David heard the wind again in the trees;
he looked down at his hands, clasped together. He could
see the sunlight on them, and the ordinary shadows of
mid-morning.

Suddenly the light on his hands seemed to brighten.
He watched, holding his breath. Was it his imagination?
The shadows grew darker for a brief moment, throwing
each wrinkle and fold into bold relief. Then all shadows
disappeared.

There was a brightness just above them, in the air.
It hurt his eyes to look at it. As he blinked, wondering,
the light came down until they were encircled by it. It
seemed to extend for some distance around, but they were
in the center of it.

As his eyes became adapted to the light, it no longer
seemed intensely bright, but softer, like a glowing white

mist. The light itself was like an actual presence, an entity. Then he saw the figure standing before them. The figure was clothed in white, and in his hands were the plates they had prayed to be able to see. David could see strange engravings on the metal. They seemed to stand out with great clarity in the glowing light.

The angel looked directly at him and said,

"David, blessed is the Lord, and he that keeps his commandments."

Then in the mist he saw a table, and on it were other plates like the ones held by the messenger. The angel placed the record on the table. David could see the metal leaves of the book as they were turned; there were more of the curious engravings on each leaf.

While they were gazing at the plates, a voice spoke to them out of the bright light.

"These plates have been revealed by the power of God, the translation of them which you have seen is correct, and I command you to bear record of what you now see and hear."

A voice. Light. A light more brilliant than any he had ever known. Stabbing his eyes, rousing his mind, awakening it to pain and new knowledge. Like Moses on Mount Sinai, Saul on the way to Damascus... seer after seer, prophet, wise man, struck anew by the light that radiated from the very core of all things. He, David, was changed in an instant, at a touch; he would never be the same. He knew then what Oliver had seen and felt, knew that Oliver's devotion was now his own. All his life would be a looking back to this moment, a remembering and retelling...he would tell anyone who would listen to him. He had seen the ancient plates with the woods full of a light brighter than the sun...he had heard the voice of God.

Dimly he was aware of Joseph getting to his feet.

123

"I've got to go find Martin. You stay here."

* * * *

Joseph found Martin further off in the woods, kneeling in prayer. Joseph went to him. Martin asked Joseph to join him in prayer.

"For I have not yet prevailed with the Lord."

Joseph and Martin prayed together, each one in turn, that Martin might receive the same blessing that the others had just received.

While Joseph was in mid-sentence. he was aware of the light and the presence he had felt before. The same vision he had just seen was opened to him again — the brilliant light, and the angel with the plates in his hands.

Again the voice spoke out of the cloud of light, saying that the book was true and the words correctly translated.

Joseph looked at Martin; the man had not moved. His eyes were wide in amazement, his mouth open. Suddenly he cried out,

"It is enough! My eyes have beheld!"

He jumped up, shouting,

"Hosanna! Praise the Lord! Hosanna to God, and the Lamb!"

"All right, Martin. Take it easy, now. Martin, wait-"

"Hosanna! And again, hosanna!"

"Martin, don't run like that! Here, wait a moment-"

"Praise be to God! I have beheld!"

Together they returned to the house to tell the others what had happened. Joseph left Martin in front of the hearth and went to find his parents.

Joseph's mother and father were sitting in one of the bedrooms talking to Mrs. Whitmer. Joseph came in and threw himself down beside his mother.

"Father! Mother!" he exclaimed, breathing hard. "You know what just happened? They *saw*, all three of them! They saw the angel, and the plates. Yes, Mother; they really did. Now they know for themselves that I was telling the truth. I don't have to carry it alone any longer!"

His mother reached out and put her hand on his shoulder. Just then Martin Harris burst into the room.

"Praise God! I have seen! Mine eyes have beheld...it is all true! Everything he said is true!"

David and Oliver were close behind him, each one eager to tell of his experience. They drew up a statement, as they were commanded to do, a signed document testifying of what they had seen.

> Be it known unto all nations, kindreds, tongues and people, unto whom this work shall come, that we, through the grace of God the Father, and our Lord Jesus Christ, have seen the plates which contain this record...

* * * *

Mother Whitmer was tired that evening. She didn't like to admit she was tired, or that things were happening a little too fast for her. She loved her young people, wanted her house to be a haven, a place of gathering for them and their friends.

But there were a lot of friends about lately. Martin Harris, and people from as far away as Colesville, and assorted members of the Smith family, all coming over to see how things were going. And while she wanted to believe in the divinity of the work — in the book the two young men were translating — it was hard to keep providing meals for so many.

Emma and her own Elizabeth Ann helped in the kitchen, to be sure. But they were young; they didn't take the housework seriously. She remembered them last night, laughing together over something the shy Oliver had done. And was she mistaken? It seemed that Elizabeth Ann and Oliver were spending more and more time together, away from the rest of the young people.

Imagining things. Part of getting old. But the truth was, the burden of the work was on her. Like the milking, for instance. All those able-bodied people in the house, and she had to do it.

She finished the milking and got up from the stool.

Just as she was about to put the milk in the milk pans, she became aware of the growing brightness.

She looked up. There was light all around her. Then she saw the figure standing in the light.

He was an elderly stranger, standing between her and the door. Her heart leaped; her first reaction was one of fear. But he made no more toward her. He stood looking at her, and she began to breathe easier.

When he spoke, his voice was gentle.

"You have been faithful and diligent in your labors. But you are tired now, because of the increase of your toil. It is proper that you should receive a witness, that your faith might be strengthened."

In his hands were the plates, of shining metal — just as the others had described them. He turned over the leaves; they made a strange metallic rustling. She could see the engravings on them, and the rings holding them together. She could also see that a portion of them was sealed together.

In a moment the messenger was gone; the light faded into the softer radiance of twilight. But she felt warmed by the glow of it. She poured the milk into the pans and went back to the house, no longer tired.

She told of her experience that night, tears streaming down her face.

"I too have seen … all my life I will remember. The work is true."

* * * *

The elder Smiths returned to their home in Palmyra. A few days later they were followed by Joseph, Oliver, the Whitmers, and Hiram Page, the Whitmer's son-in-law. They planned to make some arrangements about the printing of the book.

During the visit with the elder Smiths, eight more people, including Joseph's father and brothers Hyrum and Samuel, viewed the plates in the woods near the Smith home. The other witnesses were the Whitmer brothers — Christian, Jacob, John, and Peter Whitmer, Jr., and Hiram Page.

Together they drew up their testimony.

"We should keep it as simple as possible. Just say that the translator has shown us the plates."

"We should say they were gold."

"They had the appearance of gold."

"That's even better. And that we saw the engravings on the plates."

"And how curious they were … we should tell about that. They looked ancient."

"Of curious workmanship."

"We should say that we lifted the plates too … we felt them and hefted them."

"We should put that in first thing."

"No. We'd better describe them first."

"We'd better say something about being sober."

"And we bear record, with words of soberness … "

"That's it. That's what I meant to say."

In the end it looked like this:

Be it known unto all nations, kindreds,
tongues and people, unto whom this work shall
come, that Joseph Smith, Jr., the translator of
this work, has shewn unto us the plates of
which hath been spoken, which have the appearance of gold; and as many of the leaves as
the said Smith has translated, we did handle
with our hands; and we also saw the engravings thereon, all of which has the appearance
of ancient work, and of curious workmanship.
And this we bear record with words of soberness, that the said Smith has shewn unto us, for
we have seen and hefted, and know of a surety,
that the said Smith has got the plates of which
we have spoken. And we give our names unto
the world, to witness unto the world that which
we have seen; and we lie not, God bearing witness of it.

On the eleventh of June, 1829, the title page was
deposited with R. R. Lansing, clerk of the United States
District Court in northern New York. To protect himself
against the kind of loss he had sustained earlier, the
translator signed his own name, Joseph Smith, Junior,
as "author and proprietor." This gave him protection
under the law, as provided by act of Congress.

The title page made it clear as to the nature and intent
of the book, so that no one would be deceived. The
description, according to Joseph, was taken from the
plates themselves.

...an abridgement of the record of the people
of Nephi, and also of the Lamanites; written to
the Lamanites, who are a remnant of the house
of Israel; and also to Jew and Gentile; written
by way of commandment, and also by the spirit
of prophecy and of revelation. Written, and
sealed up, and hid unto the Lord, that they
might not be destroyed; to come forth by the gift
and power of God unto the interpretation there-

of; sealed by the hand of Moroni, and hid up
unto the Lord...
   ...to shew unto the remnant of the house of Israel what great things the Lord hath done for
their fathers; and that they may know the covenants of the Lord, that they are not cast off for
ever; and also to the convincing of the Jew and
Gentile that Jesus is the Christ, the Eternal
God, manifesting himself unto all nations...

Arrangements were made for Egbert Grandin of
Palmyra to print the book.

Martin Harris applied for a bank loan of thirteen
hundred dollars from the bank in Geneva, New York.
When the purpose of the loan was discovered, the bank
refused to grant it. He then made preparations to
mortgage his farm for the cost of printing the book —
three thousand dollars. He pledged himself to pay the
full amount within eighteen months.

Grandin prepared to print five thousand copies. John
H. Gilbert, master type-setter, was to set the type.

The rest of the Whitmers went back to Fayette, with
the exception of Peter Whitmer. Joseph stayed at his
parents' home and prepared to sign the final papers in
regard to the printing of the manuscript.

* * * *

Just as Joseph was about to leave for the printer's office,
there was a knock on the door.

Lucy opened it. It was Dr. McIntyre, one of their
acquaintances.

"I came to warn you," he said. "There're forty men
out there, a mob if I ever saw one. They plan to waylay
Joseph if he ever sets out on his way to the printer's."

"Oh, no!" Lucy cried. "Why can't they let him alone?"

Joseph came into the room. "What's all this about a mob?"

"They're all on the other side of the woods, near Jacaway's field. At least, that's where I saw 'em last. They aim to keep you from ever publishing that book. They asked me twice to take command of things, and I refused. So Mr. Huzzy offered his services — you know, the hatter."

"Oh, not Mr. Huzzy," Lucy said.

"Like I said, there's about forty of them-"

"Well, that settles it," Lucy said. "Joseph, you'd better not go."

"Of course I'm going, Mother."

"No. No, please don't go."

Dr. McIntyre said, "I'd be very careful if I were you. Some of those fellows, they get together, and they lose any sense they ever had."

"Oh, he's not going. At least wait a little while — they'll get tired and go home."

Joseph looked at the doctor. "Thanks for the warning. I'll be careful."

"I'd better be going," Dr. McIntyre said.

Lucy closed the door after him. Before she could speak, Joseph said,

"Never mind, Mother. Just put your trust in God, and nothing will hurt me today."

He was smiling. She turned away, and he knew she was hoping he would change his mind.

"It's all right, Mother. You'll see."

He set out a short time later.

The road led through a heavy strip of timber. Beyond it, on the right side of the road, was the field belonging to David Jacaway. When Joseph reached the field, there was the mob seated on the fence that ran along the road.

Joseph went up to Mr. Huzzy. Taking off his hat, he said pleasantly,

"Good morning, Mr. Huzzy."

"Uh - good morning."

He greeted the next man in the same way, and the next one, all down the line.

Taken by surprise, they looked at each other, as if confused about what to do next. Joseph passed them, and kept walking toward town.

When he returned home, after drawing up the agreement for publication, he said,

"Well, now, Mother. The Lord has really been on my side today. Now, didn't I tell you it would be all right?"

"What happened?" she asked. "What about the mob?"

"Well, they thought they were going to do great things, I'm sure. I just left 'em all settin' on that fence like a bunch of roosting chickens. I went on into town, and not one of them stopped me. On the way back, I saw the fence was empty — they had all gone home. I bet they wish they'd stayed there in the first place."

Before the book went to the printer's, Joseph had further instructions for Oliver. Oliver was to copy the entire manuscript, so that if any of it were lost or destroyed at the printer's, they would still have a copy. Also, Oliver should have someone with him as he went to and from the office, to help protect the manuscript. Someone should be constantly on the watch around the house, both night and day, to protect the manuscript from those who would try to destroy it.

With these precautions, the family and friends of Joseph Smith waited in anticipation. By August the book was in the hands of the printer. The first copies would not appear until March of 1830.

131

11

The townspeople viewed the undertaking with interest and hostility.

"You gonna buy one of them gold bibles?"

"Not on your life."

"You know what it says in the newspaper? Why, it says, right here in the *Palmyra Freeman*...it's the 'greatest piece of superstition that has come to our knowledge.'"

"If that don't beat all. Derned if I'll buy one of them books."

"Well, boys, it looks like we won't have to. It looks like Dogberry's gonna print some of it, maybe in the *Reflector*. That's what the advertising says, anyway. See? It says how parts of the Book of Mormon are gonna be printed in the paper, so the subscribers won't have to buy it."

"That Dogberry. Trust him to think of that. He's sure one smart fellow."

Obadiah Dogberry was the pen name of one Abner Cole, a former justice of the peace.

Hyrum and Oliver found him working in Grandin's office one Sunday.

Hyrum had felt uneasy about the pages that had been left there over the weekend. He had asked Oliver to go to the office with him. Oliver had agreed, even though it was Sunday.

The shop was open. They went in. There was Cole, his hands smeared with ink.

"Well," Hyrum said in surprise. "How is it, Mr. Cole, that you are so hard at work on Sunday?"

132

"It seems I can't have the press in the daytime during the week. So I'm obligated to do my printing at night, and on Sundays."

"May I see what you're doing?"

"Can't stop you."

They looked over the prospectus of his paper.

"Look there," Oliver said.

It was an agreement with his subscribers to publish one part of 'Joe Smith's Gold Bible' each week.

Oliver picked up the paper, something entitled *Dogberry Paper on Winter Hill*. There indeed was a portion of the Book of Mormon, Across from it was a parcel of the most vulgar, disgusting prose he had ever seen.

Oliver winced; he passed it to Hyrum.

There was a pause while Hyrum looked at it. Then he said,

"Mr. Cole. What right have you to print the Book of Mormon in this manner? Don't you know we have secured the copyright?"

"It's none of your business," Cole replied. "I have hired the press, and I'll print what I please."

Hyrum's voice rose. "Mr. Cole, that manuscript is sacred. I forbid you printing any more of it."

"Smith, I don't care a fig for you. That blasted gold bible is going into my paper, in spite of all you can do."

"But...but this is downright dishonest. You've pilfered it — stolen it. You just can't do this."

"I already have. As a matter of fact, half a dozen issues are already out. I took them out in the country, and your so-called prophet never even knew it. And as for stopping now — well, I just won't. And that's final. Now, if you'll get out of here, I can get my printing done."

Hyrum and Oliver looked at each other in dismay. Joseph had already gone back to his home in Pennsylvania.

"Let's go," Oliver said in a low voice. They went back to the elder Smiths' home.

"What on earth do we do now?" Hyrum asked his father. Hyrum was still fuming. Oliver stood looking discouraged.

"I think Joseph should know about it," Father Smith said.

Father Smith himself set out for Pennsylvania, and came back with Joseph the following Sunday.

The weather was extremely cold. Joseph stayed just long enough to get warm, then he headed for the printing office.

There was Cole, busy with the *Dogberry Paper*.

"How do you do, Mr. Cole," Joseph said. "You seem hard at work."

"How do you do, Mr. Smith," Cole answered.

Joseph took up a copy of the paper and examined it. He waited, then said firmly,

"Mr. Cole, that book, and the right of publishing it, belongs to me. I forbid you meddling with it any further."

Suddenly Cole threw off his coat and rolled up his shirt sleeves. He rushed toward Joseph.

"Do you want a fight, sir?" he roared. "Do you want to fight? I'll publish just what I please. Now, if you really want to fight, just come on!" He was smacking his fists together.

The man looked ridiculous; Joseph couldn't help smiling. He said,

"Now, Mr. Cole. You'd better keep your coat on — it's cold. I'm not going to fight you. Nevertheless, I assure you, sir. You've got to stop printing my book. I know my rights, and I intend to maintain them."

Cole was still shouting. "Sir, if you think you're the best man, just - just pull off your coat and fight me!"

"Mr. Cole." Joseph kept his voice low, but the words were distinct. "The law is on my side, and you'll find that out, if you don't understand it. But I'm not going to fight you."

Cole stood blinking as he realized there wasn't going to be a fight after all. He began to back away. He put on his coat again (for it *was* cold). Finally he was calm enough to agree to arbitration. The result was that he stopped his proceedings, and made no further trouble.

The next trouble came from the townspeople, who called a meeting. There they organized a committee and resolved not to purchase any of the books, once they were printed. They sent a smaller committee to Grandin the printer, to inform him of their resolution. They also hinted of evil consequences for him if he persisted in printing the book.

"For, you know the Smiths have lost all their property. They have no money. Unless they sell the books, they won't be able to pay you for your work. And they never *will* sell any, for no one's gonna buy them."

At this, Grandin became alarmed. He stopped the printing and asked for immediate payment in full, even though Martin Harris' contract with him had almost a year to run.

Lucy said, "You mean we have to send for Joseph *again*? What are we going to do? These trips back and forth are taking every cent we have."

"It can't be helped," Joseph's father said. "We have to get him up here."

When Joseph reached Palmyra, he had to find Martin and urge him to make payment. Martin sold part of his farm to a neighbor, despite his wife Dolly's objections. Then he paid Grandin.

The printer resumed his work.

* * * *

"What's all this talk about a book — some ancient record written on gold plates?" the young man asked.

"Well, where you been, stranger? That's been goin' on fer more'n a year now. They're gettin' that book printed up now."

"There really *is* a record? Something from a past civilization?"

"Well, that's what they say. But, *you* know...I mean, it sounds pretty far-fetched, don't it?"

"But - but what's *in* it? What message — I mean, if the thing is true, and really *does* exist, then what story did those ancient people think was worth preserving? I mean, what did they think was so important, that they had to engrave it and hide it in a hill?"

"It beats me. Why don't you go down to the print shop and find out?"

Stephen Harding decided to do just that. In 1829, he was a young man home from college for the summer. The first thing he heard were the rumors about the book being published. In fact, he could hardly avoid them; the whole town was a-stir.

Joe Smith, they said. Why, that had to be the same boy...he'd seen him years ago, fishing in the pond at Durfee's gristmill on Mud Creek. Stephen remembered... the boy was three years older than himself...long-legged, tow-headed.

Curious, Stephen went over to Grandin's print shop.

There he found Joseph, now a tall, rather pale young man, beardless, his hair a light auburn. With him was Martin Harris.

136

Joseph didn't have much to say; he was engrossed in what was happening to the pages coming off the press. But Martin Harris talked freely to Stephen, and roused his curiosity even more.

"I'd sure like to read the book."

"I'm afraid you can't — not till it's published. It should be ready next spring."

Then Joseph spoke.

"If you want to come around to my parents' home tomorrow evening, Oliver Cowdery will be reading from the Book of Mormon. You can hear it then."

Stephen couldn't pass up such an invitation.

* * * *

Imagine, for a moment, that time has gone back; it is over a hundred and fifty years ago, and you are at the Smith home on that night. If you are as lucky as Stephen was, you will be treated to a supper of rye bread (homemade, of course), milk, and fresh raspberries picked by Joseph's younger sisters.

Then it is time for the reading. You are sitting in the main room. By the light of a tallow candle in a tin candlestick, Oliver is reading. He is a thin young man. In the candle's glow, his face has a brooding sensitivity.

You are in the company of farming people, honest, backwoods folk, dressed in plain working clothes. There is a feeling of high expectation in the room. They are leaning forward, listening intently. Listen with them, and even if you are familiar with the book, imagine that you are hearing bits of the story for the first time.

You learn that it is the story of two major migrations to the New World in ancient times. First, there were the Jaredites, led by divine direction from the Near East approximately two thousand years before Christ.

137

The second group of people, the Nephites, came out from Jerusalem around 600 B. C., just before its destruction. It is the history of the Nephites that takes up the major portion of the book — their wanderings, their growth, their eventual destruction. Mormon, one of the last of his people, made an abridgment of other records which he had; the book thus bears his name. His son Moroni was the one who hid the collection of abridged plates at last in the hill.

It is a story of sea voyages, the settling of a new land, the journeyings under the leadership of prophet-kings. One thing you discover is that the people in both migrations had a profound knowledge of God. Their religious lives were as rich as some of those depicted in the Old and New Testaments; in fact, the same religious principles predominated.

What intrigues you, and what grips the other listeners most powerfully, is the Christian nature of the Book of Mormon. For these early believers, the book is full of the spirit and teachings of Jesus.

"Now, wait a minute," you say. "That book is not Christian. It can't be...I mean, I've heard that it isn't."

Now you have put us time travelers in a bit of a spot, for the earliest believers in the Book of Mormon did not question as to whether or not it was 'Christian.' Why else would it have passages like the following?

> And as I spoke concerning the convincing of the Jews, that Jesus is the very Christ, it must needs be that the Gentiles be convinced also, that Jesus is the Christ, the Eternal God, and that he manifesteth himself unto all those who believe in him, by the power of the Holy Ghost.

> I glory in plainness;
> I glory in truth;
>   I glory in my Jesus,

138

for he hath redeemed my soul from hell.

I have charity for my people
 And great faith in Christ
  That I shall meet many souls
   Spotless at his judgment seat.

—Second Book of Nephi

And whatsoever thing is good,
 is just and true;
  wherefore,
Nothing that is good
 denieth the Christ,
  But acknowledgeth
that he is.

— Book of Moroni

Lucy Smith says,
"Oliver, read the part about King Benjamin, where he says Christ would come."
"Let's see — Book of Mosiah..." Oliver is turning the pages.
While he is looking for it, someone else explains to the new listeners...the ancient people had a prophetic knowledge that Christ would come into the world, much as the prophet Isaiah did. Benjamin, one of the prophet-kings, made such a statement in 124 B. C.

> "For behold, the time cometh, and is not far
> distant, that with power, the Lord Omnipotent
> who reigneth, who was, and is from all eternity
> to all eternity, shall come down from heaven,
> among the children of men, and shall dwell in a
> tabernacle of clay.

139

And shall go forth amongst men, working mighty miracles, such as healing the sick, raising the dead, causing the lame to walk, the blind to receive their sight, and the deaf to hear, and curing all manner of diseases;

And he shall cast out devils, or the evil spirits which dwell in the hearts of the children of men.

And lo, he shall suffer temptations, and pain of body, hunger, thirst, and fatigue, even more than man can suffer, except it be unto death;

For behold, blood cometh from every pore, so great shall be his anguish for the wickedness and the abominations of his people.

And he shall be called Jesus Christ, the Son of God, the Father of heaven and earth, the Creator of all things, from the beginning; and his mother shall be called Mary.

And lo, he cometh unto his own, that salvation might come unto the children of men, even through faith, on his name;

And even after all this, they shall consider him a man, and say that he hath a devil, and shall scourge him, and shall crucify him.

And he shall rise the third day from the dead; and behold, he standeth to judge the world."

It is apparent by this time that the central figure in the Book of Mormon is not one of the prophets or leaders, but Christ himself. As one of the family explains, in no way does the Book of Mormon contradict any of the teachings of the New Testament; if anything, it reinforces them. For in the course of the book, the Lord Jesus himself appeared to the righteous part of the Nephite nation after his crucifixion and resurrection. He taught them as he had taught his people in the Old World, where he had said,

"And other sheep I have, which are not of this fold; them also I must bring, and they shall hear my voice, and there shall be one fold, and one shepherd."

According to the Book of Mormon, as long as the ancient ones heeded his teachings, they were at peace with one another; they knew prosperity and harmony, and a great flowering of their civilization.

> And it came to pass that there was no contention in the land, because of the love of God which did dwell in the hearts of the people. And there were no envyings, nor strifes, nor tumults, nor whoredoms, nor lyings, nor murders, nor any manner of lasciviousness; And surely there could not be a happier people among all the people who had been created by the hand of God.

But as soon as greed and violence superseded the gentle teachings of Christ, then that civilization disintegrated in a series of wars. They broke up into bitter factions, among which were the warlike Lamanites. Eventually the Nephites were destroyed.

The lone Nephite survivor, Moroni, recorded the end of his people.

> ...their wars are exceedingly fierce among themselves, and because of their hatred, they put to death every Nephite that will not deny the Christ. And I, Moroni, will not deny the Christ; wherefore I wander whithersoever I can, for the safety of mine own life.

For the nineteenth-century listeners, and for future readers living at a time when greed and violence would fill the world, a warning was given;

> And this cometh unto you, O ye Gentiles, that ye may know the decrees of God, that ye may repent, and not continue in your inequities until the fullness come, that ye may not bring down the fullness of the wrath of God upon you, as the inhabitants of the land have hitherto done.

141

> Behold, this is a choice land, and whatsoever
> nation shall posses it, shall be free from bon-
> dage, and from captivity, and from all other na-
> tions under heaven, if they will but serve the
> God of the land, who is Jesus Christ who hath
> been manifested by the things which we have
> written.

The candle is sputtering; the reading is over for the evening. We are returning you to your own century, with its noise of jets, rock videos and game shows. Behind you, perhaps forever, is the quiet of the lake country, the forests and farmlands, the smell of homemade bread. You are free to read and study the Book of Mormon, or to forget about it, if you choose.

It is interesting to note that at the time the plates were translated, people had little knowledge of the pre-Columbian civilizations, of Toltec, Maya, Inca, Aztec... the ruins of the ancient cities were just beginning to attract attention. *Quetzalcoatl, Kulculcan, Viracocha, the Great Spirit, Lord of Wind and Water... the white bearded God of the Toltecs...* all of these meant nothing to Joseph Smith and his circle of friends. Yet these were the names mentioned in the traditions of the various native American tribes, whose legends universally told of a great white teacher who had lived among them and instructed them in the ways of peace.

Joseph and his friends were unaware of these things. All the knowledge they had was in the book — that Christ himself had visited the ancient people, the ancestors of the Indians.

They also had the exhortation of Moroni, one of the last things engraved on the plates.

> Behold, I would exhort you that when ye shall
> read these things, if it be wisdom in God that ye
> should read them, that ye would remember how

142

merciful the Lord hath been unto the children of men, from the creation of Adam, even down until the time that ye shall receive these things, and ponder it in your hearts.

And when ye shall receive these things, I would exhort you that ye would ask God, the eternal Father, in the name of Christ, if these things are not true; And if ye shall ask with a sincere heart, with real intent, having faith in Christ, he will manifest the truth of it unto you, by the power of the Holy Ghost; and by the power of the Holy Ghost, ye may know the truth of all things.

12

We obtained...the following, by the spirit of prophecy and revelation; which not only gave us information, but also pointed out to us the precise day upon which, according to his will and commandment, we should proceed to organize his church once more here upon the earth.

We...made known to our brethren that we had received a commandment to organize the church, and accordingly we met together for that purpose, at the house of Mr. Peter Whitmer, Sr. (being six in number) on Tuesday the sixth day of April, A. D. one thousand eight hundred and thirty.

—Joseph Smith

Somehow they managed to work in a baptismal service (in nearby Seneca Lake), a prayer service, the meeting in which the church was organized, the ordination of both Joseph and Oliver to be elders of the new church, and a service of communion. Then Joseph and Oliver laid their hands on each person who had been baptized, that he or she might receive the gift of the Holy Ghost. This act also confirmed each one a member of the Church of Christ. During this part of the meeting, some prophesied; all of them praised the Lord and rejoiced in the happenings of the day.

Among those baptized that day were Martin Harris, Orrin Porter Rockwell and his mother Sarah, and Joseph's parents. Joseph stood on the shore to watch the baptisms. When his father came out of the water, Joseph took his hand and exclaimed, weeping,

"Oh, my God! I have lived to see my own father baptized into the true church of Jesus Christ!"

Joseph was so overcome that he went off by himself for awhile. Oliver Cowdery and Joseph Knight, Sr., went after him and stayed with him.

"I never saw anyone so wrought up before," Mr. Knight said to David Whitmer. "You can believe it; his joy was full. I think — well, it was like he suddenly realized what he had begun, and was anxious to carry it out."

"Do you see how full the house is?" David remarked. "I didn't know you could get that many people in there. I swear, there must be at least fifty-five people crowded into those two rooms. Let's see — about twenty from around here, fifteen from Manchester — how many did you say from Colesville?"

"At least twenty," Mr. Knight said. "Why, let's see, there's Polly and me, and there's my son Joseph..."

In addition there were the "six elders," the ones whose names were needed according to law, in order to incorporate as a religious body:

Oliver Cowdery	Peter Whitmer, Jr.
Joseph Smith, Jr.	Samuel H. Smith
Hyrum Smith	David Whitmer

The organizational meeting was opened by prayer. Then those assembled were asked if they accepted Joseph and Oliver as their teachers in the things of the kingdom of God. The people were also asked whether they were satisfied that they should be organized as a church according to the commandments which had been received. They consented with a unanimous vote.

145

It was a quiet, orderly event. Although there were only six members at first, provision had already been made for a complete organization.

"Yes, sir." Mr. Knight was trying to explain to one of the Whitmers' neighbors. "There's revelation providing for a quorum of apostles...for priests, elders, deacons and teachers-"

"Each with their duties defined," Oliver said.

"It puts you in mind of Paul, don't it?" Mr. Knight said.

"Paul?"

"In the New Testament. Where it says, 'And God hath set some in the church...' Oh, what's the rest of it, Oliver?"

"'...first apostles, secondarily prophets, thirdly teachers, after that miracles, then gifts of healings, helps, governments, diversities of tongues...'"

"See?" Mr. Knight said to the neighbor. "He knows everything."

"We have provision for bishops, too," Oliver said. "And even a church recorder. We've received instruction regarding local churches, transferring of membership, holding of conferences..." He was ticking them off on his fingers. "Ordination, granting of licenses, blessing of children, the manner of baptism, administering the sacrament of the Lord's Supper-"

"All that was received by revelation?" asked the neighbor.

"Down to the last detail," Mr. Knight said. "I guess he really *is* a prophet. It don't seem likely he could think of them things all by himself."

"He would have to be inspired," Oliver said. "I know for sure he's no genius."

With the organization of the church came the question of leadership.

"We need a leader. The church should certainly have a leader."

"Every church has a leader. Brother Joseph, wouldn't it be possible for you to inquire of the Lord? Maybe the Lord has someone in mind."

"Yes. Please do. Surely the Lord will direct us in this matter."

Accordingly, Joseph asked, and received the following, directed to himself and to the church:

"Behold, there shall be a record kept among you, and in it thou shalt be called a seer, a translator, a prophet, an apostle of Jesus Christ, an elder of the church through the will of God the Father, and the grace of your Lord Jesus Christ...

"Wherefore, meaning the church...give heed unto all his words, and commandments which he shall give unto you, as he receiveth them, walking in all holiness before me; for his word ye shall receive, as if from mine own mouth, in all patience and faith..."

Not everybody accepted it whole-heartedly. David Whitmer was especially troubled. Was it wise for one man to have so much responsibility?

"He's taking too much upon himself. Don't you see? It's too much power for one man. The people are receiving his words as if they came from God's own mouth...they look upon him as their lawgiver."

"I wouldn't worry," Oliver said. "He's not one to misuse it. He's the soul of honor and truth; I know him. And *someone* has to lead."

"But what if he changes? Sometimes power goes to a man's head-"

"Don't be ridiculous. It won't happen to him. Besides, look how the people love him."

"Yes. Yes...I suppose it's all right."

147

When most of the others had gone back to their homes, Oliver stood out in the road talking with Joseph.

"'Too much power,'" Joseph said. "That's what they're saying, is it?"

"Well, some of them. They-"

"That makes no sense at all. I have a responsibility — I feel it so strongly. First, to reveal the will and mind of God-"

"I know all that. I feel it, too."

"And it's not just for us. Not just for me, or for my family... my friends. It's for the whole nation. Don't you see? The world."

"I know. I do see. I think it's a matter of not going too fast just yet. I mean, we want people to understand-"

"Too fast?" Joseph smiled. "Are you the one who wants to slow down now?"

"No. Not me. But you said something a while back about not stirring things up-"

"But that was when we were threatened with mob violence. Before the translation was even finished. Things are different now. These are our own people. And for one thing, there's so little time. Don't you see? The millennium is almost here!"

Oliver did understand. Zion, the place of safety, the Peaceable Kingdom, had to be made ready. The message of the gospel, and the coming Kingdom of love and brotherhood, based on gospel principles, had to be preached to all who would listen.

"Oliver," Joseph said. "You know as well as I do that the choice of leadership was not in my hands."

"Of course I know that."

"Well, then, are they questioning God's authority?"

"Oh, no. They're just a little concerned...I'm sure they'll accept it. In fact, they have accepted it."

148

But Oliver could see David's point of view. He also understood how Joseph, caught up in his greater vision of things, might be impatient with those who quibbled over details.

The next Sunday, April 11, Oliver preached the first public sermon. The Whitmer house was full of people. Five more of the Whitmer family were baptized that day, along with Hiram Page, the Whitmer's son-in-law. Later in the week, Oliver baptized seven more people.

In Manchester, Joseph's father and brothers were ordained and sent out on missions to preach wherever they could find an audience.

Just after the church was organized, Joseph went over to Colesville and visited his old friends, the Knight family. He began holding meetings in the neighborhood. Among those attending were Joseph Knight's son Newel and his wife, Sally. When Joseph urged Newel to pray in public, Newel found he could not. Newel said he would rather pray by himself. He went out in the woods the next morning to do so.

While he was attempting to pray, he began to experience guilt and uneasiness, to the extent that he felt downright ill. He stumbled home. His appearance was so altered that his wife was alarmed. He managed to say,

"Please go find Joseph Smith, and bring him here."

When Joseph got there, he found Newel lying on the floor. Newel's features were distorted into a grotesque, almost inhuman, expression; he didn't look like Newel at all. His arms and legs were twisting, contorting into unnatural positions which hurt to look at them. Finally he went into convulsions, his body shaking, heaving itself off the floor and back down again.

By this time there were neighbors and relatives crowding in, watching. Finally Joseph managed to get hold of him by the hand.

Newel looked at Joseph. With great earnestness he requested that Joseph cast the devil out of him.

"I know he's in there. I also know you can cast him out."

Joseph replied,

"If you know I can, it shall be done."

Then Joseph rebuked the devil, and commanded him in the name of Jesus Christ to depart. Immediately Newel cried out,

"He's gone! I saw him leave! I saw him, and he just vanished, like that!"

Newel was so weak he had to be put to bed and cared for until he recovered. But the seizures were gone; he declared that the visions of heaven had opened to him.

The people watching were astounded. The news spread quickly. Joseph had to explain to more than one person:

"*I* didn't do it. It wasn't done by man, nor by any power of man. It was done by God, and by the power of godliness. Therefore we must let the honor and the praise be ascribed to the Father, Son, and Holy Spirit..."

Most of those who witnessed the healing — the first miracle in the church — became members. Newel himself went over to Fayette at the end of May and was baptized by David Whitmer.

The first conference of the new church was held on the first day of June, 1830. Again the Whitmer house was crowded, with all twenty-seven members in attendance. There were others present too, either believers or those anxious to learn.

* * * *

150

She was not yet thirteen, a young girl with large brown eyes, and mud-brown hair hanging down her back. Her name was Bethia Paige. She had ridden over with an aunt and uncle from Palmyra.

Now she sat in the third row of chairs, beside her aunt. As the conference began, she was thinking of many things besides the new church that had been formed. People were always forming new churches, and her Aunt Sarah seemed to seek them out. As if they couldn't start a new religious movement without her. Bethia smiled briefly and tossed her hair back over her shoulder.

Samantha. She thought of her favorite cat, all tawny and soft. A big, orangish cat, ready to have kittens. She hoped her brother would be kind to Samantha and not tease her. What if they should be born early, like today? Would he leave the little door into the shed open, so Samantha could get in?

"Don't worry, child," her Uncle Jake had said. "Cats manage very nicely. They always have."

There was an attractive young man up in the front row. Bethia wondered if he were related to the Smiths.

Then Joseph Smith himself stood up before them, in front of everyone. He welcomed them and made some introductory remarks.

They began singing a hymn, some hymn that Bethia didn't know. She wasn't much for hymns anyway. She thought of Samantha, and how the cat hadn't wanted to eat that morning.

Mr. Smith was praying very earnestly, up there in front. He was a large man with light hair. She remembered how some people had said he was a prophet. His voice was expressive, pleading, asking God to direct them in the proceedings of the conference. He spoke simply, as if the words came right from his heart. He didn't dress them up in flowery language the way most clergymen

151

did. Bethia liked that. She figured if God listened to any prayers, he most certainly heard that one.

"In Jesus' name we pray..."

"And bless Samantha, too," she added in her mind. "Let her be all right."

Another man was saying a prayer, something about blessing the bread to all those who partake of it. Then the men in front were offering bits of bread on a tray. They had a prayer over some glasses of liquid, too. Bethia wondered if it were real wine. It looked rather pale.

"What's happening?" she asked her aunt.

"Hush, child. Those are the emblems."

"Emblems?"

"...the emblems of the body and blood of the Lord Jesus Christ."

Oh. So it *was* the bread and wine, just like in the New Testament. So far, they hadn't done anything too strange. She had wondered why a lot of the Palmyra people were angry at Joseph Smith. Maybe she wasn't going to find out that day.

"What are they doing now? What's that fat man doing?"

"Hush. They're confirming him a member of the church."

"Who? That big fat man?"

"Oh, child, hush. Just watch. First they were baptized, see, and then they lay their hands on their heads...oh, I'll explain later."

Bethia watched with interest as they confirmed three more people. Then they ordained four men to be priests, and two to be elders. She listened to the prayers, to Mr. Smith's voice in particular. There was a kindness about it, as if he cared not only about people who were grown up and important, but about children and animals too.

Then different people were standing up and saying things — mostly things about what they were supposed to do as Christians, and how they were going to work until everybody was Christian, a part of the kingdom that was coming.

Was that why some people were angry at Mr. Smith, she wondered? He wanted everyone to be like he was? She personally couldn't see anything too terrible about that.

Suddenly things began to happen. A large woman stood and shouted,

"Praise the Lord! Hosanna!"

She had been blessed, she said, because her daughter had been ill and was getting better.

An older woman, a spry little lady, stood up and told how God had healed her long ago, and had always taken care of her family.

"That's Lucy Smith," Aunt Sarah whispered to her husband. "Joseph's mother."

Then others were standing up, some to prophesy, some to praise God and tell how he had helped them.

"When I went out into my field, six to seven acres had already been plowed, in the night..."

"...Brother Joseph laid his hands on my head, and, praise God! The convulsions stopped! The evil spirit left me; I even saw it leave! I was healed! Praise to the Lord God of Israel!"

Bethia couldn't remember much about the prophecies. They were mostly about the rise of the church, and how the numbers of Saints would increase. One did stick in her memory. A middle-aged man got up and said, in the first person,

"...for thus saith the Lord: Ye are my people, and the sheep of my pasture. Ye are mine, saith the Lord; even as I led my people Israel in former times, so will I lead you..."

153

Was that true, Bethia wondered? A people like Israel of old? While she was pondering, other voices rose.

"The heavens are open to my view!"

"I see angels, and the Lord God himself! It is the Lord! Saints, look!"

People were weeping, crying out. Joseph Smith moved down to the first row of chairs and stood quietly among the people. His face was pale, his hands trembling. Bethia could not see anything out of the ordinary, but she felt a strange heightened expectancy. It wouldn't have surprised her if an angel *had* appeared; it almost seemed as if the light were growing brighter.

Then one of the women fell in a faint. Mr. Smith went to her and lifted her up. He and another man carried her to one of the couches.

"Hosanna!" cried the man who had been healed of the evil spirit. Then he dropped to the floor.

"Brother Newel!" Mr. Smith exclaimed. "Are you all right?"

They stretched him out on the large settle, against the wall. Then the fat man, who had been confirmed, fell off of his chair.

"We'll put him on the bed, Hyrum," someone said.

"Praise the Lord!"

"Catch Sister Rebecca, there! Don't let her hit her head!"

Three others were laid out on beds in a nearby alcove. Mr. Smith said,

"My friends, we have great cause to rejoice this day. These people, our brothers and sisters, are asleep in the spirit. No harm can come to them. They have been overcome by the visions they have seen."

The room was full of the sounds of sniffing and sobbing. Someone else said,

"Praise the Lord for this great work!"

The man called Newel got up off the settle.

"Why did you lay me down like that? I didn't even feel weak!"

"Be careful, Newel," Mr. Smith said. "Don't fall again."

"I'd be right annoyed, except my heart is full of love and glory! Brothers and sisters, listen! I've had a vision! Yes, a vision of the Lord Jesus Christ, on the right hand of the majesty on high!"

"Hosanna!"

"I was given to understand, dear brothers! To my great joy, someday I will be admitted to the divine presence!"

"Hosanna to God, and the Lamb!"

Then, to Bethia's delight, they were all shouting it. "Hosanna! Hosanna, hosanna to God and the Lamb!"

They repeated it, starting it softly, like a chant, and then building to a mighty crescendo. Everyone was standing; Bethia, her aunt and uncle, even the ones who had been lain on the beds. They shouted it again and again, as if they couldn't get enough of it. Bethia's aunt and uncle were looking at each other, a bit bewildered; they were not members, and in their search for new religious groups, they had probably not expected this. Bethia laughed. She caught their eye and shouted with the others.

"Hosanna! Hosanna, hosanna to God and the Lamb!"

Then Joseph Smith moved up in front of them. He raised his hand. The hosannas died away.

He waited a moment, while the silence filled the room. When he spoke, his voice was gentle, strangely subdued.

"My dear friends, you see that we are engaged in the very same order of things as the holy apostles of old. We witness, and feel with our natural senses, the same-" Here his voice broke. He wiped his mouth with a white handkerchief and went on. "-the same glorious manifestations of the power of priesthood, the gifts and blessings of the Holy Ghost-"

155

"Praise God!" someone cried.

"-and the goodness and condescension of a merciful God, unto such as obey the everlasting gospel of our Lord Jesus Christ."

"Amen!"

"We must take with us our sense of rapturous gratitude...our fresh zeal and energy in the cause of truth-"

They ended with another hymn, and a pale thin man named Brother Cowdery offered a closing prayer.

"They're going to stop for the dinner hour," Bethia's uncle said. "Do you want to stay a while longer?"

"I think we'd best get her home," Aunt Sarah said.

"Oh, I want to stay!" Bethia said. "I think this is marvelous. I want to join this church!"

"Uh, no, Bethie." Uncle Jake exchanged glances with Sarah. "Your father would never hear of it. We just came over out of curiosity, and because the Rockwells told us-"

"But I think it's wonderful. I want to be baptized!"

"We'd better get her out of here right away," Aunt Sarah said.

"Aren't we going to meet the prophet?" Bethia said. "He's right up there. Look."

"The prophet. You mean Mr. Smith. There's a lot of people around-"

"We can at least shake his hand," Sarah said.

"I don't see him anymore. He must be outside. We'd better get home. Maybe your cat has her kittens by now."

"Oh, Samantha. Oh, yes." She'd almost forgotten. "But I want to come back. I must — I want to be-"

"All right, Bethia. Let's go now."

Bethia waited with her aunt while Uncle Jake went to get the wagon. There were groups of people outside, talking. The smell of fresh-baked bread drifted to them.

Jake came up with the wagon.

"Some prophet," he said as he helped them in. "He's around in back, telling jokes and wrestling."

* * * *

The Book of Mormon had been on sale in Palmyra since March, 1830.

Right after it was published, Martin Harris set out to recover his investment. He walked the streets of the town, clad in a suit of gray homespun and a large stiff hat. He had books under his arm, trying to sell them for $1.25 a copy.

He was not able to sell very many.

Joseph's brother Samuel, and other members of his family, trudged through the countryside with a load of books

* * * *

It was the thirtieth of June. Samuel was tired; he had walked twenty-five miles that day. In his knapsack were copies of the Book of Mormon. They felt heavier with each step.

He saw the inn from a distance. As he drew closer, he noted the signs of prosperity...the buildings freshly painted, well cared for...the aroma of fresh bread, roast chicken. The prospect of supper made him quicken his steps. Perhaps there would be a chance to sell one of the books.

He tried not to think of the four times he had been turned away that day. But the words seemed to follow him.

"What do you mean, gold plates in a hill? I never heard of such nonsense! Get out of here with those books!"

Samuel entered the inn. The landlord was just inside.

157

"Excuse me, sir," Samuel said. He reached in his pack for a book. "Would you be interested in buying one of these? It's a book — a history. It tells about the origin of the Indians."

The landlord frowned. "I don't know. How did *you* get hold of it?"

"It was translated by my brother, from some gold plates he found buried in the earth."

"You damned liar!" the landlord shouted. "Get out of my house! You aren't staying one minute with your books!"

Samuel was sick at heart. He felt faintness and discouragement sweeping over him. He left the house and went down the road a little way. He washed his feet in a small brook, as a testimony against the man. Then he walked about five more miles.

An apple tree was growing just back from the road. He decided to spend the night under it. He lay all night upon the ground, feeling less than warm, with only his sackful of books for company.

In the morning, he woke up and was preparing to go on his way again. There was a small cottage just down the road. He went toward it, hoping to get a bit of breakfast.

The only one there was a widow. She provided Samuel with some food. She listened to him, but because of her poverty, she was unable to purchase a book.

"Here," Samuel said. "Just take it. It's yours."

"Thank you very much. That's right nice of you, young man."

In Bloomington, eight miles further, he stopped at the house of John P. Greene, a Methodist preacher.

"Well, now, sir," the preacher said. "A dollar twenty-five, you say? I don't want to spend all that money on something that sounds like a nonsensical fable. Tell you what, though. I'll take up a subscription paper, and if anyone wants one, I'll take his name. You can check back here in two weeks. If anyone's interested, we'll know by then."

Samuel agreed to this arrangement.

"Here," he said. "I'll leave one of the books with you."

Samuel checked a few weeks later on the book he had left, but no sales had been made. The third time, he found Mr. Greene gone, and his wife there.

"My husband's away from home right now. I'm sorry about the books. There's just no prospect of selling them. Even this one — the one you left — I expect you'll just have to take it away. My husband doesn't seem to want to buy it. But I've read it, and I like it very much."

Samuel talked with her a little while. He bound his knapsack on his shoulders and prepared to leave. As he said goodbye, he had the strong impression that he should leave the book with her.

"Here," he said. "It's yours, a present. The Spirit forbids me taking it away."

She burst into tears, and asked him to pray with her. He did so. Then he explained to her the most profitable way of reading the book.

"You ask God, as you read it, for a testimony of the truth of what you are reading. Then you will receive the spirit of God, which will enable you to discern the things of God."

Then Samuel left. But Mrs. Greene repeated his words to her husband when he came home.

"Please. I would like you to read it, and at least give me your opinion of it."

Mr. Greene at first refused. Finally his wife persuaded him, and he read it as Samuel had suggested.

Both of them were convinced, and were baptized in a short time. Mrs. Greene gave the book to her brother,

159

Phineas Young. He read it, became converted, and started preaching from it.

The same book was handed to Brigham Young, and to his sister, Mrs. Murray. They both read it without hesitancy, and accepted it as true.

Then Brigham took the book, and hurried to find his brother Joseph, who was preaching Methodism in Canada.

Being a dynamic, straight-forward person, Brigham didn't waste any time.

"Hey, brother Joe! Stop whatever you're doing. You have to read this book! No; I mean, right now!"

Joseph Young read the book, and became convinced of its truth.

From one copy of the book, left as a gift in a preacher's home, came the conversion of a whole family.

13

I have to tell you, it wasn't easy, back in those early days. Don't think for a minute that things went smoothly, the way you read about them in the history books. No, sir. The trouble was, most people was pretty set in their ways. They knew what they believed. And they didn't need some young upstart of a prophet to make them feel uncomfortable.

Even the folks around Colesville, the ones that knew my father — I was surprised how they turned against us. I guess I shouldn't have been, considering how the truth has always had its enemies. But I didn't think they would actually tear down our dam, so that we couldn't have our baptismal service, and turn over our wagons and pile wood on them, and sink them in the water.

It was my father's household that bore the brunt of it. Everyone knew Joseph Knight, Sr., and what a friend he had been to young Joseph Smith. From the time Joseph was old enough to do a good day's work, my father had hired him. That's how we all knew him, and knew about the gold book buried in the hill. Because of the kind of person he was, many of my family believed him, and hoped to become members of the church.

That Sunday my father said to me,

"Come on, Newel. We'll just sneak down and build us another dam."

That's just what we did.

The next day — Monday, it was — we finally had our baptismal service. But before we was even finished, here come our neighbors, jeering at us.

"Watcha doin'?" they called. "Washin' sheep?"

We started for my father's house, with these people right behind us. By the time we reached the house, that mob must've numbered about fifty. Well, they started rampaging around, working themselves into a rage. They surrounded the house, and it sure looked to me like they was ready to commit violence.

We got Joseph and Oliver out of there and over to my house. The mob soon found out where they were and came tearing over to my place. We tried to stay as calm as possible. I know it was only through God's help that they were kept from laying violent hands on us.

The brethren decided to go ahead with the evening meeting, to confirm those newly baptized. Well, the time came, and all our friends began to gather together. But to our great surprise and sorrow, here came the constable and arrested Brother Joseph Smith. The warrant charged him with being a disorderly person — setting the country in an uproar by preaching the Book of Mormon.

The constable then told Joseph about the plan of those who had got out the warrant for his arrest. It seems they just wanted to get him into the hands of the mob. They were outside, lying in ambush for him. The constable said he was determined to save Joseph from them, as he found him to be a different person than what had been represented.

So Joseph went with the constable. They had not gone far from the house when the wagon they were in was surrounded by the mob. But the constable gave the horses the whip, and the mob fell behind.

Then, darned if one of the wagon wheels didn't come off. There they were, sitting in the dark going nowhere, with the mob getting closer and closer. But the constable was an expert man. He managed to get that wheel on, just in the nick of time. They drove off, leaving the mob in the rear once more.

They reached South Bainbridge, where the constable lodged Joseph in an upper room of a tavern. To protect his prisoner, the constable slept during the night with his feet against the door, and kept a loaded gun by him. Joseph occupied a bed in the same room.

The next day a court was convened to investigate the charges against Joseph. My father got two of his neighbors, Mr. Reid and Mr. Davidson — farmers well versed in the law — and retained them to defend Joseph.

There was a lot of excitement   the trial opened with a crowd of spectators. They called up old Josiah Stowell, a gentleman Joseph used to work for. But Mr. Stowell wasn't much help in proving anything against him. They even tried to get Mr. Stowell's daughters to testify. Now, Joseph had once kept company with these daughters. But everything the ladies said about him was in his favor.

Well, they couldn't prove anything against him. But they prolonged that trial until after midnight, drawing things out as long as possible, so another warrant could be brought from another county.

They had given Joseph nothing to eat or drink the whole day, if you can imagine such a thing. No sooner was he acquitted, then another constable arrested him. He was hustled out, hungry and exhausted, and taken fifteen miles away to Broome County. The constable took Joseph into a tavern, and I'll be darned if the men didn't spit on him and yell "Prophesy! Prophesy!" They acted just like those who crucified Christ.

163

The constable finally gave him some crusts of bread and a little bit of water. Then the constable made Joseph lie down on the bed, next to the wall. The constable then laid himself down and threw his arms around Joseph, as if fearing that he intended to escape. That's the way Joseph was compelled to spend the night.

That was the night the mob piled rails against our doors and sunk chains in the stream. A lot of mischief was done, and like I said, my father bore the brunt of it.

But he was adamant; he went and got the same two lawyers to go over and defend Joseph in Broome County.

I have to tell you about Mr. Reid, one of the lawyers. When he was first told of the case, he was pressed for time; he was going to refuse it. Then he thought he heard someone say,

"You *must* go, and deliver the Lord's annointed!"

He said to the man who had come to hire him,

"The Lord's annointed? What do you mean by the Lord's annointed?"

The man was perplexed. "What do *you* mean, sir? I said nothing about the Lord's annointed."

Reid told Mother Smith afterward: "I was convinced that he told the truth, for these few words filled my mind with peculiar feelings; I had never known anything like them. I immediately hastened to the place of trial."

Mr. Reid was quite a fellow. At one point, he was afraid the mob would go after Joseph and do him injury (this was when he had just been acquitted). So Reid invited a bunch of these fellows into another room for drinks. Meanwhile, Joseph made his escape.

Mr. Reid went over to see Sister Emma, Joseph's wife, between the trials. She was staying with her sister Elizabeth and brother-in-law, at their home between Colesville and Harmony. During the two days of waiting, the church women met often to pray for Joseph's freedom. Mr. Reid commented later that Emma's face was "wet with tears...her very heartstrings broken with grief."

The next trial opened before the magistrate's court of Colesville. Joseph's friends and lawyers were there, and so were his enemies, in full force.

Well, they called up a lot of witnesses, and got them to swear up and down to the most incredible falsehoods. But they contradicted themselves right and left — the court wouldn't even admit their testimony. They called others who were so enraged they would have tried to prove anything against him. But you know what? The best they could do was repeat some lie they'd heard from someone else.

Then it was my turn. I was examined by one Lawyer Seymour, who had been sent for, I think, especially to deal with me.

As soon as I had been sworn, Mr. Seymour proceeded to interrogate me as follows:

Question — "Did the prisoner, Joseph Smith, Jr., cast the devil out of you?"

Answer — "No, sir."

Question — "Why, have you not had the devil cast out of you?"

Answer — "Yes, sir."

Question — "And did he not cast him out of you?"

Answer — "No, sir. It was done by the power of God, and Joseph Smith was the instrument in the hands of God on this occasion. He commanded him to come out of me in the name of Jesus Christ."

Question — "And are you sure it was the devil?"

Answer — "Yes, sir."

Question — "Did you see him after he was cast out of you?"

Answer — "Yes, sir. I saw him."

Question — "Pray, what did he look like?"

Here one of the lawyers on the part of the defense told me I need not answer that question.

I replied, "I believe I need not answer that question. But I will do it if I am allowed to ask you one, and you can answer it. Do you, Mr. Seymour, understand the things of the Spirit?"

"No," answered Mr. Seymour. "I do not pretend to such big things."

"Well, then," I replied. "It will be of no use for me to tell you what the devil looked like, for it was a spiritual sight and spiritually discerned, and, of course, you would not understand it were I to tell you of it."

The audience laughed loudly. The lawyer — well, he just looked down, but you could tell he was mighty embarrassed.

After a final attempt on the part of Mr. Seymour to blacken Joseph's character, the two gentlemen Davidson and Reid followed on his behalf. They spoke as men inspired, and even though they were not regular lawyers, they managed to silence their opponents. The court was convinced of Joseph's innocence.

Then that constable, who had made so much trouble, came up and apologized to Joseph, and asked his forgiveness for the ill-treatment he had given him. The constable said that the mob had resolved to tar and feather Joseph and ride him on a rail, if he were acquitted. The constable offered to lead him out another way, so he could get away in safety.

"Quickly. This way."

So Joseph succeeded in escaping from the mob once again, thanks to his new friend, the constable.

Joseph hurried to where his wife Emma was waiting for him, and together they went back to their home in

Harmony. I know they were both more than a little shaken by the course of events.

A few days later, Joseph and Oliver came to my house, intending to confirm those who had been baptized. The mob began to collect again, and this time they were really mad. We decided it best for Joseph and Oliver to make their escape. They didn't even stop to eat. They left, with the mob in full pursuit. They managed to get away, after traveling all night.

At the beginning of August, my wife and I went over to visit Joseph in Harmony. We found him and his wife well, in good spirits. We had a happy meeting. It truly gave me joy to see his face again.

As neither Emma nor my wife Sally had been confirmed, we concluded to attend to that holy ordinance at that time. We also wanted to partake of the sacrament together before we left for home. In order to prepare for this, Brother Joseph set out to procure some wine. But he had gone only a short distance when he was met by a heavenly messenger. The angel said that it did not matter what the Saints ate and drank when they partook of the sacrament, but they should not purchase wine or strong drink from their enemies.

In obedience to this revelation, we prepared some wine of our own make and held our meeting. There were five of us, Joseph Smith and wife, John Whitmer, and myself and wife. We partook of the sacrament, after which we confirmed the two sisters into the church. It was a glorious evening. The spirit of the Lord was poured out upon us. We praised the God of Israel and rejoiced exceedingly.

So you see, there were wonderful times too, along with the times of persecution. And new converts were coming to us all the time. I have to tell you about my wife's sister, Emily Coburn. Emily was staying with us for a little while — this was just before the mob started harassing us. Well, this certain minister — Reverend Shearer was his name — got all upset because Emily was being exposed to our doctrine. It seems he thought she was one of his parishioners, and his own special property. He came over and spent some time "laboring with her," but he couldn't persuade her against us. So finally he tried to get her out of the house; he told her one of her brothers was outside waiting for her, to take her back to her father's house.

Well, she went outside with Mr. Shearer, but there was no one waiting for her. She refused to go any further. Then he took her by the arm to force her to go along with him. She set up a cry, and Sally (my wife) ran out of the house to help her. Those two women together were too much for him. He had to leave without her.

That didn't stop him. He went to her father, told him some lie about us, and convinced the old gentleman to give him the power of attorney. After our Sunday meeting, the reverend appeared, served notice upon her, and carried her off to her father's residence. This was done in open violence, against her will.

Nothing he could do, however, was any avail. A short time later Emily was back with us. She was baptized and confirmed a member of the church.

The Saints were having trouble in other places, too. About this time, up in Manchester, they arrested Father Smith on the pretext that he owed money. They said they would let him go if he would renounce his belief in the Book of Mormon. Well, this he wouldn't do, so even though he was ill at the time, they put him in jail. They tried to arrest Hyrum too, but they couldn't find him. They ransacked the Smith property, and pretty much tore things up.

Father Smith was finally allowed to work off his "debt" by coopering. He was in jail for thirty days. On Sundays they let him preach, and before he left, he managed to convert two people who were in prison with him.

About the last of August, 1830, I took my team and wagon to Harmony to move Joseph and his family up to Fayette. I stood by while he locked his door, with his furniture inside. I suppose they knew, the two of them, that they would never see the place again. Living there in peace was simply out of the question. For Joseph's wife Emma, it meant leaving her father's family, and the place where she had grown up.

I took them to Fayette, to Father Whitmer's house. Then I went back to my own place, to settle some affairs. Soon I set out for Fayette again, for the second conference of the church.

When I arrived, I found Brother Joseph in great distress of mind. He not only had outside persecution to contend with; he now had trouble from his own brethren, those who should have supported him.

It seems that Hiram Page had found a certain peep-stone, which he claimed had special powers. He had managed to stir up the brethren by giving "revelations" concerning church government, and even the building up of Zion, and other matters. He had quite a roll of papers, full of these pronouncements, and many in the church were led astray by them. Even Oliver Cowdery and the Whitmer family were taking them seriously, though they contradicted the New Testament and our own latter-day revelations which we already had.

Joseph was perplexed, not sure of what to do. That night I stayed with him, and we spent the greater part of the night in prayer and supplication. After spending time and care laboring with those brethren, we finally convinced them of their error. They renounced Hiram's writings as not being of God, and acknowledged that they had been misled.

Because it was such an important issue, Joseph inquired of the Lord before the conference commenced. He received a revelation in which the Lord's will was explicitly stated. Only Joseph was to receive revelations for the church, for he "receiveth them even as Moses." Oliver, and others, were to be obedient to the things which would be given to Joseph, and to declare them faithfully.

Also, Oliver was to be sent on a mission to the west, unto the Lamanites — the remnant of the Book of Mormon people. And the promise was given that the location of Zion, the place of peace and righteousness, would soon be revealed. It would be on the borders by the Lamanites.

With the question of Hiram Page's "revelations" resolved, the most beautiful peace and harmony prevailed during the remainder of the conference. It was wonderful to witness the wisdom Joseph displayed on this occasion. For truly God gave him great wisdom and power. It seems to me that none who saw him administer righteousness under such trying circumstances could doubt that the Lord was with him. He acted not with the wisdom of man, but with the wisdom of God.

The Holy Ghost came upon us and filled our hearts with unspeakable joy. Before this conference closed, three other revelations, besides the one already mentioned, were received from God by our prophet. We were made to rejoice exceedingly in the goodness of God.

14

The thing about sorrow is that it keeps coming back. You think you are healed; you think the past is behind you. Then you hear a familiar sound...a door closing, or a creak from a hardwood floor. You glance out the window, at tall grasses moving in the wind. Or you see a little mound of earth under the trees. And the pain comes rushing back...the buried child, the lost home...the parents you would not see again...

"They said such things about Joseph that made it impossible for me to go back."

It was mid-morning. Emma sat sewing, in a house not her own. When she looked out the window, she saw Father Whitmer's fields, with the forest rising beyond them. She was pregnant again, and not feeling well. But the ache in her chest was not from hunger, or any physical cause.

They had left Pennsylvania in such a rush, she and Joseph. Hardly time to gather the things they would need. They had left most of their furniture behind. Joseph had locked up while Newel Knight stood by with the wagon. There was not enough time for a last look at the house where they had been happy together, or the fields of farmland Joseph had purchased from her father. (Two hundred dollars he had paid, for the thirteen acres.)

And certainly not enough time to look at the river, or Ichabod Swamp, or the place under the trees where their first born lay buried. Alvin, they had named him...he had lived only three hours. From the upstairs window, facing east, she had been able to look out at the grave. Now, most likely, she would never see it again.

That was hard enough. But to know her family no longer understood, no longer even tried to sympathize...that was the chief burden that lay upon her heart.

They had tried to protect Joseph at first. But when the persecutions became too severe — in fact, when Joseph's very life was in danger, they had listened to the lies about him. Her father had decided that the persecution was probably justified.

And he had thought Emma a fool for staying with him, let alone marrying him in the first place.

The final parting had been bitter...it pained her to think how bitter. When she turned from them, she knew it was as if she had no family at all. The estrangement was complete.

To keep busy — that was the thing. Then she would forget.

Emma didn't have any trouble keeping busy. Four missionaries were going to the west. Besides Oliver, there was Peter Whitmer, Jr., Parley Pratt, and Ziba Peterson. They needed to have clothing furnished for their journey. And most of it had to be made out of the raw material. Emma and several others had decided to undertake the project. She sat and sewed in Mother Whitmer's house, working until her fingers were stiff and the cloth blurred before her eyes.

"Emma, my dear. You must rest now. You're working much too hard."

Mother Smith, also a visitor in a house not her own. Would they ever live in their own homes again?

"The work has to get done," Emma said smiling.

"Well, let some of the others work as hard as you do."

"Oh, they're busy too." Emma paused a moment, resting against the back of the wooden chair.

172

Mother Smith's bright, inquisitive eyes went over her as the old lady leaned forward in her rocker. Emma knew she was being scrutinized.

"You look a bit peaked. We don't want you getting sick again."

Emma was annoyed at first. Then she realized that she was being cared for — here was Joseph's mother, as solicitous as a mother hen...fretting over her more than her own family would ever do. In fact, her husband's family *was* the only family she had now. Touched, Emma said,

"I promise to rest a little while. Then I'd better work some more. And I shall take a long nap this afternoon."

"Good. We'll see that you do."

Emma sighed and looked out the window. The tall grass was yellowish-brown with the coming of fall. Harvest colors. A cloud-shadow fell over the fields.

"I'd better see about that bread," Mother Smith said. "Folks'll be hungry before long."

She got up and went into the next room. Emma could hear her getting out the bread pans, then kneading the dough to put it into the pans.

With such a large household, Emma was seldom alone. There was the Whitmer family, and now herself and Joseph, Joseph's parents, and the missionaries who were getting ready for their journey. Parley Pratt's wife, Thankful, was with them too (the other three missionaries were still single). At conference time it was even more crowded, but right now things were quiet.

Most of the men were busy outside. Joseph and Oliver were occupied with church business. The women and girls were busy in other parts of the house, some preparing the next meal, others sewing for the missionaries and the family. For once, Emma was entirely by herself.

173

She knew it would not last long. She picked up her work and began stitching again. Mother Smith was right; she had to be careful. She had been ill for four weeks. But now she was better. She thought of the thing that had sustained her through her illness, that even now helped her spirits to rise (like the bread, now in pans on the sideboard).

The blessing. The message that had been given, just for her. Addressed to her, with her hopes and doubts, her anxieties, her special gifts. It had come to her through her husband last July, when they were still in their home in Harmony.

She was amazed, even now, at the completeness of it — at the way it had answered questions that had been with her since she'd first heard of the work Joseph was to do. It had been a source of strength to her when it was first received. She marveled at the way the words could comfort her now, months later.

It was written down and kept with her few possessions upstairs in their bedroom. But she knew certain phrases of it by heart. She thought of her questions, both past and present. And she thought of the answers and promises in the revelation.

—Am I truly loved by God? Am I acceptable to him?

"...Emma, my daughter in Zion..."

His daughter, he had called her. She who was disowned by her father, was a daughter of God.

"Behold, thy sins are forgiven thee, and thou art an elect lady, whom I have called."

—Why was I not allowed to see the plates from which the Book of Mormon was translated? I was faithful and steadfast — that is, I tried to be. Many others saw them, and I did not.

"Murmur not because of the things which thou hast not seen, for they are withheld from thee, and from the world, which is wisdom in me in a time to come."

—What is my work, and my calling? What would you have me do?

"And the office of thy calling shall be for a comfort unto my servant Joseph Smith, thy husband, in his afflictions, with consoling words, in the spirit of meekness. And thou shalt go with him at the time of his going, and be unto him for a scribe, that I may send Oliver whithersoever I will."

—I am a woman, and there are those who tell me my place is in the home. But I have a mind that ranges over many things... I have a knowledge of literature and poetry, of the Bible, and history. I have a love of music, and a gift of song. Shall I ever use these things?

"...thou shalt be ordained...to expound Scriptures, and to exhort the church, according as it shall be given thee by my Spirit...thy time shall be given to writing, and to learning much."

—Will there be enough for us to eat? What about the necessities of life? How on earth shall we support ourselves?

"...thou needst not fear, for thy husband shall support thee from the church; for unto them is his calling, that all things might be revealed unto them, whatsoever I will, according to their faith."

—My furniture. My house, that we have left behind. It had a beautiful maple floor. I had a bureau, of lovely burnished wood, and bowls of birds-eye maple-

"...thou shalt lay aside the things of this world, and seek for the things of a better."

—My voice. At least I didn't leave that with the other things. I still have a voice, and the sound of it gives me joy. I sing when I work. When I worship, I feel like singing also. I know many hymns, and old songs from when I was growing up.

"And it shall be given thee...to make a selection of sacred hymns, as it shall be given thee, which is pleasing unto me, to be had in my church; for my soul delighteth in the song of the heart; yea, the song of the righteous is a prayer unto me. And it shall be answered with a blessing upon their heads."

—That I will do gladly. I *will* be used. My mind, my voice, my gifts...I will be used for the cause of righteousness, and the good of the kingdom which is coming.

"Wherefore, lift up thy heart and rejoice, and cleave unto the covenants which thou hast made. Continue in the spirit of meekness, and beware of pride. Let thy soul delight in thy husband, and the glory which shall come upon him."

—That means he will live, at least for a time. Maybe a long time. The mobs that harass him will not take his life.

The last thought was a comfort to her. She'd had great fears for his safety.

A shadow fell over her then, a cloud passing overhead. To lose Joseph, her husband...at that moment, she could think of nothing worse.

Faith...she must have faith now, as never before. God, who had called her his daughter, would surely not forsake her.

176

The fields were bright again in the sunlight. From the next room came sounds of pans being moved, of the hearth being prepared for the baking. She had lost a family, she reflected. She was beginning to realize she had gained a much larger one. Not just the older Smiths, but the Whitmers and Oliver and all the others. For they were all sons and daughters of God.

What would happen if they all saw themselves as members of one family? If they truly saw that they belonged to each other and to God, then they would be a mighty force indeed. What couldn't they accomplish? What would prevent them from actually establishing the kingdom of God upon the earth? Perhaps all the unrest and turmoil — the loss of homes and former friends — was simply a prelude to that kingdom. They were being forced to leave their former lives, to break old patterns and create new ones.

If they belonged to each other, then, in a sense, everything they possessed was for the good of the other members of the group. The fields which she saw out the window, owned by Father Whitmer, were being used to feed them all. In a sense, they were her fields, and this was her house, even though she did not own it. She felt more at home already.

That was it. In their wanderings — and she sensed there might be many — home would be wherever they happened to be. Wherever she and Joseph, or any others of the family of God, happened to be staying, that would be her home.

She was conscious of warmth and sunlight, of new life within her...the child to come. The scent of baking bread filled the house. There were voices from the next room, the sounds of the meal being prepared. She thought of the many hands that would prepare the food, which they would all eat together.

Other people were coming into the room; she was no longer alone. Elizabeth Ann Whitmer, fifteen years old, darted over to the window and looked out.

"Have you seen Oliver? He should be here by now."

Emma smiled. Mother Smith said to her,

"I thought you were going to rest awhile."

Emma said,

"But I've had a good rest. And, look. This is almost finished."

She held up what she had been working on — a coat for Oliver. In a sense, it was hers too...part of her would go to the western lands.

Mother Smith looked at it critically. "That should keep him warm enough."

"Oh, there he is, " Elizabeth Ann said. "There's Oliver."

Emma said, "I trust Joseph is with him."

"Oh, yes . He's there, too. They're going around in back."

In a few moments the men were inside. Elizabeth Ann flew over to Oliver and began talking excitedly.

Emma rose from her chair and went to meet Joseph. Their eyes met; he put his arm around her.

She smiled and said,

"Welcome home."

15

When earth in bondage long had lain,
  And darkness o'er the nations reigned,
And all man's precepts prove in vain,
  A perfect system to obtain...

—Parley P. Pratt

Parley Parker Pratt had given up on the world at the age of nineteen.

"Is that right, sir?" the youthful interviewer asked. "Did you really give up on the world, the way it says?"

"Well, now, son, that's a strange way of putting it. It's a little more complicated than that. Oh, I was nineteen, all right, and I was pretty discouraged. You see — the civilized world, or what we call 'civilized,' hadn't been exactly kind to me. I had met with disappointment...that's right, and sorrow, and unrewarded toil. What really disgusted me were the sectarian differences — the things 'religious' people squabble about. And the ignorance — it was enough to drive a man crazy.

"Well, I figured I could get away from all that by heading west. Even it if meant spending the rest of my days in solitude, among the natives of the forest.

"You see, I thought I could find a place where there would be no cheating, no buying and selling of land — no law to take all one's hard earnings to pay a small debt. And above all, no wrangling about sects, creeds and doctrines. Life among the Indians. The more I thought about it, the more I wanted to be off, to the great west."

179

"You were interested in the Indians even then, I take it."

"Oh, let me tell you. I had all these grandiose ideas. I thought things like, 'I will win the confidence of the red man...I will learn his language...I will tell him of Jesus. I will read to him the Scriptures...teach him the arts of peace, to hate war, to love his neighbor...to fear and love God...to cultivate the earth...' Oh, I was full of romantic ideas back then. But as I say, I was only nineteen — and I meant well."

"What *did* you do?"

"Oh, I left, of course. It was in October of 1826. I said goodbye to my friends and started out westward. Well, I got to Rochester, and instead of saving my money, I spent most of it on a small pocket Bible. I made it as far as Buffalo. Then I found a steamer bound for Detroit. I had no money left, so I had to agree to work for my passage."

"And did you?"

"Well, I started with that intention. But it was a rougher passage than I care to talk about. Countless delays, and then this tremendous storm — we were forced to land at Erie, Pennsylvania. Well, I'd already decided a sailor's life was not for me. I managed to stagger ashore.

"I didn't stop there long. I set out on foot, always going westward. It was November — the rainy season. Those roads were a mess — all mud and mire. There I was, struggling through that mud, with the forest dripping about me. I began to wonder if it was wise to go on."

"So then you came to Kirtland?"

"Now, wait a moment. What I found was a small settlement, about thirty miles west of Cleveland. It was so little, I can't recall it even had a name. Well, I was destitute. No money, no food, in a land of strangers. And

I wasn't yet twenty years old. Talk about discouragement. I said to myself,

"'Reckon I might as well stop for the winter anyway.'

"Well, I tried to think what to do. I approached one of the settlers and asked if I could do some work for him. With the money he paid me, I bought me a gun. Then I earned enough for an axe, and some flour and such like.

"I found me a hut — it was a small log cabin, about two mile off in the forest. It was empty — no one had been in it for a while. So I just moved on in. I began to fix it up some, for the winter."

"Did it have furniture?"

"Furniture? Good heavens, child! In the middle of the wilderness? I just brought in leaves and straw for my bed, and enough kindling for a good fire. I suppose you'll be asking about running water next. Well, I had that, too. There was a stream near the door — fresh, sweet water. Animals came down to drink. I was able to bag my own fat venison. I had that to eat, and bread from the settlement. That's how I survived over the winter."

"Wasn't it hard, being all alone?"

"Son, it was never easy. But I wasn't alone; I had books for company. Besides the Holy Scriptures, there was McKenzie's travels in the Northwest. Oh, yes, and Lewis and Clark's tour up the Missouri and down the Columbia Rivers. I had a blazing fire, and I sat reading by the light of it. All this, while those winter storms raged outside. Why, I could hear that wind shaking the forest. And in the distance, I could hear wolves howling. I remember an owl hooting close at hand — oh, that's a mournful, chilling sound. But I was warm, with my fire and my bed of straw.

"Well, spring came, and the woods were alive with birds and wildflowers. I came out of my cabin and looked around. And do you know what? I had never seen a more beautiful place. All thoughts of wandering had fled. I was where I wanted to be...so attached to my new home that I had no desire to leave it.

"I went and bargained for a piece of forest land. I promised to pay for it in a few years. Then I began to clear a farm and build me a home. By this time I was twenty years old. And I had plans. I was aimin' to make some improvements and preparations. Then I planned to go back to my native country — New York State. There was one there, you see, whom I had loved for a long time. I wouldn't have stayed away so long, except for misfortune."

"And did you go back for her?"

"I did indeed. It was Thankful I went back for — Thankful Halsey, she was then. She married me on September 9, 1827. I brought her back to our Ohio clearing.

"Now wait till you hear what we did to that clearing. The forest had been cleared for some distance around, thanks to the labors of those first settlers. We had a small frame house, yes, and a garden. There was a lovely meadow in front, and flowers all about our door and windows. In back we had an orchard of apple and peach trees, and beyond that, our fields of grain. There were other houses and farms around. And do you know what? On the very spot where I had lived for months without seeing another person, my wife now had a school for twenty children!"

"What about Sidney Rigdon? When did you meet him?"

"Oh, he came into the neighborhood as a preacher. It was rumored that he was a kind of Reformed Baptist. He and Mr. Alexander Campbell, and some other gifted men, had dissented from the regular Baptists and were

182

preaching a different doctrine. Well, finally I went to hear him.

"To my astonishment, I found he preached faith in Jesus Christ, repentance towards God, and baptism for remission of sins. He also taught the promise of the Holy Ghost to all who would come forward, with all their hearts, and obey this doctrine!

"Well, I don't have to tell you that here was the *ancient gospel* in due form. Here were the very principles I had found years before, but could find no one to minister in. One great link was still missing to complete the chain of the ancient order of things...the *authority* to minister in the name of Jesus Christ. That thought went through my mind as soon as I heard Mr. Rigdon speak.

"I went to hear Mr. Rigdon several times after that. Finally I joined a number of others, and accepted the truths he was teaching. We met frequently for public worship.

"As the year 1830 began, I felt drawn to search the prophets, and to pray for more understanding. To my joy, I began to comprehend the things which were coming on the earth — the restoration of Israel, the coming of the Messiah...the glory that should follow. I felt compelled to preach concerning these things, and to prepare people for the coming of the Lord."

"So what did you do? You began preaching?"

"Well, we left our wilderness home that August. We took passage on a schooner bound for Buffalo. Then we transferred to a canal boat going to Albany. About one hundred miles out of Buffalo, I had a strong feeling I should leave the boat. It was as if I had some sort of work to do in that region. So I left the boat and my wife — I planned to join them later.

"I remember it was early in the morning, just at the dawn of day. I walked ten miles into the country. I stopped

183

to eat breakfast at the home of a Mr. Wells. I told him I wanted to preach that evening. Mr. Wells went with me through the neighborhood to visit the people, and give them news of the preaching engagement.

"We just happened to visit an old Baptist deacon — Hamlin was his name. After he heard about the evening appointment, he mentioned a book, a very strange book which he had. It had just been published. He said it claimed to have been translated from plates of gold or brass, found buried in the earth. It had been discovered and translated by a young man near Palmyra, New York, by the aid of visions, and the ministry of angels."

"Did you read it then?"

"Well, no. I asked him where I could get the book. He said I could look at it if I would come by his house the next day.

"Well, I had this strange interest in the book. He had said it was written by a branch of the tribes of Israel. I kept thinking of it all during my sermon that evening. The next morning I called at the old gentleman's house. And there, for the first time, I saw the Book of Mormon. Little did I know, as I started to read, that it would direct the entire course of my life.

"The first thing I did was read the title page. I read the testimony of the witnesses in relation to the manner of its being found and translated. Then I just began reading. I read all day; eating was a burden. I had no desire for food. Sleep was a burden when the night came, for I preferred reading to sleep.

"As I read, the spirit of the Lord was upon me, and I knew that the book was true, as plainly as a man comprehends and knows that he exists. My joy was full. I rejoiced sufficiently to more than pay me for all the sorrows and toils of my whole life.

184

Lo, from Cumorah's lonely hill,
There comes a record of God's will,
   Translated by the power of God,
His voice bears record to his word.

A voice commissioned from on high!
   Hark, hark! It is the angel's cry,
Descending from the throne of light,
   His garments shining clear and white![1]

"I soon determined to see the young man who had been the instrument of its discovery and translation."

* * * *

The shadows of late afternoon fell across the road. He had been walking all day; he stopped in the village to ask directions.

"I'm looking for the residence of Mr. Joseph Smith. Can you help me?"

"Joe Smith? Why, sure. Just go two or three miles that way. Keep walking. You can't miss it."

It was early evening as he approached the house. There was a man driving some cows just ahead of him on the road.

"Excuse me, sir. I'm looking for Mr. Joseph Smith, the translator of the Book of Mormon. Can you tell me where I might find him?"

"I'm sorry. He's not here."

"But - but I understood he lived here."

"He *used* to live here. He's living in Pennsylvania now."

"How far is that?"

"About one hundred miles."

Parley took a deep breath. It was hard to conceal his disappointment.

---

[1] From the hymn, *When Earth in Bondage Long Had Lain*, by Parley Parker Pratt.

185

"Well...what about his father? Is his father here? Or - or any of his family?"

The driver of cows was watching him closely. "His father is away from home right now, but he lives in that small house over there. As for his family...I guess I'll have to do. I'm his brother."

"His *brother*! Well, why didn't you say so? You see, I'm Parley Pratt. I've come all this way looking for him — for anyone — who can tell me more. It's the book...the interest I have in the book..."

The cow driver extended his hand. "I'm Hyrum Smith."

They shook hands.

"Oh, you're one of the witnesses — your name is in the front of the book. This is wonderful. There's so much you can tell me...I must know more about it. Let's start at the beginning."

"First, welcome to my house. I'll just drive the cows around in back, and get my younger brother to milk them. Then we'll get you something to eat...you look as if you could use a meal, and some rest."

"Oh, I'm not tired. In fact, I'm ready to talk all night."

That's just what they did. They stayed up all night, for neither one felt sleepy. They talked, and Parley told Hyrum about the things that had happened to him.

The next morning Parley had to leave, as he was supposed to fulfill a preaching appointment that evening, some thirty miles back. Just as Parley left, Hyrum presented him with a copy of the Book of Mormon. Parley was delighted to have his own copy; he had not yet had a chance to finish the book.

After walking a few miles, he stopped to rest. He got out the book and began reading it.

He sat in the shade of a tree and read. As he turned over the page, he thought of how much the book had come to mean to him. At that moment, he esteemed it more than all the riches of the world. He would not have exchanged the knowledge in it for anything — not even for a legal title to all the beautiful farms and villages he had passed on the road.

With that thought, he returned immediately to Hyrum Smith's residence and demanded baptism. Hyrum waited, and took Parley to the Whitmer household in Fayette the next day. They walked the twenty-five miles together. They found a welcome reception, and the day after (about the first of September, 1830), Parley was baptized by Oliver Cowdery in Seneca Lake.

He was confirmed a member of the church and ordained an elder that very night.

He returned to the old homestead, where his kinsfolk lived, and began preaching the restored gospel. Most of his family believed "in part," but his brother Orson, nineteen years old, received it whole-heartedly, and was baptized at that time.

Parley went back to the family of church members further west and found that Joseph Smith had returned from Pennsylvania to his father's residence near Palmyra. Here Parley had the pleasure of meeting him for the first time.

* * * *

"So what did he say?" the interviewer asked. "The prophet Joseph. What was he like?"

"Well, child, I don't recall his exact words. But he received me with a hearty welcome, and with that frank and kind manner which he always had.

"What was he like? President Joseph Smith was — well, in the first place, he was tall. Tall and well built. The first impression was of a strong, active man. He had a light complexion — light hair, blue eyes, very little beard.

"But you want to know what he was really like. Well, let's see... he had an expression that was unique to him...as if he were fully awake, more intensely alive than most folks. You never got tired of looking at him. His face had a gentle look, and pleasant...he seemed to beam with intelligence and kindness. He had an unconscious smile, a — well, a cheerfulness. There was no restraint, or pretended seriousness, the way some religious leaders have. He had a steadiness in his glance, as if he could look into the deepest places of the human heart.

"What else can I tell you? You would've had to know him, to understand."

"I see. I wish I could have known him."

"If I had to describe his character, I'd say he had a noble boldness — he was independent. His manner was easy and familiar. When he spoke for any length, his language had a sort of original eloquence. It wasn't polished, or studied. But it seemed to flow with its own native simplicity.

"His words were interesting, edifying. But at the same time he amused and entertained. I tell you, nobody ever got bored when *he* was speaking. Why, I've seen him hold a congregation of listeners for hours together, even when it was cold or raining. He had them laughing one moment and weeping the next. Even his most bitter enemies were generally overcome, if he could once get their ears."

* * * *

During the first visit with Joseph, Parley was invited to preach at the meeting on Sunday, after which Joseph also preached. They went to the water's edge, and at Joseph's request, Parley baptized several persons.

Shortly after, Parley learned what his work was to be.

> And now concerning my servant Parley P. Pratt, behold, I say unto him, that as I live I will that he shall declare my gospel and learn of me, and be meek and lowly of heart.
>
> and that which I have appointed unto him, is that he shall go with my servants Oliver Cowdery and Peter Whitmer, Jr., into the wilderness, among the Lamanites;
>
> and Ziba Peterson, also, shall go with them, and I myself will go with them and be in their midst...

He was to carry the book and message to the Indian, as he had dreamed of doing in his younger days...*I will tell him of Jesus... I will teach him the arts of peace, to hate war...*

As he walked to the west with his missionary companions, his head was full of the things he would do.

I will win the confidence of the red man...I will learn his language...

Walking was the easiest and cheapest form of locomotion; they walked everywhere. But for some, it was easier than for others.

"Slow down a little, Parley," Oliver said. "You'll wear us all out, at that pace."

"We'll never get there, if we don't press forward."

"How many more miles do you figure we should go today?" Ziba asked.

"I'd say about ten," Parley said. "That should put us close to Buffalo."

"*Ten!*" Peter said. "We've gone a good twenty already!"

There was a groan from Oliver.

"Come on," Parley said. "You can make it. We'll slow down a little, if that'll help."

"My feet are aching," Oliver said. "Isn't it time for something to eat? Or- I know. It's time for a season of prayer. Off there, in the woods. It's just the place."

"Why don't you pray while you walk?" Parley said. "That's what I do."

Later, as they neared Ohio, he told them about Sidney Rigdon.

"Who?" Peter asked.

"I never heard of him," one of the others said.

Parley said, "He's one of the greatest orators in the Western Reserve. Probably the greatest."

"Preaches well, does he?"

"Not only that, but he's very learned. One of the best educated men you'd ever want to meet."

"If that's the case, what's he doing way out in the middle of the wilderness?"

"Well, that's his territory," Parley explained patiently. "That's where he was sent to preach, by the Reformed Baptists. And you should hear him! I swear, he's one of the most intelligent men I've ever heard."

"I thought it was *us* that was supposed to be doin' the preachin'," Ziba said. "Now you want us to go listen to *him*."

"Listen," Parley said. "I *know* this man. I think he'd be interested in what we have to tell him. I propose we go to Mentor, stop off and see Rigdon-"

"But it's out of the way," Oliver said.

"Not that far out of the way. Maybe two hundred miles or so."

"Two hundred miles!"

"We're supposed to be going to the Indians," Peter said. "Not some civilized Reformed Baptist preacher."

"I tell you," Parley said. "If we could just convince him of the truth, it would be the greatest thing you could imagine. Why, he would-"

"What if he won't listen to us?" Peter asked.

"He *will* listen," Parley said. "Anyway, it's worth a try."

"As for the Indians," Ziba said. "We've already seen that one group. The Catteraugas."

"Too bad we couldn't have stayed longer," Oliver said.

"We did the best we could...in spite of the language barrier. I don't know what else we could have done. And some of them knew English — at least they accepted two copies of the book."

"Do you think they'll read it?" Peter asked.

"We can only hope," Ziba said. "They seemed interested."

"They liked it when we said the book contained the history of their ancestors," Oliver said.

"And they thanked us, remember? You can't say they weren't gracious."

"Some of the other tribes may not be as friendly."

"Let's get back to Sidney Rigdon," Parley said. "I propose we head for Mentor, and stop first thing at his house."

"Well, I don't know," Oliver said. "Winter's coming on. And we've got a long trek ahead of us."

"His wife's an excellent cook," Parley said.

"Well...we sure can't stay very long."

At last Parley convinced them. They would go to the area just east of Cleveland, and stop at the town of Mentor.

"It's a nice little settlement," Parley said. "Good farmland, near the lake. And wait till you see Mr. Rigdon. Wait till you *hear* him."

His fondest dream was about to be realized. To carry the new-found message, the news of the restored church and the Book of Mormon, to the man who had once convinced him to work for the restoration of all things...it was more than he dared hope.

In his eagerness he pushed forward, and his footsteps made a steady pounding on the forest path. The rhythm wove itself into words in his mind.

> The morning breaks, the shadows flee;
>   Lo, Zion's standard is unfurled!
> The dawning of a brighter day
>   Majestic rises on the world.
>
> The clouds of error disappear
>   Before the rays of truth divine;
> The glory, bursting from afar,
>   Wide o'er the nations soon will shine.

—Parley P. Pratt

16

The four missionaries could not have picked a better time to visit Sidney Rigdon.

Since 1826, Rigdon's congregation at Mentor had been affiliated with the teachings of Alexander Campbell, and the idea of restoring the "ancient order of things." But he and Campbell began to have serious disagreements about just what things belonged in such a restoration. Sidney Rigdon held that spiritual gifts and miracles should be a part of it. Campbell said that the miraculous work of the Holy Ghost was "confined to the apostolic age, and to only a portion of the saints who lived in that age."

They also differed on the issues of a communal society and the doctrine of the millennium. Rigdon believed passionately in both of these things; Campbell did not. Their dissension led to a complete break in 1830. After a heated argument at the Mahoning Baptist Association's annual ministers' meeting, Rigdon returned home, his ideas rejected. In a short time he had persuaded his large congregation to abandon the leadership of Campbell.

Now, in the fall of 1830, they were on their own. Their minister was faced with a decision. Should his congregation remain independent, or should they affiliate with another religious denomination? He spent sleepless nights pondering and praying — what was God's will for his congregation?

In the midst of his spiritual searching, the four young men appeared on his doorstep.

He tried to conceal his impatience. With all the questions on his mind, he felt a little too busy to be bothered with unexpected visitors. Nevertheless, he welcomed them.

What they had to say was both intriguing and puzzling.

"Now, wait a minute, Brother Parley. Slow down a minute. Repeat that. You say you're special messengers of the living God, sent to preach the gospel in its purity?'

"As it was anciently preached by the apostles," Parley said.

"And we have a book — a new revelation!" one of the others said.

"A - a *new* revelation?" Rigdon said eagerly.

"The Book of Mormon, translated from gold plates deposited in a hill. Our prophet was shown its location by an angel."

"Oh," Rigdon said, his enthusiasm waning. Angels and gold plates, indeed. "I - I see. Uh…pardon me for being a bit skeptical, But, frankly, gentlemen-"

"It *is* the truth. In fact, I'm willing to debate you, sir!" Parley said. "Choose the time and place, and we'll debate the matter."

"Yes. Let him debate you!"

The others waited, expectant. The one they called Oliver was holding a copy of the book.

Rigdon reached for the book.

"I have a better idea. Leave the book with me, and I'll read it for myself. Instead of debating, just tell me about your young man who claims to be a prophet. I prefer to learn about him — from you — and to simply read the book."

The four glanced at each other. Oliver quickly handed him the book.

Two of them spoke at once, breathlessly.

"His name is Joseph Smith, and in 1823 he was living near Palmyra, New York-"

194

"He's young, about twenty-five, and he lives in Seneca County — Fayette-"

Rigdon had to smile; they were so eager. He glanced at the book, turning the pages, then looked up at them.

"I must confess...I have one Bible which I believe is a revelation from God, and with which I pretend to have some acquaintance, But with respect to this book...I must say I have considerable doubt."

Then Oliver and the others began to speak at once, Parley Pratt gesturing excitedly. Rigdon said,

"No, young gentlemen. You mustn't argue with me on the subject. But I will read your book, and see what claim it has upon my faith. I will endeavor to ascertain whether it be a revelation from God or not."

They talked for a while, this time one at a time. The young men asked if they could lay the subject before the people — they requested the privilege of preaching to his congregation. Sidney Rigdon consented, and arrangements were made for them to speak in his church.

A large and respectable-looking congregation came to hear them. Oliver Cowdery and Parley Pratt both addressed the meeting. At the conclusion, Sidney Rigdon, their own minister, got up. He told them,

"...the information you have received this evening is of an extraordinary character. It certainly demands your most serious consideration. As the apostle advised his brethren 'to prove all things, and hold fast that which is good,' so I would exhort you to do likewise, and give the matter a careful investigation. Do not turn against it, without being fully convinced of its being an imposition. God forbid that we should, possibly, resist the truth."

After the meeting ended, the missionaries returned home with Elder Rigdon. They talked more about the things they had proclaimed.

"I shall read the Book of Mormon," Rigdon said. "I shall give it a full investigation. Then I shall frankly tell you my mind and feelings on the subject. Meanwhile, you're welcome to abide at my house until I have read it."

One of Rigdon's basic differences with Alexander Campbell's group had to do with the matter of a communal society. Sidney Rigdon himself believed that the early Christians lived together in harmony and had all things in common; thus members of a restored New Testament church should do the same. Campbell maintained that such a thing did not have to be a part of the restoration of the primitive church.

Sidney Rigdon had convinced a group of his followers to experiment in the building up of a communal society. The group lived about two miles from Rigdon's home, at a town called Kirtland. The leaders of "The Family," as it was called, were Isaac Morley, who had given his farm to the endeavor, and Lyman Wight, a dynamic preacher.

While Sidney Rigdon was engaged in reading the Book of Mormon, Parley and the three others went over to Kirtland and proclaimed the gospel to the members of the communal group. The preaching fell on fertile ground; seventeen of them asked for baptism in a short time.

The missionaries had much to occupy them. They visited and talked with the Kirtland people, some of whom had known Parley Pratt before he left Ohio. The four also kept in close contact with Sidney Rigdon. When they made visits to him, they found him still reading.

"It's been almost two weeks," Oliver said to Parley.

"Well, we know he's praying for direction. And he's meditating on all that he's heard and read. You can be sure he's not taking it lightly."

"If he does become convinced,.I feel it will be something wonderful."

"Didn't I tell you? He's an extraordinary man. And if he believes something is true, he'll uphold it with all his strength. No matter what it costs him. Did I tell you that back in Pittsburgh, he was the pastor of a large church? He became convinced that they were not following the doctrines of Christ. So he deliberated, and resigned his pastorship. He gave up wealth, popularity, and honor for the sake of what he thought was true. And it wasn't easy; he had a family to support, and he knew no trade...his great gift was preaching, and oratory. Mental labor."

"What did he do?"

"He became a journeyman tanner."

"A a tanner? Him?"

"Yes. He worked as a tanner for about two years. He said that when he was engaged in that humble occupation, dressed in the garb of a tanner, many of his former friends would hardly speak to him."

"He's not afraid of persecution, then."

"He's had his share of it," Parley said. "I don't think he's afraid of anything men can do. Anyway, after his stint as a tanner, he went over to Ohio and started preaching from the Bible, not advocating any creed. The congregation at Mentor invited him to be their pastor — around 1826, I believe. He was in this area when I first heard him — when I was converted."

Oliver nodded. "And he's been here ever since?"

"Yes...preaching, baptizing. Marrying people. Hoping for the restoration of all things."

* * * *

197

Sidney Rigdon sat in his study, with the book before him on the desk. It was late afternoon; he could hear Phebe and the children in the keeping room, where the evening meal was being prepared.

From the window, golden shafts of light fell on the pine bookshelf and rows of books. There were pools of light on the floor, illuminating more books piled against the wall. Some of the piles had collapsed; books and papers lay scattered on the floor.

Books were everywhere...history, philosophy, grammar, poetry and literature...books about other books, and especially about the greatest historical record ever produced — the Old and New Testaments. More than anything else, Sidney loved to read. He had longed for a proper education when he was young.

Sitting there in the golden light of afternoon, he let his mind go back to the fields and farmlands of Pennsylvania, where he had grown up. He remembered his brother Loammi, who was unfit to work in the fields because of illness.

The light shifted, and it was late afternoon on that day of his boyhood, the day he had lived over and over again. It was just like this, with the golden light flooding the room, and then he was back there. His father was saying,

"I've arranged to send Loammi away to school."

"To school! What school, Father?"

"It's the Transylvania Medical School, over in Kentucky. Lexington, Kentucky."

"Oh, please! Please, Father. Let me go too!" In his eagerness, Sidney's eyes filled with tears. "May I, please? You know how much I've wanted — how I hoped I could go to school-"

"No. Loammi is the one who's going. Now, stop pestering me. Have you finished your chores?"

198

Loammi was sent off to school. Sidney begged and begged to join him.

"Please, sir. I won't eat very much. And I'll study-"

"You're not being sensible, son. I have only money enough to send one of you. Now, *you* are strong and well. You can do a day's work on a farm."

"Yes, but I can study, too! I can learn — I'll be a good student."

"Loammi can't work — he's ill most of the time. *He's* the one who needs the higher education. Not you."

Finally Sidney's pleadings turned to rebellion.

"I *will* become educated! I will! You'll see! I'll have as good an education as Loammi! And you can't stop me!"

A shadow passed overhead; the light dimmed. The memory faded. Sidney was back at his desk, looking at his rows of books. He remembered how he had worked to carry out his vow...how he had borrowed books from his neighbors. He would read them at night by the light of a hickory fire — his parents would not even let him have a candle.

Now he had a knowledge of history and the Bible that was second to none, a most valuable tool in his ministry. He had a command of the English language and the gift of oratory, thanks to his years of study. He had books of his own, in profusion, and not space enough to keep them.

Things were crowded, but it was only temporary. When his congregation finished the new house they were building for his family, there would be room for every book and pamphlet, for all his papers and notes.

He shifted in his chair, and his foot brushed against something. Another book. He reached to pick it up. His Greek grammar. He'd been looking for it only a few days ago.

He sighed and put it on one of the piles on his desk. Then he turned his attention to the book before him.

The Book of Mormon. He had already read most of it. There were some things he wanted to check on again. Even now he was weighing the final decision in his mind. In the light of all he knew, all he had read, it seemed possible that his ten year search for the fullness of the New Testament gospel had reached its end.

It was so simple, and yet so wonderful. He kept a tight rein on his emotions — it would not do to let his intellect be swayed by anything other than reason...not yet. But parts of the book were so marvelous; he wanted to weep at the wonder of it.

Point by point, he considered again the things he had disciplined himself to look for.

First and foremost, did the doctrine of the book compare favorably with that of the Bible? So far, the two seemed consistent.

First there was the question of miracles — one of the subjects on which he and Alexander Campbell had differed. According to the Bible, angels had appeared to such Old Testament patriarchs and prophets as Abraham, Jacob, Moses, and Daniel. In the New Testament, such disciples as Philip, Paul and Cornelius had also seen angels. Now here was the Book of Mormon, whose translator claimed to have been shown the location of the plates by an angel. If God were indeed going to restore his gospel, it would be reasonable that he would have angelic assistance.

In the book itself, the very question was asked; whether miracles had ceased because Christ had ascended into heaven. And the answer was given:

"Nay, neither have angels ceased to minister unto the children of men."

Baptism by immersion for the remission of sins was another teaching that was consistent with the Bible. The Nephites were instructed, "...ye shall go down and stand in the water...and then shall ye immerse them in the water, and come forth again out of the water."

In the Book of Moroni, the gifts of the spirit were given:

Wisdom	Prophecy
Knowledge	Speaking in tongues
Healings	Interpretation of tongues
Miracles	Discernment of spirits

He knew that these things were not present among the followers of Campbell; the fact had caused him much grief.

Another point was the restoration of Israel. He believed in the literal return of the Jews to their homeland, as promised in the Bible. And here was the Book of Mormon, with its prophecy in the second book of Nephi:

"And it shall come to pass that my people, which are of the house of Israel, shall be gathered home unto the lands of their possession."

Then, last of all, there was the principal claim of the book — to bear witness that Jesus was the Christ, "manifesting himself unto all nations," and that he had established a church in the new world with twelve disciples who were to carry on his work when he ascended into heaven.

Sidney finished the remainder of the book and sat in silence for a while. The light of afternoon was fading into dusk. But still he sat, even when it was too dark to read, thinking of what he had just finished, and what his reaction to it would mean.

"Papa!"

His children were calling him; the evening meal was ready. He closed the book and got up slowly. Then he went to join them.

All through the meal he wondered about how to tell Phebe, and whether she would understand. So far, she had been very understanding indeed, and had supported him in all his undertakings. But this last... it might be too much to ask.

He waited until all six children were in bed before he told her.

"My dear," he said finally. "I have given considerable thought to the new things we have been hearing. I've been praying and thinking."

"I know, dear," she said. "So have I."

"I'm convinced that the new religion brought by the missionaries is truly the apostolic church, divinely restored. I am ready to embrace its doctrines."

Phebe looked at him. "I've sensed that, too."

"You - you know?"

"How could I not know? I've watched you for two weeks. You haven't slept, you've barely eaten. I've seen how absorbed you are in the book."

He was touched. "You know, even now, what I'm about to say?"

She smiled. "Go ahead. Say it anyway."

"My dear," he said gently. "You have followed me once into poverty. Are you willing to do the same again?"

He knew they were both thinking of the new house, which now they might never live in.

Phebe said, "I've been weighing the matter. I've thought of the circumstances in which we could be placed. I have counted the cost."

He waited. She said, "I am perfectly satisfied to follow you. It is my desire to do the will of God, come life or come death."

202

"Dear Phebe," he said, and took her in his arms. They stood there together, beside the table in their main room; she patted his shoulder. Then one of the children called — eight year old Nancy. He let her go, and she went to see what was needed.

The next step was telling his congregation.

The church was full that day as he stood up to address his followers. He looked at their faces, knowing as he stood before them that he was regarded as one of the most influential and prestigious ministers in the Western Reserve. What would they think of him when he had finished?

Well, that was no matter. Like Phebe, he had counted the cost. He took a deep breath and began.

"For some time past I have been engaged in a search for religious truth, but I have not been satisfied in my spiritual yearnings until now."

He couldn't remember all that he said to them. He mentioned how at night he had been unable to sleep, walking and praying for more comfort in religion...how finally he had heard of the revelation of new truth brought by the four missionaries. Under this new truth, his soul had found peace. The message of the missionaries, and the truths contained in the Book of Mormon, had filled all his aspirations.

When he had finished, there was utter silence. He stood waiting, his head bowed, while in the first row Phebe touched her handkerchief to her face.

* * * *

In the public house a few days later, Cuyahoga County sheriff John Barr was talking to a friend.

"Lord Almighty, Ebenezer. Did you see that? They were stunned."

"I don't care what Elder Rigdon says. I need a drink."

"Church is sure gettin' exciting these days," said someone from the next table. "What with Rigdon steppin' down, and those missionaries preachin' for all they're worth."

"I heard they baptized over a hundred and twenty-five people already," someone else said. "A lot of folks down around Kirtland."

Ebenezer lifted his glass. "I bet Elder Rigdon takes most of that congregation with him."

Sheriff Barr said, "Did you hear them all sniffin' and cryin' when he stopped? I never saw anything like it."

"You gonna join the Mormons, Sheriff?" the man at the next table said.

"Not me."

"Well, *I* might," Ebenezer said. "I been studyin' some..."

"Hah! You ain't been in a church since you was married. That was more'n ten years ago!"

"That's not true. Sheriff, *tell* 'em. I was there last Sunday, when Elder Rigdon preached his last sermon."

"Do you really think it was his last sermon?" someone asked.

"Why, sure," another man said. "They ain't gonna let him stay, after he said them things. People are sayin' they're not gonna let him move into that fine new house, neither."

"I wonder who's gonna live in it?"

"Well, it ain't gonna be Rigdon. I heard someone sayin' just the other day. He said, 'Mr. Rigdon's really done it now. Givin' up *everything*, just to follow some fool of a boy.'"

"How old is this Joe Smith feller, anyway?"

"I don't know. Twenty, maybe."

Ebenezer put down his glass. "Elder Rigdon said he was twenty-four."

"Twenty-four," the sheriff said. "That's still pretty young."

"In fact," Ebenezer said, "Elder Rigdon said Joseph Smith couldn't have written the Book of Mormon, 'cause he was too young and didn't have enough education. That's how he knew it was from God."

"What's your Elder Rigdon gonna do now?" the man at the next table said.

"I heard tell," Ebenezer said, "he's gonna move over to Hiram, and live with some people there...some other Mormons. There's about twenty of them livin' over there."

"There's nothin' but little ol' log cabins over there. Nothin' like the fine new house he coulda had."

Sheriff Barr said to Ebenezer, "You really fixin' to join 'em?"

"I think so, John," Ebenezer said. "See, I thought a lot of Elder Rigdon. Still do. I figure, what's good enough for him oughta be good for me, too."

* * * *

Parley Pratt had baptized Sidney and Phebe Rigdon, along with some other converts at Kirtland. One of the new converts was a woman named Lydia Partridge. Her husband, Edward, was not as eager about the new church as she was.

"I want to know what kind of man that prophet is," he remarked to his wife.

Edward Partridge, a hatter by trade, was a member of the Disciples of Christ. He had followed Sidney Rigdon when the latter had broken away from Alexander Campbell. Sidney Rigdon was his close friend; both men were the same age: thirty-six.

He had seen his wife and the Rigdons baptized into the new church. He had stood by when Oliver Cowdery ordained Rigdon an elder. But he himself was plagued with doubts.

He was gentle and unassuming, but when it came to the subject of the new church, he had to speak his mind. He even said to Oliver Cowdery

"I don't want to sound harsh, but the kindest thing I can say is that I think you are imposters."

Oliver looked him directly in the eye and replied,

"I'm thankful there is a God in heaven who knows the hearts of all men."

That set him thinking. After the missionaries had left, he read the Book of Mormon.

"The book seems to make sense," he said to Sidney. "I wish I could see this so-called prophet for myself."

"That's just what I intend to do," Sidney said. "I'm planning to go east — to New York State — and pay him a visit. Why don't you come along?"

"That's an interesting idea. Yes...I'd like to do that. Where does he live?"

"They tell me he's either in Palmyra, or Fayette, where the church was organized. Both towns are just beyond Rochester."

"When do you figure on going?"

"I'd like to leave as soon as possible. I know it's been cold, but I should like to start out before it gets any worse."

"That sounds wise. Yes. I'll make arrangements, and be ready to leave with you."

They left late in November of 1830. It was unusually cold, but they kept on, determined to see the young prophet.

"I hope I shan't be too disappointed," Edward remarked.

"I don't know what you're expecting," Sidney said. "He's a human being, like ourselves. But the indications are that he's been especially touched by the hand of God."

"I wish I could believe that."

"Let's wait and see. I don't think you'll be disappointed."

17

...go unto the Lamanites and preach my gospel unto them; and inasmuch as they receive thy teachings, thou shalt cause my church to be established among them...

First there was the cold — numbing, bone-chilling cold, pervading everything. It was there when they took up their packs and started out in the morning; it deepened toward the late afternoon, as they began looking for shelter.

There were five of them that walked out of the Kirtland area and headed west along the lake toward Sandusky. In addition to the four young men, there was Frederick G. Williams, a middle-aged physician who had just been converted. He had elected to leave his farm and medical practice, and accompany the missionaries.

"If it gets much colder, my feet are gonna turn to ice," Oliver said.

"Just don't stop walking," Parley said.

They spent a few days with Wyandotte Indians near Sandusky. Then they pushed on to Cincinnati.

Wherever they stopped, they brought news of the new religion. They preached in log cabins by flickering firelight...in assembly halls, in churches, in dwellings of animal skins where the Indians lived. In some places, they were successful enough to leave branches of the church. In other places, like Cincinnati, they roused very little interest.

"I'd be in good shape if it warn't for all this walkin'."

"Well, we figure we can get passage on a steamboat. That'll take us at least as far as St. Louis."

"That'd be good news. My feet are just about wore out."

Around the twentieth of December, they took passage by steamboat for St. Louis. But the Mississippi was so blocked with ice that the boat only got as far as Cairo, Illinois.

"Illinois! We're only in Illinois?"

"What'll we do now? It's a long time till spring."

"Well, my feet are rested some."

"You mean you - you want to *walk* to St. Louis?"

"It's either that or wait till the ice melts."

They decided to set out on foot. It was two hundred miles to East St. Louis.

"I didn't know winters got this cold."

"The fellow back there in Cairo — he said it was the worst winter he could remember."

"And we aren't even through December yet."

The snow was at least one and a half feet deep on the prairie. No sooner had they weathered one storm of snow and ice, then they were hit with another one. On January 5, at least two feet of snow fell.

"It sure snows easy these days."

They pressed ahead into Missouri. By now they were gaunt and grim-faced. They plodded over snowfields, struggling against the constant cold. In places the snow had drifted to four feet deep. The shocks of grain were deep under the frozen snow. They had to make their way over the limbs of trees, as the trunks were covered by ice and snow.

"Horses couldn't even get through here," Parley said. "Their hooves would break right through the crust."

"It ain't supportin' *us* too good, either," Ziba said.

"But we can keep going, whereas a horse couldn't."

The top layer of snow was as light and fine as ashes. When it blew in their faces, it felt like sand. A wind sprang up from the northwest, hurling snow into the air; it flew all around them, blinding them, stinging their eyes. When it cleared, the sun glinted on the landscape, dazzling in its cold brightness.

They went through St. Louis, then St. Charles, and continued out over the frozen prairie.

Parley was used to walking, and traveling long distances. But this journey was harder than anything he had experienced. They were alone in a wilderness of snow, with no beaten road. The houses were so few that often they traveled whole days, from morning till night, without seeing a dwelling or a fire. They were wading in snow up to their knees at every step. And, if that weren't enough, the west wind was blowing in their faces with such keenness that their skin was almost raw.

Parley had never known such cold. It was so intense that the snow didn't melt on the south side of the houses, even in midday. Life during the daylight marches became a struggle for survival, a fight to keep going, their packs getting heavier with each step.

All familiar objects were made strange by the snow. The few fences were covered, the low buildings completely buried. Parley thought of his first winter in Ohio...the storms raging outside his cabin while he read by the fire. Now he was outside, with the wind and snow whirling around him. Would he ever be warm again?

The cold made him ache with hunger. He said,

"How about some food, Oliver? What shall we have today?"

"What do you mean? You know all we got's corn bread and raw pork."

"Oh, that's fine. I'll have mine frozen."

"That's the only way you're gonna get it."

"If the bread were just a little warmer, you could almost eat it," Peter Whitmer said.

"All I can even get my teeth into is the outside crust," Ziba said.

"Well," Parley said, "we'll have that today, and the rest tomorrow."

"I tell you," the doctor remarked. "I'm gettin' mighty tired of johnnycake and pork."

Finally they reached the settlement of Independence, on the western frontier. They found shelter at the home of Colonel Robert Patterson, over near the state line.

"I'm surprised you even got through," their host said. "I reckon there's been no mail delivery for weeks. No newspapers."

"It sure wasn't the easiest stroll we ever had," Parley said.

"There's a right smart chance there's other travelers under that snow — ones that didn't make it," Colonel Patterson said. "I reckon they won't find the bodies till spring."

"It was fierce. Especially when that wind got to blowing," Peter Whitmer said.

"Where you fellers from? I heard you say you walked all the way from St. Louis."

"We walked all the way from Cairo, Illinois," Parley said. "But we came from further east than that. Kirtland, in Ohio."

"Ohio! I reckon that's a far piece! That's more'n eight hundred miles, I reckon."

"It's more'n that, if you figure where we started from," Peter said. "New York State. Make that about fifteen hundred miles."

"Well, now! What news do you bring from them eastern parts?"

Oliver reached into his pack and pulled out a Book of Mormon. He put it on the table.

"The best there is," he said.

Later, the five talked about how to proceed.

"Our main objective is to go to the Lamanites," Oliver said. "I hear there's some Indians living just over the state line. Shawnees, as I remember, and Delawares."

"We're gonna have to find a place to stay. And some way of supporting ourselves."

"It's too cold to chop wood."

"I bet this place could use a - well, say, a tailor shop. Suits made in the latest eastern style."

"That's a good idea," Ziba Peterson said. "Peter and I — we could do that easily."

"And we'd be inside — we'd be warm. I've had enough of the outdoors for awhile," Peter said.

Oliver said, "That way, you could find out what the settlers are like — maybe make a few friends. I think we're going to need them."

"Do they all say 'I reckon' every other sentence?"

"I reckon so."

It was agreed that two of the missionaries would find work while the other three went across the border to the Indians.

* * * *

Even in dreams Parley could remember that final push to start a mission among the Indians. He and Oliver, in company with Dr. Williams, found their way to the Shawnee tribe and stayed one night with them. The next day they crossed the Kansas River and entered Delaware territory.

"Quick, Parley. They're coming toward us. Say something. They don't look too friendly."

"Why don't *you* say something? You're supposed to be in charge."

The doctor said, "Well, *some*body had better speak up."

By this time they were surrounded by at least eight of the Indians. Parley said,

"Excuse me. We're looking for the - uh, the chief - the residence of the chief."

The Indians looked at each other. One of them grunted, then said something in his language.

"I think your choice of words is too fancy," the doctor said. "'Residence' is too long."

"Well, you can have a shot at it, if you want."

"They're motioning to us," Oliver said. "Let's follow."

They came to a cabin, which was apparently the lodge of the chief. Inside, they were introduced to an aged man. He was seated on a sofa of furs and skins, before a fire in the center of the lodge. Parley could see that the lodge consisted of two large rooms.

As the old man took them by the hand to welcome them, an interpreter told them that the chief was revered as the Great Grandfather, or Sachem, of ten tribes; Anderson was his name.

His wives stood near him, neatly dressed, partly in calicoes and partly in skins. The light glinted on their silver ornaments.

The chief motioned the three men to be seated on a pile of blankets and robes. It was a comfortable seat; Parley settled back and began to feel at ease. The chief gestured and said something in his language.

The wives set a tin pan before them; it was full of beans and corn boiled up together. One of them handed Parley a wooden spoon.

Parley tasted the food; it was good. Oliver said,

"I think we're supposed to share it."

Parley handed him the spoon. Oliver dipped it into the pan and ate. Then he handed the spoon to F. G. Williams.

The doctor looked at the spoon and hesitated. The chief was watching him. He took a spoonful of food, then another. Then he handed it back to Parley.

When all three of them had eaten, so to speak, the chief said something. The interpreter asked them what errand they had come on.

"O Chief," Oliver said. "We have come from the eastern lands, over much snow, and we have a book, called the Book of Mormon. We want to tell you of this book, and to teach your people about it, for it will be of much benefit to you."

When this was translated, Oliver said,

"We desire that you call the council of your nation together, and give us a hearing as we tell you what is in the book."

When this last had been relayed, the chief sat in silence for a while. Then he said he wanted to consider it until the next day. In the meantime, he recommended that the three of them stay with a man named Mr. Poole — he was their blacksmith, employed by the government.

They found lodging with Mr. Poole, and went back the next morning to visit the old chief again. Oliver tried to explain a bit more about the book.

"...it will be the source of much good for your people, much new knowledge, and happiness..."

But the chief was unwilling to call his council. At first he made excuses. Then he flatly refused. The interpreter said,

214

"He says he has always been opposed to the introduction of missionaries among his people."

Undaunted, Oliver and Parley talked a little more.

"We have come so far," Parley said. "We wanted to bring you the book that tells about your ancestors."

"It tells of the first of your people. It was written on gold plates and hidden in a hill-"

The chief began to show some interest. Finally he made them wait until he could call a council. He sent off a messenger. In about an hour, forty men had assembled in the lodge. Each man shook hands with the three missionaries. Then they seated themselves, and waited in silence. Parley was impressed with their grave and dignified manner as they waited. Then the chief asked Oliver to begin where he had begun before, and to complete the explanation.

Oliver rose to his feet.

"Aged Chief and Venerable Council of the Delaware Nation..."

The doctor leaned close to Parley and whispered,

"I think he's got their attention. His voice is really forceful."

The translation commenced. They were all looking very intent, with the same dignity Parley had observed before. He tried not to stare, but he was fascinated by their faces. He sensed a strength, a solemnity about them that few white men had.

Oliver was saying something about the long distances they had traveled in order to bring the glad news...the wilderness, rivers and snows they had braved. He reminded them of the days when the red men were many, and occupied the country from sea to sea. But now, he said, they were few in numbers; their possessions were small, and the pale-faces were many.

215

"Thousands of moons ago, when the red men's forefathers dwelt in peace and possessed this whole land, the Great Spirit talked with them, and revealed his law and his will, and much knowledge to their wise men and prophets. This they wrote in a book, together with their history, and the things which should befall their children in the latter days.

"This book was written on plates of gold, and handed down from father to son for many ages and generations."

While his words were being translated, Oliver stood motionless, waiting. The doctor whispered to Parley,

"He's doing very well."

"I just hope his feet don't give out now."

Oliver was speaking again, relating how the people had prospered. Then they had become wicked, killing each other and shedding much blood. The Great Spirit then spoke with them no more; they had no more dreams and visions, no more angels sent to them.

"...and the Lord commanded Mormon and Moroni, their last wise men and prophets, to hide the book in the earth, that it might be preserved in safety, and be found and made known, in the latter day, to the pale-faces who should possess the land; that they might again make it known to the red man..."

Oliver went on to say that if the red men would then receive the book and learn the things written in it, they would be restored to their former prosperity. They would cease fighting and killing each other, and would be one people, cultivating the earth in peace.

When this was translated, the council members began talking to each other in an undertone. The doctor whispered,

"I hope that's a murmur of approval."

"I think so," Parley said. "Unless it was mistranslated."

There was silence as Oliver started speaking again.

216

"Then should the red men become great, and be in favor with the Great Spirit and be his children; while he would be their Great Father, and talk with them, and raise up prophets and wise and good men among them again...

"This book, which contained these things, was hid in the earth by Moroni, in a hill called by him, Cumorah..."

Oliver was more animated now; he was moving around, shifting his feet, gesturing.

"In that neighborhood, there lived a young man named Joseph Smith, who prayed to the Great Spirit much, in order that he might know the truth; and the Great Spirit sent an angel to him..."

"He's going to wear himself out for sure," Parley whispered.

"We may have to carry him home."

Oliver was telling about the translation of the book from the ancient tongue to the language of the pale-faces.

"...and wrote it on paper, and caused it to be printed..."

He ended by presenting a copy of the Book of Mormon to the chief of the Delawares.

There was a pause. The council members began talking to each other, while the missionaries waited. Finally the chief spoke, and the interpreter said,

"We feel truly thankful to our white friends who have come so far, and been at such pains to tell us good news, and especially this good news concerning the book of our forefathers; it makes us glad here." The interpreter indicated the region of his heart.

"It is now winter; we are new settlers in this place. The snow is deep, our cattle and horses are dying, our wigwams are poor; we have much to do in the spring — to build houses, and fence and make farms; but we will build a council house, and meet together, and you shall read to us and teach us more concerning the book of our fathers and the will of the Great Spirit."

* * * *

Afterward, Oliver was jubilant.

"Praise God!" he said. "What more could you ask?"

"It's what we had hoped for," Parley said.

They went back to Mr. Poole's lodging and told him the news.

"That is good," Mr. Poole said. "That means they have much interest. And they want *you* to read to them and teach them. That is — how to say — not usual."

Parley didn't see anything out of the ordinary about it. But Mr. Poole said,

"They have been taken away from their homes, their lands. They have been put in this strange place. They do not trust many white men."

"Hm," the doctor said. "We have a lot to understand, I see."

"Now," Mr. Poole said. "You better finish telling *me* about the book. I want to be your interpreter."

* * * *

Oliver and the others went to work eagerly. Every day they met with the old chief and instructed him further. Every day more and more people crowded into the lodge to hear.

"The whole tribe is interested," Parley remarked to Oliver. "You can just feel this - this spirit of inquiry and excitement."

"I found one who reads English," the doctor said. "I gave him a copy of the book."

"There's another one — a young man, the son of one of the council members," Oliver said. "I'll have to get a copy for him."

"Mr. Poole says some of them are even telling each other about the book — in their own language. And they're rejoicing."

Mr. Poole became a believer, and a great advocate for the book. Oliver and Parley spent most of their time in conversation with the people, much as they had done in Ohio. This time they had the services of Mr. Poole as interpreter.

Some of the Indian agents and other missionary groups became disturbed at the excitement.

"What's that Cowdery feller tryin' to do?"

"I reckon he's gonna start a full-scale uprising. Actually tellin' them Indians that they're gonna be restored to all their rights and privileges."

"Yeah. Talkin' to them like they was really worth somethin'. Jest like white men. I mean, what does he think he's doin'?"

"I don't think it's fair, those missionaries gettin' to go in there."

"I don't care what they're tellin' them Indians, but it can't be good. Else why would they be so interested?"

"Well, I reckon. There's somethin' mighty funny goin' on."

* * * *

The Indian agent, Major Cummins, spoke to the missionaries and told them they were disturbing the peace.

"I think he's being too strict with us," Oliver told Parley. "I'm afraid the freedom to visit our Lamanite brethren isn't going to last too long."

Parley said, "Why don't we go over his head?"

"What? You mean, to God?"

"Not that far. What about the Superintendent of Indian Affairs? General William Clark, at St. Louis. The governor."

"Now, that's a thought. It's probably our last hope. I'm writing to Joseph — I've already told him about our success among the Delaware Nation. I told him about the Indian agent. I shall tell him you're going to General Clark to see what can be arranged."

"*Me*? Now, wait a minute-"

"Why not? It was your idea. A fine idea, I might add."

"Well, on second thought-"

"And one of us has to go back East anyway. We're almost out of books."

The other three agreed, when the five missionaries met together again. Parley should be the one to go back.

"You're better at walking than any of us," Oliver said.

"Yes, but I'm not feeling as well as I usually do."

"Oh, nonsense. How soon can you be ready?"

They decided that, since they were now threatened with military force, they would stay out of Indian territory for a while. They would direct their attention to the white settlers of Independence and outlying areas.

"But, Parley," Oliver said. "When you see General Clark about the Delawares, be persuasive."

* * * *

Parley had some trepidations about approaching General Clark. This was, after all, one of his heroes — the same Clark who had taken part in the famed Lewis and Clark expedition. Clark was a frontiersman and Indian fighter from way back, and had participated in many military skirmishes against the Indians. His

220

daring and resourcefulness had saved the famous expedition on more than one occasion, and he had lent his skills as map maker and artist to the expedition.

For his services, the government had appointed him Superintendent of Indian Affairs west of the Mississippi, his base of operations being St. Louis. He had been appointed territorial governor in 1813, and was now governor of Missouri.

In spite of his years as an Indian fighter, it was now said that he had an intense concern for Indian affairs. He had appealed to the federal government on several occasions, asking them to show justice and humanity to the tribes.

Parley thought of these things as he made the journey back to St. Louis. But he had an uneasy feeling — the governor had seen a different picture than that glimpsed by Oliver and himself. It was difficult to know what to say.

He reached St. Louis, made an appointment with the secretary, and waited to see the governor.

* * * *

You heard some strange things when you were Superintendent of Indian Affairs.

William Clark was an old man now — sixty-one. His days as Indian fighter were long gone, and even his time as Indian advocate and governor would probably not be much longer. He sat in his office, with his own meticulous drawings of the great West on the walls, and permitted himself the luxury of reminiscence.

He was tired that particular day; he had not slept well. Dreams troubled him...or recollections of real happenings, made more vivid by the night. Strange things. Even as recently as March, strange things had happened.

Clark was a tall man, well built, suited to a life in the wilderness. Even now, old as he was, he looked and felt out of place behind a desk. There was a determined, set look to his mouth, a tightening of the lips at the corners. He had the look of one accustomed to taking control, to making decisions. He found himself thinking of some of the decisions he had been forced to make.

That Parley fellow. What was his last name? Pratt. The missionary fellow. Clark remembered how Pratt had come into his office and presented his case, asking for permission to proselyte among the Delawares.

The interview had been brief. Clark had said no, of course. The Indians had enough troubles without some do-gooder missionary taking advantage of them.

But Pratt had told a strange story. It had to do with a gold book buried in a hill, with engravings in a forgotten language...something about the ancestors of the Indians. When Pratt had started talking about the book, and some young man in New York State who had found and translated it by the aid of supernatural power, Clark had come to another decision. Parley Pratt was crazy.

Clark pointed out that there was a regulation forbidding white men to enter Indian territories to trade or for any other purpose.

This was news to Pratt; he mentioned all the other agents and missionaries who were on Delaware lands. But he conceded...you couldn't argue with a regulation.

Clark explained further how one had to be careful in dealing with the Indians...they were touchy, easily upset. Too many incidents had happened already. The wrong word or action might mean the deaths of many white settlers.

The meeting had ended; Pratt had thanked him for his time and shaken his hand. Then Pratt had left.

It was a trivial incident. He would have forgotten it entirely, except for something else that happened a short time later.

Two Nez Perce Indians had come to him, or had been brought to him, as they knew very little English. Through interpreters, who had only a rudimentary knowledge of the Nez Perce language, he put together their story.

They were part of a group of four; one Flathead and three Nez Perce Indians, who had made a difficult journey from the Northwest, across the mountains and through hostile territory. They had come in search of Clark, whom their people had remembered from the expedition. When they reached St. Louis, two had died. These two were left; their names, in their own language, were Rabbit Skin Leggings, and No Horns on His Head.

"What do they say they want?" Clark asked his interpreter.

"They say - they say they need 'better medicine.'"

"For illness?"

"No. They say they are not sick."

"'Better medicine.' Do they need more prestige? More power?"

"They say no. They say they want a - a book."

"A book? Well, give them a book. We've got a whole library full."

"No. Wait...please."

With sign language, and words in his own Indian tongue, the interpreter tried to communicate. They replied with grunts and more sign language.

The interpreter said,

"It is not just any book, they say. It is a special book."

"That's not it," Clark said. "It can't be a book. What do they want with a book? I know what to do. I'll send a runner down to get Old Sam. He's that old half-breed, lives down by the river. He's been all over the west; if anyone knows their language, he will."

Old Sam was sent for, and came in later that afternoon. He was bent and wizened, and most of his teeth were missing.

"Sam," Clark said. "Can you tell me what these Nez Perce want?"

Sam straightened up and looked at the two travelers. He said something to them, a greeting. They responded.

"Now we're getting somewhere," Clark said. "Ask them what they want."

"I don't know very good their language. A few words only I know."

"Well, that's more than we know. Ask them."

Sam asked, and said,

"They have something to tell you."

"Well, all right. Ask them what it is."

Sam said something else. One of the Nez Perce began to speak, with Sam translating. Clark indicated to the first interpreter that he should write the words as they were translated.

"I came over the trail of many moons from the setting sun. You were the friend of my fathers who have all gone the long way. I come with one eye partly open, for more light for my people who sit in darkness. I go back with both eyes closed.

"How can I go back blind to my blind people? I made my way to you with strong arms through many enemies and strange lands that I might carry much to them. I go back with both arms broken and empty.

"Two fathers came with us. They were the braves of many winters and wars. We leave them to sleep by your great water and wigwams. They were tired of many moons and their moccasins wore out."

There was a pause. Clark asked,

"But what was it they came to get?"

The Nez Perce spoke again, and the translation resumed.

"My people sent me to get the white man's Book of Heaven. You took me to where you allow your women to dance, as we do ours, and the Book was not there. You took me to where they worship the Great Spirit with candles and the Book was not there. You showed me the images of the good spirits and the pictures of the good lands beyond, but the Book was not among them to tell us the way.

"I am going back to the long sad trail to my people in the dark land. You make my feet heavy with gifts and my moccasins will grow old carrying them, yet the Book is not among them. When I tell my poor blind people, after one more snow, in the Big Council, that I did not bring the Book, no word will be spoken by our old men or our young braves. One by one they will rise up and go out in silence. My people will die in darkness, and they will go on the long path to the hunting grounds. No white man will go with them and no white man's Book will make the way plain."

When the interpreter had finished, Clark stood deep in thought.

"A book," he said, half to himself. "The Book of Heaven."

They had said they had visited churches. Had no one given them a Bible? Apparently that was not what they sought.

Clark looked at Sam.

"Tell them we do not have the book they want. We do not know of such a book."

Sam spoke to them, and they talked among themselves for a brief time. Their words were slow, sounding as sad as the speech Clark had just heard. Then they took leave of him.

When the Indians and the interpreters had left, he sat alone at his desk for a while. He was troubled, deeply shaken. Not only had he no help to give them...what they wanted was something completely beyond his power of understanding.

* * * *

Now, weeks later, he sat thinking of it again; the incident had a sorrowful, haunting quality. Why should it matter to him, that they had come on such a long journey looking for something that didn't exist? It was of no consequence, anyway...two deluded Indians, misled perhaps by some dream or vision...

Then he thought of Parley Pratt, and the tale of the gold book buried in the hill. Most likely it was something of that nature they were seeking...visionary...shrouded in superstition...

He wondered briefly where Pratt was now. Probably miles away by this time. At any rate, there was no proof that such a gold book ever existed.

You did hear strange things. It was best to take them in stride, and not get bothered over such a little matter. It was haunting, to be sure, and puzzling. But at least no one was being killed over it.

A drink. That was what he needed. Something to put the whole incident out of his mind.

"I'm going home now," he said to his secretary in the next room. "I think I'll stop in over at the Whiskey Bend, and see if I can get the news of the day."

226

18

Sidney Rigdon and Edward Partridge looked for Joseph around Palmyra. They learned that most of the Smith family was living in Waterloo, just north of Fayette.

When they finally reached the house where Joseph's parents were living, they found a service in progress. They went inside and sat down in the congregation.

People looked up as the two well-dressed strangers took their seats. Then all attention turned back to the speaker.

Joseph was preaching that day. When he had finished, he asked if anyone else had any remarks to make. Edward Partridge stood up.

First he introduced himself. He mentioned the journey he and Sidney Rigdon had made from Ohio.

"When we were in Manchester, I hoped to obtain further information about the doctrine you are preaching. We weren't able to find you, but I made some inquiry of your neighbors concerning your family and the kind of people you were. They — at least the ones I talked with — all said your characters had been unimpeachable. Everything had been fine, they said, *until* Joseph had deceived them concerning the Book of Mormon.

"While I was there, I walked over your old farm. I saw the good order and industry displayed there. I then realized what you had sacrificed for the sake of your faith.

"Having seen that, and hearing that your veracity was not questioned upon any other point than that of your religion, I became convinced of your testimony."

Here he paused and glanced at his traveling companion. Sidney Rigdon was smiling. Edward Partridge looked at Joseph.

"I am now ready to be baptized, if Brother Joseph will baptize me."

Joseph replied, "You're very tired now, after your journey, Brother Partridge. You'd better rest today, and be baptized tomorrow."

"Just as Brother Joseph thinks best," Edward said. "I'm ready any time."

He was baptized the next day in the Seneca River.

Joseph was overjoyed with the two Ohio converts; he soon had Sidney Rigdon preaching at Fayette and other places in the area.

Joseph inquired of the Lord and received a lengthy revelation for Rigdon. The specific things Rigdon was directed to do were to tarry with Joseph, to preach the gospel, to write for him, and to "watch over him, that his faith fail not." Edward Partridge also received a revelation through Joseph, in which he was "called to preach my gospel, as with the voice of a trump."

Joseph was spending more and more time in close association with Sidney Rigdon. David Whitmer and some of the others began to feel uneasy.

"I *know* Brother Sidney has talent and education," David said to his brother, Christian. "He has everything that we most need. But don't you see what's happening? He's - he's working his way deep into Brother Joseph's affections. It wouldn't surprise me if he had more influence over Brother Joseph than any man living."

"Oh, now, David," Christian said. "You're always getting worked up over little things. I can't see Sidney's influence as being anything but good."

"But he's only been here a short time. Already he's Joseph's special counselor, and close friend — his scribe. They're even revising the Scriptures together."

"Still, I can't see any harm in it."

"Well, just wait. Do you know he's been urging Joseph to return with him to Kirtland?"

"What? But that's impossible! They wouldn't — I mean, John's already been sent out there. They don't need Joseph too!"

John Whitmer had been sent to take charge of the Kirtland Saints and provide leadership, as requested by the four missionaries before they left Ohio. David said,

"They say there's hundreds of converts out there. There's a lot more of us out there than there are in these parts."

"Still, Joseph wouldn't go out there! How can you think such a thing?"

"It's just a feeling I have. Maybe John needs help."

"Not him. I hope you're wrong."

* * * *

In the latter part of December, John sent back a letter asking for Joseph's immediate assistance in regulating the affairs of the church there. Joseph inquired of the Lord, and received word that he was not only to go to Ohio, but that the whole church should "assemble together at the Ohio, against the time that my servant Oliver Cowdery shall return unto them."

But first, they were to preach in the region where they were, and especially in Colesville, to strengthen the church in those areas.

"What did I tell you?" David Whitmer said to his brother.

"Well, you didn't say we *all* would be going."

"Isn't that something? We're supposed to just up and leave this farm, I suppose, that our family has worked so hard on."

"Well, if the Lord said so, there must be a reason-"

"There'd better be a mighty good reason. Joseph is gonna have to do some pretty fast talking to get all those people to move. Those Colesville Saints? You think they're just gonna pack up and leave?"

"Some of them are mighty stubborn. Joseph and Sidney will have their hands full, that's certain."

* * * *

Together Joseph and Sidney worked with the people, especially the ones who were not convinced that moving to Ohio was what they wanted to do. Sidney preached, giving powerful sermons and substantiating his words from the Scriptures. Joseph spoke in prophecy, explaining the need for the gathering of the people. At the conference early in January, more light was received:

"...that ye might escape the power of the enemy, and be gathered unto me a righteous people, without spot and blameless; wherefore, for this cause I gave unto you the commandment, that you should go to the Ohio: and there I will give unto you my law; and there you shall be endowed with power from on high..."

They were told to look to their poor and needy, and prepare them for the journey. Those with property were to sell it, leave it, or rent it.

"I don't know," David Whitmer said. "Things are happening mighty quick for my liking. Seems to me we should think a little more about this business of gathering."

* * * *

Snow was falling around the sleigh, big, soft flakes out of the gray sky. One of the snowflakes landed on the blanket across Emma's lap; she looked, marveling at its symmetry. Then another fell beside it, and another.

"We're in for some weather," Edward Partridge remarked.

"Just keep going," Joseph said. "I don't think it'll last long."

"We may have to hole up at the next town," Sidney Rigdon said.

"No. Let's keep going."

They were skimming over the snow at a dizzying speed. Emma could hear the sound of the sleigh runners sliding through the snow, and the crunch of the horses' hooves. It was Joseph Knight's sleigh, and Edward Partridge was driving, guiding the horses lightly over the snow-packed road.

It would have been pleasant, Emma thought, even with the four of them packed into the sleigh, if only they could have gone slower. But they were on their way to Ohio, and Joseph was in a hurry to get there. Things were happening there that only he could deal with; she had heard the men talking about "strange spiritual manifestations... things not of God."

"Are you warm enough, Emmy?" Joseph asked.

"Oh, yes. I think so."

"Well, let's be sure. We don't want you taking cold." He pulled the blanket up around her.

As there were already two other blankets around her, she felt well-protected, warm as toast. The snow was coming down around them, making little patches of white in the folds of the outside blanket. She leaned against Joseph, wishing she could sleep.

But her mind kept racing, like the sleigh. She wondered what was waiting for them in Kirtland, and if she would finally have a house of her own. Probably not right away. She thought of the Rigdons, and how they had lost their fine new house. But all of them were sacrificing...the people at Fayette...Colesville...most of them preparing to leave property and take a loss in order to move west. She would try to be cheerful and make the best of things, no matter what she had to face.

If only she felt better. Her baby was due at the end of April. She no longer felt sick to her stomach, as she had at first. But she didn't feel completely well, either. The fast pace of the ride didn't help.

Still, there were compensations...views along the way. Brief vistas that lasted for clusters of seconds, instead of moments. Once she had awakened to see the woods full of a soft light, like mist... muted sunlight streaming down through the tree branches. One late afternoon she had seen the western sky a glowing saffron, with the shapes of trees dark against it. And the pines...nothing was more beautiful than the dark green of pines and evergreens, with the snow lying in lacy patterns on the tops of branches.

"There're more and more evergreens," she remarked to Joseph. "And less hardwoods."

"Yes. White pine. It just takes over."

As they stopped to change drivers, Emma heard the call of chickadees in the pines overhead. She looked up, trying to see the tiny birds. They were high up, little black shapes among the branches.

Once a deer bounded across the road, not fifteen feet in front of them. One of the horses nickered. It was a doe; Emma turned to watch it as long as she could. She saw the graceful, familiar shape, the dainty, delicate neck and tiny hooves. Then the white tail flashed up; the doe disappeared into the trees. They could hear it crashing through the underbrush a long way away.

"Emma, are you sure you're warm enough?" Joseph asked. "You keep throwing off your blankets, here."

"Oh, I'm sorry. I'll be good."

She let him bundle her up again. Then she closed her eyes, wishing she felt well and could drive the sleigh herself. That might be fun. She would drive slower, to be sure. But at any rate, with all this speed, they would soon be there.

At night they stayed in farmhouses or in public houses — one night they stayed with Joseph's sister, Sophronia, who had married Stoddard the carpenter. Emma slept and woke to take up the journey again. The days and nights began to blend together in a series of snow pictures... fences and outbuildings almost covered by the drifts, cabins with snow-laden roofs, trees bent with the weight of it. She could no longer remember where she had spent the previous night, or the night before that. It was a blur of whiteness and snow, the sound of hoofbeats and the constant motion of the sleigh.

They drove through a forest encased in ice, the tree branches arching overhead like sculptures of crystal. The sun touched the ice arches alive with tiny sparkles. In the snowbanks at the side of the road, countless particles glistened, caught by the light.

Toward late afternoon, the snow drifts were pinkish in the fading light. The tree shadows were blue-gray on the snow. There was a cabin, then another close by.

Suddenly they were there. The sleigh went around a bend, slowed down...there were three or four small log houses, some other buildings, and a general store.

"We're here !" Sidney Rigdon said eagerly.

"Praise God!" Brother Partridge said. "We made it safely through."

"Just pull up in front of the store there," Brother Rigdon said to Brother Partridge.

"This is it!" Joseph said. Emma could sense the excitement in his voice. Before the sleigh had even stopped, he was out and striding through the snow.

She looked around at the cabins. They looked even smaller now than when she had first seen them. *This is it?* she wondered, and her heart sank.

Then she realized that Brother Sidney was watching her. He smiled.

"It doesn't seem like much, now," he said. "It looks rather desolate, I fear. But in the spring, it's lovely, with wildflowers everywhere. And the summers are most beautiful."

Emma smiled weakly. "It just looks a little different, that's all."

"The trees are taller...there's more pine. This was all wilderness, just a short time ago."

Sidney and Edward Partridge were getting out of the sleigh. Sidney was folding up the bearskin rug from the front seat. Joseph had already gone into the store.

"That's the Gilbert and Whitney store," Sidney said. "All this is Main Street, believe it or not. Now, Brother Gilbert and his partner — they're about the most prosperous people in these parts. In just a few moments, we'll take you in where it's warm — you'll probably be staying with the Gilbert family."

"They have more room than most," Brother Partridge said.

Suddenly there was a commotion inside the store. The door opened and a man rushed out. His shoes clattered on the wooden porch boards.

"It's Brother Whitney!" Sidney Rigdon exclaimed.

"Without his coat!" Brother Partridge said. "He'll catch his death of cold!"

The man ran across the road to the largest of the cabins. He was yelling,

"Elizabeth! Elizabeth! The prophet is here! Joseph is here! The prophet has come to Kirtland!"

Joseph walked out of the store. There was another man just behind him. They came over to the sleigh.

"Whatever did you say to him?" Emma asked Joseph.

"I said, 'Newell K. Whitney, thou art the man!' And when he expressed surprise and said he didn't know me, I told him who I was. I said, 'You've prayed me here, now what do you want of me?'"

Joseph introduced Emma to Whitney's partner, Brother Gilbert, who had come out of the store with him. Then people began rushing out of the house where Brother Whitney had run with his message. The sleigh was surrounded by people — Brother Whitney's family, and people from the other houses.

"This is my wife, Elizabeth Ann," Brother Whitney said.

Other introductions were made, but there were so many names that Emma could not remember them all. She was tired; she tried not to show it. In the crowd of unfamiliar faces, she was drawn to one — that of Elizabeth Whitney. Elizabeth had an honest, open face, and at that moment she looked hopeful, eager to the point of tears. Weary as she was, Emma smiled as she stood beside Joseph. Elizabeth was looking at them both as if they were indeed the answer to prayer.

It was arranged that they should go to the Gilberts' house and choose a room. Their belongings were transferred from the sleigh to a wagon. Emma was to ride on the wagon, while Joseph went ahead with Gilbert.

The driver clicked to the horses, and they started down the hill toward the Gilberts' house. Suddenly the wagon slid on the ice; it overturned, spilling Emma out into the snow. She screamed.

There were voices, quick footsteps in the snow. Then Joseph was beside her, lifting her to her feet. He was breathing hard, his face flushed from running.

"I'm all right," she said, in answer to his look.

"Are you sure?"

She thought so, although by this time she was exhausted. He didn't leave her. When the wagon was righted, they walked down the hill together.

The Gilberts' house was large, but it was also full of people. Emma was afraid things would be too crowded if they stayed there.

"Let's go back to the Whitneys'," she said.

"Would you prefer that?"

"I think so."

The Whitneys gladly took them in. Later, after the evening meal, Elizabeth Whitney told how just a few days earlier, they had prayed for help and religious instruction.

"I heard a voice...we both did. Newell said he heard it too. It said — it said, 'Prepare to receive the word of the Lord, for it is coming.'"

"And now you're here," Newell Whitney said, looking at Joseph. "Things will be put in order, now."

"What things?" Joseph asked.

"Well...there're some strange doings at the services — some of the people are confused about them. You see, folks have come into the church so quickly, it seems like. There's not enough people to teach them, it seems, and lead them."

"That's understandable. Tell me about the 'strange doings.'"

"Well...it's the younger ones, mainly. Oh, they jump around and act like Indians...they go through scalping motions. They scoot around on the floor and say they're sailing to the Lamanites — taking the gospel to them, you see."

"I see," Joseph said.

"Why, just last week, young Jeff Ford was down on the floor, scooting around on his seat. I was hopin' he'd pick up a splinter. And there're other things. Old Brother Whitlock pretending to be the devil. And Sister Hubble gettin' up and prophesying. Oh, she'll prophesy at the drop of a hat. And her prophecies...well, they don't make too much sense. We're getting a bad reputation because of these things."

"Our people have to be taught," Joseph said. "They need to know the things that are of God, and the things that are not."

"And what's more, folks are saying-"

Elizabeth said to Emma, "You're looking tired. Let me show you where the blankets and things are kept. Then you can get to bed."

Elizabeth showed her over the house. "I'm so glad you are here with us at last."

"It's nice to be here," Emma said, "and not out in that sleigh."

They laughed together in the hallway, as if they had known each other a long time.

One member of the family was not all that happy about their presence — Elizabeth's elderly Aunt Sarah. Emma heard her mutter something about a "self-styled prophet."

She would try to keep on the good side of Aunt Sarah, if there was one. Meanwhile as Elizabeth lighted the candle in the guest room, Emma knew she had found at least one friend in Kirtland.

237

* * * *

In Colesville, New York, Newel Knight tried to prepare his group of Saints for the move west.

"But, Brother Newel," one of the older men said. "I don't even *want* to move."

"Now, Ben," Newel said patiently. "You *know* we've been instructed to begin the gathering of Israel, and we must do it as a people-"

"Well, can't you do it without me?"

"I don't know, brother. That's up to you. I'd sure be sorry not to see you there when all the good things start happenin'."

"It's just that I'm not young like I used to be. And too much sacrifice is required — to give up all I have-"

"I know, Ben. But it's a revelation — from God, to our prophet. We're called upon to sacrifice — for the sake of the glorious time that is coming."

"It don't seem fair," someone else said. "Brother De Mill is sellin' his thirty-six acres, and he's gettin' twice as much as me."

"And I'm getting less than you," Newel said. "I'm selling my sixty acres anyway. My good land, that I got from my father."

The complainer brightened up right away. "You're gettin' less than me?"

"Yes. And I'm not complaining. We get what we can, and do the best we can."

Joseph, Newel's brother, said,

"I talked with Brother Culver and the others just across the county line. I told them to head for Ithaca, and wait for us there. Brother Willis wanted to know what we're gonna do then."

Newel said, "We're gonna get everybody on a boat, cross Cayuga Lake, and get a canal boat at Cayuga Bridge. That oughta get us into — let's see, there's the Cayuga and Seneca Canal, then the Erie Canal — why, we can go as far as Buffalo, I figure, before we have to get out into the lake. Then it's Lake Erie, and points west."

"Why, sure. You get as far as Lake Erie, you're almost there."

"The Broome County folks are all set," said one of the others. "They're ready to travel."

"In fact, they're more than ready. The neighbors are gettin' really mean."

"Ithaca it is, then."

"Right. We'll meet you in Ithaca."

* * * *

Well, there I was, in Buffalo, New York. And it was raining. A drenching downpour. I was trying to find shelter for my people. You should have seen that city in the rain...all ugly and dismal.

I started walking. Already I was soaked to the skin. And I was thinking, *what am I doing here*? I was used to country mornings... to fresh fields, and tall grass. Lakes and forests. *What am I doing so far from home*?

Then I thought, *what home*? Right then I had no home.

Well, to tell the truth, my home was on a boat. It used to be my brother's own boat. *General Jason Mack*, he was. It belonged to Captain Blake now, who was captain under my brother.

That was a stroke of luck, remembering about the boat. You see, we'd just left the canal boat at Buffalo, and we had a long way to go before we reached Kirtland. So I sent Brother Humphrey and Brother Page out to

239

look for Captain Blake. By incredible luck, and the grace of God, they found him.

"Mother Smith," Brother Page said. "The boat is crowded already. He offered us deck passage — it was all he had. We said we'd take it."

"Good," I said. "Let's get everybody on board."

There was eighty of us, brothers and sisters in Christ. Young ones, old ones, married couples, families. There would have been more, but Joseph (my husband) was sent off with Hyrum to help one of the other groups — the ones from down around Colesville. Samuel had left soon after they did.

Well, to get back to the rain, by that time I was gettin' mighty damp. I turned down one of those little streets. I hoped I wouldn't forget how to get back to the boat. I thought, if my people weren't so sick, and always complaining, I wouldn't be here. But I had to find a house for them, shelter for the night. It was so crowded on the deck, and cold. And the boat not leaving till morning.

There was a tavern ahead, on the side street. I walked toward it, trying not to slip on the icy ground.

We had just met up with the Colesville Saints — their boat had reached Buffalo a week before ours did. They were still waiting for the ice to break. My husband and Hyrum weren't with them — they had already gone on to Kirtland by land. I thought, at this rate, a good part of my family will be there before me.

I reached the tavern, opened the door. It was good to get in, out of the cold. There was light and warmth. I rubbed my hands together, to warm them.

The landlord was there. He looked kind...a tall man with gray hair, a bit stooped.

I explained what I wanted. A room for some women and children who were sick.

"Of course," he said, nodding. "We can easily make room for them."

Then I saw the woman. Why didn't I notice her before? She was richly dressed, standing there by the window. She turned then, and I couldn't believe what she was saying.

"Now, wait. *I* have arranged to stay here myself. And I'm not going to have anybody's things in my way. I'll warrant, those children have whooping cough or measles, or some other contagious disease. If *they* come, I'll go somewhere else!"

"Why, madam," the landlord said. "That isn't necessary. You can still have one large room."

"I don't care." Her eyes flashed. "I want 'em both. And if I can't have 'em, I won't stay — that's it."

"Never mind," I said. "It is no matter. I - I suppose I can get a room somewhere else, just as well."

"No, you can't," the lady said with a sniff. "We had to hunt all over town for this one."

The landlord said, "It's the ice. People holed up all over town, waitin' for that ice to break."

I tried to pretend it didn't matter. The landlord looked apologetic. I went out quickly, into the rain.

I prayed. I said, *Oh, Lord, help. You have led us this far. I need help. Help for my sisters and the sick children. This way? Which way should I go?*

That they should make me a leader. *Incredible.* I tried to get Brother Humphrey to lead the group, when they gathered at our home on the Seneca River. But he refused. He said,

"Everything shall be done just as Mother Smith says. Does everyone agree?"

And they agreed. We boarded the boat we'd hired from the Methodist preacher. The crowd of friends...all the people that came to say goodbye —it was touching. We

241

wept. And the gift — a gift of seventeen dollars from Esquire Chamberlain.

A good thing I had that. Most of the others hadn't even brought food. I furnished them with food from day to day. And the children. They just let the children run, without regard for their safety. Finally I called the children to me and took charge of them. They would come rushing to me whenever I raised my hand.

Our people sang as the boat moved. The captain was delighted. He had his assistant take over the wheel so he could listen to the singing.

They sang in the morning, and the early evening. But when the canal broke, halfway to Buffalo, I found they could complain even better than they sang.

"Well, the canal is broke now, and here we are. Here we're likely to stay, for we can't go any further."

"We might as well just tie up and *live* here."

"We've left our homes, and we have no way of earning a living. I guess we'll just have to starve."

"It would've been better if we'd stayed where we were. There we could sit in our rocking chairs and be comfortable."

"That's right. Now we're tired out, and we don't even have a place to rest."

O, the flesh pots of Egypt. I didn't feel like Moses, or any other leader. I tried to soothe and encourage them. Then people came on board, asking for preachers.

"You say you're Latter Day Saints? Mormons? We can arrange for a meeting, if you have preachers."

They held a meeting the next day, with Elders Humphrey and Page in charge. It was on a pretty little green next to the canal. The people listened — oh, they were attentive, and they even asked for another meeting the next day. But the canal was repaired before then, and we had to be on our way.

One odd thing...the Colesville Saints were very fearful about anyone finding out they was "Mormons." The thirty members of Brother Marsh's group, who reached Buffalo just after we did, also warned me about mentioning it.

"You'll never get a boat, or a place to stay, if you tell them your religion."

Well, I was determined. I wasn't ashamed of who I was. And I wasn't going to be quiet about it for anything. We were going to keep singing and praying, and having our services.

I found another side street, and a long row of rooms. One of them looked vacant. I knocked at the first door.

An older woman answered — she appeared to be about seventy. She seemed cheerful, looking at me in the rain.

"I was noticing that room," I said. "It looks almost empty. I was hoping it could be rented for a couple of days. I'm with a group of people from my church — we're just passing through. I need a place for my sisters, and some children who are sick."

"Well, I don't know," she says. "Where be you a-going?"

"To Kirtland," I say.

"What be you?" she says. "Be you Baptists?"

"We are- we are Mormons."

"Mormons!" She still sounds good-natured. "What be they? I never heard of them before."

"I told you that we are Mormons, because that's what the world calls us. The name we acknowledge is 'Latter Day Saints.'"

"Latter Day Saints?" she says. "I never heard of them either."

"Our church was brought forth through the instrumentality of a prophet. His name is Joseph Smith, and I am his mother."

"What? A prophet, in these days? I never heard of the like in all my life! I'll tell you what. If you will come

243

and sit with me, you may have a room for your - your
sisters and their children. But you yourself must come
and stay with me, and tell me all about it."

"Praise God! I will do it!"

I ran rejoicing to the boat, in spite of the rain. If they
could see me now, the brothers who said I should tell
no one who we are! I found the sisters, who were getting
better at complaining than any folks I ever knew. I got
the little ones, the children who were sick. I tried to
explain what was happening, and how God was helping
us. I had them follow me to the long row of rooms and
the cheerful old lady.

"You mean we all have to be crowded together in one
room, while Mother Smith gets to stay with the lady?"

When I heard that, I almost gave up, I tell you. But
I prayed that I wouldn't lose patience entirely.

It must have worked. I was able to sit up till two o'clock
that morning, talking with that good lady and telling
her our whole story.

* * * *

When Mother Smith's group of Saints finally reached
Fairport Harbor, William Smith and his friend Jenkins
Salisbury decided to walk the eleven miles to Kirtland.

"I tell you," William said. "I was never gladder to get
off a boat in my life."

"I never saw such a storm," Jenkins said. "It was bad
enough with all the thunder and lightning. But when
everybody lined up at that rail-"

"You couldn't've got another person in there, even if
you tried."

"At least they weren't complaining any more."

"I wouldn't say they were exactly praying, either."

"What I can't understand," Jenkins said. "After all the bickering and carrying on, the fights, the complaints about being too crowded... Well, *now* they want to stay together. They don't want to be separated. They want to settle all together, with the other New York Saints. Can you figure that out?"

"Maybe they're afraid they might miss an argument." William shook his head. "With my people, who can tell?"

There was a team of horses and a wagon coming toward them. The driver looked familiar.

"Look! I know that person," William said. "It's - my heavens! It's my brother!"

"Which one?"

"My brother Joseph!"

"It is! It's Joseph!"

William ran to the wagon. The driver reined in the horses. He jumped down to the ground and embraced both young men, one after the other.

"Is Mother all right?" Joseph asked.

"She's fine," William said. "A little weary."

"Brother Humphrey left the boat at the last port and came walking in. He said I was to meet her and take her away from the company — she needed rest. In fact, he feared for her health."

"She could sure use some rest. Let's go get her." William hoisted himself over the side of the wagon.

"How are the others? Are they well?"

Jenkins climbed into the wagon. William said,

"They're fine. They're just over being seasick, and they're cold and tired. But no one's really sick."

"Thank God," Joseph said. "Do you know we'd heard they were dead? The newspaper report said the boat had sunk in a storm."

"Oh, there was a storm, all right," Jenkins said.

"One of those terrible storms," William said. "Thunder and lightning...the kind where everybody repents-"

"But they're not dead — not by a long shot. They're so happy to get off that boat, they're ready to kiss the ground."

"Sister Page — she said if she ever got on another boat again, it was because she was either dead or out of her mind."

"All right, boys," Joseph said. "I get the idea."

Joseph spoke to the horses, and the wagon lurched forward. William told him how their mother had taken charge of the group and brought them through.

Joseph said, "Brother Humphrey mentioned how she had everyone pray, and then the ice broke up."

"It was a tremendous noise," William said. "The ice parted just enough to let us through. The Colesville Saints were right behind us, on the next boat. The ice came together again, and we left them behind. I would've liked to see their faces. They'd been waiting there a week already. They're probably still waitin' for that ice to go."

"Oh, she was magnificent — Mother Smith was. They couldn't have made it through without her."

"Well, now," Joseph said. "It's time for her to rest."

William and Jenkins were treated to the sight of Mother Smith greeting first Samuel, who had come by a different route, and then Joseph. Samuel had received a dream concerning her arrival, and he had been afraid all was not well.

"If they cry any more," William said, "the lake level's gonna rise for sure."

"Oh, hush up, William," Mother Smith said through her tears.

Joseph was ready to take her away for some rest, but the sisters, whom she had cared for, didn't want her to leave. They got as many people into the wagon as they could, and went off to Edward Partridge's for breakfast.

"What a breakfast!" William said. "The first real meal we've had since we left Waterloo."

"This is better than three Christmas dinners put together," Jenkins said.

During the meal, William noticed that his brother Joseph appeared subdued. The laughter and gaiety went on around him, but he seemed untouched by it, as if his thoughts were somewhere else. Oh, he was pleasant enough, to be sure. But it was as if there were a shadow over him.

Are the burdens of his office that much, William wondered? Later he learned that Emma had just given birth to twins; they had lived a few hours, and then died.

* * * *

The arrival of the newspaper, *The Wayne Sentinel*, was a big event for the Palmyra townspeople.

"Would you look at that?" the woman of the house said. "Fifty souls, it says. Right here, it says, right in the *Sentinel*."

"It says that? Where?" her husband asked.

"It says, 'Several families, numbering about fifty souls, took up their line of march from this town-'"

"Why don't it just say, 'they left Palmyra?' That's what they mean, ain't it?"

"Listen," she said. "It's about the Smiths, and that strange religion. They all left for the 'promised land,' it says. And then it mentions Martin Harris — it says he's one of the original believers in that Book of Mormon. He left with them."

"Poor old Martin Harris. I seed him, just a few days ago. He was lookin' a little weary. I figured Dolly'd been at him again."

"It says he was one of the early settlers of this town...an honorable and upright man...an obliging and benevolent neighbor. A respectable fortune-"

"What?" he asked.

"It says he had a respectable fortune. I presume he's left most of it behind — 'cause you know Dolly sure wasn't goin' with him."

"Benevolent and upright, huh? It says all that?"

"Yes," she said. "Look. Right here."

"Well, he was all them things, and more, till he got mixed up with that Mormon foolishness."

"That's what it says. You ought to read it. It says, 'he has left a large circle of acquaintances and friends to pity his delusion.'"

"That's right. And not only him. Fifty souls. Just think of it. That's what it says, don't it?"

"Here," she said. "Why don't you read it for yourself?"

* * * *

While the people from New York State were traveling west, Parley Pratt was heading east.

He had left his four missionary companions in Independence and walked the three hundred miles to St. Louis. It took him nine days. He spent some time around the St. Louis area, notably East St. Louis, where he had friends. Then he boarded a steamboat for the trip to Cincinnati.

He got off the boat. It was March; the big snow had started to melt. Everything was a-wash in mud and water. He started to Kirtland on foot.

It was hard going, in the mud, but nothing like the rigors of the winter crossing he and the four others had made. Why, then, did he feel so weak...so weary? He pushed on, day after day — one hundred miles, one hundred and twenty. His head ached, and he had muscle pains at each step. Was something wrong with him?

Two hundred and fifty miles from Cincinnati, he knew he could not go on any further. He reached the village of Strongville, Ohio, about sundown. He knocked at the first door he saw.

"Excuse me," he said to the man who answered. "I'm looking for Latter Day Saints? Do you know of any in this vicinity?"

"Oh, you mean Mormons? Try the Coltrin family — about two mile east. Jest keep on the main road — you'll see a crick and a little log house. Their's is the next one after that."

Parley was so worn out by this time that it was a struggle to keep the simple directions in his mind. Keep on the main road...look for the creek...

He knocked at the door, hoping this was the right place. A man opened the door. The man was of medium height, clean-shaven. He drew in his breath when he saw Parley.

"Please, my friend," Parley said. "Could you entertain a stranger who has no money?"

The man hesitated, then said, "Of - of course. Come right in. Just let me say a few words to my wife. She's having ladies in to tea."

Parley stood just inside the door as the man of the house went into the next room to speak to his wife. There was a mirror on the wall, surrounded by hooks for hats and coats. On an impulse he looked in the mirror.

Staring back at him was an apparition smeared with mud, the face lined with weariness, the eyes inflamed. The beard was longer than he'd remembered. *Is that*

249

me, he thought? No wonder Brother Coltrin had hesitated. What would his poor wife do, with the "ladies in to tea?"

He didn't have long to find out. The wife hurried out to meet him, smiling as she took his hand.

"You are welcome here," she said. "Come sit down, and have some tea with us."

Parley was feeling deathly ill by this time. He summoned all his strength in an effort to be agreeable. After washing up, and trying to look presentable, he sat down at the table with them.

His hostess said,

"You look so weary, stranger. You must have traveled a long distance."

"I've come all the way from Independence," Parley said.

The host and hostess exchanged glances, and the two visiting ladies looked closely at him. Sister Coltrin said,

"Did you hear anything of the four great prophets out that way? There were four men...four strange men...who came through this country, and preached, and baptized hundreds of people. After ordaining elders and organizing churches, they went on westward, as we suppose, to the frontiers — on a mission to the Indians. We have never heard from them since."

"Yes," said one of the visiting women. "They were dressed plainly and comely, very neat in their appearance. Each one wore a hat of a drab color, low round crown and broad brim, after the manner of the Shakers. So it is said, for we had not the privilege of seeing them."

"They had neither purse nor script for their journey, neither extra shoes, nor two coats apiece," the second visitor said.

"Yes...I have seen them," Parley said.

"Will they return soon?" the first visitor said. "Oh, who would not give the world to see them!"

250

Then Parley began to laugh (for he remembered his face in the mirror). They looked at him, wondering. When he could speak again, he said,

"My name is Parley P. Pratt, one of the four men you described. Not much of a prophet, I'm afraid. As to a sight of me in my present plight, I think it would not be worth *half* a world!"

To his joy, he found he was among fellow-Saints; they were delighted to have him there. But his illness was getting worse. The next day, he was too weak to lift his head from the pillow.

"Measles," they said.

Measles it was. A childhood disease, that most everybody had at one time or another. But Parley had suffered such a long exposure to cold, rain, and mud, that the illness almost killed him. He was watched over day and night by the people in that place, and given devoted and loving care. As soon as he had recovered, they gave him a horse so he could finish the trip to Kirtland.

When he reached Kirtland, he found that the Ohio church had increased to more than a thousand members. The New York Saints now numbered several hundred.

There was a letter from his wife, Thankful, whom he hadn't seen in six months. She wrote that she had been baptized, and the whole church in the state of New York was moving to Ohio as soon as the way was open in the spring.

His brother Orson, whom he had baptized in the fall, was now a missionary, out preaching and baptizing as Parley had done.

Edward Partridge, who had called the missionaries 'imposters' before they left for Missouri, was now the bishop for the church. He had been called to the office by revelation, in February. Together he and Joseph Smith were teaching the people, especially those engaged in communal living, about a new financial law in which all goods and land were to be consecrated to the church.

So much had happened, just since he had left for Missouri. He wanted, more than anything, to see his wife again.

Since it was almost April by that time, he decided to wait in Ohio for the arrival of Thankful and the others from New York State.

19

...the land of Missouri, which is the land
which I have appointed and consecrated for the
gathering of the Saints... the land of promise,
and the place for the city of Zion.

...Behold, the place which is now called Independence, is the Center Place, and the spot for
the temple is lying westward upon a lot which
is not far from the courthouse...

—The Lord to Joseph Smith
July, 1831

Tuesday, August 3. Joseph stood at last upon the
appointed place. He was on a little knoll, about half a
mile from the town of Independence. All around him was
a dense thicket of woods and underbrush. The west wind
moved in the tops of the trees, making a sound like the
faint rushing of water.

"Look at the flowers," Edward Partridge said, just
behind him. "So many of them."

"It's a lovely spot," Oliver said. "I've been here so long,
I tend to forget how beautiful it really is."

Joseph turned suddenly and looked at Oliver.

"This is nothing," he said, "compared to what will be
here in the future."

Oliver met his gaze steadily and nodded without
smiling.

Joseph had sensed the change in Oliver at the time
they had first seen each other again. No more a physical
weakling, subserviant, Oliver was self-assured, assertive
— independent to the point of being defiant. So far he

had done nothing which could be construed as questioning Joseph's authority.

Joseph said, "Where's Brother Sidney? When he gets here, we can begin."

"He can't walk as fast as the rest of us," Edward Partridge said.

"There's so much more of him," someone else said.

"I'll see if I can find him," Oliver said. He turned and headed back toward the settlement.

Joseph began to walk in the opposite direction, his head full of the ancient prophecies, and the things that would come upon the land in the future.

...the glory of Lebanon...the fir tree, the pine tree and the box together, to beautify the place of his sanctuary...where for brass he will bring gold, and for iron he will bring silver...

Joseph was a little dismayed when he had first seen the area. Not because of the aspect of the land (for it was beautiful, with fertile soil, flowering shrubs and trees). It was the inhabitants that had made him uneasy.

"A rough lot," someone had said.

Even Oliver had remarked, a few days ago, "You can see the degradation of the people settled here — there's a certain leanness of intellect. The ferocity and jealousy are part of it. They don't call them Missouri 'pukes' for nothing."

"And yet this place will blossom as a rose," Joseph had answered. "The vain glory of the world will vanish, and God will shine — the perfection of beauty out of Zion."

"Yes," Oliver had said. "Well, it may take a while."

Joseph knew there were some things in the revelations that even he didn't fully understand — things that would not be immediately understood or fulfilled. But in this case, he hoped Oliver was wrong.

254

In fact, things were happening fast. It was just a short time ago, in early June, that the designation of Missouri as the land of promise had been revealed. Certain of the elders had been instructed to travel to Missouri in pairs, taking different routes and preaching by the way. They were to meet together in Jackson County, where the first missionaries had gone.

Joseph and his companions had left Kirtland on June 19. They were among the first to reach Independence.

After that, one event hastened upon another. Images flashed through his mind. Their first Sunday, with W. W. Phelps preaching to the mixed audience — white pioneers, a few black people and some Indians. The two baptisms that same day. Then the arrival of the whole Colesville branch — most of the New York Saints — a few days later. Sidney Rigdon and his wife, with two other elders, had come in about the same time. By mid-July, most of the elders had assembled, and the location of the Center Place and the temple had been made known.

Just yesterday they had placed the first log for a house, the foundation of Zion in Kaw township. The location was twelve miles west of Independence. Twelve men had carried and placed the log, in honor of the twelve tribes of Israel. Then Sidney Rigdon had given a dedicatory prayer, consecrating the land of Zion for the gathering of the people.

The first conference in the land of Zion was to take place tomorrow, in Kaw township. Joseph felt tired and a bit rushed, with all the activity. But the knowledge of where he was, of the great things that were about to happen, buoyed up his spirits; he felt a surge of exhilaration. There was a warm wind from the west. He felt it on his face...felt it lifting the ends of his hair. The wind was full of the scent of wild things, of fresh-blooming flowers and damp earth, and in it was all the exciting sense and promise of the new land.

There was a hand on his shoulder. Brother Partridge spoke beside him.

"Brother Joseph. Sidney is here, and Oliver's with him."

"We're ready to begin, then. Is Oliver ready with the eighty-seventh Psalm?"

"Yes. I presume so. He has his Bible."

They gathered in a half-circle, there in the forest. Joseph made a few opening remarks concerning the thing they were about to do. Then Sidney Rigdon began to speak in his impressive oratorical style.

There was a strange sense of time being suspended as they stood there. Joseph, looking around at the little group, found himself thinking of certain men among them, and the part each had played in the events that had brought them to that place. .

For there were only eight of them, gathered there that day, and each man's role was different.

First there was Martin Harris, robust, with a determined, set look to his jaw...the stocky New York farmer, who had left home, farm and wealth for the sake of his beliefs. He had been the first one outside Joseph's family to believe in the Book of Mormon. He had tried to help in the translation, had encouraged Joseph, had given money, and finally had paid for the printing of the book. In the process he had lost his wife and the rest of his property, but he had also been privileged to give his name as one of the three witnesses.

Oliver stood, waiting to read the psalm. He was still slender, with the same gentle, sensitive look, the thin lips. He was broader in the shoulders and chest than when Joseph had first known him. Joseph thought of the younger Oliver...the faithful scribe and second elder, who had overseen the publication of the Book of Mormon.

256

He had taken part in the restoration of the priesthood and the organization of the church, and had carried the news of the restored church to Ohio and finally to Missouri.

There was Sidney Rigdon... portly, a man with presence and fire... converted by the four missionaries when they had reached Ohio. His amazing gifts of oratory and writing, his knowledge of the Bible, were even now a blessing and strength to his people.

There was Edward Partridge, Rigdon's friend, a man "like unto Nathaniel of old, in whom there is no guile," as the Lord had said of him. Joseph thought of how a skeptical Edward had made the trip to New York State with Sidney Rigdon, with the intention of meeting the prophet for himself and seeing what kind of person he was. Edward's talents as bishop had been well-used; his honesty, his knowledge of business and financial mat ters, had helped the church in Ohio with its temporal affairs.

There were W. W. Phelps, journalist and writer, and Joseph Coe, both new members. The future belonged to them, and perhaps they would play as much of a role as the others had.

There was himself, Joseph Smith, Jr., whose own story he could not begin to tell or understand. That he, an ignorant farm boy, should have been called of God through the maze of back-country superstition and folklore that had pervaded his boyhood, was a miracle in itself. That the work should come forth and grow out of such a background was amazing, and that he should be used, and continually used, was one of the greatest wonders of all.

There were eight of them, and on that day, with prayer, they dedicated the spot where the temple of the Lord would stand in the last days. Joseph placed the marker himself, on a rise of ground near the foot of a sapling. He put earth over the stone, and planted a small bush, to mark the spot. Then he blazed the sapling with a knife, carving letters in its bark as an additional marker.

"It's time for the psalm," Joseph said to Oliver.

Oliver nodded, and the look they exchanged reminded Joseph of the early days, when they were the only ones to know of the magnitude of the work.

Oliver cleared his throat, and struggled to hold down the page (for it fluttered in the wind). Then he read:

> **"His foundation**
> **Is in the holy mountains.**
>
> **The Lord loveth the gates of Zion**
> **More than all the dwellings of Jacob.**
>
> **Glorious things are spoken of thee,**
> **O city of God.**
>
> **And of Zion it shall be said,**
> **This and that man was born in her;**
> **And the Highest himself shall establish her.**
>
> **The Lord shall count**
> **When he writeth up the people**
> **That this man was born there.**
>
> **The singers as well as the players on instru-**
> **ments**
> **Shall be there..."**

Oliver paused and looked around at his companions. The wind had stopped. There was a hush; even the bird voices sounded far away.

He drew a deep breath, and his eyes went back to the printed page.

"'...All my springs are in thee.'"

20

"Brother David, be true to your testimony of the Book of Mormon."

—Oliver Cowdery on his deathbed
Richmond, Missouri
March, 1850

"Dissenters."

David said the word aloud. That indeed was what they had been called.

It left a bitter taste upon the tongue. A painful word, a harsh one. Hardly the right word for those who had labored so hard, had sacrificed so much for the common cause. Yet in the end, that was what they had been labeled, termed by their own people. *Dissenters*.

David Whitmer sat in the sun, his back against the wall of the stable. He was an old man now, almost eighty-two. From his seat on the wooden bench, he could see the sign for his place of business.

'The Old Reliable Livery and Feed Stable.'

Under that was printed,

'Hacks, Buggies, and Saddle Horses
Richmond, Missouri'

In addition to renting horses and conveyances, and selling feed, they boarded horses by the day, week, or month. He had people to help him now; he wasn't able to do much of the heavy work. But he liked to be around the stable anyway. He liked the sound and scent of the horses, the smell of leather and hay. He knew each horse by name, like an old friend, and greeted them in turn every morning.

Not a bad life. A strange turn of events for one who had once been President of the Church in Missouri, and had sat at the same rostrum with the prophet Joseph Smith during the Kirtland Temple dedication. For they had indeed built a temple, his people...in Kirtland, Ohio. In his mind's eye he could see the white building, beautiful in its simplicity, shining as if new-washed in light. They had toiled and sacrificed to build it, and the women had even brought their good china to be crushed for the outside so that it would glisten in the sun.

He thought of the New York Saints, who had wanted to remain together in one body after their trip to Ohio. It was decided that they would stay together and be known as the 'Colesville Branch.' They had settled for awhile at Thompson, Ohio, and then Joseph had sent them to Missouri, to cultivate the land of Zion.

And so they had, with schools and a printing press, and the news of the restored gospel.

But the free-spirited Missourians, already settled there, looked askance at these Easterners who wanted to live as a community, worship together, and till the land. The Latter Day Saint farmer was as different from the independent Missouri frontiersman as day from night. One could not live without antagonizing the other.

David bowed his head as he thought of the sufferings of his people in Missouri. Persecuted, harassed, finally driven out, their homes and crops burned, their women raped, men, women and children killed...

The forced exodus from Jackson County...Zions' Camp...the fruitless attempts to obtain redress from the courts and civil authorities...the attempt to gather together, further to the north, in Caldwell and Daveiss

260

Counties...the settlement of Far West...more persecutions...the massacre at Haun's Mill...the arrest of the church leaders...

The list of troubles ran like a plaintive chant through his mind as he sat hunched over. A violent and disturbing time. So turbulent, in fact, that those who managed to live through it intact were lucky to have survived. The amazing thing was that it had all happened so quickly. Within a span of eight years, the violent events had occurred, one upon the other.

Strange to think how long ago it was now...almost fifty years. Not many of the participants were still alive. Joseph Smith and Sidney Rigdon were dead. Joseph and his brother Hyrum had been assassinated at the hands of a mob over in Illinois. That was in 1844, and not long after — 1850, it was — David's own beloved brother-in-law, Oliver Cowdery, had died of his illness...the weakness in his lungs.

He thought of the letter he had just received from his sister, Elizabeth Ann. She had married Oliver, back in the Kirtland days.

The letter...he got it out of his pocket. It was dated March 1, 1886, sent from her in Southwest City, Missouri. He smoothed it out on his lap. His eye lingered on one particular paragraph. In the bright sunlight, the words seemed to leap out at him from the page:

> In answer to your question, Oliver at no time ever faltered from his testimony of the truth of the Book of Mormon. I will write more of this later...

Oliver's wife, who had loved him all those years, would have known if it had been otherwise. David nodded and began folding the letter.

How could they have done it to him?... to one as faithful as Oliver? To any of them, for that matter... for David had been involved too, along with his brother John, and W. W. Phelps. *Dissenters*. Excommunicated, without even a legal trial. In the midst of that terrible time, it had happened. The Saints, harassed and persecuted, had turned to persecute each other.

Selling their lands in the Center Place. That was one of the charges. Oliver had insisted the lands were legally theirs, and they had a right to sell them. Then there was the matter of the two thousand dollars.

"What two thousand dollars?" David had asked.

"Oh, you remember," John had said. "The money we were supposed to be collecting for the temple in Independence."

"Oh. *That* two thousand dollars."

Then he was back there with his friends; it was forty-nine years ago, and Oliver was saying,

"They can't be serious. Everyone's lost everything they had. Homes've been burned, crops destroyed — and they want two thousand dollars?"

"Oliver," John said. "Joseph and the bishop want to see that money."

"I don't know how much of it they're gonna see."

"They sure can't build a temple *now*," David said. "Why, a Mormon couldn't even put up a privy in Jackson County now, without that mob gettin' riled-"

"Listen," John said. "Let's give them what we have, out of our own resources. Then we'll ask them to pay us back, over, say, a two-year period..."

The high council that tried them claimed they were not entitled to this money, any more than any other man. David was censured for his use of tea, coffee and tobacco. W. W. Phelps and John Whitmer were "given over to the buffetings of Satan, until they learn to blaspheme

262

no more against the authorities of God, nor fleece the flock of Christ."

"Fleece the flock of Christ!" John exclaimed when he heard about it later. "Is *that* what we were doing?"

Oliver had written a letter claiming that the trial was contrary to their religious principles and the laws of the land, in view of the fact that those being tried were not even present. This only served to incense the members of the high council.

In the end, all four were excommunicated — John, Brother Phelps, Oliver, and himself. While they were wondering what to do next, Sidney Rigdon discovered that they were still living among the Mormon people, as if nothing had happened. He preached a sermon denouncing dissenters. Eighty-three people signed an ultimatum informing these particular dissenters they had three days to get out of Far West. Together, Oliver, the Whitmer brothers, and Lyman Johnson rode to Liberty seeking legal advice. While they were gone, the people turned and drove the dissenters' families from their homes, doing the very thing that had been done by the mob in Jackson County.

David and most of the Whitmer clan went over to Richmond and tried to make some sort of life for themselves among the people there. As to how well he had done — the stable and all its furnishings was a tribute to his industry. His private assets, he knew, were worth at least ten thousand dollars.

In the forty-nine years he had lived in Richmond, he and his family had done hauling, livery work, selling of feed and grain, sand and gravel, and met two trains a day at Lexington Junction to transport the passengers into town. More than that, he had served on fair boards, participated in public meetings, served as city councilman, and was even elected to fill the unexpired term of mayor in 1867.

"Grandfather," his grandson George had asked. "Are you ever bitter about what happened? You know, over in Far West, when the Mormons drove you out?"

"Oh, no, George," he had replied. "Not bitter. Saddened — yes, saddened a great deal. I don't quite understand fully how it could've happened. Oliver, now — that's Aunt Elizabeth's husband. He was deeply grieved. You see, he had a special love for Joseph Smith. Matter of fact, I did too, except I didn't think he was right all the time. I don't think Joseph had much to do with this — he was away when the trial was held. But Oliver was never sure — he was hurt, absolutely incredulous. It was like a shadow over his life."

Oliver had moved back to Ohio after the excommunication. He taught school for a while until he was admitted to the bar as a lawyer. He practiced law there, and built up a respectable reputation as an attorney. He worshipped for a while with a Methodist congregation in Tiffin, Ohio. There were various rumors of his trying to run for public office, only to be defeated when his former Mormon activities were made known.

In 1843, Oliver received an invitation from Joseph Smith urging him to return to the church. Oliver waited, expecting an apology for what had happened. None came; Joseph was killed the next year. The Cowderys moved to Elkhorn, Wisconsin, near Oliver's brother Lyman; Oliver's health was deteriorating, and it was thought the climate would do him good. Then, in 1848, Oliver initiated his return to the church and was reinstated in Brigham Young's faction at Kanesville, Iowa. After that, he lived in Richmond, near the Whitmers.

Oliver's health grew worse. At his deathbed he was surrounded by members of the Whitmer family. As they cared for their brother, David was reminded again of the log house in Fayette, the farm between the lakes...the miraculous things that had happened there. The translation of the plates, the restoration of the church...the closeness they had felt, to each other and to God.

What had gone wrong? Now the prophet was dead, the church was scattered, split into many factions, and some of those factions were teaching things that were never in the Book of Mormon, or the New Testament either. Plurality of wives, indeed. And the name. What was all this Church of Jesus Christ of Latter-day Saints business? It should have been just the plain Church of Christ, as it was in the beginning.

As for Oliver's last words to him, David had never ceased to be true to his testimony. Thousands of people had come to him over the years, sometimes as many as fifteen to twenty in a day. To all he had given the same story, in his own words.

"My testimony is true. I did indeed see the plates, and hear the voice of the angel."

He remembered how his grandson George had begged him to unfold the fraud, as he had all to gain and nothing to lose by finally admitting the truth.

"George, what I have said *is* the truth, and the only truth. It is the same as when I first gave it, and so shall stand throughout eternity."

"All right, Grandfather. All right."

Other voices spoke in his mind...other people who had come seeking his story.

"But, why," one of them said. "Why, if you believe this is true, did you turn against the Prophet Joseph and desert him? He needed all the friends he could get."

"*I*...desert him? I never turned against him! He changed, from when we first knew him. *He* was the one

265

who changed. As a matter of fact, I saved his life, even after they cast me out for being — what was it? Oh, yes — 'of the same spirit as the dissenters.'"

There was dust from the road, and the sound of something squeaking. That squeak...it was the way his old wagon used to sound — the one he used for hauling, just after he left Far West.

Then he was back there, driving his squeaky wagon out of Richmond with a load of baggage bound for Far West. He had just been conscripted by General Parks, who had pressed both David and his team into service. He was making this hauling trip to Far West under protest, being threatened with force if he did not comply.

"If I have to go to Far West," he had said before starting off, "I will take no gun."

"All right," they had said.

David knew with awful certainty that the Mormon people were being driven from their homes; the events in Jackson county were being repeated, this time by a military force. Now here he was, riding into the very thick of things. He knew if the people spotted him, they would think he was on the side of the mobbers and destroyers. How could he explain about being conscripted?

Shots rang out, There were people shouting and running, horses whinnying. In the middle of the road, a wagon toppled over. David felt the dust in his nose and throat.

"They've got 'em!" someone shouted. "They've rounded up Joseph Smith and the whole pack of 'em!"

There was a crowd at one corner of the square. David recognized some of the church leaders.

"Here!" One of the officers handed him a musket. "You! Go over and shoot Joseph Smith!"

"What?" David asked.

266

"I'm ordering you to shoot Joseph Smith! The tall one, over there by the wall — Hurry!"

David stood up in the wagon and threw the musket to the ground.

"I will die before I harm the Lord's anointed!"

"Of all the— Get down, then, or you *will* die. You want to draw their fire?"

David delivered the load of freight and got out of there fast. He wondered who they would find to shoot Joseph.

Later he heard Joseph was in jail with the other leaders. He was safe; no one had shot him.

The squeaking was getting louder. David raised his head; he was sitting on the bench by the stable again, in the year 1886. There was a cloud of dust just ahead.

Two figures emerged from the dust, two boys from the town. They were both about eleven years old. He knew them; they began calling to him.

"Uncle Davy! Uncle Davy!"

They were leading a half-grown retriever-mix pup by a rope around his neck. It was the pup who was squeaking, a series of short, high whines. The dog was hobbling on three legs; the fourth, the right rear leg, was in the air.

"Mornin', boys. What's the matter with Cap'n, there?"

"He's got a misery in his paw," the tallest boy said. He pulled the dog over to the bench.

The smaller boy was freckled, with hair the color of river mud. "We figured you could help him, Uncle Davy."

"Why, land, boy. If a wagon squeaked that bad, I'd grease the axle."

"Grease won't do him no good," the tall boy said. He had a thin, angular jaw and hair like dirty straw. David liked his eyes; they were green, like the river in the shallows.

"Bring him closer here, Bert," David said to the tall boy. Reaching down, he scratched the pup behind the ears. The squeaking stopped.

As David reached for the paw, he kept talking in a gentle voice. "Once I had me a wagon that squeaked all the time. No matter what I did for it, it would always squeak. Finally I just let it squeak."

As he talked, he felt between the pads of the paw. He found the tip of the thorn. The pup tried to pull away. With thumb and forefinger he grasped the tip, then gave a quick pull. The dog yelped.

"Well, there it is," David said, holding it for them to see. "There's your misery."

They drew closer. "That's a mighty big thorn."

"Here," he said to the small freckled boy. "Here, Jerry. You take it."

"Oh, that's bully! Thanks." His voice was ecstatic.

"What happened to the wagon?" Bert asked. "The one that squeaked."

"Oh, that was a long time ago," David said. "Almost fifty years ago. I forget what we ever did with that one. I might've sold it." Out of the corner of his eye he saw his friend the newspaper editor walking toward him.

The pup sat down in a patch of sunlight. He scratched at his ear with his hind foot. Bits of whitish hair floated down in the light.

"Well, I *reckon!*" Bert said with admiration. "He's even scratchin' with the sore foot."

"I don't think he'll have any more trouble," David said. "Hello, Jake," he said to the editor.

"Mornin', Dave. How're you feeling this morning?"

"Right tolerable," David said. He'd been ill earlier in the spring, a touch of influenza. Now he was much better.

"You're looking good," Jake said. "I'm pleased to see that."

"I thank you."

David leaned back against the rough stable boards. Jake, the editor, stuck his hands in his pants pockets and leaned up against the side of the stable.

"I'm looking for news," he said.

"Uncle Davy just took a thorn out of ol' Cap's paw," Bert said.

"Don't tell him that," David said. "He'll put it in the paper."

They laughed together, David and the editor. The boys looked puzzled, as if they weren't quite certain. David gave the dog a final pat.

"You really oughta get Cap a proper collar," he said. "He's liable to hang himself on that rope."

"We're studyin' on it," Jerry said.

"We figure in another two weeks, we'll have the money saved."

"Oh, hang the money," David said. "Bring him down here tomorrow, and I'll make him one from scraps. I think I got some, in the back with the reins and harnesses."

Their eyes widened; they looked at each other.

"Thank you."

"Thank you, Uncle Davy."

"Well, it's for the dog. Not you."

The boys started back the way they had come, with the dog in tow. The animal stopped to do leg-lifting exercises by the hitching post.

"He's traveling on all four feet now," Jake observed.

"He'll be fine. He picked up a big ole thorn, about this big."

Jacob Child was about thirty years younger than David. He had a wide, thin mouth and dark eyebrows. He was clean-shaven, and his dark hair hung in an unruly strand down over his forehead. David liked him;

269

in some ways he reminded David of Oliver Cowdery. He was less gentle than Oliver, and, of course, without the weakness in his lungs.

"So you're up to your old tricks," Jake said, his wide mouth curving in a smile.

"What do you mean?"

"Helping people. Going out of your way. I didn't know you were a vet, too. That's something new."

"You stay around animals long enough, you learn all kinds of things."

Jake nodded, looking at him. "I figure you know a good lot about people, too."

"After this amount of time, it'd be strange if I didn't know *something.*"

Child was editor of the *Richmond Conservator,* and a staunch supporter of David over the years. David thought briefly of how his friend had given regular progress reports in his paper after David's bad illness in 1882:

'We were glad to see Uncle David Whitmer on the street looking remarkably well.'

And later, at the marriage of David's granddaughter, Josie: '...the silver haired patriarch, whose form is as erect and his eyes as bright as when he gazed on the Lord's messenger.'

That statement was most interesting, because he knew Jake was frankly skeptical and puzzled about the angel testimony.

"Grandfather?" It was George's voice, from inside the stable.

"Out here!" Jake Child shouted.

George came outside, followed by a tall man with a bushy beard. The tall man looked somehow familiar; David couldn't place him.

"Grandfather," George said. "This gentleman came looking for you and your testimony. Sir, this is my grandfather — the one they call Father Whitmer. He's the gentlemen you're looking for."

"Good morning," David said. He got to his feet.

"Hello, Father Whitmer. My name is Hiram Mills. We've met before."

"Yes," David said. "I felt sure I had seen you before." He introduced Jacob Child.

Then Mr. Mills asked a few things about the testimony. David hadn't thought Jake would stay, but he remained where he was, leaning against the stable wall.

"...occurring about noon, in an open pasture?"

"Yes," David said. "That is correct."

"Well," Mills said. "I have heard you give your story before, and all the details seem to fit, I had only one question I wanted to ask."

A horse neighed inside the stable; a wooden door banged shut. David said,

"What's the question, sir?"

"I wanted to know if you have ever given that testimony in the face of great personal danger — for instance, possibly facing death for your beliefs?"

"Oh, my. Oh, glory, yes." And David went on to tell him.

A horse was neighing and somewhere an unfastened door was banging in the wind, wood upon wood. There were men's voices in the distance, a shout from somewhere, and then David was back there in Jackson County, fifty-four years ago. He had just been dragged from his home by the mob, and marched at the point of a bayonet to the public square. All was confusion; there

271

was the neighing of horses, people shouting, men's voices raised in oaths. But etched in his mind like letters of fire were the words he had heard, back at his home.

"Bid farewell to your family, for I swear you'll never see any of them again!"

Isaac Morley was on his right, coughing (for he had a bad cold). There were others, too — those men whom the mob considered church leaders. David wasn't sure who else was there; everyone was shouting at once. There was the sound of the door slamming again, of wood hitting against wood.

He was being stripped of his clothes. He tried to struggle, but it was no use. The 'pukes' outnumbered him. He felt the gooey, sticky tar being smeared on him, and then they were rolling him in the feathers. It wasn't a thorough job, more like a token gesture. They tarred and feathered Isaac (who coughed and shivered the whole time). Then they started on the others.

"I want twelve good men!" someone was shouting. He was a tall man, heavy-set, and he was chewing tobacco. "Twelve men who ain't afeard to spill Mormon blood!"

He soon had his twelve volunteers. In a matter of minutes, David, Isaac, and the others were facing twelve men with guns cocked and aimed at them.

"Be ready to fire when I give the word!" yelled the tall, heavy-set man. He spat into the dust at David's feet.

Isaac started to cry. "Oh, my Lord," he sobbed. "This is it."

"Be still," David said to him. The one in command was saying,

"All right. You ring-tailed roarers have one more chance. Yes, one more chance." He was grinning, chewing. "Come on, now. Deny the Book of Mormon — confess that it's a fraud. Or, by the living jingo, it's instant death for all of you!"

272

As the words sunk home, the men looked at each other. The mob was silent, waiting. David had a few seconds to wonder how he could possibly deny his testimony.

"Deny it, and you will live!" The leader spat again. "You will yet enjoy the privileges — Hear that, boys? The privileges of citizens."

"Oh, my Lord," Isaac Morley said again.

David lifted up his hands and cried in a loud voice,

"I can never deny what is true! I *know* the Book of Mormon is the word of God!"

He closed his eyes and waited. There was a deeper silence. Then the mob began to murmur among themselves. The murmur grew louder.

When David opened his eyes, those with guns had turned away. The ringleader had disappeared into the crowd. The leaders of the church in Missouri looked at each other, blinking, standing there in their tar and feathers. Then David turned to help Isaac, who was coughing again.

"I see," Hiram Mills said, when David had told him. He sounded subdued, as if at a loss for words.

David said, "One gentleman, a doctor — an unbeliever — told me this afterward. He said the fearless testimony borne on that occasion — and the fear that seemed to take hold of the mob — had made *him* a believer in the Book of Mormon."

"My stars," Jake said, when Hiram Mills had left. "It's enough to make *me* want to believe it. And I haven't even read it. Say, Davy. Whatever happened to those gold plates anyway?"

"What?"

"Well, obviously, no one got rich off of them. So where did they end up?"

"Oh. Well, according to Joseph, when the translation was finished, he gave them back into the hands of the angel. That's all we know."

David started to take a step, then faltered. He leaned against the side of the stable.

"Are you all right?" Jake asked. "You want some help?"

"No. No, I'm fine. I'm a little tired, that's all. I'm just going to go home and rest."

"You want me to go with you?"

"No. No, I'm all right, Jake. I'll go on home by myself."

"If you say so."

He hadn't had too much sleep the night before. That was the trouble. It was his sister's letter that had done it. Triggering memories, causing him to dream. For in the night, he had heard Oliver's voice, seen Oliver's face... Oliver, who had been dead for thirty-six years.

That morning, he got up feeling as if he'd just seen and talked with Oliver — the way he had felt long ago, when they were friends together back in New York State.

Now, halfway down the block, trying not to appear too tired under Jake Child's watchful eye, he thought of Oliver again, of what Oliver might say if he were still on the earth.

—Brother Dave, have you been true to your testimony?

How much longer was left to him? A few years, perhaps, at the very most... a few more years to testify and relate and affirm...

—Dear brother Oliver, I have done my best. I have been true in any situation you can imagine... before all manner of people... even in the face of death itself. Sometimes I have felt too tired and weak to tell it — overburdened with the things of the world. But I have told it anyway, and have gained strength by it. What I have said, I will keep saying, until the day I can say it no longer.

Yes, my brother. I have been true.

21

Jacob Child was in the newspaper office, in the same room that had been his old headquarters when he was editor. There were notes and papers everywhere, scattered on the desk and on the floor. Back issues of the newspaper were piled on top of the bookshelf.

He was hunting through the back copies, looking for an editorial that had appeared three months ago. The current editor, Mr. Trigg, was in the outer office, giving instructions to Matt, the young secretary.

Jake had just come back to Richmond after an extended stay in the Far East. Even now, it was hard to imagine he had traveled so far, had seen the exotic lands and people of Southeast Asia. He had been appointed Consul-General to Siam by President Grover Cleveland, in the spring of 1886. For almost five years, his time and energy had been taken up with the affairs of that far country.

Now he was back in Richmond, his valise full of notes for a book about Siam. He had brought his family back, and left them at the home of friends while he visited the newspaper office. He was trying to find out what had happened in the way of local politics while he had been away.

The town seemed the same. A few minor changes...a bit more traffic on the main street. A few of the old timers gone. Davy Whitmer had died, a few years ago. He'd heard the news when he was overseas. He shouldn't have been surprised...the old man must have been eighty-three, at least. But the thought of not seeing his old friend again made him feel sad.

He flipped over another issue of the paper. There was a knock at the door.

He looked up, his mouth tightening at the corners. The secretary, a young man in his twenties, opened the door and said,

"Excuse me, sir. There's a gentleman who wants to see you. He said he heard you were back in town. Mr. George Sweich."

"Oh, yes. Of course. Old Davy Whitmer's grandson. Yes, Matt. Have him come in."

George came into the room. Jake put down the newspapers and moved around to the front of the desk. He shook hands with George.

"Hello, George. It's good to see you again."

"Oh, Mr. Child. I was just passing by, and I - well, I wanted to thank you. I didn't get a chance to tell you, before you left town. Those last articles, about my grandfather. It was - well, it was just very nice of you to say those things."

"Oh, not at all. I thought so highly of him. You know...I miss him very much. More than I like to admit. He was like a regular fixture around this town."

George said, "Thank you. We miss him too."

"I'm sure you do. It's hard to believe he's been dead four years already."

"Yes. He went in January of 1888. Eighty-three years old, he was. And twenty days."

"It's strange to walk down toward that stable and not see him there."

"Yes. I know what you mean."

Jake said, "There's one thing that's always amazed me. That story he told, about the angel. It seems amazing, almost incredible, in fact, that a man so highly respected, revered for his truth and honesty, should *insist*- oh, not that the story was false. I'm not saying that. But if it

277

had happened to me, I would have sort of kept it quiet, you know-"

George was laughing by this time. "Yes. He was pretty insistent about it."

"It's the one thing that doesn't make sense. That he should maintain all his life that he actually saw this thing — the angel with the gold plates-"

"I thought it might have been hypnotism," George said. "But whatever it was, it was real to him."

"And the way he'd tell it. He'd stand up, and there'd be this spark, this fire — his face would be alive with it. I never saw anything so convincing."

George nodded, smiling. Jake said,

"All that enthusiasm. I wonder that he didn't unite with one of those other Latter Day Saint groups. Not Brigham Young's group — I know how he felt about plural marriage. But there must have been others-"

"Oh, there's others," George said. "Grandfather knew about most of them. We had our own little family group — the Church of Christ. Then there was James Strang, up in Michigan...Lyman Wight, in Texas. Alpheus Cutler, McLellin. Shucks, there's about as many different Latter Day Saint groups as there are holes in grommets."

"And he knew about them. I was just thinking...what history that man could've told!"

"Oh, you can believe that. He was there when the Mormons were chased out of the Independence area. They had to flee for their lives."

"I know all about that," Jake said. "The early thirties. A shameful chapter of Missouri history."

"But they're going back," George said. "I've heard there's Latter Day Saints down in Independence now. They're going in very quietly, to live."

Jake was intrigued. "Is that so? They're going in there again? They must really want to live there."

"Well, it's their promised land, according to revelation. Zion... the Peaceable Kingdom. They call it the Center Place."

Jake laughed. "Independence? Well, I was hoping it was good for something. The promised land, huh?"

"Something like that."

Jake grew serious again. "And there's no trouble? The people are settling there...apparently without any violence?"

"From what I hear, it's peaceful. At least, for the ones that are going in there now. They're members of something my grandfather called the 'new organization.' The Reorganized Church. Their leader is Joseph Smith III — the oldest son of the prophet."

"I see. The prophet being the one who translated the Book of Mormon?"

"Right."

Things are starting to fall together. I never did pay too much attention to the religion...but the history part is fascinating. So Joseph's son's group is going in there, to live?"

"So I understand."

Jake was beginning to talk to himself, to think out loud, a habit he had. "It's really amazing, when you think of it...how quickly the world changes. The people that persecuted the early Mormons are all gone now — dead, I would imagine. That Southern slave-state mentality — it's gone forever, praise God! That's what those persecutions were all about, from what I can tell. The issue of slavery. The treatment of the Indians — I bet that was part of it, too. Those first Mormons believed that the slaves and Indians were real people. Davy told me that a couple of times."

"That's right," George said.

279

"Well, I'd better let you get back to work," Jake said. "I get side-tracked on history — it fascinates me. I guess you can tell."

"If ever you get the time, you really oughta go up and see that marker," George said.

"Marker? Oh, for the grave."

"Yes. The family just had it put up. They're right proud of it."

"Oh...well, maybe I will. Thanks, George. Thanks for stopping by."

"Thank *you*, Mr. Child. It's good that you're back home again."

When George had gone, Jake went back to what he was doing. But it was hard to concentrate; thoughts of David Whitmer filled his mind, and the sense of history...the things they had just been talking about. He found the back issue of the paper he was looking for, and put it on the desk.

It was too nice a day to stay in an office. He got his coat from the rack, and picked up the newspaper from the desk. Then he opened the door to the outer office.

"Well, Jake," the editor said. "Did you find what you were after?"

"I believe so. It's a help, at least. Now I have some other things to do."

"Don't forget. We're expecting you tonight at six o'clock, and we want to hear as much about Siam as possible."

"I promise you, we won't talk of anything else."

"Goodbye, now," Trigg said. He turned to go back into his office.

"Goodbye," Jake said.

"Oh, Mr. Child, there's some mail for you," the secretary said. "Shall I get it now, sir?"

"I'll pick it up later, Matt," he said to the young man. "I'll be back later this afternoon, most likely. Right now I'm going in search of history."

"All right, sir." There was no reaction on the secretary's face.

Jake went outside, wondering if Matt were very dull, or simply used to the eccentric ways of his old employer.

The mid-afternoon light fell on the western sides of the buildings, throwing jagged shadows across the main street. He walked in and out of the shadows, down toward the spot where the line of buildings stopped. He left the business section behind; he was on a country road, with a few frame houses alongside it. He was climbing now, following the road uphill as it led west of town. Tall grasses grew by the wayside; the spring flowers were blooming, patches of yellow and purple on the hills. It was early April, and there was still a chill in the air.

Like most old newspapermen, he thought of the stories he could tell, the books he could write, if only he had the time to write them. There was the story of the colonization of this western land — the towns springing up on the prairie, the westward movement of a whole people. And it wasn't an easy story either — there was hardship, and bitter fighting, sickness, Indians, wild animals, the perversity of weather...

He thought of the Mormons then — the group from New York State, who had somehow got it into their heads that the Missouri frontier was the promised land. What a strange and moving story that was...some novelist of the future would have his hands full. For it was a story of wandering and trying to settle and moving on again...a story of struggle and sacrifice, of cities abandoned and fields left unharvested, of temples built and left in haste by those who would have worshipped in them. He thought of Nauvoo, the empty, ruined city

— once the largest in Illinois. He thought of the prophet and spiritual leader, slain with his brother at the hands of a mob, and the remains of the magnificent temple, now burned.

All the elements were there, for tragedy in its highest form. And what of Missouri itself — their promised land, where they had been driven out so cruelly? But that had a happier ending — they were coming back. After all the persecution, the abuse, they were coming back again to live upon the 'goodly land.'

Dave Whitmer had used that phrase once. It was a good one. Jake prided himself on his level-headedness, his lack of sentimentality. Yet he found himself profoundly moved by the story...for in a sense it was a story of everyone and of all people — the continual aspiration and hope, the striving for the golden city, the place of promise...the disappointment, even the destruction of that hope, and the courage to try again.

And now, at last...the new generation returning, the reconciliation... He thought of his favorite lines from Whitman:

> Word over all, beautiful as the sky —
> Beautiful that war and all its deeds of carnage
>   must in time be utterly lost,
> That the hands of the sisters Death and Night
>   incessantly softly wash again, and ever again,
>   this soil'd world...

He entered the city cemetery with the western light falling on the hills in a glow of green and gold. He knew where the Whitmer plot was, from other graveside services; he didn't have to hunt.

He was a practical man, not particularly religious. The church he belonged to — one of the social churches in the town, where he rubbed shoulders with its most influential citizens — didn't hold with angels, at least

282

not ones with golden plates. Of all the leading citizens, only Davy, his friend, had kept aloof from the big social churches and had quietly worshipped with the peculiar little group known as the Church of Christ.

What a story his life would make! Upright, honest, influential... a force for good all his days...with that strange aberration, the story about the angel. The incredible tale he had insisted was true.

There was the tombstone — tall, gleaming white. It was a handsome marker, as George had said. A fitting tribute.

Well, Davy, he thought. *Rest in peace, old friend.*

He had heard that Dave himself had written out the words he wanted engraved on the stone. He went closer, and stopped at the point where the words became clear

THE RECORD OF THE JEWS, AND THE RECORD OF THE NEPHITES ARE ONE.
TRUTH IS ETERNAL

Even in death, Jake reflected. Even in death his friend had done it. Left his affirmation, his conviction carved for all to see.

Then, even though he was a practical man and non-sentimental, the marker seemed to blur before his eyes; grass and sky swam together in a whitish mist. For a moment, the message on the stone was the only stable thing in a nebulous, hazy world.

He blinked, and the green and gold of the afternoon returned. There was the tombstone in its new whiteness, the shadows dark, well-defined upon the grass.

He stood a few more moments, looking. Then he turned to make his way back down the hill.

EN GORDON, ENGINEERING MAJOR WITH A MINOR IN *individualism*.

The Optima® Card from American Express has the kind of benefits every student can appreciate:

No annual fee.

A low introductory interest rate

Big savings from MCI and Continental Airlines

Special student offers

The unsurpassed service of American Express

So why settle for an ordinary card? Declare yourself a Cardmember today.

To apply, call 1-800-344-4053.

Cardmember since TODAY

AMERICAN EXPRESS OPTIMA
7907
373.7 321345 61008

THE CREDIT CARD *from* AMERICAN EXPRESS

Visit American Express University at http://www.american express.com/student

erican Express Travel Related Services Company, Inc.

Cards

$9 IN FREE from 1-800

STEPPING OUT INTO THE WORLD IS JUST AROUND THE CORNER ...

And so are great savings. By dialing **1-800-COLLECT** you can keep in touch with friends and family and <u>**save**</u> **up to 44%***.

Here's how: Mail in the coupon and we'll send **$9 in <u>free</u> gift certificates**. Give them to the person you call collect.

1-800-COLLECT ®

It's Fast. It's Easy. It Saves.*ˢᴹ

COLLECT CALLS
1-800-COLLECT®

So even if you're moving up in the world to a big job in a big office, it's still nice to get something for <u>FREE</u>. So try 1-800-COLLECT today.

FREE COLLECT CALLS · FREE COLLECT CALLS

Harvad

CareerPak™

. . . .

A 7 year effort, it's the greatest collection of tips, techniques and tools that help you succeed.

"As your pocket reference or gift, this stunning fact-filled guide helps you: get promoted, influence & win, manage time & people, get organized, make presentations, plan projects, get a job, change careers, achieve your goals and more! Use it all your working life!"

Success
Occurs
When
Opportunity
Meets
Preparation.

Harvad CareerPak

For MJ and to Success

The Harvad Group, Inc.

Harvad CareerPak™

© Copyright 1988, 1992, 1996 The Harvad Group,

ISBN 0-9651812-0-0

For information about becoming a distributor (individual or organization),
ordering MGR forms or group sales please send a postcard to:
The Harvad Group P.O. Box 3021, Andover, MA 01810

Table of Contents

ABOUT CAREERPAK

Harvad CareerPak is a unique system that helps you develop essential skills and provides important information needed to succeed in your career. Information by itself, however, has no impact until you use it in some way to achieve your goals. Therefore CareerPak introduces MGR forms that help you "exercise" and actively implement the ideas and techniques essential for career success. Using CareerPak everyday can lift you to greater achievement in every area of your working life.

Each Day, CareerPak Can Help You:

- improve your productivity
- be more organized and effective in handling daily activities, projects, plans, meetings, addresses, expenses, and scattered information
- get a job, from the resume to the interview
- gain positions of power and influence with associates, customers and clients
- realize your potential for achieving financial and career goals
- have greater confidence
- develop superior business writing skills
- manage time, to get control of your business and personal life
- reduce stress, through better control of time and responsibilities
- deliver professional-looking presentations
- become a successful manager in carrying out responsibilities for staff, team, club or family
- get higher performance levels from those you work with

WHO SHOULD READ CAREERPAK

If you are a student looking to enter the job market or a working professional looking to advance, change careers or improve your job skills then you can benefit from CareerPak.

HOW THIS BOOK IS ORGANIZED

To learn the concepts and retain the ideas presented in CareerPak you can use MGR (manager) forms. You may order these forms separately or you can apply the techniques using your own personal organizer or notepad. This book is composed of two sections. The first section discusses the MGR forms and the second section presents easy business applications that help you develop essential skills. While the concepts and tips take only a few minutes to learn, the benefits will last a lifetime.

Section 1 - MGR Forms

ACTIVITY MGR

· for daily activities, to do's, expenses, personal achievements, time log

COMMUNICATIONS MGR

· organizes verbal and written communications, scattered notes, ideas, plans, meeting notes

PLAN MGR

· manages projects, plans, lists, people

ADDRESS MGR

· keeps addresses, phone numbers, personal information, travel directions

Section 2 - Applications

How to Get Organized

· Managing information from conversations, phone calls, letters, memos, appointments, promises, schedules, outlines, ideas, mental notes, and meeting notes.

Getting a Job

· Developing a complete job search plan.
· Finding and researching prospective employers.
· Getting in the door for interviews.
· Making cold calls to prospective employers.
· Writing resumes and cover letters.
· Interview tips.

Managing Tasks, Meetings, Projects and Plans

· Developing objectives and action items.
· Organizing a project from beginning to end.
· Keeping track of persons involved in group projects.
· Planning and facilitating meetings.

How to Make Effective Presentations

· Preparing and organizing a presentation.
· Tips for handling audience questions and answers.
· Presentation techniques: flip charts, overheads, slides.

Career Planning

· Planning and achieving short and long-term goals.
· How to work with your manager to create a plan for getting promoted, recognized and developing your potential.

Business Writing Tips that Get Results

· Creating memos with the MGR forms.
· Writing memos and letters that command attention, compel action, and create an outstanding impression.

Networking for Career Advancement

- Tracking and organizing information on important contacts.
- Developing and maintaining relationships with persons who can help advance your career.

How to Influence Clients, Customers, Vendors and Associates

- Professionally handling contacts, requests, communications and follow-ups.
- Organizing your objectives prior to meetings or calls.
- Gaining commitment for a desired action.
- How to sway customers and associates to achieve your goals.

Tips on Becoming a Winning Manager

- Establishing goals for your staff.
- Developing a system of positive reinforcement to get superior performances from your team.
- How to motivate and get more out of your staff.

Time Management

- How to get control of the time robbers in your life.
- Analyzing how your time is spent for better performance.
- How to work easier and get more accomplished in the day.
- Reducing stress; enjoying yourself more and doing those things you've always wanted but never had the time.
- Delegating work.
- How to have more productive meetings.
- Getting more out of yourself and the people you work with.

ACTIVITY MGR

The Activity Mgr is the form which will help you manage all your
daily and future activities. The form also has sections for
recording business expenses, improving time management and a
section for noting personal achievements.

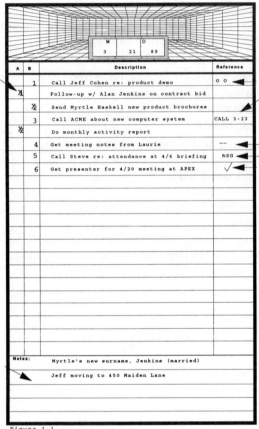

Figure 1-1

Using The Activity Mgr

The top section of the Activity Mgr is for entering activities
dealing with your work or things to be done in the office. The A
and B columns are your priority columns. You can numerically
rank your activities (A and B separately) with A items having top
priority and B items having medium to low priority. An A1 item,
for example, would be completed before a B1 item. Once an item

is completed put an "X" over the number in the priority column as illustrated with A1 in Figure 1-1.

Reference Column

The Reference column is for you to note the status of your activity during the course of the day. The following are the suggested markers for use in the Reference section:

O   Attempted a call but the line was busy or you did not get through (if you called twice and the line was busy both times, you would enter two O's)

___   Did not start the activity and will move it to another day.

✓   Activity has been started but not yet completed.

MSG A message was left for the intended party.

CALL The party you attempted to contact was out and a follow-up call must be made at a later time or date [CALL 10:30] or [CALL 8-22].

Time Activation

The Activity Mgr works on a system called "time activation". Time activation allows you to enter activities for completion on future dates. For example, today is Monday, August 5th and on Thursday, the 8th, you have to "Call John to discuss new tax laws". In this example what you would do is enter the August 8th date on a new Activity Mgr form and then enter the to do item. Since Thursday (8th) is three days from Monday, you probably want to fill out a form three pages behind the current one your working on (5th). When Thursday rolls around, you open your binder and turn to the Activity Mgr form marked with 8/8. Your time sensitive activity has already been entered and can be "activated" for completion on that day.

Time activation helps you to remember and monitor future action items.

Notes

Use the Notes section as a scratch area. Jot down quick thoughts, phone numbers, descriptions, incidents, etc. - as they pop-up during the course of completing your activities.

Business Expenses

Inevitably, during the course of business you will have expenses which must be tracked for reimbursement or for the IRS. The

Activity Mgr allows you to keep a record of the day the actual expense(s) was incurred. Use the following guidelines when entering expenses in this section of the Activity Mgr (see Figure 1-2).

Travel : mileage, tolls, parking, personal car expenses (repairs, oil)

Meals : breakfast, lunch, dinner and tips

Transportation : airplane tickets, taxis, tips (baggage, etc.) , rental cars

Hotel : all hotel fees

Entertainment : non-meal expenses (drinks, shows, gifts, etc.)

Miscellaneous : everything else (phone, supplies, etc.)

Time Audit

This section of the Activity Mgr should be used as part of a time management program. Knowing how you actually spend your time, is the first step to improving your time management skills.

At the end of the work day describe the activities you engaged in during that day. For example, Figure 1-2 shows an entry "Returned phone messages" in the 1:00 time period. In the Comments column you note the things that were particularly good or bad in your performance of that activity. The objective here is to analyze how you might have used your time more efficiently if you had to do the same things again.

Successful management of your time is crucial to you becoming effective and productive in your job and career. You will learn how to develop good time management skills in the TIME MANAGEMENT: TIPS & TECHNIQUES application. More in-depth discussion on how to use this Time Audit section is also reviewed in the DAILY TIME MANAGEMENT AUDIT application.

Personal Activities

Next, in the Activity Mgr, is your **personal activities** section. You will record personal to do's. Use the priority column and the Reference column just as you would in the section for business activities (see Figure 1-2).

(REVERSE SIDE)

Expenses for:	Sales call at APEX			Total
Travel	50 mi @ .24	$5.50 Toll	$16.50 PK	$34.00
Meals	$26.45 Dinner			$26.45
Transportation	$2.00 Valet			$2.00
Hotel				
Entertainment				
Misc.	$2.10 Call Home			$2.10
Notes:	Ed Jones and Mary Hayes for dinner		Grand Total:	$64.55

Time	Description	Comments
8:00		
9:00	Meeting with APEX	Could have shortened if prepared objective
10:00		
11:00		
12:00	Lunch	
1:00	Returned phone msg's	Good, did all at one t
2:00	Reviewed new bonus plan	Should do it over l n
3:00	Had coffee with Bob	Wasted too much ti
4:00		
5:00		
6:00		

A	B	Personal Activities	Reference
	½	Deposit ck in bank	
	2	Call florist for Bday bouquet	✓

Achievements	Responsibilities	Recognition
Won award as top salesman of the month		
Closed $100K deal		

Figure 1-2

Achievements

You can use this last section of the Activity Mgr to record any significant activities, awards, assignments, promotions, accomplishments or praises that occur on that day. There is a sense of elation and progress felt by noting your achievements throughout your career. On the practical side, documenting your accomplishments is important because you will use the information in resumes, interviews or as leverage for promotions, raises or new job positions (Figure 1-2).

9

COMMUNICATIONS MGR

The Communications Mgr is used to record and organize all your verbal and written communications. It eliminates scattered pieces of paper as it handles information from meetings, classes, phone calls and is also used to log mental notes and to organize random information. A file and retrieval system can now be established for important notes as well as a way to follow-up on critical subjects.

Key Items

The top three lines of the Communications Mgr are for you to record key items. Key items are the descriptive headings for the information entered in that form. They serve as indices for filing and retrieval. Key items can include the name of an individual you are meeting, the title of a seminar you are attending, the name of a company or just about any categorical item. This allows you the flexibility to organize and reorganize Communications Mgr forms by various categories of information (Figure 2-1).

The fourth line on the form (unshaded marker) is for a non-key item. For example, in Figure 2-1 a phone number is entered in this non-key item line. **Do not** put address information in the key items section. Address data should be placed in the Address Mgr.

NOTE: Each form does not have to include three descriptive key items. Organize according to what makes sense for you and add any other key items if it helps in categorizing the information entered.

Entering Information

The Communications Mgr is divided into subject blocks. You can therefore enter information recorded on different dates, or dealing with various subjects, that are under the same key item. An example is shown in Figure 2-1 where notes from two separate meetings, with the same individual, are continued on one form.

If you are attending a meeting which has different speakers and subjects, each block can represent a new presentation (e.g., J.Smith/Finance, M.Mann/Sales) while the key item is the name of the company, sponsor or theme of the meeting.

Action Items

As you enter information in the Communications Mgr, there will be certain items, ideas, requests or thoughts which come up and require you to take some action. In these instances, simply enter an `A' (for action item) next to the information (Figure 2-1). When

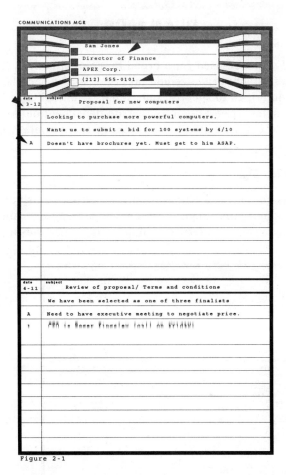

Figure 2-1

you get the opportunity, enter the item into the Activity Mgr for completion on the appropriate day. At that same time also cross

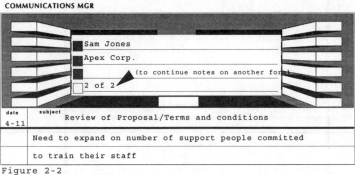

Figure 2-2

out the A in the Communications Mgr to indicate that your task was "activated" in the Activity Mgr.

11

PLAN MGR

The Plan Mgr can be used for a broad range of situations that require you to track, organize and manage a structured plan. You can assign activities to specific individuals and track due dates and completion dates. If certain activities are dependent on the completion of other items, you can manage those relationships as well.

Using The Plan Mgr

In the **Items** column you will enter all the action items you have created for a particular plan. If the current action item cannot be started prior to the completion of another item, use the **Dependent**

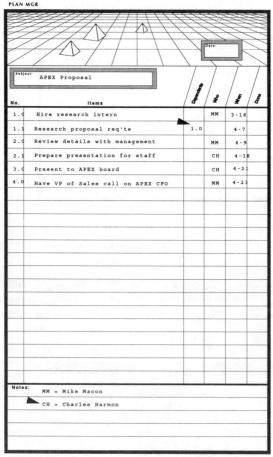

Figure 3-1

column to highlight that item. For example, Figure 3-1 shows that

12

item 1.1 ,"Research proposal req'ts" is dependent on "Hire research intern," (item 1.0) first being completed. If others beside yourself will be responsible for the completion of certain items, enter their initials in the **Who** column. Use the **When** column to highlight the

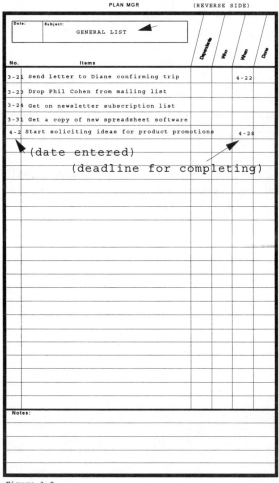

Figure 3-2

due date of the action item. When the item is actually completed, enter that date in the **Done** column.

You can use the Notes section as a scratch area (e.g., enter the full names of initials or issues which may affect the completion of certain action items).

Managing Lists of Items or Tasks

There are times when you will have a list of items (e.g., chores, monthly activities, etc.) which you are not ready to complete on a

13

given day. On other occasions information (e.g., scattered to do's) may come at you quickly and from all directions and you need a place to enter the information. Again, you are also not sure when you will get to the items and need a tool to maintain the list. In these cases use the Plan Mgr to record general lists of items or tasks in one area. If the items are related, enter a subject name in the Plan Mgr (e.g., June Activities). If the items are general and not related, enter the subject name 'General'. In the **No.** column record the date the item is entered (Figure 3-2).

If you have deadlines, enter the dates in the When column. As your schedule permits, enter items from this list into the Activity Mgr, for time activation. Once there, you will complete the activity along with your other daily responsibilities.

NOTE: You would not enter a list of items into the Activity Mgr. It is only for entering items you are reasonably sure can be completed on a particular day.

ADDRESS MGR

The Address Mgr is used to manage your addresses and phone numbers. The forms are not pre-coded to give you maximum flexibility. As you begin to use a form just designate the letter in the shaded box (Figure 5-1). You can also use the Address Mgr to gather information specific for a variety of subjects: airlines, clubs, restaurants, etc. Each subject can have its own form.

D	Airlines	Clubs

Figure 5-1

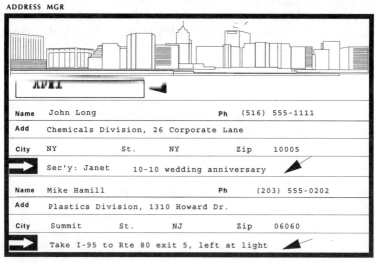

Figure 5-2

Information for individuals in the same company can also be filed on the same sheet. Just designate forms specific for that company (Figure 5-2).

Using The Address Mgr

The Address Mgr has a section marked with an arrow below each address block. This is a note or comment area (Figure 5-2). Use it to record travel directions, important dates, names of spouses, secretaries, and children. In this space you can also record second phone numbers (e.g., mother's number, summer home).

HOW THE MGR'S WORK TOGETHER

The uniqueness of CareerPak is that all the Mgr's work together as an integrated system. You can refer to information entered in one Mgr from within another.

> **NOTE:** References to the Mgr's will use the following abbreviations:

AM - Activity Mgr

CM - Communications Mgr

PM - Plan Mgr

AD - Address Mgr

For example, Figure 6-1 shows that one of your activities in the Activity Mgr is to "Call Sam Jones about terms and conditions of the contract." At the end of the item you enter "(See CM. Jones)."

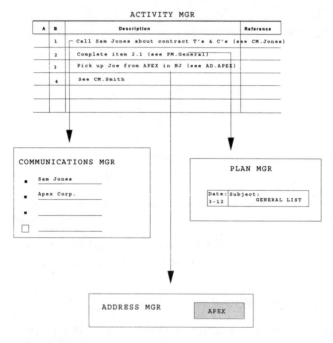

ACTIVITY MGR

A	B	Description	Reference
	1	Call Sam Jones about contract T's & C's (see CM.Jones)	
	2	Complete item 2.1 (see PM.General)	
	3	Pick up Joe from APEX in NJ (see AD.APEX)	
	4	See CM.Smith	

COMMUNICATIONS MGR

- Sam Jones
- Apex Corp.

PLAN MGR

Date: 3-12	Subject: GENERAL LIST

ADDRESS MGR   APEX

Figure 6-1

The details of the requests Sam Jones made and the information you collected are recorded in a Communications Mgr and filed under the key item `Jones.' Now once you make the call to Sam Jones you know to review the Communications Mgr filed under his name. You could have also entered "See CM. Jones" as an item by itself. You then refer to the Communications Mgr and review the pending to do's. By using this method you avoid rewriting activities or information that is entered in another Mgr form.

If a to do in the Activity Mgr needs to reference information contained in the Plan Mgr, use the same format. Enter "(see PM. Subject)" at the end of the item. To reference information held in the Address Mgr, enter "(see AD.Name)" at the end of the item (Figure 6-1).

APPLICATIONS

MANAGING AND PRIORITIZING YOUR DAILY RESPONSIBILITIES

Efficient management of day-to-day responsibilities is one of the most important skills you will need to succeed in business. The Activity Mgr is the key tool for mastering these challenges.

Prioritizing

```
                          ACTIVITY MGR
```

A	B	Description	Reference
1		Call Sam Jones about contract T's & C's (see CM.Jones)	
	1	Complete item 2.1 (see PM.General)	
	2	Pick up Joe from APEX in NJ (see AD.APEX)	
2		Submit ad to NY Times for Monday's press release	
3		Schedule hotel conference center for press announcement	
2.1		Get appointment with APEX CFO to see my manager	

```
Figure 7-1
```

Every day (morning or previous night) the first thing you should do is enter your activities for that day. You must also prioritize the activities at the same time. Ask yourself, if an item does not get done will it affect my personal reputation or harm the reputation of my company. If the answer is yes that item is an `A' activity. All `A' activities are done first. All other activities are `B' items. The next step is to rank the activities in the order you intend to complete them: A and B separately (Figure 7-1)

During the course of your business day other items may come up which have priority over previously entered items. Add these items to your Activity Mgr by ranking them with subset numbers as illustrated in Figure 7-1 (item 2.1 would be completed before item 3).

The 80/20 Rule

There is a tendency to tackle the small things first and to save the more complex activities for last. Do not get caught in this trap. The 80/20 rule says that 20% of your activities have the most significant bearing on your job, customers or general business. Do not cheat yourself, do the big items first, you'll get a great sense of satisfaction out of completing them. Do the same in the personal section of your Activity Mgr.

Managing The Activities

At the point in each day when you plan your activities, always review the previous day. The activities that were not completed or attempted must be moved forward to the current day or whatever future date is appropriate. After this step, you can then plan your current activities. By checking the previous day first, you make sure all incomplete activities are carried over and you avoid getting behind in your responsibilities.

IMPLEMENTING A JOB SEARCH

This application describes how CareerPak is used for structuring and managing a job search. Finding a job takes time and perseverance. Implementing a sound strategy, therefore, could save you much frustration while increasing your odds for success. You will use these job-seeking skills not only for your first job, but also in the future as you will likely change jobs, employers and even careers.

Establishing A Strategy

The four most commonly used methods for obtaining a job are (1) direct contact with the employer, (2) relying on personal contacts, (3) using employment services, and (4) contact through help wanted advertisements. The most successful of these methods, however, is the direct contact method. Direct contact is emphasized in this application. Use the other methods as supplemental actions when appropriate.

Step 1: Your Objectives

The first step in a job search, is to determine your objectives and criteria for evaluating job opportunities. The goal here, is to prioritize the personal factors and issues which will relate to the work situation you are considering. Use the Communications Mgr to record your objectives.

Enter **Self-Analysis**, in the first subject block of a Communications Mgr. Under this subject you will sequence those issues most important when making a career decision. For example, some people may be attracted to investment banking because of the high salaries and early responsibility. However, many early enthusiasts may not adapt well to the long hours, heavy travel demands and constant pressure to produce. Therefore, it is important to align your personal preferences with the reality of the working conditions and daily responsibilities. The following are some sample issues which you might consider:

Do you like to work with people, data, things, or ideas?	Are you patient?
Do you work well under pressure?	Are you a self-starter?
Do you mind close supervision or criticism?	How heavily do you weigh salary versus satisfaction?

Do you like to assume responsibility, or do you prefer to work under somebody else's direction?

Would you be happier in a large organization or a small one?

Do you prefer a big city or a small city environment?

Likely growth opportunities

Preferred industry

Family commitments (time, schools, work schedule, etc.)

Geographic preferences

Lifestyle as it relates to work commitments (e.g., involvement in certain athletic endeavors may have to be curtailed)

Do you prefer to work indoors or outdoors (e.g., accountant vs. sales representative)?

Are you free to relocate?

COMMUNICATIONS MGR

date 3-12	subject Self-Analysis
1	Prefer own role with [...]
2	Like feel of large company
3	West coast if possible
4	Job must have six figure potential
5	Minimum travel req'ts (baby due in April)
6	Advertising or Finance most interesting
7	Like to interact with people (no desk job)

Figure 8-1

Record each issue important to you under the **Self-Analysis** subject. You will rank the issues and use them later to help make final decisions (Figure 8-1).

After you have defined your career objectives, you must now develop your strategy for the job hunt (Steps 2-6). The Plan Mgr is the key tool for recording and organizing your strategy.

Step 2: Prospective Employers

Develop a prospective employer list by industry. For example, if you're interested in both finance and advertising, assemble company lists for both industries. Use a separate Plan Mgr for each industry/company list; sequence companies by degree of interest (Figure 8-2).

PLAN MGR

Date: 3-12	Subject: Advertising Companies	Date	Who	When	Done
No.	**Items**				
1	BBDO				
2	Grey				
3	Ogilvy				
4	Saatchi				

TIPS

[] Develop your prospect lists as well as company research information from the following sources (check your library reference section):

· Annual reports
· Business Periodicals Index
· D&B Million Dollar Directory
· Moody's News Reports
· Moody's Manuals
· S&P Register of Corporate Directors and Executives
· S&P Corporation Records
· Thomas Register of American Manufacturers
· Value Line Investment Surveys
· Magazine Marketplace
· Fortune Double 500 Directory
· National Trade and Professional Association of U.S. and Canada
  · Industry magazines (e.g., Wall Street Journal, AdWeek, Fortune, ComputerWorld)
· The Job Bank, publisher Bob Adams Inc., Boston MA 02127
· Product brochures

Step 3: Research Company Information

Before contacting prospective employers, you must be as informed
as possible about the respective companies. Being informed will
greatly increase your confidence for interviews and phone
conversations. Research is also important because you may find
out information which influences your job decision (e.g., company
is about to make layoffs or is opening a new office). In the
application ORGANIZING COMPANY INFORMATION, you will
learn how to record and organize employer data. In addition to the
research sources listed above, utilize all contacts who can get you
company leads or information. This can include friends, relatives,
recruiters, personnel agencies, professors, parents of friends, or
people highlighted in the news. Enter contact information in the
Communications Mgr so you'll have a record of important
discussions and leads.

Step 4: Resume

Once you have an idea of the types of companies you're interested
in, you should develop your resume. Emphasize experiences,
education and accomplishments that might be relevant to the
industry or particular position you're going after. Some people, for
this reason, create more than one resume with different objectives
and focus on different attributes. For example, if you're interested
in a possible finance position, accomplishments which stress your
analytical abilities might be underscored. If you're also interested
in a sales-related career, a resume which highlights marketing and
people skills might be more appropriate. Reference books that
might help you in developing your resume are: <u>Better Resumes for
Executives & Professionals</u>, R.F. Wilson and A. Lewis, publisher
Barron's Educational Series, Inc. and Better Resumes for College
Graduates, Adele Lewis, publisher Barron's Educational Series,
Inc.

SAMPLE RESUMES

SHIRLEY HOWARD

Current Address
1908 California St.
Berkeley, CA 94703
(415) 555-9999

Alternate Address
6000 Walnut St.
Philadelphia, PA 19139
(215) 555-8888

EDUCATION
University of California, Berkeley, CA
Master of Business Administration, June 1983
Major: Marketing/Finance GPA Major: 3.7/4.0

Princeton University, Princeton, NJ
BA, Architecture and Urban Planning, June 1981

Awards: Consortium for Graduate Studies in Management; Payne Fellowship; Golden State Minority Award; Phi Beta Kappa

EXPERIENCE
March 1983-
Present
Dailey Associates, San Francisco, CA
Intern: Conducting marketing research in high technology industry to assess the advertising needs of computer and software manufacturers.

Summer 1982
IBM Corporation, San Francisco, CA
Financial Marketer: Provided marketing support for marketing representatives and system engineers. Performed financial analysis of purchase versus lease alternatives. Participated in planning and implementation sessions for customers. Prepared presentations for top management on revenue forecasts and operating expenses.

Summer 1981
Philadelphia Urban Coalition, Philadelphia, PA
Project Manager: Initiated and developed guidelines for the Federal National Mortgage Association's Rehabilitation Mortgage Program. Prepared and coordinated media releases for rehabilitation program. Designed marketing strategies of refurbished homes.

Summer 1979
INFORM, New York, NY
Marketing Developer: Prepared analytical marketing reports. Developed system of efficient worldwide distribution of promotional books published by INFORM. Oversaw maintenance of sales record and performance targets.

ACTIVITIES
Finance Club, Marketing Club, Graduate Student Organization - Secretary, and Graduate Minority Business Association - Secretary

SKILLS
Basic Plus computer language; moderately fluent in Spanish; drafting skills; IBM Personal Computers

INTERESTS
Photography, drawing, painting and modeling.

REFERENCES Available upon request.

Figure 8-3 (new graduate)

24

OBJECTIVE   To obtain a position in investment banking with growth potential, that utilizes my sales, financial and business skills.

SUMMARY   Proven ability to interact with corporate senior management in achieving multimillion dollar sales. Aggressive and creative approach to marketing and sales. Excellent business and analytical skills. Strong team player skilled in account management.

EXPERIENCE   **IBM CORPORATION,** New York, NY

1984
to
Present

Account Marketing Representative
Managed corporate accounts with combined assets of over $1 billion
- Responsible for all customer service aspects, including account administration

Strategized with executive management in developing long range information systems plans

Analyzed the impact of changing financial factors on account acquisition decisions. Financial analyses include: capital structure, capital budgeting and management of working capital

Demonstrated superior account leadership in coordinating marketing support (technical specialists, engineering administration and management) to develop new accounts in the face of strong competition
- Generated $1 million in computer sales revenue from competitive wins

Marketing Representative
Prepared and presented proposals to executive management analyzing the following areas: return on investment, cash flow, financial justification,   cost/benefit analysis and systems implementation

Developed successful management information systems solutions to meet the business needs of corporate accounts
- Generated $6 million in sales of computer systems

Marketing Trainee
Completed intensive marketing training program as Top Performer
- Areas of study included: business analysis, finance, sales, marketing and computer systems

Awards: Regional Managers Award
Achieved two 100% Clubs
Eastern Area Star of the Half
Branch Managers Award
Top Performer Award

EDUCATION   **BOSTON UNIVERSITY**, Boston, MA
1984 - B.A., Psychology

Honors: Psi Chi, National Honor Society in Psychology

Figure 8-4 (experienced)

TIPS

[] Keep it to one page, unless you have an unusually long background or diverse experiences.

[] Use quality offset printing when possible.

[] Have name, address, and telephone number centered at the top.

[] *Leave* out your job objective when sending your resume to a personnel department, or recruiter.

[] *Include* your job objective when you are certain of the job being offered or professional field.

[] List current or last job first and other work experience in reverse chronological order.

[] Emphasize results and contributions in your work experiences (accomplishments, promotions, recognition).

[] Use short concise phrases with lots of action words.

[] Highlight credentials and some affiliations if career-related.

[] Do not include informati Xon on references.

[] Do not include a photograph.

Step 5: Making Direct Contact

It is now time to contact your target company to arrange an interview. The best way is the direct contact method. In the application PREPARING TO CALL A PROSPECTIVE EMPLOYER, you will learn how to effectively make contacts within the company and how to obtain an interview.

After you make contact it is important to send a follow-up letter, confirming the points you discussed and any additional information that is requested (e.g., resume, transcripts, references). Usually your interview date will be confirmed after this information is received (Figure 8-5).

Cover Letter

An effective cover letter should have four parts:

(1) An introduction which explains the purpose of your letter, the position you are seeking, and if you were referred.

(2) The reasons why you're interested in the particular company, position, product or service.

(3) Why the company will benefit from considering you as a prospective job candidate. Summarize your qualifications, training or experience (refer to enclosed resume).

(4) What the next action steps will be. Indicate your desire for a personal interview and a date when you will call or will be in the city where the company is located.

74-24 250th Street
New York, NY 11004

May 11, 1999

Ms. Thora Levinson
Chase Manhattan Bank
One Chase Manhattan Plaza
27th Floor
New York, NY 10081

Dear Ms. Levinson,
Pursuant to our conversation of May 9, Margaret James recommended I discuss with you the opportunities in the area of institutional sales. Chase Manhattan is establishing a growing and dynamic presence in the investment banking community. This growth is being fueled by a corporate commitment to being the best by hiring the best people possible. It is for these reasons why I am particularly interested in the opportunities at Chase Manhattan's investment banking unit.
The enclosed resume summarizes my background as follows:
> "Proven ability to interact with corporate senior management in achieving multimillion dollar sales. Aggressive and creative approach to marketing and sales. Excellent business and analytical skills. Strong team player skilled in account management."

My experience with IBM has been marked by consistently increasing levels of responsibility and achievement. Training in corporate finance has not only contributed to my success in corporate sales but has also prepared me for the opportunities I am now seeking. I am confident that my skills and commitment will make a significant impact in the growth and profitability of Chase's investment banking unit.
I look forward to discussing with you the possibility of a position with Chase Manhattan and will call within the next week to see when your schedule might permit a personal interview.

Sincerely,

Mark Midas
Encl.

Figure 8-5

Step 6: Post-Interview Follow-ups

It is a good idea to carry your binder with you on interviews so that company information and any salient points can be reviewed prior to the interview. After completion of your interviews, record notable points in the Communications Mgr. The points of information you record can be used in a post-interview follow-up letter:

> "The x,y, and z benefits we discussed are just what I'm looking for and I think I would be an excellent match for Acme Corp."

"The atmosphere at Chase seems to strongly favor a dedication to achieving the best possible results through individual involvement and team spirit. I would undoubtedly be able to contribute to the company's goals."

Send a follow-up letter immediately after your interview. In the letter briefly reiterate why the company would benefit from hiring you, the position you're seeking, and comment on significant issues discussed. End the letter with a "look forward to your response" or "hope to hear from you within the next week." If you do not hear from the company in the agreed upon time frame, make a follow-up phone call. If the company is hedging on an offer, indicate that you are considering other situations and are holding off on any decisions until you hear from them. Therefore, a timely response would be greatly appreciated.

Summary

The flow of an organized job search is illustrated in Figure 8-6.

NOTE: Each Step can have many action items.

Your Plan Mgr document should serve as an overall guide for your job search activities. The Activity Mgr should be used to manage the daily implementation of those activities. This is important, since various activities may have to be repeated. You could be fortunate enough to land a job in one week or it could take an extended period of time.

TIPS

[] As stated earlier, the most effective way to contact a prospective employer is directly. However, one of the most successful ways of getting "inside" a company is through temporary or part-time work. A short-term or part-time assignment gives you an inside view at a company that few can experience. It's a chance to make inside contacts, find out about openings, and an opportunity to actually work at various companies before making a commitment.

[] Agencies that provide "Temp" services can be found in the Yellow Pages under "Temporary Personnel," "Temporary Employment," "Employment Agencies," "Personnel Services," etc..

[] Another source is the newspaper Want Ad Sections which usually have detailed ads by "Temp" and other employment agencies. Some agencies provide temps for specific industries (e.g., health, accounting, finance, engineering) while most others are general. If you're interested in a particular company, be sure to ask if the agency services that company and about your chances of getting placed there.

[] Another, excellent way of getting hired is utilizing an executive recruiter or "Headhunter." These search firms are very familiar with many client corporations and are in direct contact with the actual person (manager) who has the opening. They are compensated (placement fee) only when one of their recruits is hired (client company pays the fee). The positions they are retained to fill are usually not advertised and if you're suitable, they can get you in for an interview immediately. Talk to friends and network contacts for referrals on quality recruiters.

[] Many can also be found in the Yellow Pages under "Personnel Consultants", "Management Consultants", "Employment Agencies" or "Executive Recruiting Consultants" (don't be intimidated by "executive" most have openings on all levels).

NOTE: When contacting a recruiter, express the same enthusiasm as if you're actually on a job interview. It will make a difference!

No.	Items	Dependents	Who	When	Done
Date: 3-12	**Subject:** Job Plan				
1.0	Develop goals and priorities (self-analysis)				
2.0	Review with family				
3.0	Assemble prospect list at library and local college's career office				
3.1	Research top 10 prospects				
3.2	Call friends/contacts for any info. on target companies				
3.3	Contact ex-professors in marketing for leads/info.				
4.0	Subscribe to W.S.Journal and Advertising Week				
5.0	Write resume				
5.1	Have Cheryl proof; then send to printer (100 copies)				
6.0	Call top 5 prospects to set up interviews				
6.1	Follow up with cover letter and resume				
6.2	Make follow-up calls to confirm interview dates				
7.0	Look at books or attend seminars on interviewing				
7.1	Practice interviewing techniques with Cheryl				
8.0	Send post interview thank-you letters				
8.1	Make post interview follow-up calls				
9.0	Contact recruiters for additional leads/prospects				
9.1	Contact other prospects on list				

Notes:

Figure 8-6

30

ORGANIZING COMPANY INFORMATION

In the IMPLEMENTING A JOB SEARCH application, one of the action items in your plan was to research a prospective employer. In this application you'll learn how to use the Communications Mgr to organize company data by various subjects. Organizing company profiles makes preparation for interviews, telephone cold calls, and introduction letters, all easier tasks.

Communications Mgr

Using the Communications Mgr, assign each of the following subjects to one subject block:

Company Officers   Major Competitors
Company Mission/Goals   Products
General Business Description   Strengths/Weaknesses
Financial Profile   Market Conditions

COMMUNICATIONS MGR

date	subject	Company Officers
		John Pratt, CEO
		Don Rank, VP of Finance
		Mike Harris, VP of Marketing
		Bill Ness, Marketing Manager

date	subject	Mission/Goal
		To be the world's largest advertising agency.
		Through acquisition to grow 20% a year
		To take a leadership position in consulting and other clien

Figure 9-1

Using the research sources listed in the IMPLEMENTING A JOB SEARCH application, enter as much relevant information as you can for each subject. Also include any information you may have received from contacts. Keep your comments brief. You won't remember all the facts in an interview so try to summarize the major points (e.g., company's mission, goals, current business issues).

PREPARING TO CALL A PROSPECTIVE EMPLOYER

You've selected a company you're interested in, completed your research and are now ready to set up an interview or exploratory meeting. The best way to make direct contact is through an initial telephone call, followed by a letter to confirm your discussion and follow-up actions. Most people aren't totally comfortable making telephone "cold calls" for the first time. Using the Communications Mgr to prepare a "script," in advance of the call, is very important in these cases. A script helps you with what you want to say and accomplish. Through preparation you can present a positive, professional image and a good first impression.

Communications Mgr

In the first block of the Communications Mgr, record your opening remarks. For example:

> "Good Morning Mr. Jones. My name is Michael Smith. I am a graduate of Brown University and have been a top performer for IBM in the area of marketing. I'm calling to discuss with you the opportunities available in your sales division. I have spent a considerable amount of time researching your organization, and believe I can make a significant contribution."

After your opening remarks remain silent and wait for a response. Don't spoil the impact of your remarks by making additional comments (i.e., nervous babbling). This is the purpose of having a prepared script.

In the following block, in the Communications Mgr, enter any questions you wish to discuss during the phone conversation (keep it brief, remember your objective is to get an interview to continue your dialogue). Also write down any information you have about the person you are talking to, for quick reference. In the next available block you write the responses from your contact and any important information which surfaces during the conversation (Figure 10-1). Again, your objective should be to get a meeting with the appropriate individual or to receive helpful information about the company.

date 5-11	subject Questions/Points◄	
1	How does hiring process work?	
2	Do you hire for West coast offices?	
3	Read that the company just won a major client. Congratulat	
date 5-12	subject Responses/Mr. Jones◄	
1	Normally 6 interviews. All with management.	
2 A	Ralph Akers sets up interview for the LA and Frisco offices	
▲		

Figure 10-1

Be sure to confirm a time for a follow-up phone call at the end of your conversation.

> "I'll send out my resume today and then call you next Tuesday to see if you have received it. Perhaps at that time we can set a date to meet for a further discussion of opportunities at ACME. Is that okay with you? What would be the best time to call you Tuesday?"

Action Items

If any important items come out of the phone conversation, such as the name of another lead that you must contact, put an `A' next to the information in the left column. For example, Figure 10-1 shows the name of a lead received from your phone contact. After the phone conversation is over you will write the activity, "Call Mr. Akers" in the Activity Mgr.

TELEPHONE TIPS & TECHNIQUES

[] Plan what you are going to say during the conversation. Write it down.

[] Rehearse your remarks - especially your opening.

[] Communicate enthusiasm about yourself and the company.

[] Smile. It will be reflected in your voice.

[] Jot down any habits you would like to break in your telephone manners (e.g., don't shout, don't interrupt).

33

[] Follow your written outline. Jot down any new questions that come to mind.

OBSTACLES/RESPONSES

SWITCHBOARD OPERATOR

Before asking the operator to put you through; (1) find out your key contact's full name and spelling, (2) check your key contact's position in the company, (3) confirm or obtain general information about the company.

WRONG PERSON

Ask the "wrong person" for your key contact's extension, or to get you back to the switchboard. Get some information: whether your contact is still in the position, when your contact may be available, is your contact the "right person" for you to be talking with.

SECRETARY

Identify yourself and ask to speak to your key contact. Have a friendly attitude, the secretary's support is helpful in getting through to the boss.

"HE'S NOT IN OR AVAILABLE"

Find out when your key contact will be in/available and leave a message that you will call back at that time.

"I DON'T KNOW WHEN HE/SHE WILL BE IN"

Avoid antagonizing the secretary. You want to find out when you might call and get straight through. Find out the boss's habits, e.g., whether she comes in early or stays late (if he/she does, call accordingly). Find out the company's normal hours, and/or when the switchboard opens and closes.

"WHAT'S THIS CALL ABOUT?"	Give a good but brief reason why the boss will want to speak to you; rehearse ahead of time. (e.g., you were referred, he/she is responsible for specific opportunities you're interested in, etc.) If, after being asked what the call is about, you are told the boss is "not available," it can mean the secretary is screening your call. If you leave your number, you lose control of the situation and leverage for reopening contact. Explain that your schedule is erratic, it would better if you called again. Try to establish a time when you can call.
"YOU SHOULD REALLY BE TALKING TO..."	If the secretary hasn't already told you the reason, ask why you should be speaking to someone else. The secretary could be correct. However, the secretary may not be correct or may be trying to give you the "brush-off." If so, agree to contact the other person as well as your key contact. But continue to be persistent in getting through to your key contact.
KEY CONTACT	Identify yourself and the purpose of your call. If you were referred by someone mention that up front. Briefly, go over your background and why you're interested in the company and the particular area/department for which your contact has responsibility. If you have already sent a cover letter and resume your objective should be to get an interview. If you have not had any previous correspondence, your objectives should be to get acceptance to review your background ("...send me a copy of your resume with a cover letter...") and a follow-up date for another call or appointment. Don't spoil it by saying too much once you have accomplished your objective.

`KEY CONTACT HESITATES IN AGREEING TO SEE YOU'	Mention something about the prospect's business that you may have learned from your research: company is expanding, just acquired another company, has moved to a new location, etc. (This is why it is important to use your Communications Mgr, with the company information, during your conversation.) Be creative and think of some way to interest your key contact personally. Mention local newspapers, radio and television, things your key contact may have read or seen which tie in with your objective: getting an interview to show why you're the best candidate for the job opportunity.
"YOU SHOULD REALLY BE SPEAKING TO..."	Thank your contact for the referral and then probe for more information. Inquire about the hiring process and any recent events or inside information about the company that could give you an edge in getting inside the door. Have your Communications Mgr ready to record the information as it is discussed.

THE NAME DROP METHOD

One of the most effective ways of getting your key contact to talk to you is by dropping names. Simply, name dropping is where you reference the names of persons familiar or influential to your contact. For example:

> "Good morning Mr. Jones, My name is Michael Smith. Ms. Harvey, in Investor Relations, suggested you would be the person to contact regarding the sales opportunities at ACME...."

Individuals are more likely to talk to a "friend" of a friend than to a total stranger. In the above scenario, Ms. Harvey could be a fellow employee who has some level of association with your key contact [Mr. Jones]. Through your inquiry, she referred you to Mr. Jones, the appropriate person for getting you hired. How can you develop references? A variety of ways are possible as discussed below.

36

MAKING CONTACTS IN AN ORGANIZATION

1. *Research the names of company officers and managers -* available for many publicly held organizations - using any of the information sources listed in the IMPLEMENTING A JOB SEARCH application. Many times the executives and managers are listed under the departments/divisions they manage. Call the appropriate individual directly, the higher up they are in the organization the more they will respect your tenacity in trying to contact them. Your contact may eventually refer you to another person who actually does the hiring. However, you will now have a gained a reference - a `calling card'- for further penetration in the organization. Once you do contact the right individual for getting you hired, you will have the distinction of being referred by their fellow associate and have a greater likelihood of being seen.

2. *You may encounter a situation where you have positively* identified the key contact for getting you hired. This individual is probably flooded with applications from prospective job candidates. Therefore, you need a way to distinguish yourself from the crowd. A personal referral would be ideal, however you don't have one. In this case you can "develop" a referral by contacting another person in the company (e.g., a manager of a different department) who you know is not the `right' contact. However, when you call this individual you follow the same script, introducing yourself, as if this is your key contact. This individual will then say you should be talking to someone else and will give you the name of the appropriate person - who you already know. If your key contact's name is not mentioned, prompt your "referrer." For example, "Is Mr. Jones an important person to also contact about this opportunity?" By having a reference, your name will surface among the crowd, and could be the first step in getting you in the door.

3. *This next tip is called the "Outside Referral" method.* It is the process of contacting someone who is not in your targeted company, but is familiar with key individuals in that company. The following examples illustrate this method.

"Rob was very interested in the APEX investment banking firm but had no contacts for getting in the door. One day

Rob read an article in the NY Times about an entrepreneur, W. Johnson, who successfully started his own investment firm. Johnson started the company with help from a mentor at the APEX company, his previous employer. Sensing an opportunity, Rob found the number of this new start-up and called. He congratulated Johnson on his success and for providing inspiration for people like himself, entrepreneurs at heart. Startled but flattered by this call, Johnson spent some time talking about his experience at APEX, the industry and his former mentor. At the end of the conversation, Rob had gotten permission to use Johnson as a reference for talking to the Sr. Vice President of APEX. The Sr.VP readily met with Rob since he felt "...a `friend' of W. Johnson was definitely worthy of consideration."

MAKING SOCIAL CONTACTS

This example is a description of a real incident. The moral here is *you never know where a contact can be made, so be open minded and creative whenever possible.*

"At a dinner party hosted by a friend, Marty mentioned that he was considering changing careers and was looking at the advertising industry. The host indicated that an ex-girlfriend was at the party who worked in a related field. Marty was introduced to this contact who was eager to talk about her work and also to refer Marty to other individuals who would be of value. In the ensuing weeks, Marty met several key people who eventually put him in touch with influential contacts at advertising agencies. So from one introduction, Marty went through a network chain of several contacts which led to an interview with an advertising agency."

Always let friends and appropriate associates know of your interests, because they are often the first link in a chain of network contacts.

Interviews

Interviewing is probably the most important part of the entire job search process. To really prepare yourself for the most challenging interviews, it is highly recommended that you get a copy of <u>How To Turn An Interview Into A Job,</u> by Jeffrey G. Allen, publisher Simon & Schuster. It is absolutely one of the best and most easy to read books on this topic.

[] Determine the skills and experience you need for the job you want (company brochures are good sources for information and potential contacts).

[] Dress appropriately for the interview (talk to people in the industry and visit the places that the prospective company's employees frequent to assess the dress code).

[] Be conversant about your five most significant accomplishments (personal and business) and your strengths and weaknesses.

[] Question your interviewer about the profile of a successful candidate for the position you are seeking. Tailor your responses to questions about background, achievements and qualifications to be compatible with this profile.

[] Rehearse your response to the open-ended question, "Tell me something about yourself." Be succinct and cover education, work experiences (achievements), why you're interested in that particular company, and why you feel you're the best candidate for the job. Don't delve into personal matters. If questioned on subjects you deem private or offensive, ask the interviewer his reasons for asking the question. This puts the pressure on the interviewer to explain his rationale.

[] Know what your long-range goals are and what interests you most about the position you are seeking.

[] Don't bad-mouth previous employers even though they may deserve it. Emphasize the positives while being able to discuss why you're leaving (e.g., looking for more responsibility).

[] Role-play with a friend.

[] Schedule first interviews with companies not high on your priority list to practice your interviewing techniques.

[] Smile on your way to the interview, during the interview and at the close. Think and visualize positive things happening.

[] Talk to the receptionist, elevator operator, secretaries; anyone you happen to meet before the interview. This helps to ease tensions and to get you into a comfortable frame of mind.

[] Be able to answer the question "What kind of salary are you looking for?" (e.g., "...should be relative to my abilities and expected contribution to the company")

[] Be able to answer the question "Why didn't you do better in school?" (e.g., "I was involved in other activities in which my efforts were recognized by _____...," "...and I was also awarded an _____ for my contributions.")

[] First impressions are very important. Practice your introduction, big smile and firm handshake.

[] Always maintain eye contact. Important in projecting an air of confidence and assertiveness.

CREATING A BUSINESS MEMO AND LETTER

Memos and letters are the most common forms of business communications. Knowing how to write correctly is important, since impressions are often based on your written communiqué. Included in this application are tips on developing a winning writing style.

Using The Communications Mgr

The Communications Mgr can easily be used to create memos

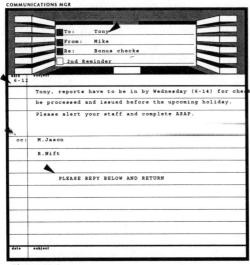

Figure 11-1

when writing to other individuals. For example, in Figure 11-1 you create an inter-office memo by entering in the key item lines: To:, From:, Re:. The non-key item line could be used for comments like `Reminder' or `Due date.'

To send copies to other people write `CC:' in the left column and follow with the required names. The Communications Mgr eliminates duplication of effort. You no longer have to take notes on a scratch pad and then rewrite for circulation.

You can keep a record of all delegated requests for future reference or verification. In a subject block note the action you would like to be taken: "Please reply below and return" (Figure 11-1).

Use the following list of writing tips to develop your business communication skills. Effective communications is essential to getting your point across and also for building a successful career.

WRITTEN COMMUNICATION CHECKLIST

PREPARATION

[] What are the facts?

[] Which are relevant?

[] What is the problem?

ORGANIZATION

[] Have I defined the WHO, WHAT, and WHY?

[] Does my opening paragraph generate enough reader interest for follow-through?

[] Can the reader follow my logic?

STYLE

[] Does it sound like me?

[] Does it express rather than try to impress?

[] Is it clearly understandable?

[] Have I used personal, action-oriented words?

[] Was I forceful?

[] Was I tactful?

CONTENTS

[] Will the reader quickly grasp the action required?

[] Was the memo necessary in the first place?

REMEMBER: Your communication is competing for your reader's time and attention.

WRITTEN COMMUNICATION TECHNIQUES

- Write the way you talk. Pretend the person who will read your letter or report is sitting across from you.
- Be direct and start right in with the most important thing you want to get across.
- A short message is more likely to get results than a long one.
- For informal correspondence, put prepositions at the end whenever it sounds right to do so. Also use contractions freely. Instead of "Enclosed please find", simply say "Here's"!

- Leave out the word "that" if it doesn't change the meaning of your sentence. You'll get a more fluent, "spoken" sentence; e.g., "We suggest (that) you...".
- Use direct questions. Replace indirect questions beginning with "whether/if" with simple, direct questions. You'll get better feedback.
- Use the active voice with personal pronouns such as "I", "we", and "you" whenever possible. Don't cling to the passive voice. Instead of, "a report will be sent to you", simply say, "we'll send you a report".
- Write short snappy sentences.
- Use short words. Replace "locate" with "find"; "prior to" with "before"; "sufficient" with "enough"; "in the event that" with "if".
- If you use abbreviations and acronyms, be sure you spell them out initially. The last thing a busy reader wants is a decoding job.
- Be specific. If you mean by July 20, say July 20, and not "by the end of the third week in July".
- Letters should be no more than one page. Additional materials should go in clearly labeled attachments
- Read and reread your prose. Eliminate needless words, shorten sentences. Avoid ambiguities.
- Rewrite and rewrite if necessary.
- When you are done, review it one more time. Put yourself in the role of the reader. Ask the questions: (1) What am I supposed to do? (2) When? (3) How? (4) Why?

PLANNING A PROJECT, EVENT OR MEETING

Planning a meeting, developing a marketing strategy or organizing a project, all follow the same process: (1) Defining objectives, (2) Highlighting the obstacles and issues to achieving those objectives and (3) Developing action items to address the issues and obstacles. In this application you will learn how to use the Communications Mgr, Plan Mgr, and the Activity Mgr for developing a structured plan.

The Five Steps To Better Planning

Communications Mgr

1. List one objective per subject block.

2. Rank objectives in order of importance (using an A-Z scale).

3. Discuss (brainstorm) the issues and obstacles to achieving each objective. Sequence issues for each objective (A1...2, B1...4, C1... etc.)

Plan Mgr

4. Develop action items for resolving each obstacle and issue. Assign responsibilities (initials in Who column) and due dates (When column). An item may sometimes depend on the completion of one or more items before it can be acted upon. Enter the item number, which must be completed prior, in the Dependent column.

Activity Mgr

5. Time activate all action items to meet due dates.

Example 1: Planning An Event

You are given the responsibility of planning a sales conference. Your responsibilities include; securing the refreshments, guest accommodations, speakers, the conference center, audio-visual equipment, materials for attendees, etc. In this example, each responsibility is an *objective*. Using the Communications Mgr you first discuss, if working with a group, all the potential issues involved in achieving *each* objective. For example, one of your objectives is to arrange the audio-visual equipment. Issues include the following:

    1- which devices are needed

    2- which vendor can supply the devices on a rental basis

    3- back-up plan if equipment fails

4- can the equipment be used in the designated room (space, power requirements)

COMMUNICATIONS MGR

date A	subject Arrange Audio-Visual equipment
1	Which devices are needed
2	Which vendors can supply the devices on a rental basis
3	Back-up plan if equipment fails
4	Can designated room handle electrical req'ts of equip.

date B	subject Secure hotel accomodations for guests
1	Availability of rooms
2	Can Corporate discount coupons be used?

Figure 12-1

PLAN MGR

Date: 6-12	Subject: Sales Conference	Dependents	Who	When	Done
No.	**Items**				
A1.0	Contact speakers to verify Audio-Visual req'ts		MM		
A2.0	Contact 3 vendors to compare rates		CH		
A3.0	Develop back-up plan with chosen vendor		CH		
A4.0	Meet with conference center to confirm electrical profile	A1.0	MM		
B1.0	Call all hotels within conference center area		JF		
B1.1	Get copy of printed travel directions		JF		

Figure 12-2

ACTIVITY MGR

A	B	Description	Reference
	1	Call Audio-Visual equipment dealers (see PM.Sales Conferen

Figure 12-3

Each issue is sequenced as a subset of the respective objective (Figure 12-1).

After all the objectives and their issues have been discussed, list the action items - in the Plan Mgr - that must occur to satisfy all outstanding issues (Figure 12-2).

Continuing with the audio-visual objective, action items include the following:

1- Contact speakers to verify audio-visual requirements

2- Contact three vendors to compare rates

3- Develop back-up plan with selected vendor (equipment, parts, location)

4- Meet with conference center supervisor to confirm electrical profile of room

Once the plan is established, use the Activity Mgr to time activate all items for successful on-time completion (Figure 12-3).

The following sections list several tips and issues to consider when planning a meeting or an event. Incorporate these ideas into your overall plan.

Facilities Checklist For Meeting

VISUAL AID EQUIPMENT

[] Film projector(s)

[] Slide projector(s)

[] Foil projector(s)

[] Projection screen (proper size for audience)

[] Check working condition of projectors and have extra bulbs

MATERIALS

[] Fresh felt tip markers

[] Chalk, erasers

[] Flip chart stands and paper

[] Lectern

[] Platform

[] Pointer (with light for slides)

[] Table for materials

[] Extra chairs by door for late arrivals, guest speakers

[] Handouts (ready for distribution)

[] Desk name cards

[] Name tags

[] Roster of attendees--copy for each attendee

[] Agenda--copy for each attendee

[] Three-prong plug adapter

[] Extension cord

[] Notepaper

[] Sharpened pencils

[] Ash trays (only if local ordinances permit smoking)

[] Extension for remote control slides

Preparation For A Meeting

[] Estimate number of attendees and determine room size or
number of chairs needed. A half-filled room with many empty
chairs destroys the feeling of closeness in the audience and
affects speaker's morale.

[] Set up a microphone to be available if the speaker finds a need
for it.

[] Set up refreshments outside the room if possible. Don't let them
draw audience's attention away from the speaker.

[] Make luncheon arrangements if appropriate.

[] Room should be equipped with:

   -lighting control (shouldn't have to turn off all the lights to
   show films/slides).

   -electrical outlets (for projectors, etc.)

   -climate control (an uncomfortably cold or warm room greatly
   detracts from the best of speakers).

[] Arrange for an assistant to be seated near the light switches.

[] Check out room and equipment in advance ("Murphy's Law:
what can go wrong, will go wrong").

[] Ensure that all visual aids are legible and placed high enough to
be seen from the back row. Use platform if necessary.

[] Rehearse the entire meeting.

[] Have a list of all the key people and their phone numbers
(suppliers, speakers, coordinators, etc.)

[] Test all presentation equipment in advance: run all films, project
all slides.

[] Arrive early to tend to last minute details.

[] Tape down extension cords, wires, etc.

[] Have a "disaster" alternate plan (especially if you depend on an audio-visual machine for part of the meeting).

[] Have adequate parking facilities (especially for a large group).

[] Confirm locations of telephones, rest rooms, vending machines.

[] Directions - receptionist alerted? Seminar posted on direction board? Seminar posted on class door?

[] Answering service - have a procedure for handling telephone messages for attendees.

[] Check sound overflow to and from adjacent rooms to minimize disruption and ensure security

Example 2: Developing A Customer Marketing Plan

Assume you are responsible for the PBH account. Your manager has scheduled a planning session to review the account.

(1) You should first prepare a profile of the account: background information on the company, key contacts, unique concerns and issues (Figure 12-4).

       BACKGROUND: PBH Inc.

A.   ORGANIZATION

       Robin Smits, President

       Bob Rump, VP Operations

       Nick Petra, Director Systems Research

       Gary Knapp, Systems Research Manager

B.   MISSION: Number one mail order subscription service

       1. Magazine promotion

       2. Increase market share (for magazines)

C   SIZE

       1. $220 million sales (1988)

       2. $25 million net profit (1988)

       3. Subscription 25 million accounts

       4. Peak period mailing: 5-10 million (December to March)

E.   INDUSTRY

       1. No. 1 in industry

       2. Competitor: AFP Services

Figure 12-4

(2) Next you must establish what your objectives for the account will be. Using the Communications Mgr, establish one objective per subject block. After establishing your objectives, rank them in

order of importance (A,B,C,etc.). The next step is the most important.

(3) Thought must be given to the issues and potential obstacles surrounding each objective; in this way you identify how you will achieve your stated objectives. List issues under each objective and number them (1,2,3, etc.- Figure 12-5).

Figure 12-5

(4) Once satisfied that you have thought through all the issues affecting your ability to achieve each objective, you then develop action items.

Developing Action Items

Using the Plan Mgr, list the item numbers of the issues/inhibitors which must be addressed with an action item - in the order of importance. For example, in the Communications Mgr under objective A, "Sell two USS transporters", you have two issues, A1 and A2 which lead to action items in the Plan Mgr; A1.0, A1.1, and A2.0 (Figure 12-6). In the Items column enter the activities that must occur to achieve the objective and resolve the potential issue or obstacle. Assign a person to that activity. If a particular item is dependent upon an issue or the completion of another item, then indicate that too.

A dependent item doesn't necessarily have to be another action item. For example, objective A in the Communications Mgr (Figure 12-5) describes issue A3, "...busy period from Sept. to Dec...", which does not need an action item but affects your ability to complete item A1.1 in the Plan Mgr (Figure 12-6).

PLAN MGR

Date: 6-14	Subject: PBH Marketing Plan	Dependents	Who	When	Done
No.	**Items**				
A2.0	Schedule seminar on transporters for PBH	mgmt	MM	6-29	
A1.0	Present cost/performance analysis		CH	6-29	
A1.1	Arrange meeting with PBH mgmt and reference customers	A3	MM	8-1	

Figure 12-6

Once the plan is completed you will time activate, in the Activity Mgr, all the items you are responsible for.

If you are the project leader, you can manage the activities of other people. As items are completed use a yellow marker (or any light color) to draw a line through the item number in the Plan Mgr. Individuals who are nearing their due dates and have not begun their assigned activities can be flagged and checked on.

MANAGING BUSINESS RELATIONSHIPS

Managing a business relationship, in its simplest form, is completing responsibilities and achieving objectives. In your career you may be called upon to manage several business relationships: with customers, associates, and vendors. CareerPak is essential to developing these skills.

Dealing With Customers, Associates And Vendors

In all businesses there are customer/vendor relationships. Whether you're a doctor, banker, clerk, manager of a department, a secretary, or an engineer, you are involved in a sales relationship. In some cases you are providing a product or a service to the public. However, as in the case of a payroll clerk - who provides checks and reports for internal company use - customers can be fellow employees or associates. Another example is the administrative assistant who supports an office staff. His/her "customers" include the managers and personnel who need his/her services to complete their duties. Customers, therefore, are those who you directly affect with the results of your work or efforts.

The principles governing customer relations is akin to all business relationships. The same techniques you apply when dealing with customers, apply to clients, staff, associates, managers and vendors. Therefore, throughout the rest of this application where customer is referenced, you can easily substitute client, associate, manager or vendor.

Customer Meetings

When calling on a customer it is important to develop your objectives and major points prior to the meeting or telephone call. Time is a very important commodity to most people and you therefore don't want to waste yours or your customer's. For these situations, use the Communications Mgr to help organize your thoughts.

NOTE: Besides not wasting time, being organized helps to project an image of professionalism to your customers and associates.

Communications Mgr

In the first subject block of your Communications Mgr, fill in the date and subject of this meeting. In the left hand column sequence the various points you would like to make and also questions you wish to ask. In the next subject block enter `Response' as the

Mike Mann
APEX Corp
VP of Sales
(516) 555-1432

date 5-18	subject	Participation in Industry Forum in August
1		Would like him to speak on new trends in marketing
2		Have him sign confidential agreement on new product d
3		What are his short term goals?
4		Can we look at the benefits of computers for his field sal

date 5-18	subject	Responses
1		He will be able to do it after getting the Chairman's
3		Wants to increase sales by 10%
		Reduce expenses by 5%
		Expand distribution network internationally
4 A		Agreed to a joint study by both companies (needs names of

Figure 13-1

heading and enter the customer's responses as each point or
question is covered (Figure 13-1).

When you call or meet with this customer again, instead of starting
a new form, just continue on the next available subject block.
Indicate the date and the subject or purpose of your current
meeting or conversation.

Action Items

During your discussion, the customer may make a request or
mention something you would like to take action on; "needs names
of individuals..." (Figure 13-1). Write an `A' in the box on the
same line as the note. After the meeting is over, enter the action
items in the Activity Mgr for completion.

Handling Incoming Calls And Casual Requests

Many times you will be the recipient of a phone call in which the
caller requests several things from you. It will be advantageous in
these cases, to have a Communications Mgr ready with a general
key item entered (a company name, general, scratch, etc.). In each
subject block you will enter the name of the caller/subject and
record the requests or information discussed. This is useful when
you don't want to devote an entire Communications Mgr to one
person (whom you don't deal with frequently) or one subject.
Instead you can have one Communications Mgr which holds

```
                    APEX

                    (212) 555-2000

date    subject
3-12            Marion Mellon/IBM PC Problem

                Has a problem when loading word processing files

A               Has to be fixed by 3/18 (goes on vacation)

A               Send new training manuals




date    subject
4-9             Ed Funt/Support Dept., x4446

A               Needs cost of new overhead projector
```

Figure 13-2

information regarding several individuals and subjects (Figure
13-3). Enter an 'A' next to each item requiring an action. At the
end of the call, time activate all requests using the Activity Mgr.

In cases when you have to return phone messages and you are
unsure of what the caller wants, use the Communications Mgr to
record important points. Use the same format of a general key item
with each subject block devoted to separate individuals and
subjects.

Verifying

At the end of your phone calls or meetings always remember to
summarize and verify the requests and key points.

> "Let me summarize what I have here. You think the product
> could meet your needs if we make the following
> modifications... Does that sound right? You would also like
> me to send you brochures on our new product line. Is there
> anything else?"

Gaining Commitment

During the course of business, there will be many situations where
you want a certain individual or party to take a desired action.

53

Gaining a commitment, as the result of a meeting or discussion, is a six step process.

Step 1: Objectives

(1) First, you must establish what your objective is - what action or commitment you want by the end of the meeting. Prior to your meeting, enter the objective in the Communications Mgr. Below the objective, list all the benefits your contact will gain by taking the desired action.

When you actually meet with your contact, first establish rapport before getting to the business at hand, this helps to create an air of comfort and friendliness. Rapport building can be of a personal nature (e.g., you talk about a family picture or plaque in the office) or have a general "What's new?" conversation.

Step 2: Introduction

(2) The next step is to *briefly* explain the purpose of your meeting or call. In the example below, your objective is to obtain commitment for a charitable donation. At the end of your statement always confirm interest.

> " I'd like to talk to you today about the PAL Fund, a charity which I believe you may be very much interested in. Why? Because the PAL Fund could have a major impact on civic issues and concerns important to many people like yourself. Are you interested?"

Step 3: Understand

(3) Before getting to the details and benefits of what you are proposing, you must establish your contact's criteria for making a decision (e.g., budget limits, others involved in decision, time frame, other competing interests, special situations affecting ability to act now, etc.). Think about the questions in advance and record the responses in the Communications Mgr.

> "Before I get into the Fund, I'd first like to understand your priorities and commitments. This will help me to describe those aspects and benefits of the Fund which may have direct relevance to you. Is that all right?"

Step 4: Confirmation

(4) After asking some probing questions, to understand your contact's ability to make the commitment you are seeking, you must confirm the information. Always make sure to ask, at the end

of your summary, if there are any other considerations before a decision or commitment can be made.

> "Let me see if I have this right. You believe that more needs to be done to help the youth in urban neighborhoods. You would make a donation to a charity only if it directly helps those in your community. Any checks over $500 must be approved by your partner, your fiscal year ends in June and you could use some tax breaks. Does that sum it up? Great. Is there anything else you need to consider before making a donation to a charity?"

Step 5: Proposal

(5) The next step is to show how the commitment or action you are looking to gain, meets your contact's decision criteria. Reference the benefits you listed in Step 1.

> "You said you will make donations to a charity which benefits your community. By donating to the PAL Fund you can assist in the development of young boys in your own area. We help them develop useful skills and to become responsible citizens. It is coordinated by our local office in the city. If you make the donation now, you can also gain a tax advantage before your fiscal year ends. To be considered a "Golden" member of the Fund, minimum donations are only $400; this falls under your limit."

Step 6: Commitment

(6) The final step, after your contact agrees that your proposed action meets his criteria, is to ask for the commitment (or sale, agreement, support, etc.).

> "Does the PAL Fund meet your standards for a charity? Great. I'd then like to ask you to make a donation to the Fund in the amount of $400."

Once you have asked for the commitment, remain silent until your contact responds. If the contact hesitates some people have a tendency to start talking; *resist* the urge and wait for a response (i.e., a pregnant pause). You lose your leverage if you start talking before your contact answers your request. If there are any objections or additional questions raised, respond to them directly and confirm your answer is satisfactory. Pause, then ask for the commitment again.

> "The PAL Fund is a reputable charity that was established 50 years ago and works closely with your local city

officials. Does that answer your question? Do you have any other concerns? I think the Fund is a charity you will be proud to be associated with and more importantly will benefit those in your community. Won't you make your donation today."

TIPS

[] Think in terms of the other person's point of view. Understand his needs and perceptions. Approach business matters unselfishly and try to help your customer meet his objectives. In doing so, you will meet your objectives many times over.

[] Meet and greet clients and associates with enthusiasm and spirit. Express your energy over the phone as well. You will leave a lasting impression on those you meet, inspiring interest in what you have to say and offer.

[] Smile, and have fun (at least give the impression) during the course of business activities. You'll be welcome in most places and will generate a "warmness" that captivates the most sullen individual. A smile could be worth $$$ in the world of business!

[] Visualize positive things happening in your business events and situations. This is a good technique to help in your motivation and the achievement of your goals and objectives.

[] Don't interrupt your customer when he is talking. Give him exclusive attention as though what he is saying is the most important thing in the world.

[] Listen, while encouraging your client to do most of the talking during business meetings. You will learn a lot more about the client and receive valuable information, information that might otherwise not have been revealed.

[] Show sincere appreciation for all parties in your business relationships. Make each of them feel important, from the secretary to the executive. You will gain more power [in your business dealings] from simple appreciation of each person's value.

[] You can never win an argument with a customer. You may be right in your points but being "right" only loses business and fosters ill will. Remember the customer "is your business" and is "never wrong."

[] Whenever you err in business, be quick to admit it. Never allow someone else the opportunity to `point out' your mistakes. Being first shows character and keeps you in control of the situation.

[] No one likes to feel pressured to take a certain action. In business dealings try to create a non-competitive atmosphere. Make the customer feel as if the action you desire him to take, is actually a result of his own decision-making process and in his best interests.

[] Customers and even fellow associates can be vociferous and aggressive species of animals sometimes. Yet until you're allowed to print your own money, you still need them to pay the bills. When confrontational situations arise try to understand the other person's problems and be sympathetic. It may be difficult to do sometimes, but you will be exhibiting professionalism. And in most situations you will gain the respect of those involved.

[] Get more business done with less effort by doing the right things the first time (think and plan before you act!).

HOW TO BECOME A WINNING MANAGER

Whether you manage a staff, a team, or even a club, it is important to track the ongoing performance of your people and to motivate and inspire them. This application can be used to help develop successful management and employee-relations skills.

Goal Setting

To become a winning manager, one of your first objectives should be to set goals for those you work with. Make sure all your people clearly understand what they are responsible for and who is accountable for specific objectives and situations. Never assume that the person understands what you're thinking. Write down the activities that will be necessary to achieve the goals that are set. Enter each goal, and activities, into a Communications Mgr and send copies to the respective people.

Establish up front with each person that you will be frank and let them know how they're performing. Give feedback on the person's performance, relative to his/her goals, on a consistent and regular basis. Don't wait for annual or semi-annual reviews.

Accomplishments

Once goals have been set and clearly understood by those you work with, it is very important that you reinforce positive efforts and accomplishments. For example, you may assign a person to a particular project or to get a sale from a customer. Don't wait until the project is finished or the sale is closed before you give praise or a "pat on the back." If the person is doing good work or making exemplary efforts, it is essential that you reinforce their performance with laudatory comments - "you're doing a great job" - and glowing acknowledgments. This is especially true for new employees who need positive reinforcement even though the final goals (e.g., project, sales, etc.) haven't been achieved yet. Always be on the lookout for good things to praise.

Reprimands

If and when a person you work with makes mistakes, or doesn't perform satisfactorily, give feedback immediately. By addressing the situation promptly, you have a greater chance of gaining the employee's acknowledgment of the problem and his commitment to change his actions. If you let negative things build up before dealing with them, the employee might resent your feedback. You will be overwhelming the employee with many negative comments, some of which he/she might dispute the fairness and accuracy of, since the incidents occurred in the past. Immediately addressing problems as they occur, allows you to deal with one situation at a time and, again, increases the chances of turning the person around.

Using The Communications Mgr

It is a good idea to prepare, in advance, a Communications Mgr for each individual with whom you have frequent contact. Whether

COMMUNICATIONS MGR

date	subject Accomplishments
5-15	Finished number 1 in training classes
5-22	Closed $50K deal at APEX
6-12	Praised by CEO at APEX for being responsive to their

Tony Brown
Sales Rep
Hired 4-18-87

date	subject Reprimands
7-12	Third time late for important staff meeting

Figure 14-1

you are a manager or work in a team-oriented environment, the same recommendation holds true.

As an example, prepare a Communications Mgr with an employee's name as the key item (Figure 14-1). In a subject block enter `Accomplishments,' in another one `Reprimands.' What you will try to do is keep a record of all the good things your subordinates do in order to give them deserved praise and recognition. Once something good has happened (e.g., a customer calls and gives a compliment), record it and immediately praise the employee. If something negative has happened record it in the Reprimands section and quickly discuss it with the employee, rectify the situation, and then move on. Do not hold any negative attitudes or grudges for isolated events.

When it is time for a formal (annual or semi-annual) employee evaluation, your job will be that much easier. You'll have a record of the tangibles and intangibles needed for a fair performance evaluation.

Also use the Communications Mgr to record important conversations with employees.

Career Goals

Most good managers are sensitive to the goals of their employees. This is important because meeting the needs and goals of your employees, is a great way to retain and motivate them.

After meeting with an employee to discuss career goals, record the important points in the Communications Mgr. Next, create a career plan, using the DEVELOPING A CAREER PLAN application as a guide. The plan should include the events, experiences, responsible persons, and training, necessary to achieve your employee's goals. Share this plan with the employee so you both are in agreement.

TIPS

[] Challenge your people constantly. Offer incentives and you will get the greatest results. This stimulates their desire to excel and promotes their feelings of self-worth and importance.

[] Establish the major goals for your people; not goals for every aspect of their job.

[] Set goals they can achieve and then gradually raise the bar and challenge them.

[] Establish a purpose (benefit) before initiating a call to action. For example, before having a meeting ask yourself what is the purpose and what do you want to accomplish (i.e., is a meeting really necessary). When asking someone to change a behavior, to begin an activity, or to achieve a goal, tell them what the purpose and benefit will be. If you can't establish a purpose or benefit to an action, then it probably isn't worth initiating or pursuing.

[] Give generous amounts of praise to all who work for you and to those who have completed activities on your behalf. The rewards will be outstanding. You will inspire confidence in those who report to you and the willingness to make further gains. An atmosphere is also created where associates look forward to offering assistance and resources when help is needed.

[] Place errors and mistakes in perspective: "You're not the only one." "I've made the same mistake myself."

[] When things go wrong, as they sometimes do, try to understand the situation (confirm facts) and the motivations of the involved persons before laying blame or condemning. Tell the person exactly what he did wrong and share your feelings about the situation.

[] When giving feedback on negative incidents, always end the discussion with affirmation of your belief in the person: "I think you have a great deal of potential and will be a success in this company." You want the person to understand you are giving constructive criticism on his actions, and not attacking the person himself. This is important if the person is to feel good about himself and will make the attempt to change his behavior in the future.

[] You may be the boss, but you'll get far more out of your people and create a positive working atmosphere by not giving commands. For example, instead of saying "I want this done by 5:00," ask "Do you think it's possible to finish by 5:00?" Instead of "Do this report differently; I don't like your format." try "You might consider this format. What do you think?" Formulating directives as questions is a more effective technique for getting things done. You make the individual feel as if he is part of the decision-making process and also lessen the chance of creating resentment.

[] For the even the smallest achievements and improvements, it is important to give praise and encouragement. The individual will gain confidence and have the motivation to produce more success stories.

[] Be consistent in your praises and reprimands. Your staff will come to expect and appreciate your awareness of the good things they do, as well as the negative.

[] Coach your staff, advise and help set goals . For them to grow professionally, however, you must let them make decisions on their own, without fear of recrimination or criticism.

[] Be sincere.

[] It is important to get feedback, from subordinates and peers, on your management style and practices. Periodically, solicit opinions through write-in surveys. Don't require people to identify themselves (on the surveys) and they will be more open and honest. Use the information to improve yourself and also to better relations with employees. You may not like and even reject opinions you receive, but being able to accept your shortcomings and then to make changes is the only way to become a winning manager.

PRESENTATION SKILLS

In this application you'll learn how to professionally organize and present your ideas. Making a successful presentation is important, whether it be for your manager or an audience of 100. Both positive and negative impressions of your abilities are often based on these events.

Organization Format

In developing a presentation, there is a three-part organizational format that should be followed. Your presentation should have an Introduction, Body and a Conclusion.

INTRODUCTION
Attention Getter:
Intent Statement:
Reason Why Audience Should Listen (Benefit):
Highlights of Presentation (Overview):
BODY
Major Point
Major Point
Major Point
CONCLUSION
Recap of Intent; Major Points; Benefit:
Next Steps Audience Should Take (Closing Challenge):
Concluding Statement:

Introduction

The *"Attention Getter"* consists of your introductory remarks, which set the tone for your presentation. Attention Getter's can include humor, personal stories, quotes, analogies or perhaps a shocking statement. Your goal here is to gain the audience's attention and to establish rapport.

The *"Intent Statement"* should tell the audience what you are going to talk about.

The *"Benefit"* statement will describe what the audience will gain from listening to your presentation. This is most important as it helps the audience focus on the content of your presentation.

The *"Overview"* briefly goes over the major points to be discussed in your presentation. This helps the audience in listening; they can follow the flow of your presentation and the subject/benefit relationships you are developing.

Body

The major points are the substance of your presentation. They are the concepts that support the intent and benefit of your presentation. To avoid confusion, you should have two to five major points, depending on the length of the presentation.

Conclusion

In your conclusion review the purpose of your presentation, the points you covered and what the benefit is to the audience. You are basically summarizing your presentation at this point and succinctly reinforcing your message.

In the *"Closing Challenge"* you ask the audience to take a desired action based on the information presented. This might consist of asking for the order, if you're in sales, or agreement to accept a proposal or consideration of new principles, for example. The Closing Challenge gives the audience a way to use the information you have presented. This increases the audience's retention of the major points discussed.

The *"Concluding Statement"* consists of your closing remarks and indicates the end of the presentation. Any tokens of thanks or recognition are given at this point. Attention Getters can be used here as well (humor, analogies, quotes, etc.).

Communications Mgr

Use the Communications Mgr to create a written outline of your presentation according to the format below (Figure 15-1).

	INTRODUCTION
Attention Getter	Good morning. How many of you find you just don't have enough time, hands or legs to cover your sales territory? Is this a problem?
Intent Statement	To discuss personal productivity techniques.
Benefit	Everyone should be more effective in his/her sales territory and have increased success with limited number of resources and time.
Overview	Time Management Verbal Communication Written Communication
	BODY
Major Point	Set your objectives each day Avoid handling the same piece of paper more than once Delegate wherever and whenever possible
Major Point	Keys to good listening: -Listen for meaning (concentrate on important points) -Verify accurate understanding -Stay tuned in (shut out distractions, be attentive)
Major Point	Write the way you talk (as if the other person is sitting across from you) Put prepositions at the end of sentences whenever it sounds right to do so Read and re-read your prose; eliminate needless words, shorten sentences and avoid ambiguities.
	CONCLUSION
Recap	Discussed ways in which you can be more productive in your sales territory.
Closing Challenge	Urge all of you to start practicing these techniques and make them part of your daily routine.
Concluding Statement	I guarantee that everyone here will benefit by being the most successful and productive salespeople in your industry today.

Figure 15-1

Q&A TIPS

How you handle direct questions and group reactions will reflect positively or negatively on your image/product/company. The following are some tips on effectively dealing with questions during your presentation.

[] Before responding to the question, pause and think about the question. Paraphrase, and repeat the question to insure clarity and full understanding of what the questioner is asking. Respond in as brief a manner as possible, while satisfying the questioner.

[] If the question doesn't deal directly with the points or intent of your presentation, don't antagonize the rest of the audience with a "unique" concern. Ask the questioner can you get back to him after the presentation so you can provide a complete response.

[] If you don't know the answer to a question, indicate that you would like to get the most accurate information - from the appropriate sources - and can you get back to the questioner (take name and number).

[] After responding to a question always gain agreement from the questioner on your response. "Does that answer your question?" "Is it okay if I can get back to you on that question?"

[] If the audience or questioner becomes hostile just empathize with their emotions. "I can understand how you feel." "I can appreciate your frustration." Then try to respond in a sincere manner, showing genuine concern about resolving the issue at hand.

[] NEVER engage in a verbal battle with the questioner; it's one you never will win, especially in front of a large audience. If you can't diffuse the hostility of the questioner, first acknowledge the importance of the question or issue and state your action plan. "I will contact the Research and Development group in our company and see if I can get an answer for you. Will that be all right?"

PRESENTATION TECHNIQUES

Flip Charts

[]Use all capital letters.

[]Letters should be at least one inch high for every twenty feet between the flip chart and the most distant viewer.

[]Space words properly by allowing the width of a "W" letter between them.

[]Don't mix colors in words.

[]Use bright, primary colors that contrast well. Avoid light (pastel) colors because they tend to disappear.

[]Don't overcrowd a page. Use 15 words or less per chart.

[]Use the unlined side of the flip chart paper.

[]Place a blank sheet between charts and staple or tape the two sheets together. This prevents show-through.

[]Write notes on the chart in pencil for a reminder of key points.

Foils (overhead transparencies)

[]Think about the audience size. Be sure the last row can read all of the foil.

[]Use special felt tip pens, designed for marking on transparent foils, to add color to your presentation.

[]Don't overcrowd a page.

[]Mask off areas on a foil and uncover them as you develop your ideas.

[]Number your foils to help keep them in order.

Slides

[]Make sure all slides have the same dimensions and horizontal orientation.

[]Make sure the room you use is equipped with light switches. Ideally only the front lights should be dimmed. A totally dark room inhibits audience participation.

[]Use bright, contrasting colors. Avoid dark, drab backgrounds.

[]Use pictures to illustrate abstract concepts. Your audience will have better a understanding of the message you are presenting.

[]Keep slides in a "start" state (correct order in carousel).

Special Considerations

[]Whenever possible provide handouts at the end of the presentation. This prevents the audience from jumping ahead and gives you their undivided attention.

[]Provide a screen on which to project if a light-colored wall is not available.

[]Remember, in-depth knowledge of the subject matter is key.

[]Be thoroughly familiar with equipment you will be operating during the presentation.

[]Have a contingency plan in case something goes wrong (e.g., slide projector doesn't work - have alternate plans or visual aids for continuing the presentation).

[]Tailor the presentation to your audience -- executives, managers, peers, etc.

[]Practice, practice, practice -- rehearse entire presentation with visual aids. You will be more confident and it WILL show.

[]Arrive early to check things out.

[]Be prepared to make changes in your presentation in anticipation of time constraints.

NOTE: Check the PLANNING A PROJECT, EVENT OR MEETING application for more tips on preparing for a presentation.

DEVELOPING A CAREER PLAN: SETTING GOALS

It is always wise to set career goals and to make plans for achieving them. You will begin to realize your full potential, and enjoy all the benefits of reaching your most cherished objectives.

Career Planning While In School

While you're still in school you can start planning for a future career with a few simple tips.

[] Many employers look for individuals with "work" experience. Volunteer and/or intern in organizations which provide valuable experiences. The list can include community organizations, student associations, alumni groups, etc.

[] Start networking early. Establish rapport with professors (many of whom have contacts in the corporate sector), alumni, friends and parents of friends. These relationships, if nurtured, can be of immense benefit.

[] Start preparing for career opportunities during summer jobs. Practice the concepts and skills in CareerPak now, don't wait.

Long-Term Goal Setting: Phase I

Developing a career plan is actually a two phase process. It includes setting short-term goals, related to your immediate occupation, and also long term goals, which may span several jobs and employers. For example, your long-term objective may be to achieve an executive position and financial independence in your chosen field. This may be possible if you parlay your experiences into higher positions at other companies or even into your own business. Therefore, your short-term goals could include achieving maximum recognition in your current job. While your long-term goals allow for career movement, as you gain higher level positions and more responsibility.

1) It is imperative that you write down your goals. Writing requires concentration and crystallizes your thoughts and ambitions. Enter one goal in each subject block in the Communications Mgr.

2) For each goal, ask yourself is it realistic or just a whim. Can you visualize yourself reaching the goal? If the goal is valid keep

it, if not cross it out. Studies indicate that most people can only seriously commit to four goals at one time. Be honest with yourself.

3) Under each goal, in the Communications Mgr, respond to the following: (a) Why is it a goal (in one sentence)? (b) What are the benefits of reaching this goal? (desired income, peace of mind, security, enhanced relationships, etc.). (c) Are there potential pitfalls to reaching the goal? - depends on some luck, out of your field of interest, unrealistic expectations (e.g., millionaire in 30 days).

4) List the obstacles and issues to achieving each goal.

5) Determine and write down the skills, education and experience needed to reach each goal.

6) Enter the names of those you may need to work with to reach your goals (e.g., spouse, mentor, key contact).

Phase II

At this point you have validated your goals, considered the obstacles and issues for each, and also established what's required to reach them. You will now create an action plan which will list the steps, target dates and responsible persons for attaining your goals.

Using a separate Plan Mgr (PM) for each goal, enter the action items needed to resolve each obstacle and issue. *Change is possible in small steps,* so set your action items to accomplish something every month. Also establish action items and dates for obtaining the necessary skills, education and experience.

After completing your action plan, you may realize some goals are not practical at this time. Accept the limitations and concentrate on the goals that are practical. However, also realize that some goals must be big to make you stretch and to develop your potential within.

Circumstances may require you change directions and action items, but don't change the decision to achieve your major goals.

This is the very reason why your action items are set up for monthly, even weekly completion. You are laying the bricks - the foundation - to reach your goals.

Monthly Action Items

Every month, enter as a to do in the personal section of your Activity Mgr (AM), "see PM.Goals Plan". Make a decision on which action items from your Goals Plan you will accomplish for that month. Enter these activities in your Activity Mgr and complete them along with your other daily responsibilities. If you do not complete a Goals Plan action item, note the status (in the AM Reference column) in red ink. Your commitment is essential to reaching your goals.

Changing Careers

Most people will change jobs and careers several times. As these events occur, use your long-term objectives as guidelines for making decisions (PM.Goals). Ask yourself, "Will this new opportunity help me achieve the long-term goals I have set for myself." Having a well thought out core of objectives, helps to avoid decisions that are detrimental, have no impact, or are a step backwards in your career.

Short-Term Objectives

For career planning, consider short-term objectives to be your occupation related goals. As an example, say your goal is to get a promotion within one year and to reach a managers level in two years. First, you should discuss with your immediate manager _and his/her manager,_ what you have to do and accomplish to achieve your goals. Your discussion should cover seven major areas. In advance, enter one topic per subject block in the Communications Mgr and record information as each topic is discussed (Figure 16-1):

1 Your interests and aspirations

2 Specific career paths from present occupation

3 Job specific achievements necessary for recognition/advancement

4 Education needs: business specific, general

5 Development needs (work assignments and opportunities that increase awareness/knowledge of various areas within particular field)

6 Management development experiences/special assignments

7 What is planned to meet objectives and development needs

-time frame

-whose responsibility to implement

COMMUNICATIONS MGR

date	subject		
A	INTERESTS & GOALS		
1	To be a manager in two years		
2	Interested in the strategic planning and financial areas of		
3	Would like to be involved in special task forces		
date	subject		
B	CAREER PATHS		
1	Sales Rep., to Senior Sales Rep, to Sales Manager		
2	Sales Rep., to Financial Planner, to Product Manager		
date	subject		
C	ACHIEVEMENTS NECESSARY TO MEET GOALS		
1	Attain 100% of sales objectives		
2	Demonstrate professionalism with peers and customers		
date	subject		
D	EDUCATION NEEDS		
1	Financial Management course 101		
2	Selling/Negotiation Skills course 202		

Figure 16-1

After these discussions, you should know your objectives and action items. Using the Plan Mgr you will organize and manage the plan for achieving your goals (Figure 16-2).

PLAN MGR

Date: 4-23	Subject: Career Plan	Dependents	Who	When	Done
No.	Items				
C1.0	Develop at least three new customer accounts		MM	7/89	
C1.1	Close sales at ACME and APEX		MM	2/89	
C2.0	Complete all reports on time: 15th of each month		MM		
C2.1	Work with administration to process sales agreements		MM		
D1.0	Have secretary enroll me in courses		DS	3/89	
A3.0	Get on the task force for "New Marketing Strategies"		MM	4/89	

Figure 16-2

72

Managing Your Plan

Use the Plan Mgr to set short-term job goals each year. At the end of *every week*, put a to do in the personal section of the Activity Mgr to review your goals plan in the Plan Mgr. You will gauge your progress towards achieving your goals. This is a dynamic plan so change "When" dates and action items where appropriate.

After you have completed your plan, review it with your manager. Always make sure your plan is a valid one, and that you and the person who most influences your career mutually understand goals and expectations.

Tips On Communicating With Your Manager

[] AVOID SURPRISES--Be the first to tell what's significant - whether it's a success or a blunder.

[] IF YOU DON'T KNOW, ASK--There can be tremendous productivity waste when people don't know what is expected. A well-organized 5 to 10 minute review will often save days of wasted work.

[] KEEP IT BRIEF--Organize what you have to say before you meet with your manager.

[] EXPRESS ATTITUDES--The normal channel for people to get their views recognized is through their manager. Pass along comments on what you'd like to improve.

[] BE FACTUAL IN YOUR REPORTING--We are often inclined to sift out the unpleasant news and pass along the good. A manager must have undistorted facts.

[] SUGGEST SOLUTIONS--If you have a problem to discuss, recommend one or more solutions and you'll both benefit.

TIPS

[] While you're employed is the best time to start looking at other job and career options.

[] Facts gained from `market research' can leverage your bargaining position with your employer. Also use the information to change jobs if required.

[] Consider all your jobs as learning experiences. Pay special attention to ideas and materials received in training sessions, as well as to unique strategies and techniques.

These "experiences" may be of value in later careers or perhaps in your own business.

[] Newspapers and industry journals (e.g., Wall Street Journal, Fortune, Inc., New York Times) are an excellent way to keep informed of what's hot and what's not, in all fields of business.

[] Utilize your personal contacts (include former co-workers) to keep you abreast of new opportunities.

[] Implement the ideas discussed in the NETWORKING application.

[] Check out advertisements for new opportunities especially if you're changing into a new field. For this method, mailing resumes is okay since your goal is a low-risk way to test your market value.

[] Career development isn't a one-time event but an ongoing process. Broaden educational experiences, part-time or evening. You'll get exposed to new ideas and skills and also be more competitive in the marketplace.

[] Decide what it is you want and go after it.

[] Establish a deadline for accomplishing what you want.

[] Decide what it will take to achieve your goal.

[] Agree to and accept only what you are willing to sacrifice in return for your goal.

[] Be mindful that while a goal may improve your standard of living, it could also ruin your quality of life.

[] Visualize and expect good things to happen.

[] Believe that you can succeed and don't ever let anyone make you believe otherwise. You are the captain of your future.

NETWORKING FOR CAREER ADVANCEMENT

Networking is an important part of any successful career plan. The old adage that says "It's not what you know but whom you know" holds very true in many aspects of business. Use CareerPak to develop a strategy for networking as well as to organize and track network contacts.

Application

As an example, say you have a conversation with a client or friend who informs you about a new position (or an event) vital to your career. You take notes in the Communications Mgr. This same individual, you also realize, could be an important contact in the

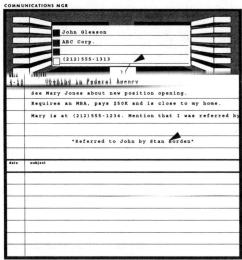

Figure 17-1

future. In the Communications Mgr enter a check mark in the center box, as shown in Figure 17-1. This allows you to quickly identify network contacts for future reference. If you were referred to this person by another contact, mention that person's name in your notes.

IDEAS ON NETWORKING

[] It is important to network on the job as well as off the job. Develop relationships with those who may have some influence in your career. Networking is also important because the average person will change careers at least three to five times in his life. Many times it is voluntary, at other times a troubled business economy, corporate restructuring or just things beyond your control, affect your employment situation. Never get too comfortable in any position, networking is a must for career growth.

[] Attend industry conferences and expand outside contacts.

[] Join organizations with potential business affiliations: fraternities, business societies, management associations, etc.

[] Many intracompany contacts are made at social events - look for opportunities.

[] Get involved in your community affairs. Besides being worthwhile endeavors, you can meet individuals influential in the political and business arena.

[] Once establishing contact with key individuals, you must nurture the relationship. Any business or personal information you have on your contact (recorded in the Communications Mgr (CM)) can serve as a platform for developing a relationship. Put an `A' for action item next to those notes in your CM.

[] Information you should have on network contacts:
· Date of birth
· Favorite sports and teams
· Hometown
· Alma mater
· Special interests (include family members)
· Life style
·Any special awards in office

[] Maintain dialogue, call and ask for advice on certain issues. Make your contact feel important and it will stimulate his/her emotions concerning you (friendship, respect).

[] Possible activities could include an occasional phone call to see how they're doing; clip and send them news articles which may be of importance to their job or hobby; send congratulatory notes or cards for promotions, anniversaries, birthdays or significant achievements.

[] Send items which may be appreciated by family members (e.g., exotic stamps if children collect stamps). Inform them of events which may be of interest to them or their family members. Invite them to social gatherings.

The important point here is that you should not neglect a relationship and then suddenly ask someone for a major favor; perception is nine-tenths of reality!

MANAGING PERSONAL INFORMATION

You will always need to keep track of personal information and data on family or relatives. Information could range from insurance policy numbers and medical information to the clothing sizes of your spouse. This application shows how to use the Communications Mgr to organize all your personal data.

Using The Communications Mgr

When establishing a personal information file, for family members for example, a form could be set up for each person. The first key item could be the person's name. Each subject block can then hold different categories of information. For example, one subject block

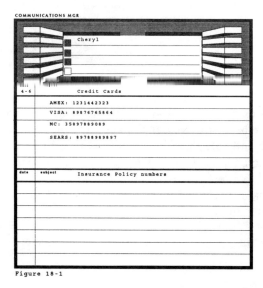

Figure 18-1

for credit card numbers, another for bank accounts, automobile information, etc. (Fig. 18-1).

You also have the option of using one form - Personal as a key item - and to use the subject blocks to separate information on several people.

Brainstorming

People often think about starting their own business. When ideas come in the middle of the night they grab the closest thing, a napkin or loose pieces of paper, and jot down their thoughts. On other occasions an individual might be thinking through an

77

important situation and want to make notes that can be referred to
later on. The Communications Mgr is great for these situations.

Figure 18-2

Establish a Communications Mgr with the name of the concept or
project you're brainstorming as the key item. As you get new
ideas, record and date them in separate subject blocks. This is a
simple way to keep all your notes together and to expand them in
an organized fashion. Use the Communications Mgr for all such
brainstorming sessions where you want to keep a chronological
record of your `mental notes.' If a thought generates an action
item, mark an `A', for action item, in the left column and time
activate it. This is a good reason to carry your binder with you at
all times.

TIME MANAGEMENT: TIPS & TECHNIQUES

In this application you will learn various time management techniques that will help increase your productivity and efficiency. When you focus on better time use, you'll find you work more easily and can do more. Ultimately earning more and enjoying yourself more. You'll be able to cope with the time robbers of your life. You'll be less uptight. You'll find you really do have time for your family and friends. Time to relax. Time to do all those things you've always wanted to do. Don't procrastinate, do it now.

Getting The Most Out Of A Time Management Program

The ideas in these pages, though simple, are powerful ideas that will help you get control of your time and your life. To get the most out of them, follow these 4 steps:

1. As you go through these pages for the first time, check off those ideas that seem particularly meaningful to you (use a pencil!). Also check the ones that you will want to apply right away. This is a reiterative process, especially if you are new in a career. So just get an idea of what's included and refer to the concepts on a regular basis.

2. After you have been through it once, go back and look at the checked items and put an `A' to the left of the ones that seem better than the rest. You can have as many `A's as you want.

3. Next, go back and look at the `A's and find five that are most important to you. Indicate them as A-1, A-2, A-3, A-4, and A-5.

4. Once you have found your five ideas, begin at once to apply them.

TIME IDEAS

__List goals, set priorities.

__Start with A's, not with B's.

__Ask the question: "What is the best use of my time right now?"

__Handle each piece of paper only once.

__Do it now!

__Work smarter, not harder.

__Make a Lifetime Goals list of what you really want out of life.

__List goals for the next six months.

__Make sure you pinpoint the really important elements in your job and life.

__List specific activities that you can do each day to move toward your goals.

__Write it down, don't try to keep your list in your head.

__Have one list, not scraps of paper.

__Make a daily "to do" list.

__Do it routinely at the same time every day.

__Update your list as new items come up during the day.

__Do the A-1 right now.

__Do first things first.

__Don't schedule every minute of the day with appointments.

__Be sure to save some uncommitted time each day to handle unexpected
events.

__Divide time and tasks into manageable parts and conquer each part in turn.

__Start with the most profitable parts of large projects.

__Remember that 80% of the value comes from 20% of your time, and put your time where the value is.

__Analyze the economics of spending another hour on a particular item.

__Don't get bogged down on low value activities.

__Select the best time of day for the type of work to be done.

__Keep in mind your long-term goals even while doing the smallest tasks.

__Lose a few battles in order to win the war.

__Plan your work and work your plan.

__Have a time budget and record how you actually spend your time (the Time Audit section of the Activity Mgr).

__Watch for time spent on trivial activities which could be avoided in the future.

__Check to see if you are putting enough time into the key aspects of your job.

__Make sure your newest responsibilities are getting their fair share of your time.

__Before you start something, consider delegating it or talking someone else into doing it.

__Concentrate on items where you personally can make an important difference.

__When appropriate, do a B item which is an A for someone important to you, but don't always do other people's A's at the expense of your own.

__Learn to say "no" graciously.

__Recognize that it is better to say "no" at the start than disappoint people later because you are over committed.

__Consider reports and paperwork as primarily for your benefit in achieving your priorities.

__Sort a pile of paperwork into A and B piles.

__Don't use desk neatening and paper shuffling as an escape from the A's.

__Ask yourself, "Is a meeting really necessary?"

__Clearly identify your purpose and objectives for a meeting.

__Try to fulfill your meeting objectives in the least possible time.

__Review old habits. Commit yourself to modify or eliminate those habits which inhibit your productivity (e.g., lengthy phone conversations during office hours).

__Find one technique each day which can help you gain time.

__Put the added meaning of self-improvement into doing routine tasks.

__Squeeze short tasks into otherwise wasted moments (e.g., read while waiting between appointments).

__Don't be a clock watcher, tense about filling every minute.

__Recognize the value of time spent truly relaxing.

__Sharpen your awareness of time.

__Consider time as money and invest it wisely.

__Do time feasibility studies before undertaking major time commitments.

__Try increasing your work pace from time to time.

__Find new ways to delegate.

__Improve your follow-up on delegated tasks.

__Require completed work from your subordinates.

__Spend more time training subordinates to do a better job.

__Use your secretary to save you time.

__Avoid tendencies to "do it yourself."

__Never put off for tomorrow what you can get someone else to do today.

__Prepare a written agenda and distribute it in advance of meetings, to give attendees time to prepare.

__Stick to the agenda.

__Give up some details to simplify the task of getting the significant items covered.

__Expect something useful to come out of each meeting.

__Print minutes of meetings, indicating decisions and next steps for follow-up.

__Quickly get to the purpose of a telephone call.

__When you have finished the purpose of the call, recognize your need to return to other priority tasks.

__Try to arrange personal visits so that you have flexibility in terminating the discussion.

__Meet visitors in the reception area rather than your office.

__Recognize that inevitably some of your time will be spent on activities outside your control and don't worry about it.

__Concentrate on areas where you have control of your time.

__Remember "There is always time for the important things."

__Concentrate on one thing at a time.

__Develop a common effort of better time usage with the assistance of others in your organization.

__Set deadlines for yourself and others.

__Arrange joint schedules with others to minimize interrupting each other's concentration and effective information flow.

__Add to the end of meetings agenda the question, "How can we spend time more effectively in our next meeting?"

__Help your boss to make better use of your time.

__Ask others, "What can I do to help you make better use of your time?"

__Whenever you have the opportunity, try to save other people's time.

__When others take action which help or hinder your efforts to make good use of time, share your thoughts with them in a constructive manner.

Time Saving Action Plan

Now that you have found your five best ideas, you should put them into practice immediately. Unless you do, you won't get the full value out of the time you've already spent in identifying them.

Take the time right now to follow these four steps:

1. Write the five best ideas from the previous pages in your Communications Mgr, one in each subject block. Rank them in order of priority, A, B, C, D, E.

2. Then, taking each of your five A-ideas in turn, write down five specific action steps under each idea (Figure 19-1). These should be action items you can take in the next two weeks to help get the maximum benefit from your ideas. For example, if one of your A-ideas was "Handle each piece of paper only once," you might decide that an action step for this week will be to dictate immediate responses after reading correspondence, or to have previous correspondence attached to current letters before they reach your desk.

COMMUNICATIONS MGR

date A	subject Handle each piece of paper once
1	Dictate reponses immediately
2	After opening mail, make decision to discard, file or
	at that time
3	Have secretary screen mail; pass along important items
	and throw out junk mail
4	Set up folders and filing cabinet for reports and letters
5	
date B	subject Set deadlines for myself and others
1	Institute penalty for staff that miss dates for submitti
	expense reports
2	Stamp due dates on all important correspondence and info
3	
4	
5	

Figure 19-1

3. After you have listed five action steps for each of the five best ideas, you will have 25 action steps. Set priorities on these 25 and find the best five, labeling them A-1, A-2, A-3, A-4, A-5. Next, use the Plan Mgr to list the five priority action steps with target dates (Figure 19-2).

4. Make sure to apply all five A-action steps in the next two weeks. As opportunities present themselves, do the other 20 items as well.

No.	Items	Dependents	Who	When	Done
	Date: 8-15 **Subject:** TIME MANAGEMENT PLAN				
A1.0	Review dictation procedures and equipment with secretary		MM	8-17	
A2.0	Have secretary complete staff distribution list		MM	8-18	
A4.0	Purchase file cabinet, folders and labels		DS	8-20	
B1.0	Get approval from executives on type of penalty I can impose for missed deadlines		MM	8-23	
B2.0	Order "Date Due" stamp from stationery store		DS	8-20	

Figure 19-2

TIME TIPS

[] Analyze the general "value" of telephone interruptions and unscheduled visitors: whether they might have waited, versus the time you lose by lack of concentration.

[] Return calls in bunches.

[] Stand-up when people "overstay;" the visitor is always in control of time.

[] Learn how to say "No." Watch out for "Will you do me a favor?"

[] Use Word Processing equipment or Personal Computers for writing.

 - four times faster than writing

 - logical arrangement and editing of data

Save Time for Others (maybe they will return the favor)

[] Don't take calls when people are in your office.

[] When possible, leave a message on the purpose of your call, when the person you are calling is not in.

[] Share prioritized `to do' list with your boss, then get his list. Helps you anticipate his priorities; helps him appreciate your organizational skills.

Discipline Yourself

[] Schedule necessary recurring tasks for set days or times.

[] Use "idle," "wait," or "commute" time productively. Travel or eat with subordinates and accomplish something.

[] A prioritized to do list is a **must:** makes you more productive in less time and helps combat mental fatigue.

DAILY TIME MANAGEMENT AUDIT

The Time Audit section of the Activity Mgr can help improve your use of time. To achieve efficiency in time management it is recommended that about once a week you perform this audit. In this application honesty is the best policy!

Figure 19-3 shows how you might describe your work day at various intervals (e.g., on the phone with customers, sales call, meetings, daydreaming, putting out fires, administrative tasks, talking to friends, waiting for appointments, traveling between meetings, etc.). Complete this section at the end of your work day.

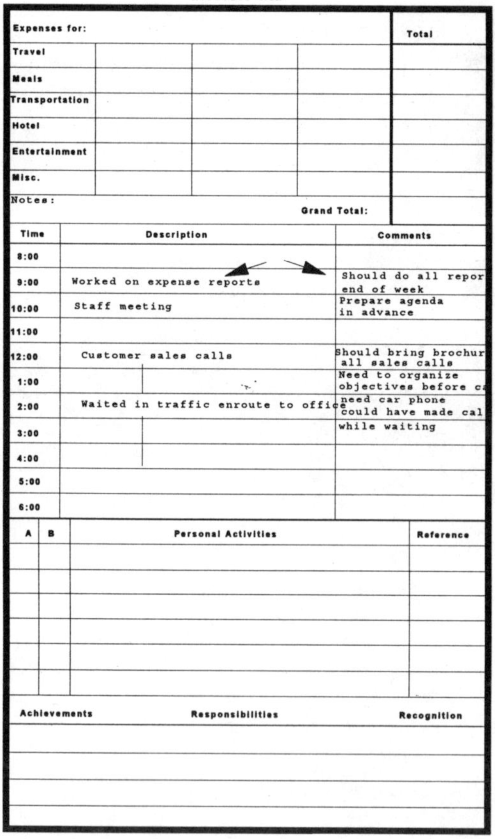

ACTIVITY MGR

Expenses for:				Total
Travel				
Meals				
Transportation				
Hotel				
Entertainment				
Misc.				
Notes:			Grand Total:	

Time	Description	Comments
8:00		
9:00	Worked on expense reports	Should do all repor end of week
10:00	Staff meeting	Prepare agenda in advance
11:00		
12:00	Customer sales calls	Should bring brochur all sales calls
1:00		Need to organize objectives before c
2:00	Waited in traffic enroute to office	need car phone could have made cal
3:00		while waiting
4:00		
5:00		
6:00		

A	B	Personal Activities	Reference

Achievements	Responsibilities	Recognition

Figure 19-3

After you have completed the time audit, critique your performance in the Comments column. Use the following questions as guidelines for your responses.

1. What were the most productive parts of the day?

2. What were the least productive parts of the day?

3. What was your longest block of uninterrupted time?

4. Who/what were your two most frequent interrupters?

5. Were any blocks of time wasted? How?

6. What were your main obstacles to greater accomplishment?

7. What did you do that your subordinates could have done?

8. What disappoints you most about how you managed your time today?

9. What is your plan for using tomorrow's time better?

Once-A-Month

At the end of each month, gauge the improvement of your management of time, the results should speak for themselves. After you feel proficient in your management of time, we recommend performing the time audit about once a month. Old habits are hard to destroy and new ones must constantly be reinforced.

Self-Examination

After you have been in your job for a while and have mastered the time audit techniques, it's time to take a look at your working relationships. Occasionally ask yourself the following questions and use the answers to improve your overall performance.

1. What is your own worst time habit?

　A. On the job?

_____

　B. Off the job?

_____

2. A. What is the most frequent way your boss wastes your time?

　B. Have you told him/her?

3. A. How do you waste your boss' time?

　B. Have you asked him/her?

4. A. What would your subordinates say about you?

　B. Have you made it easy for them to tell you?

5. A. What percent of your day are you really productive?

6. A. Are you a better manager of time now than you were six months ago?

   B. How?

7. A. Who is the best manager you know?

   B. Why did you select him/her?

8. A. Would you like to have 30 minutes more each day -- to do with just as you please?

   B. What would you do with those 30 minutes?

HOW THE EFFECTIVE MANAGER USES TIME

IDEA	ACTION
1. ELIMINATE TIME-WASTERS	Killing time is not murder; it's suicide.
2. ESTABLISH PRIORITIES	List in priority of importance those things most necessary to the welfare of your operation. Activities that only you can do. Work on these and delegate the rest.
3. SAY NO!	The more successful you become, the more people will ask for your time. There is a limit to any person's enthusiasm, energy, and hours...protect your assets!
4. DO MORE THAN ONE THING AT A TIME	Delegate to help people grow and more effectively use their time. Think and plan while waiting, polish shoes while watching TV, look for things you can do in tandem.
5. GROUP RELATED ACTIVITIES	Schedule visitors consecutively. Do dictation at one sitting. Read/sign in batches. Return calls in groups.
6. DEVELOP EXECUTIVE - SECRETARY TEAM	Review "secretarial guidelines" with your secretary. Help your secretary think as you do!
7. SCHEDULE UNINTERESTING TASKS EARLY	Tackle the task you least enjoy early in the day when you are fresh and can train the biggest guns on the problem.
8. LOG TIME UTILIZATION	Peter Drucker, the world's leading management consultant, says that "to learn how to improve the use of your time, it is imperative that you know how you actually do use your time."
10. USE DICTATION EQUIPMENT	One of the most productive pieces of equipment in business!

Dictation Techniques

[] Have necessary reference materials at hand.

[] Organize material to be dictated--make an outline or notes.

[] Have dictating unit ready to use.

[] Give instructions before content.

[] Make instructions complete as to number of copies, type of stationery, addressee, kind of communication, form, spacing, urgency, etc.

Voice Control

[] Maintain a normal pitch.

[] Maintain normal pace.

[] Don't mumble.

Dictation

[] Enunciate clearly.

[] Minimize distractions--avoid fumbling with microphone, papers, etc.

[] Understand and use unique features of your dictation system.

Instructions (During Dictation)

[] Explain corrections.

[] Indicate unusual punctuation.

[] Indicate paragraphs.

[] Indicate quotes, capitalizing, etc.

[] Give spelling of unusual words or names.

Delivery

[] Dictate complete thoughts--a phrase or a sentence at a time.

[] Avoid unnecessarily long pauses.

[] Avoid groping for words.

[] Be direct, crisp and specific in phrasing-- keep it short and to the point.

[] Avoid distracting mannerisms--eating, chewing gum, turning away, etc.

[] Use style of expression fitted to purpose of message.

M	D	Y

A	B	Description	Reference

Notes:

Expenses for:				Total
Travel				
Meals				
Transportation				
Hotel				
Entertainment				
Misc.				
Notes:			Grand Total:	

Time	Description	Comments
8:00		
9:00		
10:00		
11:00		
12:00		
1:00		
2:00		
3:00		
4:00		
5:00		
6:00		

A	B	Personal Activities	Reference

Achievements	Responsibilities	Recognition

COMMUNICATIONS MGR

date	subject

date	subject

date	subject

date	subject

Date:

Subject:

No.	Items	Dependents	Who	When	Done

es:

Date:	Subject:		Dependents	Who	When	Done
No.	Items					

Notes:

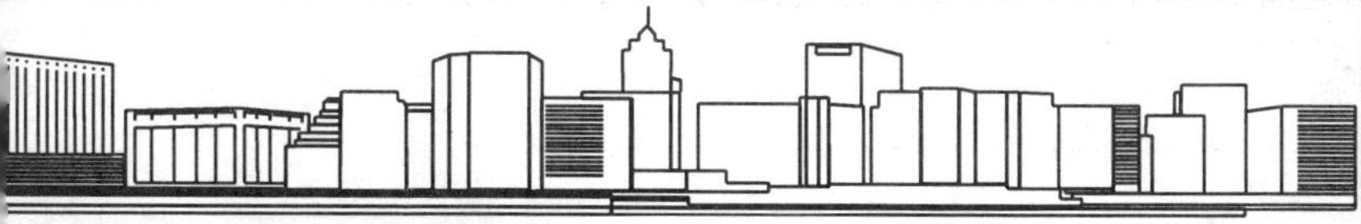

Name Ph
Add
City St. Zip

Name Ph
Add
City St. Zip

Name Ph
Add
City St. Zip

Name Ph
Add
City St. Zip

Name Ph
Add
City St. Zip

Name Ph
Add
City St. Zip

Name Ph
Add
City St. Zip

Name _____ Ph _____

Add _____

City _____ St. _____ Zip _____

➡

Name _____ Ph _____

Add _____

City _____ St. _____ Zip _____

➡

Name _____ Ph _____

Add _____

City _____ St. _____ Zip _____

➡

Name _____ Ph _____

Add _____

City _____ St. _____ Zip _____

➡

Name _____ Ph _____

Add _____

City _____ St. _____ Zip _____

➡

Name _____ Ph _____

Add _____

City _____ St. _____ Zip _____

➡

Name _____ Ph _____

Add _____

City _____ St. _____ Zip _____

➡

Name _____ Ph _____

Add _____

City _____ St. _____ Zip _____

➡